"Elliot leaves your stomach grumbling and your heart pounding, and it's hard to discern what's more delicious: the elaborate dishes or the couple's simmering chemistry."

—*Kirkus Reviews* (starred review)

"This romantic comedy from Elliot . . . is a sexy slow burn with sizzling chemistry between the well-developed protagonists. Julie and Bennett fall in love over countless meals, and the descriptions of the foods they consume are incredibly described and guaranteed to make readers salivate."

—*Library Journal* (starred review)

"This classic enemies-to-lovers plot is a slow burn, but the result is worth the wait and the food descriptions along the way will make readers salivate. Romance fans are sure to be charmed." —*Publishers Weekly*

PRAISE FOR

Sadie on a Plate

"*Sadie on a Plate* is a joyful, satisfying romp. I loved it—and I'm still hungry!"

—KJ Dell'Antonia, *New York Times* bestselling author of *Playing the Witch Card*

"*Sadie on a Plate* reads like the ultimate cooking-show comfort watch—with the added spice of a forbidden romance. A delicious love story and heartfelt ode to Jewish cuisine."

—Rachel Lynn Solomon, *New York Times* bestselling author of *Business or Pleasure*

"My goodness—Amanda Elliot knows how to write swoon-worthy food! Amidst all the inventive dishes and luscious food descriptions, *Sadie on a Plate* mixes the drama of a culinary competition, a slow-burn forbidden romance, and a salty-sweet cast of characters into the perfect bookish bite."

—Amy E. Reichert, author of *Once Upon a December*

"Amanda Elliot's debut, *Sadie on a Plate*, is a foodie delight. Fans of *Top Chef* will cheer on Sadie Rosen as she blazes through the *Chef Supreme* competition. The Jewish meals Sadie cooks are from the heart, as is her steamy romance with Chef Luke Weston. This sweet sufganiyot of a novel is deliciously delectable."

—Roselle Lim, author of *Night for Day*

"*Sadie on a Plate* is a delectable mix of humor, reality show drama, foodie vibes, and heart-fluttering love story. Amanda Elliot has crafted an endearingly imperfect heroine whose hot mess–ness and tenacity will resonate with readers. You'll swoon, laugh, and cheer as you watch Sadie earn the happily ever after she so deserves."

—Sarah Echavarre Smith, author of *The Boy with the Bookstore*

PRAISE FOR

Best Served Hot

....

"*Best Served Hot* is a sweet, spicy, absolutely delicious romance! Julie and Bennett's love story will leave you smiling, while the food scenes will leave you hungry. I recommend reading with take-out menus within reach."

—Jen DeLuca, *USA Today* bestselling author of *Haunted Ever After*

"If you're looking for a real, relatable romance, look no further than *Best Served Hot* by Amanda Elliot! The rivals-to-lovers vibes are delicious, as are all the descriptions of food. Do not read this on an empty stomach—you've been warned!"

—Alicia Thompson, *USA Today* bestselling author of *The Art of Catching Feelings*

"Amanda Elliot is a master of banter and crackling chemistry, delivering yet another winner! This rivals-to-lovers romance is spicy, lush, and addictive."

—Amy Lea, author of *The Catch*

"A winning romance that will make your mouth water. *Best Served Hot* features two rivals who come from very different worlds but who are united in their love of food. If only I could eat the meals served in this book."

—Jackie Lau, author of *The Stand-Up Groomsman*

"*Best Served Hot* was made to be savored. With a lovable cast of characters, a swoon-worthy romance, and food descriptions so vivid they'll make your mouth water, Amanda Elliot's latest is fantastic. I devoured every word!"

—Kerry Rea, author of *The Jewel of the Isle*

"*Best Served Hot* is a fun foodie romance filled with all the highs and lows of finding your passion. Every course of this enemies-to-lovers tale satisfies, from the amuse-bouche to the dessert. Anyone who loves a good meal will enjoy dining out with Julie, Bennett, and the rest of this sparkling cast."

—TJ Alexander, author of *Triple Sec*

"*Best Served Hot* is the perfect recipe for a fresh, fun, and foodie-licious rom-com: a spunky and relatable main character with a decent serving of edge and a hilarious inner voice, a sexy yet strong love interest with a side of cinnamon roll, a large helping of diverse and well-fleshed-out supporting characters, and a healthy dash of spice in the bedroom! Warning: do not read on an empty stomach unless you have seriously amazing plans for dinner! Delicious fun."

—Meredith Schorr, author of *Someone Just Like You*

"*Best Served Hot* is a delectably sweet and spicy enemies-to-lovers rom-com from an author who knows the way to a food writer's heart is always through their stomach."

—Washington Independent Review of Books

"This novel is perfect for any fans of cooking shows who also love to curl up with a beach read. It's fun [and] breezy, and [it's] clear that Elliot did her research into the behind-the-scenes world of *Top Chef*." —*USA Today*

"*Sadie on a Plate* reveals the arduous, exacting tasks of making really good food. Light as a soufflé, it's delicious."
—*The American Jewish World*

"A love letter to Ashkenazi cooking, and food in general, as a means of connecting with one's identity."
—*The Canadian Jewish News*

"Foodies with a hunger for juicy cooking-show competitions will eagerly lap up every last drop of *Sadie on a Plate*, Amanda Elliot's delicious rom-com. . . . Detailed food descriptions, recipes, and kitchen culture—along with a diverse cast—spice up a well-plotted story warmed with romance, humor, and heart." —Shelf Awareness

"Luke and Sadie are likable characters with magnetic, slow-building chemistry and sympathetic, realistic backstories. The fast-paced, delicious plot is as much about food as romance. . . . Readers, especially those who enjoy shows like *Top Chef*, won't be able to put down this fast-paced romantic comedy." —*Library Journal* (starred review)

"Elliot's first adult novel . . . has the perfect amount of reality show high jinks and food innuendos that help dial up the heat. . . . A satisfying debut for foodies and romance lovers alike."

—*Kirkus Reviews* (starred review)

TITLES BY AMANDA ELLIOT

Sadie on a Plate

Best Served Hot

Love You a Latke

LOVE YOU A LATKE

AMANDA ELLIOT

Berkley Romance
New York

BERKLEY ROMANCE
Published by Berkley
An imprint of Penguin Random House LLC
penguinrandomhouse.com

Library of Congress Cataloging-in-Publication Data

Names: Elliot, Amanda, author.
Title: Love you a latke / Amanda Elliot.
Description: First Edition. | New York : Berkley Romance, 2024.
Identifiers: LCCN 2024004326 (print) | LCCN 2024004327 (ebook) |
ISBN 9780593815830 (trade paperback) | ISBN 9780593815847 (ebook)
Subjects: LCGFT: Romance fiction. | Novels.
Classification: LCC PS3605.L4423 L68 2024 (print) | LCC PS3605.L4423 (ebook) |
DDC 813/.6—dc23/eng/20240206
LC record available at https://lccn.loc.gov/2024004326
LC ebook record available at https://lccn.loc.gov/2024004327

First Edition: October 2024

Printed in the United States of America
1st Printing

Book design byAshley Tucker
Interior art by Ann in the UK/Shutterstock

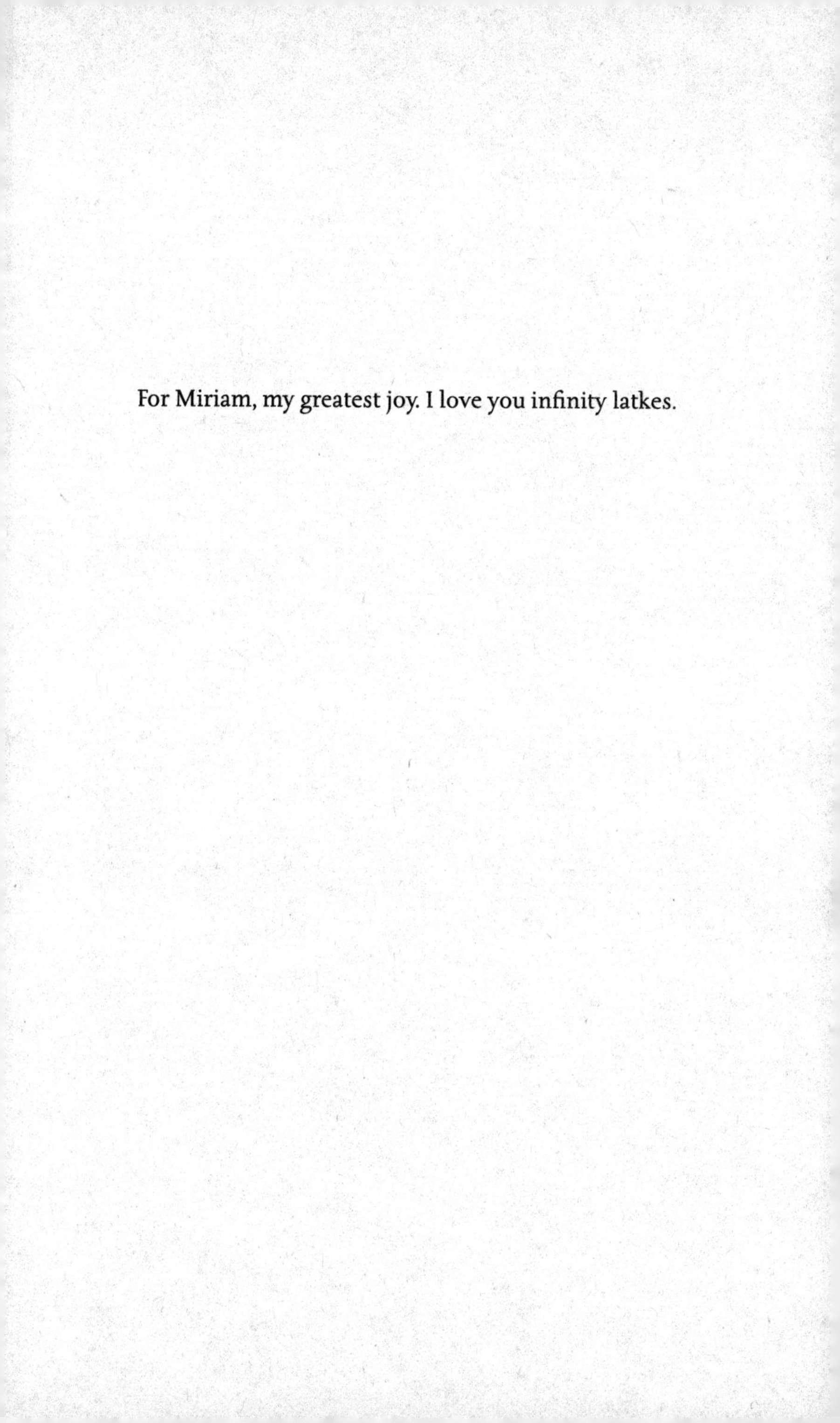
For Miriam, my greatest joy. I love you infinity latkes.

1

OUTSIDE THE PICTURE WINDOW OF THE CAFÉ, snow drifted to the sidewalk in big fluffy flakes. Sleigh bells jingled on the speaker overhead, not quite covering up the burbling sounds of the machines behind me. Scents of gingerbread and mint drifted through the air. And, in my head, a Category 2 headache was pinching the area between my eyes and radiating back toward my ears.

There are five categories in ascending order of least to most severe, in case you're wondering.

"Sir, I don't know how many more times I can say it," I told the beet-faced man on the other side of the counter. He wore flannel like most of the other people who stopped in for coffee or a pastry, but he wasn't a local. It was easy to tell who was and wasn't a local when there were only a few hundred of them. "I can't give you a refund when you drank the entire thing. I can give you a new coffee. For free. For your trouble." *So you'll get out of here and leave me alone.*

The man glowered at me like I'd told him his beard was patchy. "I could barely taste the gingerbread. It didn't fulfill the expectations I had of a gingerbread coffee. I don't want a free mediocre coffee. I want my money back."

Excuse me, my gingerbread coffee was not just far from mediocre; it was excellent: I'd spent days perfecting the exact blend of ginger, cinnamon, allspice, cloves, and nutmeg to flavor the coffee without overpowering it. I'd even added a pinch of crushed red pepper flakes in the mix to mimic that gentle burn a good gingerbread cookie gives you in the back of your throat. Whenever I finished stirring a new batch of it up, it smelled exactly like I'd dropped a warm, fresh-out-of-the-oven cookie into a vat of coffee. The first time I'd tasted it I'd literally pumped my fist in the air—that glorious sensation of achievement that comes from creating some excellent piece of art. Yes, fun drinks were art. "Then you should have said something after your first sip or two," I said. "It couldn't have been *that* bad if you drank the whole thing."

"I wanted to see if it would get better as I went on. Maybe all of the syrup had settled at the bottom."

I had to hold myself back from rolling my eyes. Except fuck it, that was a really eye roll–worthy thing to say. I rolled my eyes. My brain was now throbbing. "I'm going to have to ask you to leave."

And then he said my absolute favorite thing problem customers said, the glorious seven words that made the throbbing in my head shrink into glee. "I'd like to speak to your manager."

I drew myself up so that, despite our height difference, our eyes were level. And I smiled. Not my fake, stretched-out customer-service smile, either. A real, true, toothy grin. "Sir, I *am* the manager."

I could've gone on from there. Because I wasn't just the manager. I was the owner. Well, technically the renter. But either way, I was the one in control of this warm, cozy space and the apartment above it. Another thing that had given me a glorious sense of achievement: running my own business at the age of twenty-eight and not having to answer to anyone else about how I spent my time or what drink specials I wanted to put on the board or how I wanted to talk to my customers. I didn't think I could ever go back to working for someone else again.

"Whatever," the man grumbled. He shook his head. "If this is how you treat your customers, you won't be in business much longer." He pointed at the menu board. "If your gruesome drawings don't put you out first."

I turned to look at my menu board, where I'd written all of our seasonal specials in chalk. Next to the gingerbread coffee listing I'd drawn a cheery gingerbread man going for a quick dip in a hot tub–esque cup of coffee. Though looking at it now, the gingerbread man did kind of look like he was screaming. (I was about as good at drawing cheer as I was at faking it. In other words, not very.) And you could possibly interpret his raised arms as flailing with panic.

The man was already storming out, but I wasn't going to let him have the last word. I called after him, "It's a festive doodle!" The door slammed shut with the tinkle of a bell.

I took a deep breath. His words rang in my head. *You won't be in business much longer.* They were just the nasty words of an aggrieved customer, I told myself. Not prophecy.

Though you didn't need to be a prophet to read what the profit margins of the last few months were saying.

No matter. I didn't have time to waste stressing over it or feeling sorry for myself. I turned my attention to the next customer in line, who was bound to be annoyed after the long wait. "Good morning, how can I help you?"

As I realized who I was speaking with, that Category 2 headache slammed back into my skull so hard it flipped right into a Category 3, which would ache at least as long as the person who caused it was in the vicinity. As long as *he* was in the vicinity, I should say. Because Category 3 headaches were reserved for one special customer.

"Beautiful day today!" said certain customer chirped, beaming a mouthful of very white teeth in my direction.

The snow had stopped falling, leaving a murky gray sky behind. The temperature was supposed to hover at that sweet spot between freezing and not freezing, so that what snow was left on the ground would turn into a nasty wet slush and anything that came down the rest of the day would be a sleety, icy rain. "It's supposed to be wet and rainy all afternoon."

His smile didn't waver. "Who said rain can't be beautiful?"

Ugh. When I closed the café at four and walked outside, I'd probably find him singing and dancing as the water poured around him, his tap shoes somehow magically not slipping in the slush. "What can I get you, Seth?"

It was truly a shame he was so annoying, because if not

for the whole personality thing, he'd actually be handsome. I'd perked up the first time I saw him walk through my door, his green flannel setting off broad shoulders beneath dark hair that curled around his strong cheekbones.

And then he'd opened his mouth. Something he insisted on doing way too often each time I saw him. Now, instead of just telling me that he wanted a pumpkin spice latte with whipped cream—what he gets from October through December each year—he said, "Man, I wonder what that guy before me was going through. It must really be a lot for him to act like that."

I should have known better than to take the bait. I really should. But the man's words were still smarting at me, like poking at an already aching bruise. *You won't be in business much longer.* "Or," I replied, already mad at myself, "maybe he was just a jerk."

"Maybe he was tired and somebody rear-ended his car yesterday and his head hurt and he just wanted to feel like someone was taking care of him," Seth said.

"Or maybe he was just a jerk," I said. "Lots of people are. What do you want, Seth?"

"To continue believing that humanity is generally good, and that people who behave badly usually have a reason for it," he said. "Also a pumpkin spice latte, please. With whipped cream."

"Latte coming right up." I felt a little better as soon as I turned my back to run the machine, breathing in the sweet steam bath of coffee and sugar. He probably assumed I drank my coffee black and strong, but I actually loved a good pumpkin spice or vanilla or hazelnut cream latte. See?

Just because I saw humanity as it really was didn't mean I was some sad, bitter person who snubbed anything sweet and indulgent.

Not that he'd gotten to me, or that anything he could say would ever get to me. I was one hundred percent right, and he was one hundred percent wrong. If he thought there weren't plenty of people out there who weren't jerks just for the sake of being jerks, he clearly hadn't met very many people.

As the machine was finishing its magic, I held the cardboard cup underneath the spout to let it fill. The moment I pulled it away, steaming and topped with a thick layer of pale foam, Seth said, "I like your drawings, by the way. They're funny. I mean, it's not like you drowned a *real* gingerbread man. Or like gingerbread men are real and can drown."

I gritted my teeth. "The gingerbread man isn't drowning. He's soaking in his hot tub of coffee."

"Oh. Well, it's up for interpretation. All good art is, right?"

"It's not art," I said, just to be contrary. "It's supposed to be fun." Bah humbug. I was never making a festive doodle again.

I spun around as soon as Seth's cup was finished filling to find him looking at me with what appeared to be sympathy. "I never like to assume people are just jerks; I like to think they're having a bad day and they feel bad about it afterward. Have you ever read Anne Frank? 'In spite of everything I still believe that people are really good at heart.' I try to live by her example."

I set the cup on the counter for Seth to take. Irritation boiled inside me. Why did people always need to bring up Nazis as a rhetorical talking point? They weren't rhetorical. My great-grandmother had lost both her parents and her sister to them as a child. "Yes, I've read *The Diary of Anne Frank*. I wonder if she still would've said that after the people she was talking about killed her."

Seth frowned. I thought he'd come back with something else about the Holocaust—good luck to him; my Hebrew school education might not do me much good in this land of Presbyterians and Methodists and hard-core atheists, but I could out-knowledge anyone about the Holocaust any day. Instead, he said, "What about the whipped cream?"

"We're out," I said. It was an asshole thing to say, especially considering it was making my business look bad and I couldn't afford to lose even my most annoying customer, but I couldn't help but feel a muted sort of joy as he looked sadly down at his cup. See, Seth? Some people really did just like being mean. At least to people who deserved it. I waited for him to protest that he could literally see the whipped cream can behind me, to call me out, to do something, anything—

His lips rose in an infuriating little smile. "That's probably for the best," he said. "I should be watching my sugar intake anyway. Have a wonderful day, Abby!" He grabbed his coffee and strode off whistling. *Whistling.*

The whistling alone made my headache throb at a steady Category 3 for the rest of the morning into the afternoon, as I wound down the coffee orders and took some time to swipe crumbs off tabletops with a damp rag, then ran into the back for a sorely needed bathroom break. I washed my hands carefully for sanitary reasons, because I was *good* at what I did, damn it, and stared at myself in the mirror. My cheeks were even hollower than usual, and the bags beneath my brown eyes hung heavy enough to hold a croissant each. Or maybe the lighting was just super unflattering in here since the bulb directly above me had gone out.

I'd go with that, I thought, making a mental note to replace it and at the same time knowing there was at least a fifty percent chance I'd forget by the end of the day. It would be so much easier if I still had an employee or two I could ask while I manned the counter, but I'd had to let go both the teenager who helped out on weekends and the retiree who came in on weekday mornings for some extra cash and socialization. It was either that or take a pay cut myself, and I literally couldn't cut my pay any more without skipping meals or getting behind on rent.

My stomach clenched, as it did every time I had these thoughts. Maybe I wasn't as good at what I did (damn it) as I thought, because if I was, wouldn't I be making enough money to keep a couple part-time workers? As it was now, I could barely pay the rent, and that was with me praying that the bakery a few towns over continued to be generous enough to sell me their baked goods at cost in exchange for strategically placed advertisements. What was the point of them advertising in my café, after all, if there weren't enough people stopping in to see them? Now my stomach unclenched and rolled. If I lost my café, I'd have to start all over somewhere else. I wouldn't have the capital to start my own business again.

I could practically hear Seth's irritating chirp. *Look on the bright side! You get so much extra time to brainstorm Christmas coffee specials and draw designs on the menu board.*

My foot hurt. It took me a moment to realize it was because I'd kicked the counter.

Sometimes there was no bright side. Sometimes things just sucked.

2

I USUALLY CLOSED THE CAFÉ UP AROUND FOUR, after the lunch rush (in other words, my usual ten regulars stopping in for a salad or a fancy grilled cheese that was fancy because I used Gorgonzola and put fig jam and arugula on it). My headache was finally beginning to dissipate as I slipped my silenced phone out of my apron pocket for the first time in hours.

Some invoices due I'd deal with after I ate my own lunch (a decidedly non-fancy grilled cheese made with whatever leftover bread and cheese I had in the back before it could go stale or moldy). Some spam emails—those I deleted. A few requests for collaboration with other town businesses—the bookstore wanted to know if I'd consider stocking a few punny cookbooks to try to drive traffic to their store; the craft store asked if I'd want to sell some of their soaps in exchange for them selling bags of my coffee. Those I starred to deal with later, too.

And about a million texts, all from the same group chat. I sighed through my nose. The first one was from Lorna Begley, the president of the town's small business council, which I was on by virtue of running a small business in town. **Emergency mtg at 5pm today in craft store. Very imprt.**

I massaged my temples. Lorna held a whole lot of emergency meetings. Usually, they were because she'd spotted a mouse in her store or heard a rumor that a movie might be filming a few towns over, but occasionally they were about something serious, like when the diner on the town outskirts had burned down and she wanted to brainstorm ideas on how to raise money to rebuild, or when major floods similar to the ones that had hit our town a few years ago were forecasted again. I did not want to deal with Lorna or her weird, unintuitive text abbreviations tonight, but I couldn't skip just in case it was something real.

So instead of replying-all and blowing up everyone else's phones, I just reacted to Lorna's text with a thumbs-up.

Which she reacted to with snark as soon as I showed up to the meeting. "Oh, Abby," she said, glancing up briefly from her phone. "I wasn't sure if you were coming, since you didn't reply."

I gave her my best stretched-lip customer-service smile, trying to counter the usual resting bitch face. I'd gotten enough snark from Lorna asking why I always looked so "angry" or why I couldn't be "happier" around the "holidays." "I liked your text. That meant I was coming."

Her own return smile was equally insincere. "Oh. I see."

If my café was barely staying afloat despite being the premier (read: only) place in town to get decent coffee and a quick lunch to go, I had no idea how Lorna's craft store was still in business. She sold goods for tourists, of which there weren't enough these days: fancy soaps shaped like trees and infused with maple syrup; earrings made of wire in the shape of maple leaves; T-shirts with sayings like *I tapped that in Vermont*. I at least got business from locals. No local would be caught dead with anything in this store.

Lorna and I might have stood there giving each other dead-eyed smiles until meeting time, but someone cleared their throat uncomfortably behind me. It was a familiar throat clearing, one I was used to hearing before its owner asked me if I could show him where the cleaning products were (even though cleaning the bathroom was one of his only chores) or if I could please just apologize to his grandma to keep the family peace (even though I'd always been perfectly polite to her and *she* was the one who'd called me, to my face, a "humorless money-grubbing bitch not good enough to scrape [her] grandson's boots").

I took a deep breath, fully ready for the headache to flare into a full-on Category 4 as I turned around. "Connor."

To his credit, Connor had his shoulders hunched forward like he was trying to fold himself up and disappear, which was difficult when you were precisely six-foot-four and had ears that flamed bright red with any feeling of embarrassment or nervousness. I'd noticed it even in the near-darkness of the grubby Brooklyn dive we'd met at after matching on Hinge. Back then I'd found it endearing.

But that had been a very long time ago. He scratched his reddish curls, grimacing. "Hey, Abby. Been a while."

It really had been, which, to think about it, was impressive in a town with less than six hundred full-time residents and only one main street. I wondered where he was getting his coffee now. Probably letting his mommy make it for him in a standard coffee brewer. "Yeah, I guess," I said, like I didn't know it had been exactly eight months and four days since he dumped me. Which, in turn, was three and a half years after I moved here for him.

You might wonder if I regretted it. I didn't. Not only did I like running my café, something I could currently only have afforded in a tiny town like this, but I'd gotten used to the parade of locals. We might not all be friends—look at Lorna, for example—but we knew all of our businesses and our livelihoods depended on one another, which meant that I knew I could depend on them no matter what. And because I'd moved to town on the arm of a local, I'd been welcomed into the fold, where I'd stayed even after he dumped me.

If I lost my café and had to go somewhere else, I wouldn't just lose my own business, I'd lose all of that. Small communities like this were usually suspicious of outsiders. And I couldn't afford the delightful anonymity of a big city.

I shook off the thought. "What are you doing here?"

I didn't mean for it to sound accusing, but he still took a step back like I'd threatened him with the knife on the table beside us, which had a maple leaf–shaped handle (not just impractical but uncomfortable, too). "Uncle Joe and Aunt May are on vacation, and you know Donny's good for nothing, so they asked me to take over management while they were away."

I nodded. Made sense. Connor freelanced in web development, which made it possible for him to take shifts at his aunt and uncle's restaurant when he was needed. They'd often drafted me back when we were dating, too. I didn't miss it. If I never had to smell a maple-glazed pork roast or maple-bacon sweet potatoes again, it would be too soon.

Connor nodded back, hands stuffed in the pockets of his flannel. I had nothing else to say to him, so thank god Lorna chose this moment to announce, "Okay, looks like everybody's here. Let's get started."

I beelined toward her like I was desperate to hear every word she said, feeling a weight lift off my temples the more steps I took from Connor. Lorna raised her eyebrows at me in the barest nod of approval, which was a bonus. Not that I needed or wanted her approval. It was better for the business to have her not annoyed with me.

She clapped her hands together. "All right, everyone," she said, and the murmurs of the twelve or so business owners faded into the faint jingle of the Christmas music still playing overhead. "I'll cut right to the chase. We've all seen our business dip over the past few years, so we all know we need more people coming by or we're in trouble. I want to hold a holiday festival here in town."

The murmurs rose again, covering up the cheery tune of the currently appropriate "Santa Claus Is Comin' to Town." The thought of a Christmas festival—because, let's be real, when people said "holiday" they meant "Christmas"—made sense, I supposed. Some of the nearby towns hosted big Christmas festivals full of gingerbread houses and hot chocolate and lines to sit on Santa's lap, and they attracted crowds looking for Christmas cheer amid snow and small-town charm. I'd suggested holding one of them to the small business board years ago, when I was fresh and new here. Back then Lorna had told me there were too many in the area to make ours stand out, but she must have changed her mind.

"Awesome," Connor said. "I know Uncle Joe's always wanted to play Santa Claus. It's probably too late for him to grow his beard out, but he's got a fake one in storage just in case. Smells a little like mothballs, but the kids won't care."

Lorna gave him a toothy grin like she was ready for dinner and he was an animal who'd just walked into her trap. "Ah. When you heard me say 'holiday,' you thought 'Christmas.' But that wasn't what I meant." She paused for dramatic tension. "There are too many Christmas markets around here for a new one to stand out. What we're going to hold is a *Hanukkah* market. And Abby is going to run it."

My first thought: huh, I didn't realize there was another Abby in town.

My second thought, as all eyes in the room swiveled to me: oh, shit.

"You don't mean *me*?" I blurted.

Lorna's grin widened. I'd always thought she had too many teeth for her face. Now there they all were, wide and sharp, ready to chomp down on me. "Congratulations, Abby!" She began to clap. After a moment, the rest of the room started clapping, too.

This was all going way too fast. "Wait a second," I said, then raised my voice and repeated it so that everybody could hear me over the applause and the music (now "Silent Night," decidedly *not* appropriate). "Wait a second!" The clapping petered to a stop, but the eyes stayed on me. My skin itched. "I don't understand. Nobody talked to me about this."

"Well, I mean, it's obvious." Lorna sounded as if she were talking to a very small child. "You're the only Jewish person on the council." She left the "or in town" unspoken. "Who else could run it?"

Sweat broke out, chilly on my forehead. It was already dripping down the back of my neck and soaking into the collar of my sweater, which now itched even more against my skin.

I didn't think I'd ever talked about being Jewish with the people in town (to be fair, I didn't talk about most things with the people in town). How did they even know? I imagine asking Lorna and receiving her scornful response. *Your name is Abigail Cohen. And besides.* Her hand waving vaguely at my face, at my thick dark hair and prominent nose. There was no one way to look or sound Jewish—I'd grown up with blond Jews who had tiny noses, Black and brown Jews, Jews with last names like O'Brien and Chiang—but there would be no use telling her that.

It wasn't like I was trying to hide being Jewish. It was a part of me like my freckles or my tendency toward dark humor. It was more like, why bring it up? I wasn't observant. I didn't keep kosher or need days off for the holidays. And I certainly wasn't part of the Jewish community anymore. I'd left that behind when my parents left *me* behind.

I was certainly not going to bring *that* up with her, though. Instead, I said, "Can we talk about this more? I'm not sure I have the time to—"

"Oh, it won't be that much work," Lorna replied. "I've already gathered all the vendor info from my friends who run the other holiday festivals. You just have to tell them what they need to do. And you've got time. It's not even December yet, and the festival won't be until the end of the month."

I blinked. "At the end of the month? But Hanukkah is early this year."

Lorna wrinkled her brow. The song overhead switched to jingling bells. "What?"

It had been years since I'd lit a menorah, but all holidays were automatically filled in on the calendar app I used. "Hanukkah starts soon," I said. At her look of puzzlement, I continued, "Its date is based on the Hebrew calendar, which is a lunar calendar. So in some years it's as early as the end of November or as late as January."

Lorna shrugged. "Okay, but that doesn't change the date of our festival."

"If we're going to do a Hanukkah festival, shouldn't it take place on actual Hanukkah?"

She shrugged again. None of the other business owners seemed especially bothered, either, except for Connor, who looked kind of like he wanted to run away. But that had nothing to do with my questions about the festival. "Most of the Christmas festival revelers don't come on actual Christmas. I don't see why the date matters. Besides, that week between Christmas and New Year's is when the most people have off, whether they celebrate Hanukkah or not."

I opened my mouth to keep arguing—it just didn't seem right!—but something stopped me. Why did I care so much?

It wasn't like I was observant. It wasn't like I was planning to celebrate anyway. "Okay, fine," I said, trying to ignore the unease simmering in my stomach.

Lorna clapped her hands together. "So you'll do it, then!"

"What? That wasn't what I said." I still had so many emails to respond to, and I had to prep for tomorrow's menu, and I had to clean out the whole café and, right, change that stupid lightbulb, and that was just today. "I still don't think I have the—"

"We really appreciate it so much," Lorna said loudly, bulldozing right over me. This time the group reacted, everybody nodding, probably relieved that all this work wasn't getting dumped on their shoulders. "Can you believe there aren't any Hanukkah festivals in all of New England? Imagine the untapped market in New York City and Boston. There are a lot of Jewish people there who aren't currently being served." She gave me a meaningful look. "It's just what this town needs."

My mouth snapped shut. It was hard to argue with her about anything that would bring people to town. The numbers on my latest balance sheet floated before my eyes the way they did every night when I tried to go to sleep. If putting on a festival would keep me in business, then maybe I should just do it. It wasn't like I had to feel Irish to make mint-green coffee specials for Saint Patrick's Day or Christian to order pastel pink pastries for Easter.

Besides, Lorna said she had all the vendors already, she just didn't have the knowledge she needed. As distant as I felt from the synagogue I grew up in, I did still remember the basics. I could tell a food vendor to stock up on doughnuts and frozen latkes; I could make sure the lights guy sourced a menorah instead of an inflatable Santa. “Fine,” I said grudgingly. “I’ll need that list.”

Hanukkah was all about celebrating a miracle. If this worked out okay, I wouldn’t need a miracle to save my café—just a little extra work.

3

OR A LOT OF EXTRA WORK. BY THE TIME I'D FINished leaving messages for all the vendors—because the festival was only a month away and I needed to start planning immediately—it was almost eight o'clock, and I still had prep to do, and I needed to clean, and I ended up falling asleep facedown on a table.

So that meant a hectic morning when my phone alarm beeped me awake. I didn't have time to shower, just a few minutes to pop upstairs for a quick face wash and deodorant swab before going back downstairs to get the pastry delivery and finish the cleaning I'd abandoned last night.

Which meant that I was extra not in the mood when Seth showed up for his daily pumpkin spice latte with whipped cream, which I was benevolent enough to give him today. "Hey, Abby, are you okay?" he asked when he saw my face, his brows furrowed with concern.

I swear, if he told me to smile, I was going to dive over the counter and waterboard him with his coffee.

Fortunately for him, he continued with, "Do you want

to talk about it?" which was still irritating but not worthy of torture.

"No, I do not," I said. "Have a good day. Next!" I looked behind him. Alas, there was nobody there.

"Okay, so you don't want to talk about it, that's okay," he said earnestly. "What if I bought you a coffee so you could sit down for a minute and take a break? You don't have anyone waiting right now."

A Category 4 was already tapping at my temples, asking politely to be let in before bringing out the battering ram. I closed my eyes and took a deep breath, trying to convince it that I wasn't home. The scents of cinnamon and coffee and banana bread—today's bakery special—filled my nostrils, calming me down the tiniest bit.

"You gave me free whipped cream today," Seth said. "It's the least I could do."

My eyes snapped open. "The least you could do? Dude, I gave you free whipped cream because I charged you for it yesterday and then didn't give it to you. It was bad business that I was correcting. That is *all*." I could barely hear the guitar quartet strumming Christmas music from the speakers over the blood thumping in my head. "And thank you for reminding me that I don't have any customers waiting. I hadn't noticed how bad business is. I really appreciate it." The sarcasm was bitter on my tongue. I'd have to wash it down with a sugary coffee once Seth was gone.

Speaking of Seth, his face was dropping more and more with every word. His hazel eyes were almost hidden by those thick dark brows now. Good. He should feel bad. As bad as I did. I continued, "And even without customers to take care of at this moment, I still have so much to do. Too much. Vendors to call back, and cleaning to do, and"—*Argh!*—"that fucking lightbulb in the bathroom I still have to change!"

My words stopped at the exact moment the playlist overhead paused. The silence rang through the room, bouncing off the twinkling fairy lights I'd strung from the ceiling and the 1950s-era photos on the walls that could plausibly be this place seventy years ago but that I'd actually bought at a thrift shop for ambiance.

Seth took a step back, hands raised in front of him. At some point he'd set the coffee down on a table, like he was worried I'd throw it at him if he put it on the counter. "Sounds like a lot," he said, and now his eyebrows pinched together in sympathy.

That was the last thing I wanted: anyone's pity. Despite the roiling in my stomach, I shrugged, then crossed my arms. "It's fine. I don't know what came over me. It's not even that much compared to next month. I'm good at what I do and I can handle it."

"I know you're good at what you do. Why do you think I come here every morning?"

Because you get off on irritating people? Or maybe because I'm the only decent coffee shop in a ten-mile radius? I chose to stay silent. Instead, I grabbed a damp rag from the shelf behind me. If I was going to stand here anyway, I might as well wipe crumbs off the counter.

"Life can still get to you no matter how good you are at something."

Scrub. Scrub. I might actually scrub a hole in the cheap Formica left behind by the previous owner, which I'd never got around to replacing. I ground my teeth. Erupting like that didn't make me feel better. I felt like I'd scrubbed a hole in myself, and now anyone could just take a peek inside at my beating heart and blood vessels and pulsing lungs and see exactly where they should cut me to make me bleed the most.

"I prefer to think of myself as an open book," Seth said. "I like talking things out so that they don't just fester inside my head."

An open book? Okay, then. I was a locked diary. Or, as Connor had so sweetly put it when he dumped me, *We've been together for more than four years and I feel like I barely know you.*

Fine. Everything was fine. Love was overrated anyway. It had been almost a relief when Connor moved out. Then I knew I was safe, that there was nobody close enough where they could hurt me.

The bell tinkled over the door. *Thank. God.* I whipped my head up and pasted on my sunniest customer-service smile, lifting up on my toes to see over Seth's mountainous shoulder. "Good morning!" I trilled extra hard, showing the world and the universe and anyone who happened to be watching that I was totally, entirely *fine.* "What can I get for you?"

I threw myself into helping the customer pick between a cherry Danish and an almond croissant, a decision that from the wrinkle in his brow would make you think involved the nuclear codes, and by the time I turned back to the customer with his latte, Seth had vanished. So had the other two customers in the store. A relief, as it allowed me a moment to sag against the counter and wipe my forehead with my apron, which left crumbs clinging to my hair. Glamorous.

Off to the bathroom to rinse them out. I only remembered as I was stepping over the threshold that the light was out, which would mean trying to use the mirror would be useless . . .

. . . except that, as I automatically flipped on the switch, the light went on, too. So bright it dazzled me for a moment, made me look down at the floor and blink a few times to regain my bearings.

When I looked back up, I noticed the packaging from the new lightbulb, which I kept in the bathroom closet, sitting proudly on the back of the toilet. Someone had scrawled something on it in green Sharpie. I exhaled slowly as I read.

Hope this helps even just a little bit! —Seth ☺

Of course he'd sign with a smiley. He was probably disappointed he didn't have any i's in his name that he could dot with hearts or o's he could fill with little faces. I stood in front of the sink and washed the crumbs out of my hair with the assistance of the light overhead, leaving a big wet splotch on my apron.

And yet still, as I dried my hands on my apron—what was another splotch?—and went back out behind the counter, I had to admit it: the headache had receded. And the day felt just a little bit more manageable.

I sighed. Maybe I shouldn't have been quite so harsh earlier. Even if he *had* been extremely annoying. Changing the bulb for me hardly made up for that, I told myself. And almost believed it.

Fine. He could have real free whipped cream tomorrow.

4

OF COURSE, THAT SLIGHTLY LIGHTER FEELING ONLY lasted until the end of the day. As I closed up shop, my lips thinned as I counted the day's receipts. The numbers were even worse than yesterday's. If things didn't look up soon, I'd have to . . . I didn't even know what I'd have to do. I couldn't just close down, considering my home and my business were one and the same. I'd have to move. And where? I liked it here. I liked the cold fresh air in the morning, the idea that everybody knew and could depend on one another so that nothing felt too overwhelming, the feeling of isolation from the larger world and all the things it could do to you.

It reminded me of what I'd felt like growing up. Sure, the suburbs of New York City were nothing like small-town Vermont: I didn't know anywhere close to all my neighbors, and I certainly didn't stop and chat with them at the store.

I was thinking more of my community. Of the Jewish youth group I'd grown up in, of the people at my family's synagogue, of the way people showed up with food whenever a relative died or sang to me at my bat mitzvah even though I barely knew them or swooped in with offers of help anytime someone lost a job or hit hard times. It had been like sitting by a warm fire all my life, protecting me from the cold.

And then, well. When I got turned out into the cold, I didn't even have a coat.

It was the Hanukkah festival bringing up all these memories, I decided as I brushed a dusting of snow from the windshield of my car and got behind the wheel. It wasn't even five yet, but the sun was already setting, giving the tree-covered mountains in the distance a fiery glow. I just had to get this over with, and then I could go back to not thinking about the past.

Surely, it wouldn't be too long—I was, after all, on my way to meet with one of Lorna's vendors. I'd already spoken with the logistics guy, who was in charge of making sure the area where the festival would be held—the town's central green square—wouldn't be lit on fire by electrical cords snaking everywhere and that we'd have proper restroom and EMT access as required by law. He'd been fine. Hopefully, the other vendors would be, too.

First up was the scenery guy, who was responsible for decorating and sourcing all the physical booths we'd need along with the little extra things to make the ambiance extra festive. I was meeting him at an early Christmas festival he was setting up in a nearby town. Gravel crunched under my tires as I pulled into the parking area, noting the abundance of trucks and trailers surrounding me.

Funnily enough, the guy actually looked a little like Santa Claus, big and burly with a cropped white beard and round red nose. "Evening," he said. The sun had set fully now, but it almost didn't feel that way with the blazing lights surrounding us. "You must be Abby?"

"I am. And you must be Fred?" We shook hands. I tried to match him, but it was hard when it felt like he was trying to crush my finger bones to dust. Not very Santa-like. "Lorna spoke very highly of your work. And of course I've seen it at the Willingboro Christmas Festival."

He smiled, revealing a gap between his two front teeth. "Thank you kindly. I have to say, I was immediately intrigued when Lorna told me she was planning a Hanukkah festival. That's something new around here. Should be fun, though."

I hadn't realized I was tense until my body relaxed. There was always something about meeting a new person in an area where there weren't a lot of Jews, or even where there were a lot of Jews, actually. People could get weird about Jews in the direction of really hating us or professing to love us so much it got creepy. And I don't even want to mention the frequency with which somebody would casually bring up Jesus and wouldn't I be happier if I found him.

"Awesome," I said. "So, looking at what the Christmas festivals all seem to have and what seem to be successful at drawing people in, I think it would be fun to have some kind of 'here's the story of Hanukkah' display, and—"

"What *is* the story of Hanukkah?" Fred interrupted. He paused before a massive Christmas tree sparkling with multicolored lights. I blinked at it, dazzled for a moment, before turning back to him.

You'd think he would have googled the basics before

meeting with me. But whatever. It was fine. "Basically, Hanukkah is about a Jewish revolt against non-Jewish oppressors. In the land of ancient Israel, Jewish territory was conquered by this asshole of a king Antiochus who decided to outlaw Judaism. He made all sorts of jerk moves like putting up an altar to false gods in the sacred Temple and ordering pigs, which are not kosher, to be sacrificed on it. Anyway, this group of guys called the Maccabees revolted against the king and fought against his army and the Jews who'd gone along with their edicts."

"Sounds bloody," Fred said.

I chose not to respond to that. "The Maccabees won and defeated the king and the army, but the problem was that the Temple was still defiled. They cleaned up and everything, but the oil that was supposed to keep the eternal light lit, well, eternally, was defiled, too. They only had enough suitable oil left to keep the lamp lit for one more day, even though it would take them eight days to make more. But, miracle!" I did jazz hands, which immediately made me feel like an idiot. But letting them fall would only make me feel like more of an idiot, so I kept those things shimmering and shimmying for the whole next sentence. "That one day of oil lasted eight days instead, so by the time it would have gone out, the new batch was ready! So Hanukkah doesn't just commemorate the successful revolt, but the miracle of the oil. That's why we eat foods fried in oil and light the menorah for eight days."

Fred did not seem super impressed, not even by my jazz hands. "That's not what I expected," he said.

"Well, what did you expect?"

He shrugged. The lights blinked on and off behind him. "Something less bloody, without as much war or as many dead pigs? Something more heartwarming, I guess? Like Christmas."

I supposed it was hard to get more heartwarming than the birth of a magical miracle baby with stars twinkling in the sky and cuddly (live) farm animals all around. "Well, Hanukkah is technically a minor holiday. It only gets so much attention in Western culture because it's right around Christmas." He squinted at me. I continued, "Besides, most of our holidays aren't really the heartwarming sort. Mostly, they commemorate times different groups have tried to kill us and failed. Or trees; we as a people really like trees. Great food, though." He squinted at me even harder. I wasn't sure why I felt the need to go on. "Except for the holidays that involve fasting. But even they have good food at the end of them, usually."

"All righty, then," Fred said, with the tone of a doctor telling a patient that the ache in their ankle didn't mean they had cancer. "Well, we work with what we have. This festival demonstrates our inventory pretty well, I think." He gestured at the tree behind me. "We have all sorts of lights. Hanukkah colors are blue and white, right? We can deck your tree out in blue and white lights."

Now it was my turn to squint. "What tree?"

"There's always a tree at these festivals," he said. "And it shouldn't be hard to put one of those Jewish stars at the top instead of a golden angel or a regular star. What do you think?"

What did I think? I thought that he was totally missing

the point. “Decorated trees aren’t really a Hanukkah thing,” I said. “I don’t think we’ll want one for a Hanukkah festival.”

He sighed heavily. “All right. Let’s take a walk around, then.”

As he led me around the ghostly grounds, all set up yet empty of people, I wondered why I cared so much. The easy thing to do would be to just nod and agree with whatever he told me. It wasn’t like I was the one paying after all. Tourists would still come, curious at the novelty of a Hanukkah festival if they weren’t Jewish or, if they were, thrilled by the crumbs thrown their way. I still remembered being a kid when Hallmark’s one Hanukkah movie aired every year in the middle of their Christmas marathon. No matter how terrible the movie was, no matter how inaccurate it felt to our experiences or pandering it felt to the general non-Jewish audience, it was still so exciting to feel like someone was speaking to us.

Fred stopped before the Nativity scene, whose life-size plastic figures glowed in pale blues and pinks and whites. “I have a bunch of sets of these guys. I don’t think it would be too hard to set them up differently to show the Hanukkah story,” he said, waving his arm over them. “Would a sheep work in place of the pig? And we could put those little hats on the Three Wise Men and make them into your rebels.”

I exhaled deeply through my nose. “No, a sheep wouldn’t work in place of the pig. The whole point is that pigs aren’t kosher, so sacrificing a pig in the Temple was profane in a way a sheep was not. And no, we can’t just put yarmulkes on the Three Wise Men and turn them into Maccabees.”

He threw his hands in the air. "I didn't even get to my idea of using a Frosty the Snowman as the evil king! You know, it's symbolic. A cold heart and all that."

The rest of the tour didn't go much better. He tried to sell me on garlands of holly as a generic wintertime decoration and on using light-up reindeer noses for a menorah ("There are eight of them! It's perfect!") and did not take kindly to my telling him there were actually nine candles on a hanukkiah, counting the shammash that lit the other candles. By the end, I was shaking my head before he could finish telling me his idea for repurposing his rental Santa outfit into a jelly doughnut costume (don't ask).

The food guy, who was supposed to coordinate vendors for the food booths and source ingredients, was just as unhelpful on the phone the next day. "Kosher?" he said. "What's that?"

At least for once, Seth didn't make it worse. As soon as I'd seen him walking past the window toward the door, I'd started preparing his pumpkin spice latte. That way I'd have it ready by the time he made it to the counter, meaning minimal time for talking. Though of course he tried anyway. "Is there any coffee in there under all that whipped cream?" he asked, picking up the cup, his glancing smile telling me he was joking. "How much did you charge me for this?"

Had he not even looked at the screen before blithely swiping his card? He was lucky I wasn't a scammer. I always carefully examined any receipts before paying for anything to make sure nobody was trying to take advantage of me. "It's free," I said. "In appreciation for changing my lightbulb yesterday."

I expected him to crack another joke or smile and say thank you, but his response surprised me in its seriousness. "You don't have to give me anything for it. Knowing I helped you out is enough."

Ugh. His sincerity made me want to empty the whole container of whipped cream into a pretty white tower on his head. "Whatever," I grumbled. But he didn't push it. He just took a sip, gave a happy sigh from underneath his whipped cream mustache, and walked away with a spring in his step.

Given my difficulties with the vendors, when Lorna's name popped up on my buzzing phone, I was not all that eager to pick it up. And not even because I'd just closed the café and plopped down on my secondhand cracked leather couch upstairs to take a much-needed break. "Abby," she said without preamble. The force of her voice practically shook the leaves of the half-dead plants Connor had left behind on the windowsills due to his mom's allergies. "I hear you didn't hire the decorator or the food vendor I sent you to."

I slipped off my Crocs—ugly, but nothing else kept my feet from throbbing after a long day the way they did—and tucked my legs under me. "Neither of them knew what they were doing."

Lorna sucked in a deep breath. I braced myself for her to yell, but the quiet, deadly voice that came out was somehow even scarier. "Of course they know what they're doing. They run all the Christmas festivals in the area. If they don't know what they're doing, then nobody up here knows what they're doing."

I focused on the crack that ran from the ceiling to the floor right next to where my living space turned into the tiny kitchen. My apartment hadn't fallen apart yet, so I hadn't bothered to call the landlord about it. Something that had always bothered Connor, but then why hadn't he just called the landlord himself? "I'm sure they run amazing Christmas festivals. But Hanukkah festivals are different. We need different things, different foods, different setups. You can't just put blue and white lights and a Star of David on a Christmas tree and say it's for Hanukkah."

"Why not?" asked Lorna. I almost laughed before I realized she wasn't joking.

A chilly wind blew in through my window, making me shiver. The window was closed. That was probably a problem. Maybe I *should* call the landlord. "If we're not going to do it right, why bother holding a Hanukkah festival at all?"

"For the tourism dollars," Lorna said bluntly. "That we need to keep this town alive. That, need I remind you, *you* need to keep your café alive."

She let the words hang there in the air between our phones. I focused harder on the crack in the wall. Maybe, if I was really lucky, the ceiling would fall in and entomb me. Like, not enough to kill me, but enough to land me in the hospital for a little while. I'd be out my deductible, which might lead me to financial ruin, but at least I wouldn't be expected to put together this festival from my sickbed.

Lorna sighed. "You know, it's okay if you want to bow out. I can take over, or give it to someone else."

Someone else who would go back to the vendors and say that, sure, telling the story of the Maccabees with the

Nativity figures seemed cool, and sure, who needed a giant menorah when we could have a big tree, was what she meant. Despite literally thinking moments before that I'd rather put myself in the hospital than do this, the thought of her doing it wrong felt even worse.

It was already bad enough that the Hanukkah festival couldn't be held on actual Hanukkah. I could just imagine the Jewish tourists traveling up from New York City and Boston, so excited by their little scrap of representation, only to find a Christmas festival colored blue and white.

I hated the thought. I hated that I cared so much when I felt like I no longer belonged among those very same people I was trying to impress. It wasn't like I could fill the hole that they left in me by putting on an incredible festival. And yet. "No," I told her. "I can do it. Give me a few days to find other people."

Just the thought of dedicating more of my vanishingly rare free time to hunting down appropriate vendors threatened to bring on a Category 4. Lorna asked, "Where are you going to find them?"

"I'll ask the local Jewish community," I said, trying to sound as confident as I could.

A confidence I was pretty sure was misplaced, which I confirmed as soon as I hung up and googled it. There *was* no local Jewish community. Vermont only had a few thousand of us in the first place, and those of us who were here were scattered all over the state. There were some congregations in the bigger cities, like Burlington. I could theoretically make the long drive there and ask around.

But what if they could just look at me and know how

much I felt like a fraud? How much I felt like I no longer belonged? I hadn't been to a synagogue in years. I hadn't celebrated any holidays, or exercised my rusty Hebrew, or observed the rest day of Shabbat, since I left home. What if they took one glance at me and told me I wasn't one of them?

Just the thought made my long, low exhale shake.

Maybe I could find somebody nearby who wasn't a fraud, who knew things I didn't or could ask around in my place. I mean, there were Jews in places like Nepal and Tanzania. There had to be at least a few of us within fifty miles in this country with the second-highest Jewish population in the world. But how to find them? If only there was an app for that.

Wait. There *was* an app for that. Wasn't there? For dating? Like Tinder, but for Jews. I wasn't looking to date, but as long as I made that clear on my profile, nobody could fault me for trying to connect. Right?

Before I could convince myself it was a terrible idea, I'd opened up the app store and begun the download. Only a few seconds and, with a ping, it was prompting me to set up my profile. I had to look like someone nice and friendly who probably wouldn't try to murder a potential partner, so I took a few minutes to scroll through pictures on my phone. There weren't a lot of great options: I wasn't one for selfies, and . . . was it sad to say I didn't get out and do much worth taking pictures of? It wasn't like I could populate my profile with photos of my lunch specials and seasonal coffee offerings.

Sad or not, the thought was making me feel some kind of way, so I hurriedly picked a few that weren't terrible—one the local paper had taken of me at work at the café; two of me and Connor together where I had to crop him out—and made my profile go live. Heart pattering with anticipation, I went to start swiping. And I swiped.

Once. Because there was apparently only one other Jew—or at least only one other Jew on the app—within fifty miles of me. I stared at my empty screen, blinking not so much with shock but with maybe a little surprise. I'd been so amped to go that I hadn't even looked at the profile of that one person, assuming I'd have at least a few more to go.

My phone buzzed. Match! Could it be bashert?

I rolled my eyes. No, we were probably not soulmates.

A fact that became even more obvious when I saw the profile photo. That cheerful grin not even slightly impeded by the dark beard surrounding it. That stupid name I didn't even bother scrawling on the coffee cup anymore.

Seth.

I didn't like to think much about my parents, but my mom popped into my head right now anyway. She was short, like me, and just as pale, her dark hair cropped into a pixie and her lips always pursed. Or at least they had been the last time I'd seen her, over five years ago—it was an undeniable fact that I'd gotten my resting bitch face from her, though she was a lot better at covering it up with genuine-looking smiles. She'd always claimed to "just know" if someone she met, or an actor on a show she was watching, was Jewish. *It's all our shared trauma as a people,* she said once, tone grandiose. *It reaches out to the other. Forms an immediate connection knowing that we've survived all the same things.*

Apparently, my own Jewdar was broken, because I'd

never felt anything like that from Seth. Just grating annoyance and the overwhelming desire for him to leave my presence immediately.

I had to unmatch him. Whether it killed the festival or not, there was no way—no way—I could let him see my face on this app or let him think that I'd purposefully swiped right on him. Ugh. The Hanukkah festival could burn like the First Temple. Just the idea of him thinking there might be more than a business relationship between us made me want the ceiling to collapse on me again—this time leaving no survivors.

But just as my thumb reached for the bright red button, my phone buzzed. With a message. And considering I'd only swiped right on one person, there was only one person it could be from.

Ugh.

Well, what was done was done. I might as well read it. Hey! Is this the Abby from Good Coffee?

I briefly fantasized about saying no, then letting him think I just had a look-alike in the area with the same name. But that was not plausible, given how few people there were around here. Yup.

His response came immediately. I see! I wasn't sure. I thought there might be another Abby in the area who smiled every so often.

I raised my eyebrow at the gall. I was smiling a lot more in my pictures than I did around him, but there was a reason for that. Maybe I smile all the time when you're not around.

No response came immediately that time. I sighed. God

help me, I was actually feeling a little twinge of . . . bad. So I added, grudgingly, By the way, thanks again for changing that lightbulb. That was a nice thing to do. It really helped me out.

Those three little bubbles indicating typing appeared, then disappeared. To distract myself from what he might be struggling to say—not like I cared—I clicked over to his photos.

His profile pic was a full-body shot from far enough away where you could barely see his face, a posed shot of him standing triumphantly atop the summit of a—hey, I knew that mountain. Back when I had days off instead of "days off," I used to drive an hour east toward the New Hampshire border and do this exact same hike. I'd had to hike a lot of mountains to find this perfect one: a steep enough slope where I sweated and panted going up but that wasn't so steep where I felt like I might fall off or had to clamber my stumpy legs up too many menacingly smooth rocks; long enough where I got a good workout but short enough where I didn't have to stress about being stuck there overnight if I twisted my ankle; a stunning view of rolling trees and sky and tiny dollhouses to reward me for making it to the top.

Maybe I'd even hiked by him at some point. Nodded at him in the universal greeting of hikers.

So that I didn't have to think too much about how there might have been a time when I didn't find him extremely annoying, I swiped to the next one. This one was a close-up of him mid–giant smile, eyes half-closed as the pudgiest corgi I'd ever seen licked his face.

I was not immune to the power of an adorable corgi. It took me a few seconds to swipe past it, and I had to make myself scowl to erase the tiny smile playing on my lips.

The rest of his pictures were standard dating profile flair: him with a group of carefully less-good-looking friends; him smiling with a young child to show how unthreatening he was; even one of him in a suit wearing a kippah, a nice pander to the more observant users of the app. No photos of him with a fish he'd caught or with a tiger, which I'd learned over many years of swiping were often warning signs of bro-dom.

My phone buzzed with a message. You're welcome. So. Want to meet up and talk about something other than coffee?

That corgi flitted through my mind. Maybe if he brought his dog, spending time with him wouldn't be quite so insufferable, because I could ignore him and play with the dog.

No. *Down, Abby. You're here for a reason, and you need to be up front about it.* Which was a good thing, actually, because it would immediately take whatever expectations Seth might have from me off the table. Just FYI, I'm not on here looking for an actual date. I've been drafted into planning a Hanukkah festival and am looking for help from whatever local Jew I can find. Could you maybe help with that?

I stopped. Wondered why he might offer to help me without anything in return—there was only so far this sunny "all I want is to know I helped you out" attitude could take me, surely. So I added, Free pumpkin spice lattes all winter if you can. I stared at the screen grudgingly for a moment. With extra whipped cream.

Those three little typing bubbles popped up, then

disappeared. Popped up again, disappeared again. Sweat prickled on the back of my neck. What if he blew me off? Took a look at what I'd asked for and what I'd offered, and figured it wasn't worth it?

The typing bubbles appeared again. This time words came after them. I am susceptible to bribery, he wrote. But I just had a better idea. Maybe we can help each other.

What do you mean?

Let's talk in person.

I hated myself for thinking it, but, well: I was intrigued. I suggested meeting at the café to make things easy. He said that would be fine if that's what worked best for me, but he'd really been wanting to check out this holiday pop-up bar a couple towns over. Maybe it could inspire your festival.

It was an interesting idea. And honestly, I wanted to get out of my café for a bit. So even though it meant an extra half hour of driving and the associated gas money, I agreed.

It couldn't be that bad, right? What were the odds I could convince him to bring the dog?

5

AS IT TURNED OUT, THE CORGI WASN'T EVEN HIS. Which means I'd basically agreed to this meeting under false pretenses. "I only agreed to come because of the possibility I might one day get to play with your fat corgi," I said, then realized how that had sounded.

Fortunately, Seth either had a less dirty mind than me or was polite enough to snicker only on the inside. "Sorry. He's my friend's. So is the cute kid."

That, at least, was a relief. I didn't even know if I wanted kids, and I definitely wasn't ready to be a stepmom.

Not that that had anything to do with anything right now. There was no chance of me being anyone's stepmom. This was just a business meeting. A business meeting at a holiday pop-up bar.

By "holiday," the bar of course meant Christmas. Christmas music was jingling over the speakers, and the warm wooden walls were strung with garlands of tinsel and twinkling multicolored lights; a tall Christmas tree glittered in one corner, and the bartender and servers were all decked out in Santa hats. The menu included such gems as the "Naughty but Nice" (lots of cinnamon and some chili pepper) and the neon Day-Glo green "Grinch" (melon liqueur and vodka). The one token Hanukkah cocktail was called the "Hebrew Hammer" and was not only a disconcerting shade of blue but consisted mostly of tequila. Hammer, indeed.

I went with a simple cranberry cordial, and Seth got an eggnog. "I've never really understood eggnog," I said, grimacing at the thick white liquid in his crystal glass from where I sat beside him at the bar. "It's just . . . like, milk and alcohol together. Gross."

"You're missing out." He took a sip. "It's like drinking cake."

"Like I said, gross," I said. "Though maybe it's because I never really had it until I was older. It could be an acquired taste. Like gefilte fish." I still remembered the time my cousin brought her non-Jewish boyfriend to the family Passover seder. He'd gamely eaten the matzah and the egg in salt water, but when she passed him the little paper plate of mushy gray fish cylinder topped with glistening globs of gelatinous slime, he'd quite literally gone green.

"Gefilte fish is delicious, though," Seth said. "I like the stuff from the jar—classic—but have you had the fancy kind that comes in a loaf from a good deli? Fantastic."

I shook my head. "I'm a jar girl all the way." Though I hadn't had it in so many years. They probably didn't even carry it at the grocery stores up here.

It felt nice to talk to someone who didn't just know what gefilte fish was, but didn't gag at the thought of it, even if that someone was Seth. I took a sip of my cranberry cordial. Nice and sweet and tart enough to make me pucker up.

"I wouldn't have pinned you for a jar girl," Seth said with an easy smile. "I would've pinned you as a girl who goes to the river, catches her own carp, and bludgeons it to death in the bathtub."

"I'll take that as a compliment," I said.

"I meant it as a compliment."

"Good." I wasn't sure how to take *that*. "Anyway, about why we're here." I'd already told him a bit about the Hanukkah festival in our messages, but now I elaborated, going into what Lorna had asked me, what I thought would make for a good Hanukkah festival, and my disastrous talks with the Christmas vendors. "So, I was really hoping that you might know . . . well, anything and anyone more than me. If you know anyone I should contact, especially if they can source kosher food or happen to own an enormous blow-up menorah, that would be amazing."

He leaned into me, so close I could see a few crumbs of sugar from his drink rim clinging to his beard. They glittered like tiny snowflakes. I breathed in deep, trying not to think about it, but that only made me realize that he smelled like oranges and campfire. Which I really shouldn't have been able to smell, considering the strong odor of mulling spices drifting my way from behind the bar. "Abby," he said solemnly. "I can solve all of your problems."

"You definitely cannot solve all of my problems. You don't even know what all my problems are." And I certainly wasn't going to share them.

If I were him, I probably would have rolled my eyes. But

he just grinned. "I mean all your problems related to the Hanukkah festival." Dramatic pause.

Which I did not have patience for. "Spill it."

"So I'm from New York," Seth said. "And there's a reason they call it Jew York City."

"I've literally never heard anyone call it that," I said. "Except maybe on 4chan. And those aren't the people you want talking about the Jews."

"You're familiar with 4chan? I have so many questions. But anyway, I grew up in one of those Jewish families who knows everyone. Between my parents and my cousins and my Hebrew school friends and summer camp pals, I'm probably connected to every kosher food vendor or enormous blow-up menorah owner in the city, and that's not even mentioning the theater players with a skit about the Hanukkah story and the Hanukkah craft ladies and the—"

"I got it," I interrupted, solely because I was sick of hearing his voice and not at all because of the stab of jealousy that hit me upon hearing about his close-knit community and family. Or at least that's what I told myself. "So you'll help me? In exchange for all the free coffee and whipped cream you can drink?"

What I expected based on my past experiences with him: him to smile big, nod like he'd just downed a glass full of sugar (which he had), and gush about how helping people gave him such a high he'd never even thought about taking drugs.

What I got: a keen glint in those hazel eyes, a cock of his head like he was considering pushing me off my stool, and his arms crossing over his chest.

I was immediately intrigued. When he spoke, the intrigue rose even higher. Also the annoyance, but that tended to rise whenever anybody spoke, honestly. "It'll cost you more than free coffee."

"I don't have any money," I said. I had a sense that wasn't what he was talking about, but I wanted to get it out of the way anyway. "And I own nothing of consequence, unless you want a collection of vintage fast-food glasses I've accumulated at yard sales or a bunch of half-dead plants. And honestly, you can take the plants. They're too much commitment for me."

"I mean, I'll take your plants. I'm a great plant dad," he said. "But I meant more a price of your time, and also maybe your sanity."

"That would scare me if I had any sanity left after sitting here with you for an hour."

He pointed at me. "See? That's what I need. Say that around my mom and she'll love you forever. She loves it when people take the piss out of me."

I blinked. Maybe that explained why he kept coming back to the café and trying to befriend me no matter how many times I rebuffed him: he was used to snark meaning love. "Why would I be talking to your mom?"

He folded his arms on the bar and leaned into them, almost knocking over his nearly empty glass. "Because if you want me to help you create the Hanukkah festival of your dreams, you'll be coming home with me for Hanukkah."

I laughed. When he didn't, my own laugh fell off my face. "Are you joking?"

I already knew he wasn't, but he confirmed. "No. Hanukkah starts next week, and I'm supposed to spend it in New York with my family. I want you to come home with me and pretend that we're dating."

Okay, this time I couldn't hold the laughter back. "That we're *dating*?"

He cast his eyes down at the bar and traced a crack there with his index finger. "You don't have to remind me that you find the thought of it so hilarious."

"I . . ." He was right. I was kind of being a dick. But it wasn't even the thought of me dating him that I found so hilarious—it was the thought of him wanting to date *me*. Me, whose own family had cast her out. Me, who was barely even Jewish. Me, who was hanging on to her café and her place here in the community by a thread. I said, "That wasn't what I meant. I was just surprised."

His shoulders relaxed a little bit. "Okay. I get that. So, are you in?"

"I still have so many questions," I said. "Why do you want me, of all people, to be your fake girlfriend? Why do you need a fake girlfriend in the first place?"

He answered me with a question of his own. "Why do you think I was on that app at all?" He didn't wait for me to respond. "My parents don't love that I moved so far away from them."

"You're not that far," I said. "You don't even have to fly to get down there."

"I know, right?" he said, shaking his head. "I could be living across the ocean or something. And they're worried about me being all alone in a Jewless land. When I say *worried*, I mean there are weeks where my mom calls me crying every day about how she's devastated I'm so far away from my family and my community and my people. So if I can bring home a Nice Jewish Girlfriend I met up here who's keeping me connected, she'll stop stressing out so much."

"Aw, you're a mama's boy," I teased. It was maybe the least surprising thing I'd learned about him.

He grumbled, "If I was that much of a mama's boy, I wouldn't have moved so far away from her." He perked up. "So what do you say?"

"Still not done with the questions," I said. Behind me, a group of guys burst into a rousing chorus of "Jingle Bells." I sipped my cocktail quietly, waiting for them to finish in a round of cheers, before continuing on. "Obviously, we're not really dating. Won't people pick up on that? Like, no offense, but I don't really want to cuddle up each night in your childhood twin bed."

"My bed at home is actually a full, thank you very much," said Seth. "And you don't have to worry about that. My parents might be Jewish, but they're pretty WASPy Jews as far as things like PDA go. Nobody's going to be expecting us to cuddle or kiss. And as far as bed sharing goes, my parents have a rule that under their roof you can't sleep in the same room unless you're married. Used to drive my ex crazy that one of us had to take the couch."

"You're taking the couch," I said. "I want the bed." The words had barely come out of my mouth before I realized what they were. A confirmation. I was . . . actually considering doing this?

I could ask Maggie, the retiree, to come back in for a week and take care of the café—she already knew what she was doing, and I trusted her. I'd be out the money I had to pay her, but I'd basically be breaking even, which I could survive for a week. And if I could put on the absolute best Hanukkah festival that would already be pricking the ears of all these New Yorkers jonesing for a winter-break getaway . . . well, I'd be repaid many times over. Like investing in the stock market. Or so I imagined. I didn't have enough money to invest in the stock market.

"You can have the bed," Seth said. "Are you in?"

It didn't seem like the worst idea in the world, but something stayed my tongue. It seemed too rash to agree to something that big on the spur of the moment. I was more prudent than that. "I need some time to think about it."

"No worries," Seth said. "Just let me know. Last minute is fine. I think the whole thing is actually more fun if I don't even warn my parents you're coming."

I choked on the last sip of my cranberry drink. It went down the wrong pipe, making my lungs way too festive. "Please don't make me surprise anyone. What if they say they have no room? Or that they don't want me there?"

"One, having no room at the inn was how Jesus was born, so maybe that's how we finally get the Messiah," Seth said. I snorted back my laugh this time so that I wouldn't drown in merriment. "And two, you clearly haven't met my parents, who are maybe the most welcoming people in the world. My mom would rather choke on a ham sandwich than tell a guest she doesn't have space for them. She'd put you in her bed and sleep on the floor if she had to." He stopped and considered for a moment. "You'd have to sleep next to my dad, though. And he snores."

The bartender stopped by to see if we wanted another round. I hesitated. "I shouldn't. I'm driving after this."

"Me too," said Seth. "I probably shouldn't have more."

I'd dreaded the thought of coming here in the first place, but now the thought of the night ending, well . . . it didn't quite fill me with dread, but it didn't fill me with delight, either.

Seth said, "How are your mocktails?"

Apparently, the candy cane mocktails were excellent. Seth said, "Great, I'll try one." And turned to me.

I sighed, hiding my relief. "Well, if you're having one, I guess I'll try one, too."

I quickly took a sip of mine as soon as it came so that Seth couldn't suggest a toast. The bartender was right: it was excellent, sweet and minty without tasting like toothpaste. I delicately speared one of the sugared cranberries from the top and popped it in my mouth.

"So, assuming you do come," Seth said, giving his drink a stir. The separate layers of whatever red and white concoctions they'd laid in the glass spun together. "Will this be your first time in New York?"

I closed my eyes. It wasn't the stirring or the alcohol, but somehow I was feeling a little dizzy. Maybe it was the glare of lights off all the garish tinsel, or the smells of Seth's citrusy campfire mixing with the mulled wine spices and mint and sweat of so many people packed close together. The conversations around me all blended into a dull roar.

Probably thinking I hadn't heard him, Seth prompted, "Have you been to New York before?"

With effort, I opened my eyes. Seth was smiling patiently

at me, eyes wide and curious, and as long as I focused on him the room didn't spin. I said, the words sour in my mouth, "Not in a while."

It wasn't a real answer to his question, but he seemed to take it as me saying I hadn't spent much time there. "You'll be in for a treat, then. The city is beautiful around the holidays. We'll take you everywhere. It'll basically be an all-expenses-paid vacation." And he went on to tell me all the things we would do, all the things his family liked to do for Hanukkah, how his friend group would welcome me with open arms.

I just sat there with my mocktail, taking sip after sip, knowing that no amount of sweet would erase that sourness from my tongue.

6

I COULDN'T SLEEP THAT NIGHT. THAT WASN'T UN-usual for me; typically, I'd get up and do some invoices or something else really boring for a bit, which would lull me to rest.

Tonight was different. It was Seth's words bouncing around in my skull, the echo a total distortion of his voice. *Have you been to New York before? You clearly haven't met my parents, who are maybe the most welcoming people in the world.*

My parents. New York.

I'd spent the first five years of my life in the city proper, and then we'd moved to Riverdale in the Bronx after that in search of more space for less money. My life didn't change all that much, though. The community around me was just as Jewish, and I could take the 1 train into the city anytime I wanted.

For all I knew, my parents were still there. Maybe Seth's were in Riverdale, too. I hadn't thought to ask specifically where they lived. If they were in the same neighborhood, if there was the chance I might round a corner and walk into my mom or my dad, I'd have to say no.

They definitely weren't dead. I googled their names plus "obituary" every so often, just to check.

Connor had never understood my relationship—or lack thereof—with my parents. "They're your mom and dad," he'd say every so often when questioning why he'd never met them or why they didn't call on my birthday. "Even if you guys don't get along, doesn't that still matter? Shouldn't you at least talk to one another?"

He didn't get it. Nobody with loving, supportive parents could get it, I think. At first I tried to be patient with him, understanding that he was looking at us through the lens of his own parental relationships (great and great), and feeling sad that I didn't have what he had. And then I got sick of trying to be patient and started snapping at him. *Stop it. My life is better without them. Don't ask me about them again.*

I couldn't tell him the exact reasons why—they were the ones who'd taught me that. I didn't think it would matter if I did, anyway. I could picture his response. *That doesn't sound so bad. It's not like we have to live next door to them or talk to them every day or anything. They're still your parents, though. Doesn't that mean something?*

The only response I could picture to that was strangling him, so I figured it was better for both of us just to stay off the topic.

Sometimes I wished I could capture for him the expressions on their faces the last time my parents and I saw each other. Frozen sneers. The last time I showed up at their door, my mom greeted me with an icy expression like I was a stranger. Which would have been preferable to being her child, probably. She'd always treated strangers better than she treated me.

But by then I had an excuse to move away. I was dating Connor, and he'd expressed how much he wanted to move back up to Vermont now that he was able to work remotely. So I just went with him, and I never went back.

It hadn't been running away. It had been running *to* something. If I had been running away, it would have been totally different. So what if I was nervous about going back? Anyone would be in this situation.

I rolled over. My stomach sloshed with the movement. My head was starting to throb, a full-on Category 4. There was no way I was going to fall asleep tonight, not when the prospect of running into my parents when I least expected it was floating around in my subconscious. And regular conscious.

I reached for my phone. The time blinked at me, making me squint. 12:30 AM. Only five more hours until I had to get up to open the café. Great. Like I wasn't exhausted enough.

Seth and I had exchanged numbers before meeting up at the bar, which meant I was able to shoot him a text before I could think it through. He was definitely sleeping, but maybe if I got the question out of my head, it would give me enough peace to sleep. **Where do your parents live?**

The three dots appeared immediately. So he was up. Surprising. It struck me that, even after spending two hours together, I had no idea what he did for a living. Maybe he did something that didn't start until later in the day, though I immediately pushed that idea aside, since he was in the café every morning. **In the city. I told you.**

I know in the city, I said, tapping each letter hard, like I might be able to communicate impatience through the screen. **Where in the city? The city's a big place.**

Upper West Side. In the 80s near Riverside Park, he said. **Is that specific enough for you?**

They lived along the same train line as my parents, then, but an hour south. We probably wouldn't run into each other, judging by simple proximity. **What synagogue do they go to?**

He messaged back a congregation I vaguely recognized, and googled to find it was Conservative. My parents were Reform and went to a Reform synagogue. So they probably didn't have an overlap in their friend groups, because they would have found their friends and community through their synagogues and the local Jewish Community Centers.

It seemed like it would be safe. To go. If I wanted to.

I messaged him, **Thanks**. And then, because I was curious, **What are you still doing up?**

Big work project due tomorrow, he said back. **I work best last minute. What are you still doing up?**

Should I ask him what he did? No. He probably told me earlier and I forgot it, and he'd be insulted now if I asked. Obviously, I couldn't tell him why I was actually up right now, either. It was easier—safer—not to share the parts of yourself that could hurt you. If my parents had taught me anything, it was that. **Just finishing some stuff up for the café**. Which, if I really was going to be beset by insomnia, I should probably actually do. No sense in just lying here wasting time when I could be doing something productive. **The grind never stops.**

At least you have good coffee to help you out, he replied. At this hour, I only have the swill I can brew myself.

Please tell me it's not instant coffee.

I won't tell you, then.

I wrinkled my nose. Café owner or not, I didn't think of myself as a coffee snob. If mediocre coffee made you happy, then you do you. But instant coffee? That was a step too far. That was straight-up embarrassing, and I'd stand by that in a court of law, if anyone ever took me to court for blaspheming the terrible name of instant coffee. Wow. I can't believe I let myself be seen with you in public.

Please don't ban me from the café.

It's tempting. My fingers went on without input from my brain, Don't worry, I can hook you up with some good beans—

No. What? Backspace. What I said instead: I'll go with you to New York. For the sake of the festival.

For the sake of the festival! he wrote back. Don't worry. It'll be fun.

I hoped he was right. My eyelids were finally getting heavy. I set my phone back on my nightstand, laid my head on my pillow, and fell off into a deep, dreamless sleep.

7

OF COURSE, I WOKE UP THINKING, *WHAT HAVE I done?* I literally went back and reread my messages to confirm that I was remembering correctly and hadn't nightmared up an agreement. But I had indeed committed. It was too late to back out, no matter how much I wanted to. And of course I wanted to. At least that's what I told myself.

So the rest of the week passed in a blur of me trying to get everything done before I left and mostly failing. Maggie the retiree was indeed glad to come back on board for the week; she even still had her old keys, which was probably not a great thing security-wise, but it worked out well for me now. I stocked up enough coffee so that we wouldn't run out—what was one more credit card extension?—and made sure my pastry deliveries were paid up. I left a ton of to-do lists, hoping that maybe she'd be a magical cleaning wizard and I'd return to the café looking better than how I left it.

Connor never came to my café, but, as if all the gods I didn't believe in were laughing at me, I did run into him the night before I left. It was chilly outside, a few flakes of snow swirling through the pools of light on Main Street; I was running out quickly to restock some tampons for next month from the drugstore (many thanks to those same gods for allowing my period to end right before this trip so that I wouldn't have to deal with it in Seth's parents' bathroom).

I had my coat and scarf pulled up to my nose, and I pulled them up higher as soon as I saw his distinctive shuffle, hoping that maybe he either wouldn't notice me or would allow himself to pretend he hadn't noticed me. "Hey, Abby," he said with a grim smile. No such luck. "How's it going?"

How's it going? I wished he'd given us both the decency of a quick nod and fast walk in the opposite direction. "I'm actually going that way," I said, pointing past him, even though the drugstore was in the same direction he was walking. I'd double back. I could use some exercise anyway. So what if I was already shivering? I wouldn't freeze to death. "Getting ready for a trip tomorrow, so I don't have much time to chat."

The latter part of my sentence apparently didn't penetrate his thick skull, since he said, "A trip? You?" Well, he didn't have to sound so surprised about it. "Where are you going? Someplace warm, I hope."

I took a deep breath. Seth and I hadn't said anything about faking a relationship up here—it would be a lot harder around people we saw every day, who knew our relationship as one of sniping and withheld whipped cream—but we hadn't discussed hiding our trip, either. "No. I'm actually going down to New York. The city."

Connor's eyebrows jumped up so high they disappeared

beneath the brim of his hat. "The city? You?" He rubbed at his reddish beard. "To see . . . your parents?"

One of the reasons he'd called me a "closed-up, frigid bitch I barely even know" (to his credit, he did later apologize) is that I'd refused to ever tell him details about my parents. I mean, why did he have to know? It wasn't like him knowing would change anything. All I'd ever tell him was that we didn't talk anymore and it was for the best. He never gave up asking, though. "It's not like I'm trying to get at some juicy gossip," he'd say, trying to look me in the eye, even though I was *obviously* busy cooking dinner or reading a book or something, anything, else. "I'm your boyfriend. We live together. If you can't tell me the things that hurt you, who can you tell?"

"No," I told him both then and now. "I'm not going to see my parents. I'm actually going with a friend."

"A friend? Who?"

"Seth. I don't think you know him. He comes into the café every morning."

"So he has good taste in coffee."

"Yup." I left out that his good taste in coffee was most of what I knew about him, and that, considering he'd admitted to sometimes drinking instant coffee, it wasn't even entirely true. "So, anyway . . ."

"Anyway." This time he took the hint. "Have a good trip, Abby. I hope you find what you're looking for."

"I'm not looking for anything," I said automatically, but that wasn't true, was it? I was looking for successful Hanukkah vendors. And that was all.

SETH WANTED TO play Twenty Questions on our three-and-a-half-hour drive to the city. I shut that down right away. "No car games," I said, fiddling with the radio. Nothing but static was coming through. "Do you not have Bluetooth to hook your phone up to the car speakers?"

"Never needed it," Seth said. "I like to sing in the car. I know some great duets, if you're interested."

"I am definitely not interested." I stared out the window, the rush of static and other cars buzzing in my ears, and watched the tree skeletons fly by. Maybe I shouldn't have insisted on taking his car, but I hadn't wanted to pay for the gas or the wear and tear on my own. Besides, he'd offered.

A few more minutes of static and he sighed. "The car doesn't have Bluetooth. But that cord there can connect to your phone manually."

"Thank god." I lunged for it before he could reach for it himself and put his own playlists of god-knows-what on. Probably Broadway show tunes or podcasts about cute animals.

But when I started blasting my favorite playlist of girl indie rock from the speakers, he shook his head. "No way."

"What's wrong with it?"

"Nothing's wrong with it. I like this stuff," he said, which was surprising, because every song on this playlist was wildly angry. "But I'm pretty sure it's a law that when you're driving somewhere for the holidays and you're not singing a cheerfully out-of-tune duet, you have to listen to holiday music."

"By which you mean Christmas music, because Hanukkah options are sparse." Unless you counted the Maccabeats, the Jewish a capella group, or endless covers of "I Have a Little Dreidel," which, just shoot me now.

"I actually have a pretty good Hanukkah playlist," he said. "Search me on Spotify."

Grudgingly, I did. "I'll try it out, but I reserve the right to stop at any time." Hitting play, I nodded in approval when the first song to come up on shuffle was a rock interpretation of "Ma'oz Tzur," electric guitar included. "Okay, this isn't terrible."

"High praise from you."

I settled into my seat as the Vermont and then the Berkshires forests whizzed by. "So," I said, once the playlist had started over (because, again, there really weren't all that many Hanukkah songs on offer, even when you included all the Israeli ones), "what do I need to know about your family and about being in a relationship with the great Seth . . ." I paused as I realized I didn't know his last name.

"Seth Abrams," he said, not sounding bothered by it.

"Seth Abrams," I finished. "Any siblings whose names I should know? Do your parents erupt at any mention of Marvel movies? Should I talk up my love of classical music to get on their good side? Do you have any weird below-the-belt birthmarks they're going to quiz me about?"

He removed a hand from the wheel to count down the list one by one. "One: no siblings. Beloved only child here, born when my parents were at the ancient age of almost-forty and were beginning to lose hope. Thus, I was spoiled for most of my childhood. I've moved past it. Mostly."

Interesting how we were both only children and had turned out so differently.

"Two: I don't think my parents have ever watched a Marvel movie, though they'll pretend to be interested if you're into them. If you want to know things that make them erupt, mention e-bikes speeding on the sidewalk or people who let their off-leash dogs tear up the protected landscapes in the park. Three: I think they like classical music, but there are other ways to get on their good side. My mother is a retired podiatrist, and my father is a semi-retired lawyer. Their jobs are very boring, so if you want some brownie points, you can always ask questions about them and pretend the answers are very interesting, since nobody else does.

"Four." He glanced at me sidelong, raising his eyebrows. "If my mother or father attempts to quiz you on our pretend sex life, feel free to pretend you have no idea what sex is or that you've even heard the word before. I don't think that'll be a problem, though. I don't think any parents like thinking or talking about their children's sex lives."

"Just making sure," I said. "Anything else I should know?"

He was quiet for a moment as he took an exit toward New York. "We probably won't just be spending time with my family. I know my friend group wants to get together, too," he said at last. "This is actually the first time I'll be seeing them since I moved. We haven't all been in the same place since before that, but the group chat is already buzzing with plans. You'll like them—they're all good guys. And girls. Just. Um." He swallowed hard. "My ex will probably be there, too. The friend group kind of absorbed her when we dated. And, um, it didn't end well. The relationship. Last year." The tips of his ears were turning a brick red. "So she might be a bit cold to you. Don't worry about it. It isn't your fault."

"Well, we're not really dating," I said. "So she can be as cold to me as she wants. I'll be a snowman. Coldness will only strengthen me."

He gave a relieved laugh. "It'll be fine, though. Here, let me tell you a bit about my friends. Any real girlfriend of mine would've heard some stories."

The rest of the drive passed quickly with all of Seth's tales; apparently, kids in the city could get up to way more trouble when they didn't have to worry about being old enough or too drunk to drive. Before I knew it, we were driving over the Tappan Zee Bridge, the tall buildings of the Bronx and then Manhattan rising up alongside the highway.

By some Hanukkah magic, we managed to find street parking right outside Seth's parents' building on West End Avenue. I stared up at the building as Seth grabbed our rolling bags from the trunk. I'd always regarded these grand architectural marvels with envy compared to the boxy modern building I'd grown up in; all the cornices and carved stone flowers decorating the brick gave the building so much charm and old-world glamour. Someone had strung around the entrance lights that would probably twinkle white once it got dark out. People walking fluffy little dogs weaved around me; tall trees made the wide sidewalk feel homey, even though the branches were bare.

"Ready?" he asked.

I drew in a deep breath. "Ready."

8

HUGGING HAS NEVER BEEN MY THING. BEING tucked up right against somebody's sweat and hair and odors, wrapped in arms so that you can't get away, and wondering if they can smell or feel anything weird about you? No thank you.

But it wasn't like I could sidestep the mother of my fake boyfriend, or ask her if she'd prefer a handshake (I would actually prefer to greet someone without having to touch their skin at all, but for whatever reason that doesn't seem to be an option. Society, get on that). So when she, upon Seth and I walking into their airy, sunny apartment and him introducing me to her as his girlfriend, swooped in for a hug, I just gritted my teeth and let it happen.

It could have been worse, I supposed. She was soft and round and smelled like cinnamon, though that only made me more self-conscious that I probably smelled like stale car sweat and my road snack of turkey jerky.

After what felt like about three hours, she released me. I took an immediate step back and sucked in a breath of clean air. The apartment itself, or at least the small chunk of it I could see upon walking into the main living area, was really nice: built-in bookshelves filled with Reese's Book Club picks and foil-bound editions of classic novels; cozy mismatched furniture in bright colors and plaids that should have clashed but somehow didn't; pictures of Seth and his parents at all ages lining the mantel above a grand fireplace. I seized upon that and figured I'd start with a compliment, because who didn't like that? "It's so nice to meet you. You have a beautiful home."

She clasped her hands before her. I'd expect a woman with an apartment like this to have polished, manicured nails, but hers were short and unadorned. "Thank you so much, Abby. It's absolutely delightful to meet you, too." She shot a chagrined look at Seth. "I only wish my son had told me you were coming. I would have been more prepared."

"I'm very sorry," I said, shooting my own annoyed look at Seth. This whole situation was weird enough; why did he have to make it weirder by springing me on his parents out of nowhere? "I didn't realize he was serious when he told me I was going to be a surprise."

"You should always take me seriously," Seth said brightly. "Come on, both of you, it's better this way. Less stress for all of us. Mom, you would've worked yourself into a frenzy trying to make sure everything was perfect. Now we can all relax."

I was truly impressed by the force in Seth's mom's glare, and truly surprised it didn't reduce him to a smoking pile of ashes. By the time she turned back to me, it had melted into a warm, welcoming smile. Kind of scary. "By the way, dear,

I'm Bev. It's short for Beverly, but nobody calls me that," she said. "Please, take a seat and relax. Let me go get Seth's father. He probably has his headphones in and is dead to the world."

She bustled out of the room and down a hallway. I obediently took a seat on the red and yellow plaid couch, perched on the edge of the cushion. Seth sat beside me, close enough to touch without actually touching me. He asked, "Everything okay so far?"

"Your mother is lovely," I said. "I like her more than you at this point."

He touched a hand to his chest in mock pain. "You wound me." He cocked his head, considering. "Though, to be fair, she probably likes you more than me right now, too."

We didn't get a chance to say anything else to each other before Bev came back down the hallway, tugging by the hand one of the tallest, thinnest men I'd ever seen. "This is Seth's father," she told me. "Benjamin, introduce yourself."

His mustache—dark hair speckled with gray—twitched. "I think you just introduced me."

"Nonsense."

The mustache twitched again, but Seth's dad stepped forward and held out his hand. That was my kind of greeting. Well, more my kind of greeting than a hug was anyway. "Hello. I'm Seth's father. My name is Benjamin." It was too bad he looked nothing like a Ben, because Ben and Bev would've sounded adorable together.

Benjamin's handshake was strong and firm without threatening to crush my fingers. "Hi, I'm Seth's girlfriend. Abby."

Somehow, between all the introducing and sitting, Bev had conjured up a platter of cookies and some teacups, which she placed on the coffee table between splayed copies of *Bon Appétit* and *Architectural Digest.* "These are lime shortbread, and these are chocolate hazelnut biscotti. Pick your choice of tea, too, and I'll bring in hot water."

I chose a floral herbal mix, not wanting to introduce more caffeine to my wired nerves, and soon enough Bev was back with hot water for it to steep. "So," she said over her own cup of tea, as she and Benjamin sat down in a pair of armchairs facing us. One was green; the other was brown leather. "Abby, since we haven't heard anything about you, you'll have to fill us in. Tell us all about yourself."

I cleared my throat and took a sip of tea to stall. It was sweet and pleasantly bitter. "Well, I grew up in the area, in Riverdale," I said, feeling a bit like I was at an interview for a job I didn't really want. "Now I run a café up in Vermont. It's a small operation, just me right now. I make and sell artisan coffee and some easy breakfast and lunch food. Um, it's a lot of work but a lot of fun."

Bev's eyes gleamed. "Oh, so you're 'the cute girl at the coffee shop' Seth looked forward to seeing every morning! How nice that worked out."

My eyes darted to Seth, who was redder than a steamed lobster. "*Mom,*" he said, his voice strangled.

"What?" she said. "You're dating now, aren't you? So she knows you think she's cute."

Something wanted to jump out of my throat. I wasn't sure whether it was a laugh or a cough. Seth must have started laying the groundwork for our fake relationship before we left so that it wasn't a *total* surprise when he showed up with me. I had to assume that, because the thought of him actually thinking I was cute and looking forward to seeing me every morning? It made my insides squirm in a way that wasn't entirely unpleasant, like going on a roller coaster.

"Anyway," Bev continued. "So that's how you met? At the coffee shop?"

Seth jumped in before I could respond, his voice still thin and oddly high. "Sure, I thought she was cute, but she was so grumpy all the time, I didn't know if we could ever make it work."

Grumpy? Me? I got my hackles up, but they deflated pretty quickly. Honestly, it fit.

"She always had this attitude," Seth said. "Sometimes she wouldn't give me the whipped cream I paid for just because she didn't feel like it. Or she'd snark at me when I wished her a good morning. You know. But I got past it."

Okay, now my hackles rose and stayed up. He *got past it*? Seriously?

Come on, Abby, I told myself. *Be a good fake girlfriend. Nice and sweet and demure and whatever. Remember the festival.*

But my mouth opened on its own. "How generous of you to get past it," I said breezily. I turned to Bev with a wry smile, hoping she'd think I was joking. "He might have thought I was grumpy and difficult at first, but I thought he was *so* annoying. Like, I'd just be trying to get through my day, get all my orders right and deal with problem customers, and he'd be in there trying to chat with me about how nice it was outside or how he just loooooves the smell of autumn."

I'd gone too far, I immediately thought, but Bev laughed. "Sounds like Seth," she said.

I should probably smile, too, to show that I wasn't being serious, even though I was. I stretched open my lips, negating my usual resting bitch face.

"So the two of you started off getting on each other's nerves, but obviously that changed," Bev said. "What happened?"

Seth glanced at me. "Well. It was a wild day."

"The wildest day," I said, jumping in. Not a chance I was going to sit here silently and let him emphasize how grumpy and difficult I was. Even if, it occurred to me a second later, that was exactly what a good fake girlfriend would do. Because what did it really matter? He was the one who would be stuck with these people for the rest of his life, while I would never see them again after seven more days, so what did it matter what they thought of me?

It was too late, though. The words were already spilling out of my mouth. "Seth had come by in the morning for his usual sugary latte, and it was storming outside. Pouring down buckets. Lightning flashing in the sky."

"Are you sure about that, dear?" Seth asked. He cocked his head at me, grinning a little. "I remember it being bright and sunny."

I felt a smile twitch at my own lips. "No, it was definitely storming. How could you forget? Considering you'd just come in for your morning sugary latte and the ceiling opened up."

"You're right, how could I forget," Seth said, raising his eyebrows at me, like he was challenging me not to laugh. "It was pretty unforgettable how the water poured right on your head."

The image was absurd. I swallowed the laugh down so he wouldn't get the satisfaction. "Seth leapt forward to rescue me, but I was screaming about the expensive coffee machine. It wasn't like I'd gotten a blowout that morning—my hair could take a soaking, and I could always wash my clothes. But my espresso machine?"

"Right," Seth said. His parents were glancing back and forth between us as if we were bouncing a Ping-Pong ball from hand to hand. "You were screaming in panic, looking like a drowned rat, scrabbling in place trying to stay upright as the water tried to drown you, and all you would say was, 'Save the machine!' So I gallantly dove into the fray and moved the machine to a dry table, then went back in for you."

"If only you hadn't slipped and fallen!" I interrupted.

"I fell?" Seth was raising his eyebrows, his lips pressing together hard like he, too, was trying not to burst out laughing. "Are you sure?"

"I'll never get the image out of my head," I said earnestly, turning my eyes up to the ceiling, because if I spent any longer looking at his face I was *definitely* going to explode. "I was standing there with the water beating down on me almost like a massage, trying to calculate how much this was going to cost to fix, only to have you come sliding into me like a soggy Rollerblader."

"How could I forget literally knocking you off your feet?" Seth's voice was strangled now.

Do not look, Abby. Stick the landing. "You're misremembering again, because I didn't fall," I said. Deep breath in.

Deep breath out. "You don't remember how I had to stoop down and drag you out of the fray so that you wouldn't be like that urban legend of a turkey who drowned because it was too stupid to stop looking up at the rain?"

"Somehow I did not remember that."

"I'm not sure how; it was very memorable."

"That's right. I'm remembering now," said Seth. "The water was so slippery and moving so much that you might not have fallen at first, but you fell after dragging me out of the waterfall. Leaving us both lying on our backs in the pool, turkeys looking up at the downpour."

My deep breath shook with the effort it took not to laugh. I almost broke when I looked at him to see him grinning at me with his eyebrows raised.

But I didn't. I held strong as I said, "And that was, of course, when you saw fit to ask me out."

That did it. He burst out laughing. I looked down, smirking with victory, as he covered his face with his hands, shoulders shaking.

"Sounds . . . romantic," Bev said doubtfully. "But what about your ceiling?"

Right. If that had happened in real life, I would've been freaking out, because I definitely would not have been able to afford the café being closed while my landlord lackadaisically arranged for the repair. Maybe I would've finally gotten to be the target of one of Lorna's emergency meetings. "Oh, it all worked out," I said, because the less specific detail I gave her, the better. "But, you know, I want to hear about you, too. Seth told me you're a podiatrist and a lawyer, right? Those jobs sound very interesting."

Immediate brownie points for me as Benjamin's face lit up. "It's extremely interesting. I've spent most of my career working with tax and estate law—"

"Oh, she doesn't want to hear about tax codes and people's feet," Bev interrupted, though the pleased expression on her face told me I'd gotten some brownie points from her, too. "I'd much rather hear more about you. What about your first date?"

Not going to lie, I was actually kind of curious to hear about being a foot doctor. What drove a person to go through medical school and residency and all the red tape and lack of sleep and everything only to focus on feet, maybe the least essential part of the body? Also one of the smelliest and the ugliest?

But I was a good fake girlfriend and I wasn't going to press. "Oh, our first date was much more romantic." The holiday pop-up bar we'd gone to had opened in October, so we theoretically could have been together for two months after going there on our first date. We expounded upon the atmosphere, the drinks, his invitation to come and meet his family. Which was all true. Technically.

"How lovely," Bev said. "Now, Abby, you said you grew up around here, didn't you? What's your last name?"

"Cohen," I said, and braced myself for the reaction I knew I'd get.

I wasn't disappointed. Bev's entire face lit up, and she clasped her hands under her chin. Benjamin's lips creased in a tiny smile. I figured those were equivalent emotional reactions for them. "Oh, so you're Jewish?" I confirmed with a nod. "How wonderful. Not that we'd have anything against you if you weren't. Where are you from?"

For the next several minutes we played Jewish geography, another thing I'd braced myself for—what if they knew my parents? Fortunately, they didn't, but they did know the parents of a couple kids I'd gone to camp with and one of my old neighbors, and we spent a few more minutes debating if they knew some of my distant cousins or if they just had common names. It was kind of nice, feeling connected to the community again. No matter that I hadn't talked to any of the people we were discussing in years. I was still a part of the web.

"Well, they're all lovely people," Bev said finally, which was a lie about at least one of my cousins. "And what brought you to the middle of nowhere in Vermont?"

"I went up for a relationship and stayed because I liked it," I said.

Bev pursed her lips. "Oh, but it's just so far away. And there's no community up there. I hate that Seth is up there all alone."

There was plenty of community, just not Jewish community. But I understood what she meant. I'd almost forgotten how nice it was to be surrounded by people who knew your inside references, who wouldn't prejudge you for your ethnicity or religion (your synagogue membership or your specific level of observance, though, sure).

But this was only temporary, I reminded myself. *So don't get too comfortable.*

The silence was stretching on too long. *You're here to be a good fake girlfriend, Abby.* So I plopped my arm over Seth's shoulders and made myself smile. The skin of his neck was warm against my bare forearm. "We're not up there all alone anymore."

Bev gave us a tremulous smile. Her eyes were just shiny enough where I suspected she might be ready to cry. "And I'm so glad for it."

My tea was growing cold. I took a sip anyway so that I'd have something else to focus on besides that gooey look on her face. My nerves were starting to dance under my skin, begging for a break from the interrogation and the cheery attitude.

As if he could read my mind—or maybe it was just the fact that my arm had tightened around his neck—Seth jumped in. "What are we going to do for dinner tonight? Should we take Abby out to one of our favorite places?" He'd barely let Bev nod before he continued. "We spent a lot of time in the car. Do you want to freshen up a bit, Abby? Maybe take a quick nap or a shower?"

Oh, thank god. I didn't even need a nap; I just had to sit by myself in a quiet room for a minute. "That sounds great."

Seth stood and motioned toward the hallway as if he were about to give me a sweeping bow. "Because I am a gentleman, I will gift you my old bedroom while I take the couch. Let me show you where it is."

I nodded with a look that I hoped expressed appreciation. It wasn't that I didn't appreciate it for real—I truly needed this break—but I'd been told my face wasn't the best at expressing emotions. Resting bitch face strikes again. I'd gotten "Why does the cashier always look so angry?" on more than a few comment cards.

I'd stopped putting out comment cards.

"Don't be ridiculous," Bev said, waving her hand in the air.

Oh no. Was she going to insist that her darling son have his old room back while I stayed out here in the main area where she could watch me sleep and force-feed me warm milk at three in the morning?

She continued, "The two of you should share the bedroom. It's fine with me."

Seth's jaw hung open. "But . . . you never let me share the bedroom with Freya. I always had to sleep on the couch."

Freya. His old girlfriend. I pictured a Viking goddess, icy blond hair swooping into braided buns and light blue eyes peering down at me from a face sculpted of cut glass. She'd definitely be cold if we ran into each other, I thought. Maybe she'd try to harpoon me.

Bev waved her hand in the air again. "Oh, times have changed."

Seth scoffed, raising one thick black eyebrow. Funnily enough, his dad was doing the same exact thing right now with his same exact thick black eyebrow. "Times have changed? Or is it the girl who's changed?" He had an edge to his voice now. "I always thought you liked Freya."

"I did like Freya," Bev said. "Must we discuss your ex-girlfriend in front of your new girlfriend? I don't think Abby came all the way here for that."

"I really don't mind sleeping separately," I said, steering the conversation away, even though I was kind of interested in hearing more about Freya. "I don't want to make you uncomfortable in your own home. I'm happy to go by your rules."

"And I really don't mind allowing you two to share Seth's room," she said. "You're welcome here."

Seth glanced at her darkly, that edge still to his voice. "This conversation isn't over."

"Of course it's not, dear," she said. Her voice was mild but hard underneath. Seth's edge wouldn't be able to cut it no matter how sharp it got. "I'm always around to talk whenever you want. In fact, we should talk more often. I'd love it if you called me more."

Seth sighed and grabbed my bag, hoisting it over his shoulder. The equivalent of a dog rolling over and showing its belly to the dog with bigger, scarier fangs. "Come on, Abby. I'll show you to my—*our*—room."

The hallway branched off the living room on the far end of the kitchen. I peeked into a small, lavender-scented bathroom before Seth opened the door across from it. "Here's my old room slash the guest room slash the office."

I stepped inside. Whatever the slashes, it was clear they hadn't changed much about this room since Seth moved out aside from maybe shoving a desk under the window and adding some decorative pillows to the head of the bed. Otherwise, it was all baseball bedding and navy blue walls covered with sports posters and framed pages from comic books. The room's bookshelf teemed with middle grade and young adult sci-fi and fantasy novels, thick paperbacks with creased spines.

Seth followed me in, closing the door behind me. He leaned in, like his parents would otherwise be able to overhear his whisper through the door and down the hallway. Though who knew? Maybe Bev had tiptoed after us and had her ear pressed against the wood. "Sorry about that. I can take the floor."

Because, of course, there was only one bed. One full-size bed, tight for two people but not too tight. It would be perfect if I were a real girlfriend who wanted to cuddle and, you know, not a fake one who had no desire to cuddle through the night even when in a real relationship. I slept hot. Cuddling all night just made me sweaty. "Okay," I said. "I guess. You don't think that'll be a problem, though? What if your mom pops in to wake us up and finds you on the floor? Won't she think that's weird?"

He didn't even bother trying to tell me that his mom wouldn't barge in on us while we were sleeping. "Probably," he said. "But we could just tell her you kick a lot in your sleep or something?"

"Why am *I* the kicker?"

He shrugged. "Because it was never an issue with past girlfriends, so it would be weird if it suddenly came up now?"

But how would his mom know, considering he'd never shared a bed with one here? Whatever. It didn't really matter. I was only here for eight nights and then I was out. "We can figure it out later. Can I have a few minutes to chill?"

"Of course. That's why I got us out of the living room," Seth said, but he didn't move. I coughed, widening my eyes and moving them meaningfully toward the door. Now he moved, but farther into the room, which was not the intention. "Anything you wanted to talk about?"

I cleared my throat. "I, um." Why did asking for a moment alone feel so awkward and weird? Maybe because

Seth didn't seem to be the kind of person who valued alone time. If anything, he seemed like the kind of person who did his best to never be alone ever. "No, I was thinking of maybe taking a nap. Like you said."

"Oh, okay. Got it. Can't blame you." He moved toward the door, hands in his pockets. He glanced over his shoulder before leaving. "Anything you need to be comfortable? Do you want to take a shower or something? Not, like, with me. That's not what I meant. I just meant, there are towels in the closet next to the bathroom and soap in the—"

"Don't worry, I didn't think you meant you wanted to take a shower with me," I said dryly. He nodded, then opened the door to reveal Bev standing there, fist raised as if she were either about to knock or punch her son in the nose. I hastened to add, "Because that would be awkward in your parents' house, obviously. Not because we haven't done it before. Plenty of times."

Nailed it. The pained expressions on both his and his mother's face testified to *that.*

Hey, maybe by the end of this Hanukkah season, I would have so horrified his mother that she'd be kissing the feet of whatever non-Jewish girl Seth dated next.

"Sorry about that, Bev," I said. "I didn't realize you were there."

The pained expression quickly resolved itself into a bright smile. "I just wanted to tell the two of you something I forgot." She produced two long strips of paper and held them out to Seth, who took them. In contrast, the pained expression on his face settled in for the long haul. If he used my own headache ranking system, I'd say he was preparing for a Category 3. "I couldn't help but get tickets for the Eighth Night Ball. They were fundraising for the HIAS, so it was for a good cause."

"Tickets for you and Dad?" Seth's voice barely strained with hope.

Bev rolled her eyes. "You know perfectly well that the Eighth Night Ball is far too fashionable for the likes of us. Also, it's much too late at night. No, they're for you and Abby."

Though I'd never gone, I had vague memories of the Eighth Night Ball from when I lived around here, because it got written up in all the Jewish publications and friends' older siblings and parents had posted their glamorous get-ups beneath twinkling white lights and garlands. The charity ball typically took place on the last night of Hanukkah; everybody got fully dolled up to see and be seen. I'd always kind of wanted to go.

"Mom, I don't dance," Seth argued.

But Seth clearly didn't want to go, and I was here to be a good fake girlfriend, not don a Disney Princess gown and be swirled around beneath glittering crystal chandeliers to the elegant tunes of a string quartet. So I said, "I don't have anything to wear."

Bev started with Seth. "You do too dance. I've seen you."

"At what? My bar mitzvah?"

"You had a very good sense of rhythm for a thirteen-year-old," she said. Point apparently made, she turned to me. "And don't you worry about that. I figured you wouldn't bring any formal gowns with you. I'll have it taken care of."

"Oh, I can't possibly." Even renting a formal gown was

expensive. I couldn't afford it, and the idea of letting my fake boyfriend's mother take care of it filled me with guilt.

"I insist. It would make me so happy."

If you've never tried to argue with your stereotypical Jewish mother about something, let me set the scene for you. Picture trying to wrestle a greased golden retriever, all while it gazes at you with big, sad puppy dog eyes. Oh, and it's also two sizes bigger than you. With large teeth. And opposable thumbs.

Point being: I'd already lost. "That's so kind of you."

She beamed at us. "The two of you are going to look so handsome together. I can't wait for all of our friends to see you."

"I'll hold on to the tickets," Seth said. "Hopefully, I don't lose them. Or accidentally light them on fire."

"Don't you worry," Bev said with an angelic smile. "I purchased them digitally. So if you lose them, or burn them, all I have to do is print them out again."

What the hell. She already had us. "It sounds like so much fun," I said. "Thanks so much."

"Of course," she said. "Well, I'll leave you to it." She stepped away, even closing the door behind her, leaving Seth and me alone in the room. He stared after her, probably thinking something about how she never would've behaved this way with his Viking goddess.

"Hey," I said, stepping closer. "It won't be so bad." It was kind of funny, this role reversal. That I would be the one telling Seth things weren't so bad. Just to make it extra ironic, I said, "Look on the bright side." But then I couldn't figure out what the bright side would be for him, so it only did so much.

He made a face, hopefully coming to a deep and powerful understanding of how irritating his personality could be. But then he smiled, as if he was indeed looking on the bright side. Ugh. "You're right. I'm glad you're excited about it, at least. That will make it fun."

What did it matter, when I was just a fake girlfriend? But I supposed he was one of those annoying people who made their day by making other people happy.

But before I could say anything about it, he was gone, leaving me totally, blissfully, alone. Or maybe it wasn't total, or even entirely blissful, because that last smile of his lingered in the air before me like the afterimage of a flash photo.

9

THE REST OF THE DAY AND EVEN THE NIGHT WENT surprisingly smoothly. Bev and Benjamin took Seth and me out to their favorite neighborhood place, a little French joint where we feasted on steak frites and duck and some truly excellent salads. When we got back to their apartment, we lit the Hanukkah candles—well, candle—for the first night. They insisted that, as their guest, I be the one to hold the shammash over the tinfoil as we sang. It was amazing how the first two blessings came back to me after not reciting them for years (the third, which was only said on the first night, had my tongue stumbling—fortunately, Seth and Bev sang loudly enough to drown out a chorus of ambulance sirens).

Bev wished us good night with a smile so gooey it made me feel like I'd eaten too much sugar (which I had, because you couldn't celebrate Hanukkah without doughnuts, and it turned out there was a Krispy Kreme a mere few blocks away from Bev and Benjamin's apartment). "Don't be too loud in there, you two."

"Gross, Mom," Seth said, scrunching up his whole face.

I struggled to keep my own face straight. "Good night."

Once we had the door to Seth's room firmly closed behind us and we'd waited a few minutes to hear Bev and Benjamin's footsteps pad down the hallway and their bedroom door close, I turned to face him. "Are you sure you don't want to share the bed? We don't have to make it weird."

"No, it's totally fine," Seth said. "I actually don't mind sleeping on the floor."

"You're really sure? I don't want you to hurt your back or anything." I'd said I was fine with it earlier, but now, looking at those hard wood planks and thin rug, I felt kind of bad.

"Absolutely," he said. "It's like camping. It feels like an adventure."

The small pile of pillows he'd arranged to cushion himself didn't look like an adventure. They just looked uncomfortable. But whatever. This was his house. He could do what he wanted.

We faced opposite walls to change into our pajamas, or what served as pajamas. I hadn't slept in pajama sets or nightgowns since I was a kid—usually, I just slept in T-shirts washed so many times they'd gone soft as silk, and boxer shorts. As I waited for Seth to finish changing into whatever he wore at night, I stared at the wall and tried not to feel too self-conscious. I was basically wearing shorts and a T-shirt. I walked around wearing shorts and a T-shirt every summer in public without even thinking about it.

And yet, as I turned around to see Seth in an outfit that all but matched mine, I couldn't help the quiver that went through my stomach. I crossed my arms over my chest, even though I'd made one concession to my usual bedtime attire and kept on a sports bra. "Well?" For some reason, my voice came out higher than usual. I cleared my throat. "Should we go to sleep?"

"You're not going to brush your teeth?" he asked. "That's bad for your dental hygiene."

Of course I always brushed my teeth before bed. I didn't know what was going on with me. "I don't need you to worry about my dental hygiene," I said, flustered, tempted not to brush my teeth now, just to show him, but knowing I wouldn't be able to sleep with dirty teeth. I went first, then Seth, and once we were both minty-fresh and emptied of excess fluids, I lay down as he turned off the light. "Well," he said. "Good night."

"Good night."

I closed my eyes and waited for sleep to come, but apparently it had been scared off by Seth and Bev's out-of-tune singing. After what felt like an eternity, I turned on my side to look down on the floor, where Seth was staring up at the ceiling. For a moment I wondered if he slept with his eyes open, but then he blinked and turned to me. "Can't sleep?"

"Nope," I said. I gave it a second to see if he'd chirpily suggest counting sheep or imagining myself on a beach, but fortunately he didn't. Instead, he asked me a question.

"What did you think of my parents?"

"They seem nice," I said automatically. It was true. They had been very nice and welcoming to me.

Seth blew out a breath. "Good. They can be kind of a lot."

These flannel sheets were incredibly warm and cozy. I imagined Bev tucking in the corners when she'd put them on the bed, smoothing out the top so that her son wouldn't suffer any creases against his back. "A lot isn't always bad," I said, burrowing deeper into the fuzziness, feeling bad again that he was stuck on the hard floor with only a few pillows trying to save his back from total ruin.

"Glad you think so." He was quiet for a moment. "They really liked you, you know. They weren't faking it."

Well, I hadn't been worried they were faking it before, but I was now. Then again, what did it matter? It wasn't like I'd ever be seeing them again after this trip. I tried to ignore the pang that thought made in my chest. "Okay. Cool."

We were quiet for a moment. It was almost companionable. Seth and me against the world, assuming his parents were the world.

And then he had to ruin it. "By the way, when my mom said that thing about how I thought you were cute." His words came out in a rush, so fast I thought they might drown me. I turned away from him, focusing on the ceiling. For some reason, I couldn't handle seeing his face right now. "I don't mean to—"

"I know what you meant." My words came out so loud they might have woken up Bev and Benjamin. I lowered my voice as I went on, still studying the ceiling. A line ran through the plaster above me, hopefully not meaning the place was going to collapse on my head. "Don't worry. I didn't take it seriously. I know you were just trying to make our relationship seem real."

I've always been someone who's appreciated a good silence—why fill up a calming, soothing quiet with unnecessary babbling or background noise?—but I couldn't take the one that fell after my words. I felt like if I didn't fill it up, I might hear something I didn't want to hear. "It was good thinking, actually," I said. "Me coming here totally out of nowhere might make them suspicious. Of the truth. That this isn't an actual relationship and we have no actual feelings for each other."

Seth was quiet for a long moment. Again, quiet usually settles me, but this one tied my stomach into a knot. "Right," he said finally. "Sure. You're right. I'm glad you're not weirded out or anything."

"Nope, all good here," I chirped, still staring at the ceiling. "Good night."

"Good night, Abby."

It took a while to fall asleep, and once I did, I kept waking up to the sounds of cars honking and ambulances blaring sirens outside. At least I didn't wake up wincing or clutching my lower back, unlike my fake boyfriend, who the next day led the way into the kitchen bent over like an old man. He straightened up when he saw his dad already in there, eating a bowl of what looked like plain oatmeal. "Good morning."

"Good morning," Benjamin said gravely. To be fair, he said everything gravely. "What's on the agenda for today?"

"I was thinking I'd take Abby downtown to check out some of the Hanukkah pop-ups," Seth said. He didn't specify that we'd be looking at them for my own Hanukkah festival, which made me wonder if he'd told his parents about that. "Where's Mom?"

"Her barre class," Benjamin said. "But don't let that stop you. Go have fun just the two of you."

I copied what Seth was having for breakfast—some Greek yogurt and fruit with granola—and then we were off. It was lucky I'd brought my winter gear with me, because the wind outside was so chilly it would've burned right through my wool pea coat. Of course, my warm winter coat and cozy hat made me sweat on the subway, so I was relieved when we climbed the steps and emerged somewhere in the Village.

I was glad to see that the years hadn't totally erased the Village's charm; glossy bank chains and Duane Reades alternated space with small, grubby, quirky stores that looked like they didn't make enough rent to pay for a square foot of their space: a place that made custom rubber stamps; one that sold dollhouse furniture; another with a display of antique teapots in the window. Christmas lights were strung on the streetlights, making glittery stars over the dirty sidewalks; every time a store door opened, a tinkle of holiday music poured out. "I always liked it down here," I said, breathing in deep the smell of pine as we passed a Christmas tree stand. "Though I didn't come much."

"Yeah, it takes a while to get here from Riverdale."

We walked by a fancy-looking restaurant that proudly proclaimed in its window that it served modern twists on traditional Jewish food. I slowed to take a look, but Seth kept moving. "I've been there with my parents and it's great, but not why we're here," he said. "Besides, we definitely couldn't afford to have them cater the festival."

I caught up with one more wistful look over my shoulder. Babka beignets sounded amazing. "We're here to scout people who might want to come do a booth for the festival?"

"Exactly," said Seth. He stopped so short I almost walked right into him. "That reminds me. I made up a Google Doc with other people you might be interested in talking to about the festival: the guys I know who perform the Hanukkah story in schools and at synagogues; the company that rents out the giant blow-up menorahs; some of my mom's friends or my friends or synagogue connections who sell various Hanukkah-related things or Judaica. Let me share it with you now before I forget."

My phone buzzed with the notification. "You're not worried I'm just going to take the info and run?"

Seth gave me a lopsided smile. "You wouldn't do that."

"How do you know?" Even though I had no idea where we were going, I started walking again. "I got what I wanted. Why bother continuing the charade of being your girlfriend?"

He didn't break stride beside me. "Because you're a good person and you wouldn't not keep your agreement."

"That's idealistic," I said as we stopped before what appeared to be the facade of an old Jewish deli. "What's this?"

Seth swept his arm out, narrowly missing hitting a pair of tourists wearing I ♥ NY T-shirts and taking photos of pigeons eating a discarded slice of pizza. "This whole area used to be pretty Jewish. My great-grandparents actually grew up around here when their parents brought them to America. But in recent years most of the Jewish delis and businesses have closed. This one among them."

I studied the big picture window, beyond which throngs of people were crowded before a counter. "Doesn't look closed to me." I left out the fact that some of my great-great-grandparents had come to New York, too, back when they'd immigrated from the old country, narrowly making it out before the Holocaust. They'd been part of this great American machine, building this city and this country into what it was now.

"Right. The building was just sitting empty, so this pop-up took it over for a few weeks. Are you looking only for kosher food for the festival?"

I shook my head. "Not only. I definitely want to have some kosher options for the more observant visitors, but everything doesn't have to be kosher. Lots of things don't even have to worry about kosher laws as long as they aren't meat or dairy. Like we don't have to worry about kosher latkes, I don't think, as long as we're careful with toppings."

"Good. Because most of the pop-ups we're going to aren't strictly kosher."

We stepped inside the former deli and were blasted in the face by doughnut steam. Every spa should have a doughnut steam room. "I see we're starting with dessert."

"It's Hanukkah," Seth said. "Eating doughnuts is a good deed."

You really can't go wrong with the food at any Jewish holiday. Well, with the exception of Passover, because matzah is terrible and eight days of no carbs but matzah and potatoes can have you crying for pizza by the end. But think bagels and lox to break the Yom Kippur fast. All sorts of exotic fruits on Tu B'Shevat. Brisket and tzimmes and noodle kugel for pretty much any occasion. And that's only the Ashkenazi food; I'd been treated to Sephardic and Mizrahi food occasionally at friends' houses growing up, and I remembered fish cooked in spicy tomato sauce, tagines with chickpeas and saffron, Yemenite braided bread with whole eggs hidden in the twists.

But Hanukkah food? Because Hanukkah celebrates the miracle of the oil, it's basically a mitzvah to eat fried foods for the holiday. And doing a good deed by eating French fries or doughnuts is the absolute best way to do a good deed.

So he was technically right. We joined the long line, which had wound all around itself to avoid subjecting anyone to the cold outside. The space was otherwise pretty spare, with a wooden counter, a chalk menu board hanging above it, and some tables and chairs pushed up against the walls.

I examined the menu as we inched closer. "What are the odds that Manischewitz grape filling will be good?"

"I never got the Manischewitz hate," Seth said. "Manischewitz is delicious. It's like drinking grape juice."

I glanced at him with dismay. "If you want grape juice, drink grape juice. Manischewitz is supposed to be wine."

"Maybe I like my wine tasting like grape juice."

"I knew you had terrible taste."

We moved forward in line. The guys in front of us stepped up to the counter, leaving us craning our necks at the menu board. "We have to decide what we're going to get. Are you okay with sharing?"

"I love sharing," Seth said. Of course he did.

Ten minutes later, we were huddled at a corner table that had miraculously opened up just as we were receiving our cardboard containers full of doughnuts. We'd left a trail of powdered sugar behind us as we elbowed our way through the crowd, like Hansel and Gretel leaving breadcrumbs in case they needed to find their way out.

Seth was even more smug after we sawed the Manischewitz grape jelly–filled doughnut in half with a plastic knife. “This is amazing,” he said around the half-chewed glob of dough and jelly in his mouth.

Like a civilized human being, I took the time to finish chewing before responding, which gave me time to think about how right he was. The wine—sorry, “wine”—really worked as a doughnut filling, the jelly tart and sweet and smooth with the ever so slight bitterness of alcohol, which perfectly complemented the rich, plush, not-too-sweet dough. The powdered sugar on the outside coated my lips with sweetness as I swallowed. “It’s good.”

The other two doughnuts we’d gotten—a chocolate gelt one that was basically just a glazed doughnut with chocolate filling and a gelt garnish on top, and a chunky apple pie one—were good, too. I grabbed their business card on the way out, though I did say to Seth as we exited the store into the cold air, “I’m not sure if I’ll call them.”

“Why not? The doughnuts were fantastic.”

“We can find doughnut vendors locally in Vermont that make doughnuts just as good, and they can give their doughnuts fun Hanukkah names,” I said. “That way we can save the budget for things we can’t find in Vermont, like kosher food and exclusive Hanukkah specialties.”

Like latkes. The next place had popped up to sell the fried potato pancakes with toppings ranging from the standard applesauce and sour cream to kimchi and trout roe.

This one had a window to order outside, so we took up our positions in line while stomping from foot to foot to keep warm.

"Anyway," Seth said. This line was moving more slowly than the doughnut line. "I'm not idealistic."

"What?" I had no idea where that had come from.

"Earlier," he said. "That's what you said about me. That I was being idealistic when I told you I knew you wouldn't just take the info I'd gathered for you and run."

"It is so idealistic," I said. "Maybe I'll take it and run right now."

"Go ahead. I won't be upset."

I stared at him. He stared back at me. My hand, holding the phone with access to his Google Doc, twitched. Why not just take it and leave? It wasn't like I cared about what he thought of me.

Except . . . maybe I did.

A tiny, little bit.

"I'm not going to do that," I said. A beat. "Did you really think I would?"

"No," he said immediately, firmly. But his face didn't match the vehemence of his tone. He actually looked a little . . . relieved?

"Oh," I said, surprised. "You didn't totally know. You wanted to make sure I wouldn't just ditch you."

I would've thought him thinking of me that way would hurt my feelings. It didn't, though. Somehow it made me actually feel better. Because he *wasn't* cartoonishly sunny after all. "You're right, I guess," I told him. "You're not that idealistic."

"I told you," he replied. "Just because I like to see the best in people doesn't mean that's all I can see." He was quiet for a moment. We took a step forward, and suddenly the smell of fresh frying latkes hit my nose. I breathed in deep. I rarely thought that anything could smell better than French fries, but this might smell better than French fries. More surface area for the oil to caress the potato. It was science.

Seth cleared his throat. "Do you think . . ." He trailed off before he could finish whatever he was going to say.

I waited. "Do I think what?"

He opened his mouth, then closed it. Pressed his lips together. Opened them. "Do you think that latkes are superior to French fries?"

It wasn't like I had an idea of what he was going to say, but I hadn't seen that coming. I guess maybe I thought he was going to continue the conversation we'd been having. Not that it mattered. So what if maybe he wasn't as annoying as I'd thought? "Yes. Latkes are obviously superior to French fries, because of the lacy, crispy edges and the pillowy insides."

"French fries have crispy outsides and pillowy insides, too."

"No, French fries have *a* crispy outside," I said. "Latkes have multiple. The more the better."

"I see," Seth said. "So would you put latkes in the pantheon?"

"The what?"

"The pantheon of the best foods," Seth said. "Don't you have a list?"

"Of my favorite foods?"

"No, of the *best* foods," Seth said. "They're different. Favorite is subjective. Best is objective."

I snorted. "There's no such thing as an objective best food. Everybody has their own individual tastes."

"Not entirely true," said Seth. "Take potatoes. Have you ever met anyone who dislikes potatoes?"

"I haven't met a lot of people," I said. Purposely.

"Or butter," Seth said. "Pizza. Macaroni and cheese. Really?"

I wanted to tell him that I despised pizza and wanted to vomit at the thought of macaroni and cheese, but of course that would be a lie. Pizza and macaroni and cheese were delicious. "There are lots of people who are lactose intolerant and can't eat any of those foods."

"Doesn't mean they don't think they're delicious."

We inched forward in line. "One of my favorite things about growing up in New York was the food," Seth said. "My dad, as you may have noticed, would be content eating brown rice with steamed broccoli and baked salmon every night, but my mom loves food. We'd travel all over the five boroughs to try all sorts of different things. Have you ever been to the Queens Night Market? It's like the Central Park Food Festival but less expensive and less pretentious." I shook my head. Queens was a long way from the Bronx. "I tried food from Sierra Leone there for the first time. Afghani food, Cambodian food, ceviche."

"That sounds like a lot of fun," I said. I'd grown up in kind of a Riverdale cocoon; sometimes my friends and I would go into Manhattan, but the other boroughs were at least an hour away by train, so we rarely made the trip. "What's your favorite food neighborhood?"

Of course he couldn't pick a favorite. As the line continued to crawl, he expounded about the Thai and Nepalese food in Jackson Heights, the Middle Eastern places in Bay Ridge, the various Chinese cuisines in the city's multiple Chinatowns. My mouth was literally watering. "Oh my god, next time you'd better take me on a food tour."

He stopped talking and stared at me. It took me a moment to realize why. Next time? There wouldn't be a next time. There was this time and this time only. I let out a weak laugh. It was okay. I could always come back on my own and seek out the fried fish salad at the Thai place, the silky-smooth hummus at his favorite Lebanese joint.

Why didn't the thought of going there alone feel better than the thought of going there with him?

As if it were a glorious sign from God to stop thinking about it, the menu board appeared ahead. I turned to face it fully, carefully avoiding Seth's eyes so he couldn't address my slipup. The main offering was singular: latkes. But the toppings were varied and delightful. "We should decide what we're going to get. I vote we get one order with sweet toppings and another with savory options. I'm intrigued by the apple chutney and the cucumber raita."

It took him a moment to talk, and in that moment I held my breath. But when he spoke, it was about the latkes. Which was what I wanted. Of course. "Any of them sound good. Get whatever you want."

"Are you sure? You can't complain if you don't like it, then."

"I'm sure."

Of course he didn't complain. We set up shop on a

nearby bench, me starting with the savory order—trout roe; sour cream; pickled radish—and him with the sweet one—spicy apple chutney; honey; whipped cream. The second savory order, with smoked salmon and dill and cucumber, we balanced between us, because I couldn't limit us to only two options after all. And really, when it came to fried potatoes, the more the merrier.

Especially these, because they were excellent: lacy and crisp, with crunchy edges and soft, pillowy centers. "I'm definitely going to call them for the festival," I said, tucking the business card into my wallet after taking a quick picture just in case I got mugged. "Hopefully, we can afford them."

"Hopefully," Seth said. His arm brushed mine as he raised a latke to his mouth for another bite. Usually, my shifting away would have been automatic, but it took me a second this time. Probably because it was cold out, and he was emanating heat like a radiator. "Hey, you know. What you said."

"About the latkes?"

"No, earlier? You said something about wanting to go on a food tour 'next time'?" I tensed again. "I just wanted to say, no pressure, but if we ever happen to be in the city at the same time, I'd be happy to take you."

I softened, like a crispy latke beneath a heavy spoonful of tangy, sweet, spicy apple chutney. "That would be really nice." We could go as friends; of course we could go as friends. If we happened to be in the city at the same time.

I kind of hoped we would be.

A FEW HOURS later, we were waddling down the sidewalk with full bellies, a snowy layer of powdered sugar dusting our coats and a stack of business cards fattening up my wallet. "This might be my favorite day ever," Seth said so sunnily I could swear the clouds overhead considered breaking open.

Somehow it wasn't annoying, maybe because I could agree that all the food had been amazing. I'd gotten some solid leads for the festival, as well as some other ideas for where I could use local vendors, which would please Lorna. I was riding high on the thought of making Lorna eat her words, even though we were back on the subway and a guy was clipping his toenails across from me. "So where to now?" I asked. It was still early, but it was already starting to get dark. "I feel like I already have the start of a great festival, but you've been full of surprises. Do you somehow know a guy who can actually time-travel into the past and bring Judah Maccabee back for a speech? Or no, a guy who can bring Antiochus back so we can all throw rocks at him?"

"I think that's called stoning," Seth said. "Isn't that illegal?"

I dismissed him with a wave of my hand, grinning. "If anyone deserves to be stoned, it's that guy."

A smile twitched at his lips. "It's nice to see you . . ." He trailed off. "Actually, I was thinking we'd check out the—"

"It's nice to see me what?"

"Nothing," Seth said. "I was saying, I think we should check out the big menorah lighting in Union Square. It's supposed to be the world's largest menorah."

I debated asking again what he'd really been meaning to say, but a different curiosity won out. "Do you think they'd bring the world's largest menorah up to our festival? That could be a draw."

Seth laughed, which was actually nice, because it covered up the sound of the nail clippers. "No, I just thought it would be fun. Besides, won't it not actually be Hanukkah during your festival anyway?"

Right. Thinking about it that way still seemed weird. We wouldn't be able to do a real menorah lighting. I mean, we could—it wasn't like anything was legally stopping us. But it didn't feel right to light a menorah outside the actual holiday. We could still have big blow-up fake menorahs with all the candles lit as decoration. But not a real one.

It was fine. It was all going to be fine. It wasn't like I cared about the actual holiday. I cared about bringing tourists to town and saving my café. "Right."

We stopped at the Union Square subway station, which was basically an underground maze swarming with people coming and going in all directions. I had to stop myself from grabbing on to Seth's sleeve like a child so that we wouldn't be separated. It was a relief to emerge into the city air, no matter how many stairs it meant climbing.

The sun was setting over the tall buildings around us, outlining them in red and gold, washing the sky a darker blue. A street busker was fiddling a rendition of "Santa Claus Is Comin' to Town" while, several feet away, a group of drummers pounded a rhythmic beat. As we waited to cross the street into the square, I inhaled deep and smelled not just the usual New York street corner smell of pee and hot pretzels and coffee but gingerbread and cinnamon.

For a moment I wondered if it was magic, and if I was that character in a Christmas movie who was about to find herself changed by holiday cheer. But if I was going to be in any movie, a Christmas movie was not it. My eyes fell upon the far side of the square, where wooden booths wound themselves into a maze, draped in golden lights and cloaked in rising steam. "Oh," I realized. "The Union Square Holiday Market."

By *holiday*—say it with me—they meant *Christmas.*

"We can check that out, too, while we're here," he said. "The menorah doesn't get lit until it's fully dark anyway."

I didn't really feel the desire to browse aisles of miniature Santas in guises from candles to soap or ornaments shaped like the NYC skyline, but enough of the doughnuts and latkes had worked their way out of my stomach for me to gravitate toward the hot chocolate booth. Seth handed me a red cardboard cup that warmed my hands. I stuck my face in it and inhaled deep. Yum, hot chocolate steam. That should totally be a spa offering, too. "Thanks."

Seth got a hot chocolate as well, his spiked with a spicy kick of cayenne. Probably didn't want to stick your face into that one. "No problem. Thanks for being here with me." He held his cup up. I stared at it for a moment before realizing he wanted to toast. That was a terrible idea. Our cups didn't have lids. If we bumped them too hard, we'd slosh hot liquid down our arms.

But what the hell. I did it anyway. He tapped my cup so gently I didn't have to worry.

The hot chocolate was thick and rich and delicious. Sipping it slowly, we meandered from the "holiday" market over to the middle of the square, where the giant menorah stood proud. When he'd told me it was the world's biggest menorah, I'd somehow pictured something the size of a building, but of course it wasn't anywhere near that size. It was about five Seths stacked on top of one another. It was tall, gold, and gleaming (probably plastic), with candles the length of my arm sprouting from it.

I wondered where they got candles that big. They probably had to special order them.

We weren't the only people drifting over that way; tens of people were beginning to gather, some wearing kippahs or long skirts, others in secular clothes, like us. I couldn't help but feel a flash of fear from being in a public space with a bunch of obvious fellow Jews, because mass shootings and hate crimes. But I pushed it down. If I lived in fear, the Antiochuses of the world won.

Once we found our positions toward the front of the crowd but not in the very front, I realized I should really thank Seth for sending me that Google Doc and taking me to these pop-ups—even if I didn't meet anyone else the whole trip, I'd have a good start for planning this festival. And all I'd had to do so far was let his loving mother hug me.

But it seemed weird to bring it up after a while like this, as if I'd been obsessing about it or something. So I just said, "I don't think I've been around this many Jews at once in years."

"Me neither," Seth said. I wondered again about the circumstances that had brought him to the middle of nowhere, Vermont, but this wasn't the time to bring that up, either. "Isn't it great? The feeling of anticipation like electricity in the air as we wait to light the menorah, the sound of all of our voices raised together in song . . ."

Having to worry about a hate crime, I didn't add. But I'd already decided I wasn't going to dwell on that. Besides, what he'd mentioned did make me feel like I wanted to smile.

Not that I *actually* smiled. As previously mentioned, my face didn't always like to listen to the rest of me. Impulsively, I asked, "What do you do?"

"What do you mean?"

"Like, your job," I said. "If you told me before, I forgot." He blinked at me, apparently surprised. "If I'm supposed to be a good fake girlfriend, I should probably know what you spend most of your time doing."

"Probably true," he said. "I'm a dog food taster."

I boggled at him. "What?"

"You know," he said. "That big factory up near Burlington? Someone has to taste the dog food and make sure it's up to par." I had no idea what to say to that. He continued, "It's not too bad. Though I have developed a taste for horse. And it's amazing how many wines you can pair with it. A good red really covers up the aftertaste."

His lips were twitching. I smacked him on the shoulder the same way, I realized a moment too late, that his mom had yesterday. "You're joking."

"I am. Though it is a real job, you know," he said. "I wish I had a more serious face so that I didn't give it away. Imagine how hilarious it would've been if we were out to dinner with my parents and you started talking about how my breath tastes like tinned horse when we kiss."

"Is horse even kosher?" I asked. It didn't matter. None of us kept strictly kosher anyway. "So what do you actually do?"

He shrugged. "The real answer is way more boring, I'm sad to say. I'm in data analysis. Not glamorous, but the pay is decent, it's remote, and the hours are pretty good."

More than anyone could say for my job, to tell you the truth. "What data do you analyze?"

He dove into a word salad of financial and marketing buzzwords that left my head spinning. It was a relief when the guests of honor—I missed who exactly they were, but they were all dressed up and grinning from ear to ear—got up to light the menorah.

The massive candle burst into flame, lighting up the night. Was it my imagination, or had the Christmas music from the fair area dimmed? Only the drummers were still going, their thuds like a heartbeat. I opened my mouth to sing the blessings, and it was like the words weren't just coming from inside me; they were flowing through me from the people all around. *Baruch atah Adonai, eloheinu Melech ha'olam . . .*

Out of nowhere, I felt Seth press something into my hand. I looked down. A tissue?

I swiped it at my cheek out of instinct. It came away slightly damp, but I was not crying. I had no reason to cry. If my eyes were a little bit shiny, it was nothing but a trick of the light.

10

THE NEXT DAY WAS A SYNAGOGUE CHARITY EVENT, which Bev was very excited about. Over breakfast, she told me about all the people I would meet (or, in her words, all the people she would "get to show me off to"). Barbara Horowitz, who had a tendency to lie about how much money her son made. Helen Goldberg, whose botched boob job had given her a serious case of uniboob. Eva Hallac, who had cheated in order to win the rainbow cookie Bake-Off against Bev last year. (Over his newspaper, Benjamin, not looking up, said, "She didn't cheat." "Did so," said Bev, which evolved into an argument that ended in Bev pettily drinking the rest of Benjamin's coffee and then making a sour face at its lack of sugar.)

During the argument, Seth popped in, freshly showered, hair curling damp around his ears. "Oh, man," he said as Bev was grimacing into the empty mug and Benjamin was smiling smugly behind his paper. "I'm really sad we're going to have to miss it."

"What?" Bev said with dismay. "But all of my friends are going to be so disappointed."

"Sorry," said Seth. He didn't sound sorry at all. "But we have big plans." He didn't specify what those big plans were. I managed to hold back on asking until he'd reached a bargain with Bev that we'd miss the event but meet them for lunch afterward and I had to ask him how I should dress for said big plans.

"These plans had better be pretty damn great for me to miss out on seeing the uniboob," I told him. "Your mom said you can see the one nipple poking through her shirt, like a Cyclops."

"Trust me, I've seen it and it's not nearly that impressive," Seth said. "Just wear your regular clothes. Anything is fine."

Clad in my jeans, a purple sweater, and my pea coat, I ventured out with Seth into the cold. Or coldish—today wasn't all that bad. "So?" I said, once we were on the sidewalk. "Where are we going?"

He grinned at me. The green of his own sweater set off the green flecks in his eyes, made them sparkle above the dark brush of his beard. "No idea. Any thoughts?"

I gaped at him, thumping him lightly on the arm. Beneath the soft weave of his sweater, I could feel his muscle flex. I pulled my hand away before it could linger too long, try to figure out how many bicep curls he'd done in the last few weeks. "I thought we had big plans."

"We do have a big plan," Seth said. "And that big plan is not going to the synagogue charity event."

"Why do you hate charity?"

That smile was still playing on his lips. "Doing good things for other people is the worst."

I rolled my eyes. He went on. "Really, it's probably for the best we aren't going. My mom will feel so guilty that she RSVP'd yes for me and I didn't show that she'll donate twice as much to make up for it. Hey, want to go see dinosaurs?"

"That transition may have given me whiplash," I said. "What do you mean, dinosaurs?"

By dinosaurs, he meant the Museum of Natural History. Having grown up in the general area, I'd of course been for a school trip back in middle school, but not since then. "Okay, sure," I said. "Why not?"

The museum wasn't a long walk from Bev and Benjamin's apartment; I enjoyed passing all the old fancy buildings, some with lion statues flanking the entrance and others covered in crawling ivy. Fifteen minutes later, we were standing at the bottom of the museum's majestic marble steps, which rose to meet an even more majestic marble building, round pillars flanking an arched entrance tall enough to admit giants.

Seth stopped at the bottom of the steps. "There. We've seen dinosaurs."

I snorted. He was kind of right: an enormous topiary sculpture of a brontosaurus stood at each side of the door, their long, green, leafy necks creating a secondary arch for people to walk beneath. Giant red poinsettia wreaths ringed each one. "And to think we didn't even have to pay the price of admission."

"Great news: my parents are members, so we don't have to pay the price of admission anyway."

"Nice. I love a deal."

Of course, we still had to wait in line and everything to

get in, then check our coats. I swiped a map from a kiosk, unfolding it before me as we walked. "So obviously we have to visit the dinosaurs. You can't come here and not get a selfie in front of a T. rex."

"That would be blasphemy," Seth agreed. "Hey, watch out." He settled a hand on my shoulder, and my heart very nearly stopped. Because of the unexpected touch, I told myself, not because of how warm and strong his hand was even through the weave of my sweater as it guided me away from a trash can I was about to walk into.

I took a deep breath. The hand fell away. My shoulder felt cold for a moment. "I'll be more careful."

"Don't worry, that's what I'm here for," Seth said amiably. "So, what besides the dinosaurs? Obviously, we can't see the whole museum in one morning."

"Just the morning?" I said. "Didn't you ever read *From the Mixed-Up Files of Mrs. Basil E. Frankweiler* as a kid? You know, where they ran away and lived in the Met? I always kind of wanted to do that."

"The fun thing about being over eighteen is that we could be arrested for that," Seth said. "I think it's trespassing."

"But think of how much fun it would be."

"Getting arrested?"

"Yes, Seth, I think it would be tremendously fun to get arrested. I've always thought prison orange was my color."

"Anyway," he said, ignoring me, "how about the hall of gemstones? I haven't been there in a while, and they're stunning. Or there's the new butterfly vivarium."

Of course he would want to see gemstones and butterflies. "I think there's an exhibit on sharks going on right now."

"Okay," he said. "We can see the sharks if we also see the butterflies."

"Deal."

But first, of course, came the dinosaurs. Seth and I maneuvered our way through throngs of lollygagging tourists toward the appropriate hall. It was almost like an obstacle course: dodge the harried dad swinging around a diaper bag; leap over the tantrumming toddler; zigzag between the couple who can't decide whether they'd rather examine a glass cabinet of fish skeletons or make out. "This is one thing I don't miss about the city," I said, sighing.

"It's not like we don't have tourists up in Vermont, too."

"Sure, but there's a lot more space to get around them."

I waited for him to tell me earnestly that he loved when tourists jostled him because it transferred some of their joy to him or whatever, but he just shrugged. "That's true, I guess." He was quiet for a moment. "I can't be too hard on tourists, considering I was one the first time I went to Vermont."

Right. He was a transplant as much as I was. "Why did you end up there anyway?" I asked, genuinely curious.

He avoided my eyes. "Hey." He craned his neck. "There's the T. rex."

Sure enough, the empty eye sockets and massive sharp teeth of the legendary carnivore loomed ahead of us. It was cool, but not cool enough for me not to notice that he'd dodged the question. I opened my mouth to pursue it, then closed it. It wasn't any of my business. No matter how curious I was. Instead, I said, "It must have been so trippy to be one of the first people to find a dinosaur bone. No wonder they believed in dragons."

"That must have been so—" His eyes widened so much in surprise that for a second I wondered if the T. rex had come back to life and chomped down on one of the tourist couple (who'd decided pretty vigorously on making out over the fish skeleton. Maybe dinosaur bones were an aphrodisiac). "Bonnie! Hey!"

I turned to find a woman about our age approaching with purpose, a high dark ponytail swinging behind her and a wide friendly smile plastered on her lips. "Seth! Oh my god, how long has it been?"

He didn't answer, just returned her hug. He then turned toward me with a weak smile of his own. "This is Abby. My girlfriend."

"Oh my god, hi, Abby!" She came in and, before I could ward her off with crossed arms or maybe a knee to the stomach, she was hugging me, too. I stood there stiffly until it was over. "I'm Bonnie. Seth and I went to school together."

I wondered if she was part of this fabled friend group. "Oh, wow. So you must have some good stories."

"Oh, I don't know," she said. "We came here for a trip in elementary school and he got lost, I think? That was you, right, Seth? Except it turned out he wasn't lost. He was hiding, because he wanted to see if the dinosaurs came alive at night."

I shot him an amused look. So he *did* think it would be cool to sleep over at the museum. Even if he was blushing about it now. "Seems like a poorly thought-out plan, considering that if they did come alive at night, you'd probably get eaten."

"I was a kid," Seth defended. "And most of my exposure to dinosaurs had come from the book *How Do Dinosaurs Say Happy Chanukah?* Where they were cuddly and friendly and giving one another Hanukkah presents."

Another girl came up beside Bonnie. Bonnie pulled her close with an affectionate arm around the waist. "This is my girlfriend, Nora."

"Nice to meet you," Nora said, resting her head against Bonnie's shoulder.

I was suddenly very aware of the two feet of space separating Seth and me. No hands being held, no shoulders being draped with arms, no cheeks pressed by lips. If we were an actual couple, wouldn't we be more comfortable with each other?

This was probably something we should have discussed. He'd specifically told me his parents wouldn't be expecting any PDA, but hadn't told me anything about friends.

Desperate times called for desperate measures. I stepped closer to Seth, so that my hip rested against his thigh, and leaned my head against his shoulder. He still smelled like oranges and campfire, despite using his family's lavender soap. "Nice to meet you, too." There shouldn't have been a pulse in his shoulder, but I swore I could feel the beating of his heart, fast and uncertain, against my ear.

Nora looked to Seth, as if waiting for him to say something. He did, a moment too late, stumbling over his words. "Nice to meet you."

I steadied myself against the warm, solid bulk of him, leaning in a little so that my hair brushed the hollows of his neck, because that was what a girlfriend would do. And what a girlfriend would do was stay there after a few minutes of small talk, then for a minute after Bonnie and Nora had bid us goodbye and disappeared back into the crowd, because what if one of them circled back or looked over their shoulder at us? It was the good, responsible thing to do, and that was it, and it had nothing to do with the warmth.

Seth finally cleared his throat. I blinked and jumped back, feeling almost like I'd been woken from a sound sleep. "Thanks for improvising."

"Of course. That's what I'm here for," I said. The words tasted a little sour. "Is Bonnie part of your friend group?"

He shook his head. "No, just an old classmate. So you really didn't have to . . ." He waved his hand around, indicating the hug and the closeness and whatever else.

I forced a smile. "Sorry if you didn't want—"

"No, it's not that," he said hastily. "I just . . . never mind." He cleared his throat again. "Maybe we should discuss our parameters for being around other people I know. So that neither one of us gets uncomfortable."

I couldn't help but shrivel a little bit at that last word. So I'd made him uncomfortable. That was the last thing I'd wanted to do. But I'd already apologized, and I wasn't going to make things awkward by apologizing again and again. "You know I'm not a super touchy person, but I don't mind if we have to hold hands or hug to make this relationship look real."

"Okay," Seth said. "So it would be okay if, like, we ran into a friend and I put my arm around you?"

"Sure."

"Okay. Sounds good."

"Okay." An awkward silence fell upon us, as thick and smothering as a wool blanket. I coughed to fill it. It did not help. Maybe more words would? "So now that we have the rules, do we have plans with your friends to use them?"

"I don't know. Hey, want to move on to the sharks?"

It was getting awfully crowded around here, and I was pretty sure we'd been in the background of at least seventy pictures of people with the T. rex. "Sure." Maybe my bones wouldn't be the only thing that future people would see of me. In fifty years kids would ooh and aah over pictures of their grandparents with me and Seth holding each other in the background. *What a cute couple,* they might say, not knowing any differently.

The shark exhibit was full of bones and teeth and models hanging from the ceiling. We strolled through it, musing on which shark we'd most like to get eaten by. "I think the little shark would be best," said Seth. "There's at least a chance of me being able to fight it off."

I shrugged. "I don't know. It still looks pretty strong. And I'd rather just get devoured in one big gulp than chewed to death by a thousand tiny bites."

It was kind of a depressing debate, and I wasn't inclined to finish it. "Hey, before, you said you didn't know if we'd be seeing your friends," I said. I wasn't prying; it was a legitimate question that applied to my job as a fake girlfriend. Right? It was only fair for me to know what the plans were for the rest of the trip. "I thought you said in the car that we would be? The group chat was buzzing."

He grimaced, either at me or at the thought of how

easily he'd fit through the jaws of a megalodon. "Yeah. The group chat's still buzzing with plans. I don't know, I just . . . I don't know. I guess I'm kind of avoiding them."

That didn't seem like him. That seemed like me. "Why? You don't miss them?"

"No, I do. I just . . ." He sighed. "I'm nervous. You know, Freya and I broke up, and then I disappeared without even saying goodbye. I'm kind of worried they're mad at me." He was quiet for a moment.

"There's no way to know without seeing them," I said. "And isn't it better to just get it over with and find out for sure instead of spending all this time agonizing about it?"

He shrugged. "Or I could just never talk to them again."

"A very adult way of dealing with your feelings."

"Thank you."

"Just to be clear, that was sarcasm."

"What?" Seth cupped his hand over his ear. "Can't hear you. Anyway, want to go see the butterflies?"

Again, it wasn't my business to pry. I was a fake girlfriend, not a real one. But still, as we paused in the middle of the butterfly vivarium to marvel at a lacy scrap of bright blue that fluttered to a rest on Seth's shoulder, our hands grazing each other with the movement, I figured that to the people around us we looked pretty real.

11

BEV WAS GLOWING AND TRIUMPHANT WHEN SETH and I met her and Benjamin outside the synagogue after the charity event. The building was a majestic beast, a massive stone structure with pointed towers and elegant scrollwork dating back to the late 1800s. "My rainbow cookies sold out much faster than Eva Hallac's. Just more proof that she didn't really win the Bake-Off."

"That was last year, Mom," Seth said. Their apartment was only fifteen blocks away from the synagogue, so the plan was to walk back and grab dinner somewhere on the way. "Don't you think it might be time to let it go? For the good of the community?"

Bev bristled, clutching her padded MZ Wallace bag to her side. "Al Gore let it go for the good of the community, and just look at what happened."

"Yes," Seth said seriously, but he glanced at me with a spark in his eye. "The rainbow cookie Bake-Off is exactly like global warming."

"Honestly, Seth, of course I didn't mean *that*."

This time I met Seth's eyes with an amused look of my

own, in on the joke. If I were a real girlfriend, this moment would become something we'd bring up to make each other laugh over the years. *I can't believe you ran out of whipped cream again. It's basically global warming.*

But I wasn't a real girlfriend, and this whole thing would pop like a bubble as soon as Hanukkah ended. I looked away.

"Personally, I find it in poor taste to joke about global warming," Benjamin said. "Haven't you seen those very sad pictures of the polar bears going around the Internet? The ones trapped on melting ice caps? And that's not even mentioning the millions of people who are going to lose their homes to rising sea levels."

"Nobody was joking about melting ice caps or rising sea levels," Seth said. We passed a normal sidewalk tree strung up with multicolored lights. A dog was peeing on the base. "We were joking that Mom thinks her Bake-Off is equivalent to the sad polar bears." He exchanged another glance with me. "Abby, do you think we're the only two who understand humor around here?"

Without having to speak, the other three turned left, taking us up a side street to Broadway. Unlike West End Avenue, where we'd been walking, Broadway was wide and commercial, bustling with fellow walkers bundled in winter wear. Stores and restaurants lined the four-lane avenue, everything from hipster-ish bars to restaurants from around the world to dog salons to human salons to salons that styled both humans and dogs. People poured in and out of them, each open door releasing a rush of warm air and a different interesting smell.

"I understand humor perfectly well," said Benjamin, sounding a little insulted. "For example, a man slipping on a banana peel. Always funny."

Ironically, at that exact moment, we passed a banana peel lying on the sidewalk. Somehow I didn't think Benjamin would find it so funny if he'd slipped on it.

"Whatever you say," Seth said.

"Seth?" The voice came from behind us. I glanced over to see one powder blue glove on Seth's shoulder, as if keeping him from running away. We all turned around.

I didn't even need to hear Seth say, "Freya," because I knew immediately who she was—she looked exactly as she had in my head. Tall and willowy, with light blond hair, icy blue eyes, and a pale, narrow face. In addition to those powder blue gloves, she'd wrapped herself up in a slim-fitting powder blue coat and a woven hat that bounced with a shiny silver pom-pom.

Forget resembling a Viking. She looked like the Snow Queen from a fairy tale.

As if I were meeting the actual Snow Queen, I braced myself for a gust of cold air as she turned in my direction. Instead, I got mild curiosity. "I heard that you were bringing someone home for the holidays. You must be Abby?"

"I am Abby," I said cautiously. Would she say something passive-aggressive? Look me up and down with derision? Freeze me out?

Instead, she smiled. And yeah, it was a little stiff, but it reached her eyes and everything. "Nice to meet you, Abby. Welcome to New York. I'm Freya." She reached out a hand. I took it. Her handshake was delicate, like I might break her fingers if I returned my usual strong one.

"Nice to meet you, too," I said, remembering too late that I probably had resting bitch face going on. I made myself smile in return.

She released my hand and turned back to Seth. "You haven't said anything in the group chat about tonight. Are you coming?"

Seth shifted from boot to boot, his hands tucked away in his pockets like he was afraid she might try to shake his, too. "Oh, I don't know. We're pretty busy. We're on our way to dinner."

I furrowed my brow, my forced smile sliding away. Here he was, doing his avoidance thing again. Trying to hide from his fears. Should I say something? Try to prod him toward what I thought was the right decision?

"Nonsense," Benjamin said. Bev was looking at Freya with a sort of pained smile, as if the situation was too awkward for her tastes. "We have plenty of nights to have dinner together." For just a moment, his eyes glinted with a sort of vicious glee. "Maybe I don't understand humor, but I do understand how important it is to spend time with your friends."

Shots *fired*. I coughed to cover up a smirk.

"See?" Freya said. She touched Seth's upper arm, then, as if realizing they weren't dating and shouldn't be touching anymore, sharply pulled it away. "Everybody misses you. Come on. We're going on an ugly sweater bar crawl to the Tree. You always had the ugliest sweaters. You can't miss it."

Seth glanced over at me, eyes helpless. "Abby?"

"I'll need to borrow an ugly sweater," I said, and that was that. Seth gave up.

"Okay. We'll come."

Freya's smile was gleaming and pearl white. "Excellent."

An hour later, Seth and I were emerging from the subway near Herald Square, both of us decked out in the ugliest sweaters I'd ever seen. When I'd heard "ugly sweater bar crawl to the Tree," I'd of course pictured traditional ugly Christmas sweaters: blinking red lights adorning a deformed knitted Rudolph; leering elves circling an unintentionally demonic Santa.

So when Seth produced a collection of ugly Hanukkah sweaters from the back of his closet, I'd been pleasantly surprised. And immediately claimed the one with the light-up menorah on the front, leaving him with a blue-and-white monstrosity covered in dreidels. Both were itchy. I didn't care.

"Is there anything else I should know before meeting all your friends?" I asked him as we pushed through crowds. We were getting some stares. Admiring ones, I chose to believe.

Seth shrugged. "I've already told you about them. They're just normal people."

"Where did you meet? Did you all go to school together?"

"No, not all of us," Seth said. "I met some of them when I went to college up in Boston, then added Freya and some more after college when we were working up there. A bunch of us moved to New York over the next few years, including

Freya and me, and we grew a little here. It's more of an amorphous blob than a tight group."

If they weren't all tied to a specific place or point in time, maybe that left room for people to still join. Like me.

No. I almost laughed at the absurdity of thinking that. I'd probably never see them again after this. Unless I happened to be in New York and Seth invited me out. After all, we were friends now. It wouldn't be absurd to become friends with a friend's friends. "Are you feeling any better about seeing them? Any less nervous?" I asked. "Since Freya didn't seem to be mad at you, and if anyone was going to be mad at you, you would think—"

"I don't want to talk about it," Seth snapped, then looked surprised at himself. "Sorry. I shouldn't have bitten your head off like that."

"No, it's fine." After all, I was just the fake girlfriend. An accessory. It wasn't for me to ask personal questions, like how he was feeling or what was going on in his head. Even if our outing to the museum, the light touches of our hands, and the slip of vulnerability he showed in telling me he was nervous about seeing his friends had given me the illusion that maybe there was more to it than that.

Frigid bitch.

I shivered at the echo of Connor's parting words. It wasn't that I was frigid. I just knew my place. Besides, if I started asking Seth personal questions, he'd start thinking he could ask me personal questions in response. And I wasn't having that.

The first bar in our bar crawl was a stereotypical Irish

pub, all dark wood walls and sticky floors and torn green cushions. As we stepped inside, I was hit immediately by a wall of sound and beer smell. The place was packed. Almost by instinct, I reached for Seth's arm so that we wouldn't get separated as we pushed our way through.

And stopped myself just in time. So what if we got separated? I'd find him eventually. I didn't want him thinking I was nervous to get stranded in this crowd or something.

"Hey." Seth's hand grabbed mine, wrapping it in warmth. I exhaled a deep breath that felt a little like relief. Good for him, keeping the ruse up and making sure we looked like a couple. Good for him.

Fortunately, his friends were clustered at a table by the window. I actually spotted them first, because, no joke, Freya was illuminated by a light from above that made her almost-white hair glow and the diamonds in her ears sparkle. She waved at us when she saw us coming, which made the rest of their group turn.

"Seth-man!" one of the guys bellowed. There were six of them in total, including Freya. "You made it! How long has it been?"

"Too long!" someone bellowed back, but nobody made it awkward beyond that. Between beery one-armed hugs and firm handshakes that made Seth let go of my hand, I was introduced to the four guys and two girls. Names were shouted at me over the noise, but, even after asking them to repeat themselves one or two or three times, I was left only reasonably certain that the guy with the scruffy brown hair was Dan and the girl who wasn't Freya was named Kylie. The other three guys might have been named Mike.

I managed to settle myself on a rickety stool between Seth, Dan, and Kylie, so that I wouldn't have to worry about names or having Freya twitch her finger and turn my heart into ice. I braced myself for answering a bunch of probing personal questions about where I grew up and what my hopes and dreams were, but nobody seemed particularly interested in that. They were more interested in our relationship. Well, our "relationship." "So, Abby," Dan hollered, blasting me in the face with a lungful of beer breath. "How did you and Seth meet?"

I glanced over at Seth, who was deep in conversation with one of the Mikes. No help there. Had he told them some fabricated romantic story about how I'd nearly slipped on an icy night and he'd caught me and noticed how the snowflakes sparkled in my eyelashes before making some crack about how he was falling for me, too? Or were we supposed to spin the same wacky water-crashing-through-my-ceiling tale we'd told Bev and Benjamin for the sake of consistency? Hopefully not. "He's a frequent customer at the café I run," I said. "Comes in every morning. We got to know each other like that. He's very . . . cheerful early in the day."

Dan laughed so wide I could see his molars. "You can say that again. We lived together in college and I swear I almost pushed the guy out a window a few times. It's like he's immune to hangovers."

There it was: an immediate sense of kinship. I'd never particularly wanted to push Seth out a window before, but that was mainly because my café was on the first floor, so I hadn't thought of it. "Clearly, you didn't push him out a window, though."

"Thank god for that, or you wouldn't have such a great boyfriend," Dan said, grinning again. I couldn't tell if he was being sarcastic or not. Probably he wasn't. A real friend wouldn't be an asshole about that. "I don't know, something about the guy's attitude was infectious. I never wanted to be told to 'look on the bright side' of losing out on the dorm we wanted or getting turned down by the guy in my history of immigration class, but I have to say, he was usually right. If we'd gotten that dorm, which was a lot nicer but less central, we wouldn't have become the kings of the party scene. If that guy had gone out with me, I wouldn't have met Mike S., who became one of our best friends." He nodded at the guy across from him, who I assumed was Mike S. He nodded back.

"Yeah, totally, I get it." I plastered a big smile on my face, the type of smile the girlfriend of a "look on the bright side" guy should have. "It's like when my grandma died, and I was like, well, on the bright side, at least I still have my other grandma."

Dan pinched his eyebrows. "Uh. Okay."

I took a big gulp of my drink.

And another.

And another.

"Hey, guys, you'd better not be telling Abby any embarrassing stories about me." Seth's attention was suddenly back on me, his smile so blinding I had to squint a little. He draped an arm over my shoulder. Don't people say that weighted blankets help with anxiety for some reason? I didn't know why I was thinking that now, but I set my drink back down on the table.

Not soon enough to keep the effects from hitting me hard, though. The drink wasn't even that good—the cranberry juice was too sugary, and the vodka was cheap, and they hadn't even given me a maraschino cherry—but it got the job done. By the time we were flowing out of the Irish bar and on to our next stop, I felt like I was floating pleasantly above the sidewalk, tethered to the earth by Seth's hand. "Are you okay?" he asked.

"I'm fine," I said dreamily.

When we stopped in front of the next bar, my jaw dropped open. Dan slapped Seth on the back so loud it echoed. "This one's for you, Seth-man!"

Seth looked stunned. "Is this . . ."

It was. A. *Hanukkah bar.*

Blue and white lights dazzled me as we stepped through the door and were met by the scents of apple and vanilla and fried potato, which—I couldn't explain it—smelled just like Hanukkah. "Apple isn't even a Hanukkah food," I murmured.

"What?" asked Kylie, who was next to me.

I shook my head. "Nothing."

Electric menorahs blazed all around the room from every surface, all lit up for the third night. Right. We'd passed sunset without lighting the candles. Had Seth's parents lit them without us?

We nabbed a circular table so that everybody could hear one another when they talked, me settling in between

Seth and Dan again. It would have been easier here even if we hadn't; the music, currently a version of Adam Sandler's classic Hanukkah song, was set pretty low. One of the electric menorahs sat in the middle of the table, along with a few extra-large dreidels. I picked one up to find a sheet of instructions beneath for a dreidel drinking game. Nun, nobody drank. Hay, you drank. Gimel, everybody drank. Shin, you got to choose someone else to drink. Simple. Elegant. Brilliant.

I didn't realize I'd said that out loud until Seth started to laugh. "How much did you have to drink already?"

"Only two drinks!" I poked him hard in the chest for emphasis. A ragged nail got stuck in the weave of his sweater, and it took a second to extricate myself. "To be fair, they were strong." It was probably a good thing that I'd stuck to one drink when I met up with Seth the first time.

"Clearly," Seth said, a smile twitching at his lips.

"What, do you find this funny?"

"Yes," he said. "You're usually so buttoned-up. It's funny to see you loosen up a little."

There was nothing like somebody pointing out you'd loosened up to make you tighten right back in on yourself. I turned away from him, feeling like I'd accidentally flashed him or something. "Hey," I said loudly, because I'd rather talk to anyone and everyone else right now. "It's after sundown and we haven't lit the candles yet, and we've got this great menorah right here."

The table sprang into action as I ordered them around: Dan loosened the lit bulbs so that they went dark, and Seth pulled up English transliterations of the blessings on his phone for the non-Jews' (about half of them—it seemed a couple of the Mikes were Jewish, but the rest of the group wasn't) reference.

They were all too shy to start off the singing. Thanks to the vodka, I was not. "Baruch atah Adonai . . ."

Everybody else joined in, the people who didn't know Hebrew butchering all the pronunciations enthusiastically. Understandable—if you didn't know that the "ch" transliterated into a sound that could be described in English as clearing your throat, you'd naturally pronounce it like the beginning of "choo choo train." But they were trying, and that was what mattered.

It mattered a lot, actually. *It's the vodka*, I told myself, but my sinuses were stinging with how much I felt it. I was so used to blending in the opposite way—buying friends Christmas presents; going to Christmas parties and singing along to Christmas music; creating Christmas specials for my menu board—that welcoming people into my own traditions felt odd. Odd, but really nice.

Nice enough that, after we'd all ordered a round of Hanukkah-themed drinks (unable to resist my curiosity, I'd selected a latke-themed cocktail that was either going to be fantastic or terrible), I insisted we play the dreidel drinking game. "It's part of the holiday," I told them all. Their faces blurred just slightly as I spun around, enough where they could've been anybody—my childhood friends, my family, the tourism board. "When you're a kid you play with gelt."

As if the waitress had read my mind, she turned up not just with our drinks, but with a little mesh bag of the gold foil–wrapped chocolate coins for each of us, too, so I didn't have to explain what gelt was. Before trying my cocktail, I ripped open the bag and tore apart one of those bad boys, popping the coin into my mouth. It took a few seconds for the cheap, plasticky chocolate to melt. Just like I remembered.

"I played strip dreidel once in college," Dan offered, and the table laughed. He nudged Seth. "If I recall, you lost pretty bad. Didn't your underwear end up pinned to the wall of the girls' bathroom?" I snorted at Seth's chagrined expression and took a sip of my latke and applesauce cocktail. It tasted mostly like apples and cinnamon, which was probably a good thing, though I did appreciate the salty potato chip garnish on the rim.

"If we do that tonight we'll probably get arrested, so let's stick to the drinking game," Freya said dryly. She'd been pretty quiet most of the night, and I'd caught her, more than once, sneaking glimpses at me. Had she mispronounced her ch's, or had she spent enough years with Seth where she knew how to properly clear her throat? I wasn't sitting close enough to hear. "You go first, Dan."

Dan anticlimactically spun a nun, so nobody drank. Fortunately for everybody who wanted to get drunk, the Mikes each spun gimel, so we all made it halfway through our cocktails.

And then it was Freya's turn. She spun shin. Her eyes roamed around the table, pausing briefly on me before settling on Seth. "Drink." She raised her glass to him. He raised his glass—a bright red concoction named after the blood of the rebellion, which was both gross and cool—and took a sip. Something I didn't quite like simmered in my belly, but

I pushed it away immediately. It had no right to be there. It must have been the potato vodka.

Eventually, drinking dreidel devolved into discussing the best Hanukkah or Christmas presents everyone at the table had received. "Back in high school, one of my guy friends came up to me with the most nervous expression on his face and was like, 'I got you something for the holidays,'" Kylie reminisced, stirring her bright blue drink with a toothpick that had once been stacked with pickled blueberries. "I opened it up and it was this absolutely gorgeous, absurdly expensive Tiffany bracelet. I totally panicked because I hadn't gotten him anything and just grabbed this Scooby Doo ornament I'd bought as a gag gift for someone else and was like, here you go! I got this for you!"

The table cringe-laughed. Kylie shook her head and took a sip of her drink. Her teeth had been stained bright blue, too. "His face lit up when he heard what I said, then fell when he saw what was inside. Poor guy. I wore that bracelet every day through college, though."

I thought for a second about volunteering my own standout Hanukkah gift. There was the year my mom had gotten me the exact dress I'd been eyeing online, only two sizes too small. She'd refused to return it, even when I showed her I could barely squeeze my bust in. "Maybe it'll serve as motivation for you." Or the year my parents had made a point of getting me a small, cheap Barbie toy while getting my cousins big expensive sets for them to open in front of me. They'd been punishing me for something. I couldn't remember what it was now. Something about how I'd forgotten to close the cabinet doors when I was done with them.

The rest of the table was laughing at something Dan said. I joined in a moment too late, then startled as Seth touched my shoulder. I braced myself for him to ask if I was okay or tell me that I looked stressed, but he only said, "Let me know if you want to head out at any point. I know they can be a lot."

I shook my head, whipping him in the cheek with my hair. "No. I'm having a good time." I was almost surprised to realize it was true. I liked their raucous energy, my immediate welcome into the circle. The way they made me feel included and listened with interest when I spoke.

And I really liked this bar, too. I swirled my drink around, tilting my head at it in interest. I'd never done a Hanukkah special at my café before. I'd never thought there would be a market. But this bar was full, and not everybody in here could be Jewish—most of our group wasn't. I could do a Hanukkah coffee special taking this cocktail as inspiration. Who didn't love a latte with apple and cinnamon flavors? And a fun potato garnish?

". . . so my grandma picked it up and shook it, and of course that's when the box started to vibrate," Freya finished, and the table burst into laughter. I didn't even have to hear the beginning of the story to know it was funny. My own laugh was genuine.

As Freya finished, she tipped her drink toward Seth. "Tell them about the cactus."

"Oh my god, the cactus." Seth's face lit up. "So you guys know I'm a responsible plant dad. Unlike *some* of us." He shot a glance at Dan, who raised his glass in our direction.

"A toast to the many dearly departed basil plants I bought at the grocery store."

"Anyway," Seth went on. "This is back when I wasn't working remotely and was in person at the office in Boston. For some reason, my boss decided that his holiday gift to all of us would be cacti. Did you know it's actually harder to take care of a cactus than you'd think? People assume they're these plants for dummies because they like sun and don't need a ton of water, but you have to be careful about how much—"

"We don't need the cactus instruction guide," Dan said. "If anything, I need the basil plant instruction guide."

Seth shook his head. "No way. You've been barred from ever buying a basil plant again. By PETA."

Kylie snorted. "Does PETA have anything to do with plants?"

"They should," Seth said. "They're living things, aren't they?"

I jumped in. "I read this article that said plants can cry and dream."

"See?" Seth said. He slung an arm around the back of my chair. The warmth of his arm soaked into my shoulders. "No more basil plants for you, Dan. By PETA decree. Anyway, my coworkers started realizing that they were killing their cacti. I, the fool, told them I would adopt any ailing cacti in need. The first one appeared on my desk overnight. The next two popped up a few days later. Soon, my desk was a sea of cacti. I didn't have time to do any work. All my time was taken by rotating them in and out of the sliver of sunlight my desk got each afternoon. My productivity reports began to fall. I started to panic."

He shook his head solemnly. "And then the CEO, Prickly Joe, stopped by my desk." He paused. "Of course, he was just the CEO, Joe, before he tripped."

Everybody laughed, me with them, and kept on laughing as Seth described how, between the red face and the spluttering, Prickly Joe had resembled nothing more than a furious porcupine. The image tickled me; I leaned my head against Seth's shoulder with a snort. His shoulder tensed for a moment under my ear, as if he were surprised, but then his arm tightened around me, drawing me closer, the way he would with a girlfriend.

Only I wasn't a girlfriend.

I'd almost forgotten that. I'd almost let myself relax.

I pulled myself away, laugh stopping short. Seth's arm dropped away. The table's eyes found me, their laughs stalling.

I forced a smile. "Bathroom. Excuse me."

The winding path to the bathroom through the crowded bar took me past not one but two large stuffed Hanukkah Harries (the secular Jewish child's joking equivalent to Santa). It felt kind of like they were watching me the way Santa was supposed to. Catching what I'd done that was nice, catching what I'd done that was naughty, catching what I'd done that wasn't right, like thinking for a moment that I was a real member of the group.

The bathroom was empty, which was a relief. I used it, because why not while I was already here, then stood at the sink and splashed some cold water on my face. Took a deep breath. Stared at myself in the mirror. Really, glared at myself in the mirror. *What do you think you're doing, Abby? This is all transactional. To save your café. You don't even* like *him.*

Except that wasn't true anymore, was it? I considered him a friend. I didn't know when my brain had made that switch, but it had. *But you're not a girlfriend. You don't want to be his girlfriend. Chill the fuck out.*

The bathroom door opened behind me as I realized I was mouthing the words into the mirror. Hopefully, I clamped my mouth shut before whoever came in noticed. I turned to go, because standing there talking to myself was weird, and found myself face-to-face with Freya.

The mirror crackled with a thin sheet of ice. The droplets of water on my face froze solid.

Not really. But that's what it felt like.

"Sorry, sorry," Freya was saying. "I wanted to wait until you got back, but I really, really had to pee, and you were taking forever . . ."

"Don't worry about it!" I rushed to say. "No worries. Go pee."

But she didn't move toward the stalls. And I couldn't move toward the door, since she was in the way. I was left staring at her ugly sweater, which wasn't even that ugly—powder blue to match her eyes, covered in snowflakes laced in glimmering silver thread—until I realized that it probably looked more like I was staring at her boobs, which was so awkward I *had* to look her in the eye.

"Well, nice seeing you here," I said awkwardly, willing her to move. She didn't, maybe because it was on the list of the weirdest things to say to someone in the bathroom.

Instead, she said, "I wanted to hate you so badly." I blinked. She clapped a hand over her mouth. Through those long, thin fingers, she said, voice muffled, "I didn't mean to say that out loud."

"Been there," I said, because I literally had been there just minutes ago. *Please move*, I willed at her with all the telepathic force I could muster. *I cannot handle a drunk girl heart-to-heart right now. Or ever.*

Alas, my telepathic force remained just as weak as when I'd spent a week in middle school attempting to bend spoons at the dinner table.

A single tear rolled slowly, glamorously, down Freya's cheek. "I wanted to hate you, but I can't. You're really cool, and Seth really seems to like you. I want to be happy for you."

I could see where this was going. I could wait for her to slowly and dramatically hiccup her drunk way there, or I could cut it off quickly and hope it surprised her enough that she'd let me goooo, damn it. "Do you still have feelings for him?" I said, trying to sound as gentle as possible.

I did not do gentle well. I was pretty sure I sounded like I'd asked her if her tires needed more air. Sure enough, she responded by bursting into tears. Not bursting into tears the way I did on the rare occasions I cried—red, snotty, messy, loud—but soundlessly welling over so that her eyes sparkled and her lashes glittered. Only the tip of her nose got a tiny bit red.

Okay, I felt like such an asshole right now. I couldn't just leave. I stepped closer and, trying to channel Bev, gingerly put my arms around her. She was tall enough where her tears flowed into my hair. On the bright side, maybe the saltiness of her tears would have the same excellent effects as a beach day, which always turned my typically straightened hair into glamorous beach waves.

Freya sniffled above me. "No. I don't. I swear I don't." I blinked, a little bit surprised, but also relieved. It made things a lot less awkward here. "Not romantic anyway. Like, I don't want to get back together with him. I just . . . It's just, our breakup came out of *nowhere*. Everything seemed to be going great and then suddenly he tells me he's moving to Vermont. Alone. After two years. I still don't know what happened. He didn't even tell any of the friend group; he just disappeared. Dan thought he hated him for ages."

I patted her awkwardly on the back. I was the worst possible person to be in this situation with her. If only I could switch places with someone warm and nurturing and comforting, someone who would know exactly the right thing to say.

"I'm sorry," I said.

She sniffled again. "It made me feel like absolute garbage. Like I wasn't even worth breaking up with properly. Has he ever said anything about me? To you?"

If Seth and I actually were in a relationship that had lasted long enough for the two of us to come stay with his parents, he might have. But all he'd told me was that things ended badly. "I'm sorry," I repeated. "That's a shitty way to break up with someone. Just moving away? Come on. Use your words like a grown-up."

Freya's sniffle turned into an elegant snort. "Right? I don't think it's too much to ask for after two years."

"Definitely not," I said. It was probably safe to pull back now, right? I did, patting the damp spot on my head. No beach waves yet. "Did he ever apologize to you, at least?"

"Nope."

Wow. "I'm impressed that you could come out and hang with him like this. Whenever I run into my ex, it's the most awkward, uncomfortable thing ever." Aside from this encounter, probably, but I didn't say that.

Freya's snort this time was decidedly less elegant, which made me like her more. "It feels awkward and uncomfortable. But I wasn't going to get pushed out of the friend group just because he'd be around. And I wanted to show him how well I'm doing." She rolled her eyes at herself. "So much for that."

"I won't tell him about any of this," I said. Even if we actually had been dating, I wouldn't share someone's vulnerability with someone else. I wouldn't want anyone else sharing mine. "So don't worry about that."

"You're so sweet." Freya pinched her nose and stared up at the ceiling, maybe trying to stop the tears. "Again, I really wish I could hate you. The ex's new girlfriend, who his mom seems to loooove even though she never seemed to like me. I bet he wouldn't just move away from you after years of a relationship."

I had two excuses for what I said next, neither one of them particularly good. The first: alcohol. The second: I'd skated too close to the line earlier by putting my head on Seth's shoulder and almost—almost—forgetting that this whole thing was fake, and part of me wanted to make sure that line stayed strong. "You don't have to hate me," I said, breath quickening. "Because Seth and I aren't actually in a relationship."

That made her choke on air or maybe spit. "What?"

I leaned in, as if there might be a listening device posted somewhere above the mirror. "I mean that we don't even like each other that much; we're just the two closest Jews in our area of Vermont. I needed his help creating a Hanukkah festival for the town, and he needed a Nice Jewish Girl to bring home to get his mom off his back. And our town is so small that we use a barter system." I smiled to show that I was joking, but her face was deadly serious. "Anyway. So I have no idea why he broke up with you, but he didn't do it for me, and you don't have to stress about saying things about him to me."

She shook her head, seemingly disbelieving. "Of course it's for Bev," she muttered. "I could never do anything right for that woman. Not Jewish enough. Didn't have a prestigious enough career. What's wrong with being a kindergarten teacher?"

"Nothing," I assured her. Owning a café required way less schooling than becoming a kindergarten teacher, and, to be honest, at this point Freya probably made more money than me. "The youth need education."

"The youth need education!" she shouted, pointing her finger up in the air as if to say THIS. "I wasn't a good enough cook. I could go down the list forever." She chewed the inside of her cheek, looking pensive. "Maybe his mom made him break up with me. I can't see him standing up to her."

"I don't know," I said, because it was true, I didn't know. "I'll try asking him and seeing what I can find out."

Her face brightened. "You'd do that?"

"Sure," I said. Why not?

She leaned in as if to hug me—oh no—but, a Hanukkah miracle: the door opened and in flowed a group of girls, eyes bright with alcohol and skirts tight and glittery. "Oh. My. God," one said. "I love your sweaters. Like, I'm obsessed."

"Oh my god, thank you," Freya said. She clasped her hands under her chin like a Disney Princess. "I love your hair. I've always wished mine curled like that."

"Well, I love your shoes," another girl said back, and before I could get drawn into the drunk-girl-in-the-bathroom compliment circle, I slipped out.

Back at the table, Seth turned to me with a concerned smile. "You were in there for a while. Everything okay?"

Great. Just what I needed: everybody at the table thinking I was undergoing some kind of smelly gastrointestinal distress. "Fine, just had to fix my makeup," I said breezily. I cast my eyes around the table, eager to find something else, literally anything else, I could use to change the subject. "People's drinks are looking pretty empty. Are we moving on to the next place soon?"

Indeed we were. Once Freya came back, her face carefully composed, we went to a Christmas-themed bar, then to a gothic place that seemed right out of a Tim Burton movie. I was careful to stick with mocktails to keep my head clear and my body under control. Every time Seth smiled at me or draped his arm casually over my shoulders, I repeated the same mantra to myself. *It's not real. You wouldn't want it to be real anyway. Do it for the café.*

By the time our final stop rolled around, I was exhausted and sick of talking to myself. To make everything worse, Seth grabbed my hand on the way out of the gothic bar. He decidedly had not been limiting himself to mocktails, and his eyes were fuzzy, his words a little slurred. "I'm really glad you're here with us," he told me, squeezing my hand.

It's not real. You wouldn't want it to be real anyway. I painted on a smile. "Me too."

"There it is!" Dan said.

There it was: the Rockefeller Center Christmas Tree. It rose tall as a building, wide and majestic, sparkling all over with red and green and blue lights. The star topper glowed gold.

A lump rose in my throat. I couldn't speak, even if I wanted to.

"Group picture!" Kylie yelled, beckoning us all in. Crowds jostled around us as we tried to meld into one selfie-able blob. Seth held tight to my hand the whole time, making sure we wouldn't be separated.

What did it matter? I pulled my hand away. "I can just take it," I said, but Kylie waved me away.

"No way. You're part of the group. Get in here!"

Later on, when she sent the picture to each of our phones, I was surprised to see I was smiling. I didn't remember doing it.

12

THE NEXT MORNING, MY EYES POPPED AWAKE with the excitement of an idea. Without bothering to think it through, I leaned over the side of the bed. "A sufganiyot latte."

Seth winced, covering his eyes dramatically with his arm as if my teeth were the sun. If anything, he should be covering his nose, I realized belatedly (the morning breath multiple drinks had given me could have wilted grass). "Good morning to you, too."

"Did you hear me?" I asked.

"I heard you. Something about a doughnut coffee that was entirely lacking in context for being shouted at me this early in the morning."

I hadn't been shouting. Had I? Maybe. The idea was that exciting. I pulled myself over to the edge of the bed, dangling my bare feet over the side, dangerously close to where Seth was stretched out on the rug with his meager pillow and blanket. It was a good thing we weren't in a real relationship, or I'd probably be self-conscious about my feet.

I'd always had ugly feet, scarred and knobbly with an oddly long second toe and a scrunched knot of a pinky.

But enough about my feet. "A sufganiyot latte," I said, then added context. "I'm thinking I set up my booth at the fair with some Hanukkah coffee specials. I already thought about a latke special based on that cocktail I got, and now a sufganiyot latte with flavors of strawberry and powdered sugar. A chocolate gelt cappuccino. I'm thinking of a few other ones, too. I can sell them at the fair and see how popular they are, then rotate the more popular ones at the café with all the Christmas specials next year."

Seth pulled himself slowly to a seated position against the wall, wincing. Hopefully, at his back and not my idea. "You look very angry about this."

"That's just the resting bitch face," I said impatiently. "I'm very excited. What do you think?"

He tipped his head as if in thought, though it might have been because he was all lopsided from sleep: his hair flattened one side and flying free on the other; all the blood in his face red in his one cheek. "What do I think?"

I realized I was holding my breath. That was stupid. I needed to breathe.

Seth cracked a smile. "I think I'd try some of those out instead of my usual pumpkin spice."

I didn't need to release a breath I hadn't realized I was holding, because I'd already realized I was holding it. So instead, I just released a breath. "Okay. Cool."

"I'm really excited about these ideas, too," Seth said, and it was truly amazing how he could be this animated right after waking up. "I can't wait to try them. I volunteer as tester."

He volunteered as tester. Which meant that he really did want to stay friends after this whole adventure.

The thought didn't make me cringe the way it might have only a few days ago. Somehow his positive attitude was less annoying here in New York than it was in Vermont.

Or maybe it was the context. Maybe it was taking him from "annoying me at work" to "showing me things he was excited about, for good reason."

Or maybe it was that I actually had things to be positive and excited about for the first time in a long while.

But no need to psychoanalyze myself. I jumped out of bed, feeling a lot more energized than someone who fell into bed after too many drinks late last night had any right to feel. "I'm going to go hop in the shower and get ready. What do we have going on today?"

Seth fell back onto his sad floor pillow. "Sleeping a little later?"

I laughed, assuming he was joking. "I'll be back in a few."

But by the time I got back, scrubbed clean and fragrant with Bev's lavender-lemongrass soap, he was snoring again, one arm draped over his eyes. I stood there and watched him sleep for a moment—that broad chest rising and falling, his lips parted in his dark beard—before shaking myself off. *Stop being a weirdo, Abby.*

I could sit there in bed and play on my phone or read a book until he woke up, or I could go have something to eat. My growling stomach solved that conundrum for me. I padded out into the hallway, closing the door gently behind me so as not to wake Seth.

In the kitchen, Bev and Benjamin turned to look at me at once, Benjamin at the table with his bowl of oatmeal and a print issue of the *New York Times*, Bev at the counter with the coffee machine. Neither of them spoke. I said, awkwardly, "Good morning."

"Good morning," Bev said, but her tone was low and deadly. I braced myself for whatever I'd done—had she discovered I was making her precious son sleep on the floor?—but exhaled in relief when she aimed her barbs at Benjamin. "Or it would be a good morning if my beloved *husband* of almost forty *years* would get off his *tuchus* and help me with the French press, considering he used the last Keurig pod."

Benjamin didn't even look up from the paper, bless his nerve. "I said I'd help you as soon as I finished my oatmeal. I don't want to eat cold oatmeal. It's like eating cement."

Eating hot oatmeal was also kind of like eating cement, but I didn't say that. Especially because Bev's brows had lowered, and thunder was on the horizon. I said, quickly, "Let me help."

Ten minutes later, Bev was awestruck at the latte I'd made her. "You even did the little leaf art on the top," she said. "Wow." She took a sip. "This is excellent."

"Thank you," I said. "Is it okay if I make one for myself, too?"

"Please," she said. "Make ten for yourself if you want."

"Only if you want me scaling the side of your building from the caffeine," I said dryly. She laughed.

Once I was done, I sat at the table with them, because to

do otherwise would be rude. Benjamin laid down his paper, which gave me a good look into his bowl of oatmeal. Again, I couldn't see any mix-ins or spices or anything. "How did you sleep?"

"Very well, thank you," I said. "How about you?"

They exchanged a glance. "Very well, thank you."

Silence settled over the table, thick and warm as a blanket. I took a sip of my coffee, my cheeks heating up. I had to break the silence before Bev did with some super personal question that would ruin my day. "I actually did some brainstorming overnight," I said. "I love it when that happens, when you come up with ideas without even having to put in any effort."

I wondered a moment too late if that would be a black mark on me—Benjamin seemed to be the kind of guy who valued effort—but whatever, too late now. I went on to tell them all about my café, about how I'd always had Christmas specials but was now coming up with ideas for Hanukkah specials. "Oh, those sound delicious," Bev said. "I don't know how I'll choose one when I visit the two of you up there."

"I'll make all of them for you," I said. And then what the hell, I went on and told them all about the Hanukkah festival, too, and how I was down here coming up with ideas for it. "I'm actually pretty excited," I said, and when had that become true? "It's going to be, from what I can tell, the first Hanukkah festival in New England outside of Boston. I'm hoping it'll attract Jewish tourists, but also non-Jews and locals, too. I really like the idea of sharing Hanukkah with people who don't know anything about it." I'd seen how much fun that could be here, playing the dreidel drinking game and lighting the menorah with Seth's friends. "I'm thinking I'm definitely going to hire the latke guy and the apple cider people from the pop-ups Seth took me to—I know apple cider isn't really a Hanukkah thing, but it was so good I can't resist. And then there's this doughnut maker up in Vermont who I think will be perfect if I can persuade them to try out some Hanukkah specials."

"We'll definitely have to come up for this! I can't believe Seth didn't even tell me about it," Bev said, and for a moment I could picture it: the four of us at the festival, Bev darting off to booth after booth and bringing back armfuls of sufganiyot and latke platters, Benjamin rolling his eyes but eating just as much as the rest of us, me and Seth strolling behind them hand in hand, wondering if that would be us in thirty years.

A moment. Just a moment. And was that really so bad? It wasn't like I was deluding myself. I knew it wasn't real.

It was just a thought that made me feel warm, as if Hanukkah candles were flickering before me, reflecting a glow from the window. Just for a moment.

I couldn't bring myself to say anything. I just smiled.

"I know a guy who makes these beautiful crafted hanukkiahs out of all sorts of found objects," Benjamin said. "Technically, he makes them out of trash, but they're quite beautiful. For being made of trash. I could give you his number if you'd like. Maybe he could sell them at your festival."

"That would be wonderful," I said. "Thank you."

Bev smiled fondly at me. For a moment I felt guilty for it, after all Freya had told me yesterday. It wasn't like she liked me for a reason I had anything to do with. "Your hair looks nice," she said.

Surprised, I touched my head. I hadn't washed my hair in the shower this morning, just tied it up out of the way, but it had of course still gotten damp. It hadn't quite reverted back to its natural curl, but the ends had gone rogue, the middle waving. "Oh, thanks. I usually straighten it."

Maybe I wouldn't today, I decided spontaneously. Maybe I'd just let it do what it wanted.

I touched my hair again. My mom's voice popped into my head. *You look awfully . . . unkempt. I don't want you going out with us looking like that. Do you want to stay home?*

But Bev had said it looked nice. And what did it matter anyway? I didn't care if Seth thought I was beautiful. And it wasn't like I was going to see any of these other people again. If I looked unkempt, then I looked unkempt.

"Is Seth still sleeping?" Benjamin asked. "He never sleeps this late. He's always been an early riser."

Of course Seth would be an early riser. He probably popped awake with the sun every morning. I rose from the table, my coffee mostly finished. "I'll check in and make sure he's still breathing."

No noise in the hallway, but everything smelled like lavender. I breathed in deep, finding it comforting. Opened the bedroom door and–

"Oh my god," I said, because yes, Seth was breathing.

He was also naked.

Not totally naked, I realized a beat later. He had a towel wrapped around his waist. Which, come to think of it, explained why everything smelled like lavender. It also explained the beads of water clinging to the black curls scattering his chest and taut stomach and the thicker trail of black hair leading down beneath the towel–

"Oh my god," Seth said, his eyes widening. "I'm changing."

Why was I staring at those glistening beads of water on his skin? That was rude. I tore my eyes away and stared up at the ceiling, my cheeks heating up. My first instinct was to shout some apologies at him and slam the door and run back out into the kitchen area.

Thank goodness I'd never really been one to trust my gut, because my second instinct told me that would look suspicious to Bev and Benjamin. I was their son's girlfriend after all. We were presumably sharing a bed and saw each other naked all the time. So, fighting that first instinct, I slid inside and shut the door behind me.

I didn't let my eyes slide back down to Seth, but I assumed his cheeks were as red as mine. "Sorry," I said, as quietly as I could, so my voice wouldn't reach the kitchen. "But your parents would think it was weird if this freaked us out, right?"

"Right," Seth said, and from how strangled his voice was, I knew I was one hundred percent right about red cheeks. The cheeks on his face. I wouldn't know about his other cheeks. They'd been covered up by the towel. Not that I'd looked. "It's fine. No big deal. Maybe just face the wall?"

I was too close to the door to turn around without hitting the knob, so I took a step forward. And, naturally, since I was still staring at the ceiling like I was trying to read a treasure map printed on it, tripped over something. One of my shoes from last night, I realized as I was falling.

"Whoa!" Seth managed to catch me in his arms before I could fall flat on my face. His bare arms. His bare wet arms. His bare wet arms flanking his bare wet chest.

Those bare arms against my shoulders, my waist, were strong and capable and warm. They cradled me for a moment, and I had to fight the urge to lean into them, to rest my head against his shoulder.

And then I realized that those arms had been holding up his towel. I lurched upright and away, my face so hot it might actually combust into flame and fry us both crispy like latkes. "Sorry, sorry," I said hastily, then noticed that the towel was firmly knotted around his waist, barely dipping under his belly button. An innie. I had an innie, too.

"Don't worry about it," Seth said, his voice still strangled. Maybe because I was staring at his belly button. Which was weird. I went to tear my eyes away, only to notice a slight bulge there beneath the knot. It could have been a wrinkle in the towel or it could have been—

Abby! Get out of here!

I spun around, feeling frantically for the doorknob. Somehow I had the presence of mind to call over my shoulder in what I hoped was a spritely and cheerful and not at all frantic manner, "Sounds good! I'll get some coffee ready for you!"

And then I was out in the hallway, the door closed behind me. I had to lean against it for a second to let my hammering heart calm down a little bit. Deep breath in. Deep breath out. Why was I so flustered? It wasn't like I was some blushing innocent who'd never seen a shirtless guy before. I saw shirtless guys all the time. Not, like, a weird amount of the time. A normal amount of the time. At the beach. Running outside during the summer. Sometimes, unpleasantly, in my café.

So pull it together, Abby.

Back in the kitchen, I managed to smile for Bev and Benjamin. "He just got out of the shower and is getting changed," I said. "He should be here soon." To avoid having to look them in the eye, I busied myself making Seth the perfect cup of coffee, even sprinkling in some cinnamon and nutmeg to mimic the flavor of his usual pumpkin spice latte.

It took him longer to come out than I expected, and I definitely did not spend those extra minutes thinking about what exactly he could be doing in there that would be taking so long, nope, not at all, my cheeks were always this red.

He finally came padding out wearing a T-shirt and jeans, hair sticking up all over his head. "Good morning," he said, and good for him, it no longer sounded like he was being strangled. "Ooh, is that for me?"

I held out his coffee mug like an offering. "It's pumpkin spice–ish," I said. My heart fluttered. There was clearly something wrong with my body today. Maybe I'd drunk too much caffeine. "Hope you like it."

"I know I'll like it." He took it from me, then focused on my face. "Oh. Your hair looks nice."

My heart fluttered again. Two people had told me my "unkempt" hair looked *nice*. "Thanks."

Maybe because Seth was still hungover and we'd had a lot of activities the last few days, maybe because we were both exhausted from the stress of the morning, we decided to take it easy this morning and afternoon, then light the fourth night of candles with his parents at sundown. "Let's go walk in Riverside Park," he said, already by the door wrapping his scarf around his shoulders. "I want to show you the gardens."

I waited until we were out in the hallway, the door shut behind us, before saying, "It's winter. Aren't the gardens all dead?"

"Hush, you," Seth said lightly. The elevator stopped on our floor with a ding. We stepped inside, where I was given the privilege of staring at my makeup-less, wild-haired self in the unflattering overhead light above the elevator mirror. "I need a slap of cold, fresh air in the face if I'm going to make it through the day."

"Fine, let's go look at dead flowers." I paused. "I'm really sorry, by the way. You know. For walking in on you getting dressed? I didn't mean to. I—"

"It's really okay," Seth said. The elevator jounced to a stop. The building should probably get that checked. "It happens. You didn't do it on purpose."

"Right."

We waved to the doorman as we passed by. Outside, the air was indeed a cold, fresh slap of air in the face. "You know, I could've done without the slap," I said. "Considering I was a responsible adult last night who stopped after two drinks and all."

"It feels like you have something you want to say."

I gave an exaggerated shrug. "Is your fake girlfriend not allowed to look out for your health?"

If I'd ever been to Riverside Park, I couldn't remember it. The long, narrow strip of green parkland snaked its way between the Upper West Side and the Hudson River, across which the buildings of New Jersey stood, looking sad and inferior (hey, as a born and bred New Yorker, it was my right to bash New Jersey as much as I wanted). It was hilly and crowded with monuments and statues. I stopped to check out the Soldiers' and Sailors' Monument, which rose up high and domed into the grayish sky, surrounded by cannons aimed at a playground below. Hopefully, they didn't actually work.

"So," Seth said, hands in his pockets as we strolled down a grassy incline and into the park proper, where the sound of the slate gray river was covered up by the traffic of the highway next to it. "I wanted to check in with you now that we're almost halfway through. Is everything going okay with you so far?"

That phrase stuck in my head. Halfway through. Tonight would be four nights, the official halfway point to returning home. When I'd go back to being the single owner of a failing café who barely remembered her Hebrew.

That wasn't totally true, at least. I'd discovered that over this trip. I guess I'd said those blessings over and over so many times growing up that it was like riding a bicycle. Which I also barely remembered how to do, but if Seth sprang a bike-riding outing on me, I could probably wobble my way through it. "Yeah," I said, clearing my throat over a lump that had suddenly risen up there. "It seems like it's all going well for me. I got so many leads for the festival. It's going to be amazing."

I let it sprawl out in my head. The wintry fairgrounds, spiky grass dusted with snow, the big lights overhead making it all glitter. The sound of a live band performing Hanukkah songs, but also other Jewish and Hebrew songs, just to break it up. Maybe even a klezmer band if their rates weren't absurd and the tourism board wouldn't laugh me out of town when I told them about the accordion. The winding rows of tents with their rising smells of frying oil and powdered sugar, the booming sound of voices reenacting the Hanukkah story, the shining lights of the big brass menorah reaching into the sky . . .

It was stunning. And it was all thanks to this deal I'd made. It was only fair that Seth feel like he'd gotten as much out of it as I had. "How about you? Anything I should work on or change for the second half of the trip?" I cracked a wry smile. "Besides maybe learning how to knock?"

His nose was ruby red from the cold, almost matching his wool scarf. "No, not at all. Like you said, it's been great. Everybody loves you, you know. They're going to be so sad when . . ."

He didn't need to say it. They were going to be so sad when we "broke up." Hopefully, Bev wouldn't be one of those weird moms who came after the ex to ask why. I had a friend back in college who'd broken up with her boyfriend and ended up having to block his relentless mother on Instagram because she wouldn't stop DMing her GIFs of sad baby animals.

I swallowed hard. Time to change the subject. As long as I was careful about it, I could broach the subject without betraying Freya's confidence. "You know, Freya told me a little bit about your breakup last night. If I were her, I would be pretty angry with you."

I watched him carefully to see how he'd react to that. If his eyes would narrow, or roll with annoyance of me butting into his business.

But his expression gave no indication of whatever he was feeling beneath. "Oh."

I gave him a second to elaborate on that "oh," but nothing came. I said, "She told me that you'd basically ghosted her after more than two years. Her and your friends, too. Is that why you were so weird about going to see them?"

That got a grudging response. Well, half response. "I didn't ghost her. I broke up with her because I was moving to Vermont."

"Why the big move? It wasn't for work, right? Since you're working for the same company, just remotely."

A chilly breeze whipped through us, making me pull my arms in tighter. We were now walking by the gardens, which were, indeed, mostly brown and dead, but the wire frame of a cat suggested topiary in the summer months. I'd kind of like to see that, the topiary cat.

Seth sighed. I wondered if he liked cats, then wondered why it mattered. "I moved to Vermont because of Freya."

"What?"

"I moved to Vermont because of Freya," Seth said through clenched teeth. "Things were good between us. I liked her, loved her. I just . . ."

He trailed off. This time, I had the sense to wait and let him continue on his own.

When he did, he was no longer speaking through a

clenched jaw. "It had been about two years, and we were getting into our late twenties. People were starting to prod about getting engaged and getting married. And I just . . . I freaked out."

"At the thought of getting married?" I asked.

"No," he said immediately, and now his eyes were large, honest. "Okay, maybe. Kind of. I imagined walking down the aisle with her, living together forever, having kids with her, waking up next to her every morning, and freaked out. Panicked. It made me feel like I wanted to crawl out of my skin.

"And again, it was nothing she did. Freya is great. Which was part of the problem. Every time I'd gone through a breakup before, I was either the one who got dumped or she'd cheated on me or something. I didn't know how to break up with someone who was perfect, just who I maybe didn't want to commit to in such a big way. And if I didn't know how to do it, I definitely didn't know how to explain it to all of my friends. I figured they'd see me as the bad guy. So I just . . . left."

I blinked. "You just left? What, did you just get in your car and drive until you got tired?"

He scoffed at me like I was the one who'd made the more ridiculous statement. "Of course I didn't just drive until I got tired. Abby, this is Manhattan. Nobody has a car." He paused. "I took a train. I'd been up in the area for a hiking trip with the guys a couple years ago and really liked it, so figured, why not? I got a car once I was up there."

We jumped nimbly out of the way of a kid barreling toward us on a bicycle, face full of panic. "So let me get this straight. You couldn't handle the thought of a mature, adult conversation with your partner *of two years*, so instead you just ran away. I can't believe you never even apologized to her. You really owe her one. A big one."

"Wow, Abby," Seth said, and this was it, this was going to be the explosion. Seth was going to say how dare I, as his fake girlfriend, question him like this, like I had any right to say such a thing.

But his shoulders sagged. "You know, you pretty much nailed it."

And that made me feel a little sorry for saying it so harshly. Not enough to actually apologize, though. I mean, it wasn't like I'd been wrong. So what the hell, I just barreled down, full steam ahead. "Do you think this might be a bit of a pattern?"

"What do you mean?"

"What I mean is, instead of having a confrontation with your parents and telling them you're happy and to leave you alone, you formulated this scheme to bring a Jewish fake girlfriend to get them off your back."

"Oh," Seth said slowly. "Oh, yeah. I see where you're getting that impression."

We walked side by side in silence for a little while. He might have been thinking over what I'd said, considering what it meant about him as a person and him as a partner and him as a son. Me? I was craning my neck over the chain-link fence to see all the dogs in the dog park. There were so many, and guess what? They were all cute. Not as cute as Seth's friend's corgi, but very few dogs could be *that* fluffy and have *that* round of a butt.

"You know," Seth said, and I was about to tell him that yes, I knew his friend's dog was so cute I was considering a kidnapping scheme, but of course he couldn't read my mind. "I guess I've never been great with conflict. As a kid my mom always kind of took care of things for me. That's not much of an excuse, but . . ."

"It's a fine excuse," I said, thinking of my own mom and dad. They were my excuse for so many of the things I'd chosen to do and be. Only . . . "How long, though, can you let it be one? You're an adult now. It can't explain everything about you forever."

My stomach flipped unpleasantly, like when you're making that first pancake and it oozes out the sides because it's not fully cooked. Maybe I wasn't just talking to Seth.

"Unless you want her to," I said hastily. "I mean, it's your life. Not really any of my business."

"No, you're right," he said. "I mean, even last night, I didn't really want to go out with the group, but they told me to go, so I went."

"But you ended up having fun, right?"

"I did," he said. "But that doesn't mean it was a good thing that I just folded."

"That's true." We were both quiet for a moment.

And then my phone trilled. I hadn't realized I'd taken it off silent, but now we both looked down to where I was trying to fumble it out of my pocket. You'd think that, after years of living through brutally cold Northeast winters, I'd be better at maneuvering my fingers through gloves.

It had already rung for so long by the time I'd extricated

it that I just answered it without even checking who it was. "Hello?"

"Abby, hello." Lorna's most businesslike tone rang out in my ear. "Is this a good time?"

"Um—"

"Good," she said. "I wanted to check in and see how things were going in regard to the festival. Since you didn't take any of my recommendations."

It's Lorna, I mouthed at Seth, grimacing as I tucked the phone into my shoulder. "It's actually going really well," I said. "I'm in New York City for a few days and have already found some vendors I definitely want to hire."

I gave her a rundown of the people I'd decided on, plus some of the other booths I was considering, highlighting the places where I planned to stick to local vendors. Lorna was silent the whole time, which, not going to lie, made the hair rise a little bit on the back of my neck the way it did before a lightning storm.

And then she struck. "That all sounds unnecessary," Lorna said. "Why do you need to call in all these special vendors from the city? I'm sure they're charging extra for travel."

I took a deep breath. The air chilled my lungs. "They do cost a little more, true, but it just means we get a smaller percentage of their—"

"And I really want to insist that we have some kind of holiday tree," Lorna said. "It's not a Christmas thing to have a tree. Wasn't it a pagan tradition to begin with that we adopted? We as in Christians. Anyway. Vermont is full of trees. There's a big evergreen tree in the middle of our flag, so you can think about it as celebrating our state. Do it in Hanukkah colors. It'll be beautiful."

But it *was* a Christmas thing to have a tree. I ground my teeth in frustration. I'd heard it so many times. *Christmas is basically secular now. Is it really that big a deal for all the kids to wear Santa hats? It's not a religious thing. We're all singing Christmas songs at the holiday concert, it's not like we're at church or singing prayers.*

Whether they viewed those things as religious or not, they were all part of a holiday celebrating another religion. "Lorna . . ." I said.

"I really must insist," she told me. "Anyone who comes up here for a holiday festival will be expecting a tree. There's a reason the Christmas festivals have been so successful. People expect certain things when they go to one."

Then why didn't you just decide to have a Christmas festival? was what I wanted to say. But my new self-righteousness was already wilting along with my curls under my hat. Was it really that big a deal to compromise a little? I didn't want to fight with Lorna. If I did, who knew what she'd do? Maybe take me off the project altogether and do it herself, a Christmas festival reskinned in blue and white. "Fine. We could have a tree."

"Wonderful. I knew you'd be reasonable," Lorna said. There was almost no ambient noise on her side of the phone, and I pictured her outside in her backyard, the mountains hushed behind her, snow falling silently on the grass. Unlike what she was hearing from me. Just in the last minute, we'd had someone cursing at an e-biker who'd almost hit them, screaming children at a birthday party, and a runner blasting his shitty music for all the world to hear. "And I was thinking a holiday light show, too. People love those. My friends tell me they're very popular at their festivals. And isn't Hanukkah the festival of lights?"

That didn't seem like so big of an ask. "I guess we can."

"Great, I'll get the vendor from my friends. I don't know how much Hanukkah-specific stuff he has, but obviously we're not going to pay to have someone lug all that from New York," Lorna said. "What else did you have in mind?"

The rest of the conversation made me feel like I was slowly shrinking, leggings puddling around my legs, feet swimming in my fluffy boots. She grudgingly okayed me bringing some kosher food vendors up from New York, but not all of them ("They're so expensive, Abby. Why are they so expensive?"), and she insisted that we include some of the vendors from up there that people were familiar with ("We already know everybody loves the corn dog guys and waffle makers. Not everything has to be a special Hanukkah food"). She understood why I wasn't going to have a Santa but badgered me with questions about a possible replacement ("Parents love having their kids take pictures with someone, and you can charge so much for them. Doesn't Hanukkah have some kind of mascot? Can we make one up? Can we just say that Santa's in town and felt like stopping by for a doughnut or whatever?").

By the time Lorna sighed heavily in my ear and said, "Okay, it sounds like we've got a good start. Let me know if you have anything else you want to run by me, okay?" all the fight had gone out of me. I was limp. All I could do was nod and give her a quiet goodbye before she hung up.

Seth had, of course, been there the whole time, looking off into the distance and pretending not to eavesdrop but obviously overhearing everything at least on my side. "Everything okay?" he asked carefully.

My mouth opened, instinct strong. I would tell him that yes, of course, everything was fine and I had it all under control. Nobody had to worry about me.

Except he'd just shared a bunch of really personal stuff and let me poke and prod at his most sensitive spots. This wasn't even one of my sensitive spots, just an annoying thing that was happening. So why not share a little bit? Maybe he'd have some ideas on how to help.

So I sighed. "I was excited about all the plans we came up with for the Hanukkah festival, but Lorna's not totally on board. I'm pretty sure she just wanted to have a Christmas festival but there wasn't room for another one in the market, so she wants to technically have this be a Hanukkah festival but have it really be a Christmas festival."

"Why didn't she just plan it herself, then?"

I shrugged. "Bad publicity? There have been all those stories about cultural appropriation and cultural insensitivity. Maybe she didn't want to be featured in one."

"So instead she piled it on the shoulders of the only Jew she knew but figured she would control it all anyway," Seth said slowly. "So that if they did get any bad publicity for this Hanukkah festival being a whole lot like a Christmas festival, she could point to her token Jew and be like, 'She's Jewish and she planned it, so it's fine.'"

Sounded like Lorna. A sour taste filled my mouth. "I don't like being used like that."

"I don't blame you. I wouldn't, either," said Seth. "What if you told her that it was your way or the highway?"

"What?"

"Like, if you told her you were going to do it the way it needed to be done, or else you were out."

"I can't do that," I said. I took a deep breath. I wasn't quite ready to share how badly my café was doing, and how much I desperately needed an influx of tourists to keep it afloat. That was too much like exposing a bruise for him to poke at. I said, instead, "Even if I can only change her plan a little bit, isn't that better than nothing? I'm just thinking of all these excited Jewish tourists flocking in for their tiny scrap of representation and finding Santa Claus and Christmas trees."

Seth squinted at me, as if he suspected there was more to it that I wasn't sharing, but he didn't press me. "I guess."

It didn't make me feel any better.

It was nice to spend the rest of the morning being lazy, considering how busy we'd been the past few days. Even if I had to be on my tip-top best behavior regarding our fake relationship, since Bev and Benjamin were around the entire time. Bev somehow produced an entire lunch spread from nowhere, bagels with cream cheese and lox and pickled red onions and capers and scallions, multiple salads on the side. The woman was a food magician.

Naturally, the bagels were the best I'd had in a very long time. To be fair, I hadn't had a bagel in a very long time. Vermont had great food, but those round bread rolls they called bagels didn't deserve the name. I had no idea if it was the New York City water or not that made New York bagels so chewy and doughy and delicious, but they clearly did something right here that they didn't do anywhere else.

"So, Abby," Benjamin said to me over lunch. "I thought your ideas for Hanukkah drink specials in your café were excellent. Have you thought about expanding or diversifying your business?"

I huffed a little laugh, spraying a few bagel crumbs back on my plate. "To be quite honest, I'm focused mostly on keeping my one location alive and running. Business . . . could be better lately. That's why I'm so determined to make this Hanukkah festival a success."

Benjamin nodded. "Smart. No sense in big dreams if you can't pull your little dreams off first."

Exactly. That had to mean I'd done the right thing on giving in to Lorna on the festival. Like he said, saving the café and the town had to come before getting absolutely everything about the festival right.

I wasn't going to say that to him, though. I'd just assume.

"What are your big dreams?" Bev asked. "Say the sky's the limit. Would you want to be a Starbucks one day? With franchises all over the world?"

I blinked and stuffed a bite of bagel into my mouth so I'd have a moment to think. I'd entertained thoughts of becoming a big CEO one day, sure. Hasn't everyone? Flying on the private jet, shuttling from beachside estate to mountain estate to city penthouse, sitting at the end of a big shiny wooden table surrounded by people looking at me with respect. The trappings sounded fun. The other aspects of the job—a grinding work schedule, constant travel, schmoozing all the time—less so.

I swallowed the bagel lump. "I honestly don't know," I said. "I mean, if some big investor came to me and was like, let me help you spread your brand all over the country, I imagine it would be hard to turn down. And it could be cool to have a few locations where I could try out experimental things or cater to different crowds. But I'm pretty happy where I am."

Cold fear clutched my chest at the thought of losing it. I hurried on to fill the space. "I like being my own boss and I like the town and I like getting to do my own thing when it comes to the menu. It would be nice to have a few employees so I don't have to be there all the time." And maybe live in a house or nice apartment instead of the shitty rental above the shop, because I liked the smell of coffee but didn't love marinating in it twenty-four seven. And not have to stress about going under all the time, but I'd already told them enough. I didn't have to share my greatest worry. "But otherwise it's all pretty good. I think I could be happy there for a while."

"That's really lovely," Bev said. "Of course, I would have preferred it if you said, 'I want to open a café on the Upper West Side and move back here soon,' but I'm glad you're happy."

Behind her, Seth rolled his eyes at me. I bit back a smile. "Maybe one day. Rent is very expensive around here." If rent wasn't so expensive? I don't know, I could almost see it. They'd been so good to me, it didn't sound all that bad to have Bev show up at the café every morning for a free coffee she protested against but never actually paid for, bullying all her friends and neighbors to make it their regular spot, Seth's friends showing up for open-mic nights and poetry readings and whatever else happened at artsy coffee shops in New York City. Me brewing up increasingly ridiculous and colorful sweet coffees for Seth to try. Unicorn lattes with sprinkles and peaked whipped cream horns. Chocolate-chocolate-chip mochas with lumps of half-melted Hershey's bars floating in them.

There I was, thinking of this as a real relationship again. My smile disappeared. A headache tingled at my temples. This wasn't real, and it was important for me to remember that.

With such small, trite topics as our hopes and dreams for the future dispatched, the conversation turned toward last night. "What did you think of Seth's friends?" Bev asked. "I've always thought Dan needs to shave. Much like Seth here, but I won't say anything about that."

"You kind of did just say something about that," said Seth.

"I like Seth's beard," I said, and now that I'd done my supportive fake girlfriend job, why not poke at him a little? "At least, as long as he keeps it groomed. Sometimes his mustache grows over his lips and it feels like kissing a Christmas tree."

"An oddly specific description," Seth said, meeting my eyes. I flushed, my own eyes dropping to my lap, because I could tell exactly what he was thinking. *How much time have you put into thinking about what it would feel like to kiss me?*

Quick, Abby, change the subject. "Anyway, what were we

talking about? Seth's friends?" I swallowed hard, raising my head, and brushed a strand of hair off my forehead as if I didn't still feel Seth's eyes hot on my cheek. "I liked them. Everyone was really welcoming." For a moment I was back there in the glow of last night, everybody laughing around the table as they stumbled through the Hanukkah blessings, the lightbulbs of the cheap menorah shimmering in my vision until they looked almost like real flames. "And even the non-Jewish ones were excited about lighting the Hanukkah candles. It made me realize how much I've . . ."

I trailed off, because the end of that sentence would have exposed a soft part inside of me I wasn't sure I wanted to put out there. *It made me realize how much I've missed this.* "This" being a stand-in for a whole bunch of different things. The community. The lights. The feelings.

"I have an idea for later," Seth said abruptly.

"Oh, for all of us?" said Bev.

"No, just for me and Abby," he replied. She didn't even look deflated, as if that was the answer she'd wanted.

My turn to ask a question. "What is it?"

"I'm not going to tell you or else you'll probably refuse to go."

"Well, that's one way of selling it," I said.

"Just trust me," Seth said, and god help me, I did.

13

I REALIZED THAT TRUST IN SETH WAS ENTIRELY misplaced when he told me we were going to a stand-up comedy night. Unfortunately, he didn't tell me until we were outside the building, which made it a lot harder for me to run away. "No way, no, no, hell no," I told him, having to raise my voice to be heard above the music thrumming all down this street of restaurants and clubs and the chatter of the crowds spilling through their doors. "Stand-up comedy is the worst. Nobody is funny, but you feel like you have to laugh or they look at you with those big sad eyes and it's so awkward."

"How much experience do you have with stand-up comics?" Seth asked, then his eyes widened. "Let me guess: you're a former stand-up comic. Performing to night after night of snarky crowds is what embittered you on life."

I snorted. "I couldn't think of anything less appealing than getting up in front of a crowd and trying to make them laugh."

That hadn't been the case for Connor, though. Before moving up to Vermont, he'd tried his hand at multiple comedy clubs. As his girlfriend, I was always expected to sit up front and laugh heartily every time he paused, which, honestly, should have been the first sign that we weren't compatible. I'd never been good at faking laughter. One time he told me it looked like I was being electrocuted, and I'd never been able to get that out of my head, so I'd just stopped trying.

"This one will be different," Seth said, opening the door and gesturing me inside with a bow that was almost courtly. I eyed the dark entryway with unease. "And if I'm wrong and you hate it after fifteen minutes, we'll leave."

"You promise?"

"I promise," he said. Okay. Even if it was terrible, I could do anything for fifteen minutes, as I'd learned at the dentist. So, with still a fair amount of trepidation, I crossed the threshold.

The main room wasn't as deep and dark as the entryway would suggest. After climbing down a set of steep, narrow stairs, we emerged into a big space that, despite its low ceiling, was brightly lit and cozy with colorful cushions scattered over chairs and benches. A stage was set up on one end of the room; I eyed the standing mic uneasily.

We took a seat at a table close enough to the stage where we'd be able to see everything but far enough where hopefully the comic wouldn't be able to make easy eye contact. The show still had a bit of time before it went on; people were still trickling in, appearing to be in no hurry as they shrugged off coats and unwound scarves. "So what's the deal with this place?" I asked. "Is one of your friends performing or something? Or, don't tell me, *you're* the former stand-up comic." I stopped and considered for a moment. "I could see it."

He snorted. "No, I don't have the intestinal fortitude necessary for getting up onstage and bombing in front of a crowd."

"Then what—" I stopped as a waiter materialized to hand us menus. I'd drank enough last night where I didn't particularly want to drink again, so I gave the alcohol menu only a cursory scan before moving on to the food. "Hey, wait."

"Cool, right?" Seth said so smugly it made me hope just a little bit that he'd give himself a paper cut.

It was cool, though, I had to grudgingly admit. The menu was full of foods that felt like home to me, but that also had a flair of originality. Brisket and matzo balls in a hearty bowl of ramen. Lox bowls with nori and crispy rice. Savory potato kugel and boureka pastries with hummus and fried artichokes with kibbeh. Knishes with kimchi and potato filling and a gochujang aioli. "This menu is so . . . Jewish."

"So Jewish," Seth agreed. "And make sure you're saving room for dessert. The rugelach is unreal, and the rainbow cookies are"—he looked around, then lowered his voice—"better than my mom's."

One of the things I actually missed about living in New York was seeing all the fun twists people put on Jewish and Israeli food at restaurants and in delis. Nobody was doing that in Vermont.

Maybe you could do that in Vermont, something whispered in my head. I was used to just pushing that voice away, but, for once, I let myself pause and consider it. Would it be that crazy to sell babka at my café? I bet people would love a thick, tender slice of the sweet bread braided with chocolate or cinnamon sugar or even something savory with their coffee. I could experiment with fun fillings, have a daily special. Or I could rotate shakshuka or sabich sandwiches on the brunch specials menu, since they both involved eggs. My regulars might see eggs poached in spicy tomato sauce and pitas stuffed with fried eggplant, eggs, and all the salad fixings as breaths of fresh air.

"Abby?" Seth said in a tone of voice that suggested this was the third or fourth time he had said my name.

I blinked. "What?"

He gestured at the menu. "Have you decided what you're going to get? Do you want to share a few things?"

"Sure," I said. And then, because he'd been so supportive when I'd raised the idea of my specialty coffees, I asked him what he thought about my idea.

His eyes lit up. "I think that sounds *amazing*. I'll be first in line every morning."

The idea of that didn't even provoke the specter of my usual Category 3. In fact, I hadn't experienced a headache like that around him this whole trip. Maybe it was something in the New York air. Probably smog. Right, fresh clean mountain air was totally known for making headaches worse.

When the waiter came back around, we ordered a few different dishes to share, and then the room quieted to a dull buzz. I glanced over at the stage to find the night's first comic setting up the mic—a twentysomething guy with a thin frame and an abundance of dark curly hair. I sighed through my nose, readying myself for some tired speech about adulting or jabs at an imaginary wife.

Instead, the comic said, "Good god, I haven't had this many people staring at me onstage since my bar mitzvah. Are you going to pelt me with candy again? I don't even have a Torah stand to hide behind."

A surprised laugh bubbled up from my throat. What the comic had said wasn't even that funny, but it struck pangs of familiarity inside me that I hadn't felt in years. I was right back there, age twelve and thirteen, hurling fruit gems as hard as I could at the heads of my Hebrew school classmates as they finished their haftarah, then pretending I was too cool to scurry up to the bima afterward with the littler kids to gather them up, no matter how much I wanted to. It was a memory of my childhood that didn't have anything to do with my parents.

I'd spent a lot of time at synagogue without them, actually. I'd almost forgotten.

The guy continued to be not-that-funny, but he kept bringing up things that sent me tumbling back down memory lane. Not like I was trapped in a car with a speeding driver, but like I'd boarded a roller coaster I was really excited about trying out. It was a little scary, but also thrilling to remember things like reading the freaky parts of the Tanakh during a boring Shabbat morning service, or substituting other words for the Hebrew in Adon Olam. Apparently, my friends and I weren't the only people to take *l'ayt na-ah-sa* and turn it into *I ate my socks.*

By the time the guy gave an ironic little bow and stepped

down from the stage, something inside me had melted a bit. I didn't want to analyze it, or I might do something terrible, like cry. So I was relieved when the food showed up and I could devote all my attention to how delicious it was rather than how glad, how grateful, I was to be back in a space like this.

The rest of the night went on much like that. All of the comics didn't necessarily bring back good childhood memories, but as they regaled us with anecdotes about how people always felt the need to ask them what they thought about Israel before befriending them and jokes about how all of our holidays followed the general structure of "they tried to kill us, they failed, let's eat" and tales about how our generational trauma from the Holocaust sometimes manifested in the impromptu running of marathons (okay, so that one was less relatable), I just felt . . . I don't know, like I was back in the club again. Like I'd been reminded that, like it or not, I wasn't a lone wolf out there; I was part of a pack.

And all while eating what were, however much I hated to admit Seth was right, the most delicious rainbow cookies I'd ever had. They were so beautiful I almost didn't want to eat them; while many rainbow cookies had only a few different layers, these literally were striped with every color of the rainbow. I kind of wanted to see if each layer actually tasted different or if they were differentiated only by food coloring, but the thought of tearing one apart felt like throwing tomatoes at a masterful painting. "Plot twist," I said, closing my eyes as I savored the chocolate edge of one cookie and debated taking another. "The guest baker tonight is your mom's nemesis, Eva Hallac."

Seth snorted. "It's the melting of the ice caps all over again. No, the guest chef tonight is some famous TV chef who has a Jewish restaurant nearby. We walked by it the other day, and you thought it looked good, remember? I heard she's taking leave from the restaurant because she just had a baby, but she can't stay away from the kitchen altogether."

Maybe she'd want to help out at the Hanukkah festival, I thought with a burst of inspiration that, just as quickly, fell flat. Seth had already said I couldn't afford her. "I understand that," I said. Understandable that someone might take a break from something to focus on another thing, and then come back to it once they remembered how much they loved it. How much they missed it over the years, how good it felt to finally come home again.

I was just talking about the chef. Obviously.

"Hey, do you want to hear a secret?" Seth leaned in, eyes sparkling. A pink crumb was clinging to his beard. I had to stop my hand in midair when I realized I was going to brush it away. What was I thinking? "Something I've never told anyone before."

I tucked my traitorous hand under my thigh to keep it in check. "Sounds like great blackmail material."

"Okay, if we've reached the point where people are willing to pay money for my secrets, I think that means I've made it."

"I don't think that's what *blackmail* means."

Seth flashed me a brilliant smile. "Well, I give you permission to blackmail me with it, if you really want to."

"That takes all the fun out of blackmail."

"Sorry," Seth said, not sounding sorry at all. "Anyway. I may have lied to you before."

"Please tell me you lied about what's under your beard," I said. "I knew you were a face tattoo kind of guy."

"I actually have a second beard tattooed under the first beard," he said. "Just in case."

"Just in case what? Just in case your face catches fire, but only in the beard region?"

"That's ridiculous," Seth said. "Any fire in the beard region would also burn my skin, rendering any tattoos pointless."

"I see."

"Anyway," said Seth. "I may have lied about doing stand-up. In that I actually may have tried stand-up before."

Somehow, it didn't strike me as a wild idea. I could see it in my mind, Seth doing his absolute best to make people laugh. "I just can't believe you lied to me. Didn't think you had it in you."

"Honestly, I forgot about it until just now," Seth admitted. He popped the last half of rainbow cookie into his mouth without asking if I wanted it. "It was right after college, when I thought I was the coolest guy ever. Which has never been true, by the way."

"Agreed," I said.

"Rude. Anyway, Dan was trying to make it as a stand-up comic, and he asked me if I would go on with him one night as moral support, so I signed up to go on right after him. Which worked out well, actually, because he totally bombed, so I figured I couldn't do worse than that."

"Let me guess," I said. "It was a huge success and you left the crowd in hysterics."

"If only," Seth said somberly. "No, I tanked, too. It just wasn't as bad because Dan laid the groundwork beforehand."

I snorted. "If I could go back in time, I would attend that comedy night just so I could cringe at how bad you were."

"Again, rude," Seth said. "And also, if you could travel back in time, wouldn't you want to do something like, I don't know, kill Hitler?"

I snorted again. "Someone else would just have taken his place."

"That was a joke."

"Was it? Maybe that's why you bombed your stand-up."

He stood abruptly. "I have to go to the bathroom," he said, and walked off. I was left watching him, blinking at how suddenly he'd left. Had I genuinely insulted him? I thought we'd been joking around.

Ugh. This meant I'd have to apologize if I wanted to keep things the way they were. Which I did. Because things were really nice right now.

Ugh, again.

Watching a terrible comic alone is way less fun when you don't have someone next to you to snicker with or roll your eyes at (one-sidedly, since Seth was way too nice to do such things when the comic could potentially see him do it if they squinted really hard). So I pulled out my phone and scrolled mindlessly through photos of old friends taking hikes and hugging babies and posing wistfully in front of flower walls and that's why I didn't realize what was happening until I heard Seth say into the microphone, "Shalom, everybody."

My head popped up so fast I heard something in my

neck crack. Okay, that would have to be looked at later. But for now, my eyes zeroed in on Seth, who was standing on the stage, his smile so bright it eclipsed the lights above. The mic only reached his chest, like it had been adjusted for the shorter person before him and he couldn't figure out how to raise it. "How's everybody doing tonight?" he said, scanning the room.

Nobody responded. He took it in stride. "So, gefilte fish, huh? What's up with that stuff?"

What the hell was he *doing*?

Again, nobody answered him, but the wattage of his smile didn't dim even the slightest bit. "I mean, how do we even know it's fish? It could be anything in there. Like they say with hot dogs. Pig snouts. Well, that wouldn't exactly be kosher. In more ways than one."

I hadn't realized somebody could cringe with their entire body. It was really not helping whatever had cracked in my neck.

He went on, either oblivious to how little the crowd was laughing or in spite of it. "And pickled herring? Which word makes it sound less appealing?"

Still no laughter. I watched his smile fade a single watt.

I don't know how to explain what happened next. All I know is that seeing his smile fade stirred something in me. And it wasn't glee, the way it probably would have been back in Vermont. Whatever it was, it made me want to do something, anything, to make that (irritating) (obnoxious) (dazzling) smile return to its former brightness.

So that's how I found myself onstage next to him. I don't remember getting up and walking over there and clambering up the low edge of the stage; my memory just blinks and it's like I teleported from my seat to the spotlight. It was shocking, but not as shocking as my appearance seemed to be for Seth. He just gaped at me, apparently forgetting how to speak.

Giving me the opportunity to take over. "I met his mother for the first time recently," I said. "And she managed to wriggle the mention of Jewish grandchildren into our very first conversation."

No reaction from the audience. Maybe I should have set the scene more. Worked in context. Isn't that what they said about comedy? That it's all in the context? Or maybe that was just my panicked brain throwing up smoke signals for rescue.

Seth seemed to pick them up. "To be fair, we'd make beautiful babies."

Heat crept up my neck. I was aware that I should be responding, but all my words seemed to have temporarily fled.

Seth added hastily, "Not that we're going to. My mom can comment all she wants."

The heat didn't recede. My neck and ears had to be bright red by now. "But maybe we will," I said, nudging him as if to say, *Fake relationship, remember?* "Either way, it's not her business. Anybody else get pressured by their Jewish mothers for grandchildren? It's a stereotype for a reason, right?"

I'd hoped that would get at least one exasperated kid to raise their hand, but nope, nada, nothing. The humiliation was acute, kept my ears and throat burning, but somehow it didn't feel as heavy as I would have expected. Maybe because Seth and I were going through it together. "Tough crowd," I said. Why didn't comedy still have a giant cane that came out of the wings to yank people who were bombing offstage? "So, anyway, gefilte fish?"

I have no memory of the rest of our set. For all I know, Seth and I could have stood up there and recited the ABC's over and over until the painful silence made us pass out from the embarrassment and somebody was finally kind enough to drag us offstage and dump us in a pile in front of the building. Outside, in air cold enough to chill some of the scorching humiliation from my cheeks, I started, "Well, that was—"

"Amazing, right?" Seth finished, which had actually been nothing near what I was going to say, unless maybe I'd decided to go with *amazingly terrible*, or *amazingly dreadful*. "I haven't had a rush like that since college."

"You're joking, right?" I said. I began walking away from the comedy club in a random direction, not caring where I was going as long as it was away. "We bombed up there. It was horrible."

My back was to him, so I couldn't see his expression, only the crowds of people dressed in far too few clothes for the weather and the cars rolling through puddles of slush in the road, but I imagined him looking bashful and unassuming as he spoke. "So what if we bombed? It was still exciting to be up there. Sometimes you have to try new things."

"Is that why you went up there? To try new things? To see if maybe somehow you'd gotten good at stand-up comedy?"

"Oh, no, I knew I'd be terrible, and I was indeed correct

when I said I didn't have the intestinal fortitude to bomb in front of a crowd, because I feel a little like I want to throw up," he said cheerfully. "But my date said that she'd rather go back in time to see my first bomb than go back in time to kill Hitler, and I figured a desire that strong couldn't be left unmet."

This time, no amount of chilly breeze or frozen sleet dripping from the eaves of restaurants could be enough to soothe the fire in my cheeks. "Well, who wouldn't make that choice?" I mumbled. Maybe he couldn't hear me over the sound of all these people going to restaurants and bars and clubs, but I couldn't bring myself to speak up. "A chance to see an extremely annoying person humiliate himself in front of a crowd, or getting all bloody and gross?" I paused. "Also, of course I would kill Hitler if I had the chance."

He continued on as if I hadn't spoken. Which in his mind maybe I hadn't, because he hadn't heard me. I was kind of relieved—I hadn't meant to call him annoying.

Not that he wasn't. Of course he was.

Anyway, he said, "I couldn't believe that you came up and joined me. Why did *you* come up there? I thought you, and I quote, 'couldn't think of anything less appealing than getting up in front of a crowd and trying to make them laugh.'" He paused and considered. "To be fair, I guess we didn't actually make anybody laugh."

This was the first time I really got to think hard about why I'd done it. I'd looked up there at Seth bombing, at the crowd wincing at how bad he was, and I'd imagined how it would feel for that to be me. I'd be shrinking with humiliation, paralyzed with it, especially going through it alone.

And I hadn't wanted Seth to go through it alone.

I sighed. "I guess I . . . care about your feelings or something? And I didn't want you to suffer up there by yourself?"

We stopped at a crosswalk. It was getting quieter around us now, the streets of restaurants and bars transforming into streets of stately brownstones twinkling with classy red and green and white lights. "Wow," Seth mused. "I'm so touched. For what it's worth, I'm really glad you're my friend, Abby."

Wait. Not all of the brownstones were twinkling with Christmas lights. In the middle of the block, one beautiful building hung heavy with strings of blue and white. We stopped in front of it to see in the window a gleaming bronze menorah, its four candles flickering low.

I was glad he was my friend, too. Not that I would ever say it aloud.

But, because he was my friend, he knew not to try to make me. He slung his arm over my shoulders. Instinctively, I leaned into him, and we stood there like that for a second, drinking in each other's warmth.

It was normal, for a fake relationship. We were performing the image of a loving boyfriend and girlfriend for anybody who happened to be around.

I chose not to think about how there wasn't anybody else there.

14

IRONICALLY, THE FIFTH NIGHT OF HANUKKAH brought us to a Christmas festival. "Kylie has a booth where she sells her homemade ornaments," Seth said. "So the whole group is going to support her. You'll come, right?"

I shrugged. It wasn't like I had much of a choice. "Sure." I was actually kind of excited. I didn't hate Christmas or Christmasy things. I'd been known to listen to Christmas music during the summer sometimes and appreciated a good holiday light show. There was nothing wrong with Christmas.

I just didn't want Christmas in my Hanukkah, the same way I didn't want to dip a grilled cheese in my cinnamon roll latte. Both were delicious, but I didn't want them together.

Speaking of coffee. Once Seth and I got up the next morning and he started talking with his parents about what we were going to do for brunch, I ducked into the other room to give Maggie a call. Everything was going great, she assured me, except that we were running low on whipped cream. I was deeply suspicious she'd been giving it out for free to her grandchildren and her grandchildren's friends, but I instructed her to pick up some more from the grocery store and told her I'd pay her back for it when I returned.

In the kitchen, Bev, Benjamin, and Seth all turned to stare at me when I walked in. I resisted the urge to pat my head to see if a bird had landed there or something. "Is everything okay?"

"Everything's great," Bev said. "We were just talking about what to do for brunch. I called up our favorite place, but they don't have any openings, and then Seth just started raving about the brunch at your café, and saying it was the best brunch food he'd ever had and how you've been talking about adding some new specialties to the menu . . ."

"Did he, now?" I narrowed my eyes at Seth, who was studiously avoiding looking at me.

"I'd just love to try it," Bev said brightly, ignoring the way I was attempting to assassinate her son with laser eye beams. "Of course, I don't want to ask it of you. I know it's a lot. Just let me know if you're not in the mood, and I'll put something together."

Inwardly, I groaned. My brunch service consisted mainly of items that were easy to make ahead and whip up quickly on order: French toast casseroles; salads with hard-boiled eggs and crispy bacon on top; cold sandwiches and a few simple egg dishes. Not the kind of elaborate meal that would impress someone like Bev, at least not yet. And while I was semiconfident in my babka baking ability, that was a several-hours-long project.

But I had to try. I'd literally just thought about how much Seth had helped me with this Hanukkah festival, no matter how Lorna was trying to fight it. I took pride in doing well at things. Including being a Good Fake Girlfriend.

I pasted a smile on my face. "Of course. I'm sure whatever I make won't compare to yours, but I'd love to thank you for having me here."

The preening, satisfied look on Bev's face told me I'd said exactly the right thing. Good Fake Girlfriend, indeed.

"I'll need a sous-chef, of course," I said, turning to Seth. "You should do adequately."

"He'll be more than adequate," Bev said. Benjamin raised one single eyebrow. "That boy grew up in the kitchen with me banging on pots and pans. It's in his DNA."

"Not from my side," Benjamin said. Which was fair, judging from the plain oatmeal he ate every morning.

Upon some urging from Seth, Bev and Benjamin went out for a nice long walk in Riverside Park for some fresh air. "I don't care about the fresh air," Seth said as soon as the door closed behind them. "If they stayed here while we made brunch, my mom would be hovering over your shoulder the whole time, sticking her nose in everything. And I don't mean figuratively."

"Should I worry you're going to do that, too?" I asked. "After all, it's in your DNA."

Seth rolled his eyes. "She sees what she wants to see. There's a reason I'm at your café picking up food and coffee every day instead of making it myself."

"And here I assumed you just enjoyed annoying your local barista."

"That, too," he said, grinning. "So? What should we make?"

"It's your house," I said. "Shouldn't you decide?"

"If you let me decide, we're doing bowls of cereal."

That would certainly not impress Bev, not even when she got her nose wet sticking it in the milk. So I did a pass-through of the fridge, the counter, the pantry, and even the secret drawer where Seth said Benjamin hid his sweets supply. (I'd fancied finding cotton candy and Pop Rocks and multiflavored jelly beans for when the buttoned-up old man let loose his wild side, but of course his sweets supply consisted of plain bittersweet squares of chocolate.)

After a bit, the two of us surveyed my finds, splayed out on the counter like treasure we'd dug up. A slightly stale loaf of cinnamon challah. Some eggs. Berries on the softer side of ripe. "Well, it's obvious, right?" I waited for him to come to the same conclusion, but he just stared blankly at the counter. "Thank god you sent your mom out, because she would be terribly disappointed in you right now," I told him. "We're making French toast. Just do what I tell you and you'll be fine."

He grimaced. "If you say so."

"I do say so," I said firmly. "Now go crack maybe three eggs and whip them up in a bowl."

"Maybe three, or three?"

I sighed. "Three."

He hadn't exaggerated when he talked about how bad he was. I realized that when, after slicing the challah into two-inch-thick slices, I found him trying to fish bits of shell out of the bowl. "Use the eggshell," I said.

"What?"

I reached over. My hand closed over his, fingers sinking into the spaces between his fingers. They fit perfectly. "The pieces of shell will run away from your skin," I said. Skin that was warm and firm beneath mine. "But like attracts like. If you use the bigger pieces of shell that aren't in the bowl to scoop out the smaller pieces you're trying to get, they'll stick like magnets."

With my hand guiding his, he clumsily managed to get the first cracked bit of shell out. "Like attracts like, huh?" he said. "I guess that explains why we're in a fake relationship and not a real one."

My cheeks warmed. "It's not personal. I'm not looking for a relationship anyway." Again, locked diary. I had no plans on giving anyone the key.

"I see," said Seth. "So it wasn't that you found me annoying."

I could've cooked one of these eggs on my cheeks right now, shell and all. "You heard that?"

"I have excellent hearing. And memory. You called me annoying both at the comedy club and to my mom when you met her."

"Well, can you blame me?" I asked. It wasn't worth denying the truth; he'd see right through me. "I'm not a morning person, and you were bright and cheerful as hell every morning. Of course I'd find you annoying at first."

"Not a morning person? You run a café," Seth said. "And that's leaving aside that metaphor. Simile? Hell is supposed to be the opposite of bright and cheerful."

"I mean, isn't hell mostly fire and screaming? Fire is bright. Some people scream with cheer."

"That wasn't the point."

"Maybe I run a café because I'm the opposite of a morning person and couldn't find decent coffee to wake me up anywhere else in town."

"Okay, that's the point," Seth said. "But you didn't answer about finding me annoying."

I surveyed the ingredients again, less because I needed time to figure out what to do with them and more because I needed time to figure out what to say back to Seth. "I need the milk. And sugar."

It only took Seth maybe thirty seconds to dig them out. I resented Bev for her well-organized and well-stocked kitchen. He said, "You know, you said 'annoying at first.' Which suggests that if you did find me annoying, you don't find me annoying anymore."

"Well, it wouldn't be a very good look for me to call my fake boyfriend annoying where someone might hear me." I poured milk into the now shell-less whipped eggs, then dumped in some sugar and a pinch of salt. "Stir this."

He grabbed the fork and went to stir. "I want to hear you say it."

"Say what?"

The eggs were whipping further, becoming perfectly pale and creamy. "That you don't find me annoying anymore."

"I don't find you annoying anymore," I said, annoyed. "Though keep trying and I bet you can get back there. Go find me the biggest nonstick pan you can."

Bev apparently kept her pans under the sink. Seth knelt on the floor and stuck his head in the cabinet. His voice muffled, he said, "The thing is, I haven't changed at all. I still do my absolute best to look for the silver lining in every situation and see the best in every person. So if the way you feel about those things has changed . . . maybe it's not me, it's you?" He stood up and presented me with the pan, grinning cheesily.

I briefly debated taking it by the handle and whacking him over the head with it, but Bev and Benjamin didn't deserve to return to a murder scene in their kitchen. "I have not changed," I said huffily. "Go on. Preheat the pan."

"What does that mean?"

"Are you kidding? Do you not know how to heat up a pan?"

"Maybe you should've just said, 'Heat up the pan.'"

I grabbed the handle from him. "I have not changed." Slammed the pan on the stove. Put the electric burner on medium. "It's just the holidays. Everybody gets more cheerful around the holidays."

"I didn't say you seemed any more cheerful than you did before," he said. "Don't worry, I think it's safe to say that you are not cheerful. Aren't we supposed to soak the bread in the eggs before cooking it?"

"Yes," I huffed. I turned the burner off. This was Seth's fault. He was getting me all frazzled by accusing me of things that weren't true, and it was making me mess up. "Find me a big casserole dish or something else to do the soaking in."

That was harder for Seth to find. Good. I stood there watching him, hands on my hips, every bit of me tense and sensitive, like even a feather brushing against my skin might make me break out into hives. Maybe it was partly due to how he looked kneeling on the ground, his head in the cabinet but his broad shoulders unable to fit through, his back flexing every time he moved.

Maybe it was because I liked the idea of him kneeling before me, looking up at me from between my legs.

Hives. Everywhere.

Finally, when I was beginning to think I might have to send him to the drugstore for some cortisone, he located a deep enough casserole dish. He placed it on the counter gently, large hands gripping the sides as he made sure it wouldn't break, then turned to me. "Now we put the bread in and pour the liquid over top?"

"Yes." It didn't take very long, after which we were left just staring at it, waiting for the bread to absorb all of the delicious, rich, sweet goo. It reminded me of when we were in the kitchen previously, when Benjamin and Bev had been asking me about my hopes and dreams, and made me realize that Seth hadn't said anything about his own. "So we covered pretty well what I wanted from my future and that I like living where we live," I said. "What about you? You ran to Vermont to escape commitment, but why did you stay? You could've gone anywhere."

"I liked where I'd gone," Seth said. "You know, I didn't even realize how much I'd like it until I got there. I grew up here, then went to college and lived for a few years in Boston, so I never really left the city environment. But when I got to Vermont and realized that all the open space around me was there to stay, that I'd get to see the same people over and over again every week, it was like I could breathe deeper than I ever had before. You know?"

"I know," I said, because I'd felt that way, too. "Though I'm amazed you became part of the town. I think the only reason they welcomed me in is because I was in a relationship with one of them."

He raised an eyebrow. "It's really not that complicated. You just be friendly to people and offer to help them out and, before you know it, you're friends."

"Whatever." It definitely wasn't that easy. Not that I'd ever tried. "What about career goals? Do you always want to be . . . a . . ." His job sounded so boring that I'd already forgotten his official title. "Data . . . person?"

He raised an eyebrow. "A data person?"

"Yes," I said. "A data person."

He snorted. "I mean, it's not quite being a professional baseball player. That's what I wanted to be as a kid, but I didn't even make the varsity team in high school. I like my job, though. It's low-stress, low-stakes, good hours, and it pays well. I like that I can do it anywhere and that I have lots of time to do things outside of work, like go hiking. Maybe I'll want to switch it up one day if I get bored, but I'm happy now."

"That's fair," I said. "Unlike when you said I'd changed. I haven't changed. I haven't." It seemed very, very important that he know and acknowledge that. My breaths were coming a little faster just thinking about it.

Before I could say anything else, his hands were on my shoulders and he was looking down at me with very serious eyes. "I know you're not a hugger, so if you say no, it's totally okay," he said. "But can I give you a hug?"

I opened my mouth to grumble no, to tell him that I'd rather spontaneously combust.

But instead I just stepped into his arms and nestled my cheek against his shoulder. Why? I couldn't tell you.

Maybe you actually have changed, a voice whispered in my head. A voice that sounded an awful lot like Seth's. When had my inner monologue started sounding like the most annoying person in the world?

Except it was like his arms around me were soothing the irritation, aloe vera on a burn. Or maybe it was more like those strong, warm arms were protecting me from whatever in the air had been causing it. Either way, I felt my shoulders relax, my heart rate slow.

It still felt important to tell him, "I haven't changed." It came out muffled by his flannel shirt.

"Of course you haven't," he said into the crown of my head. His breath ruffled my hair, sending tingles down my neck. It was a pleasant sensation. Not because of him, obviously. Because every girl knew that getting your hair played with or rustled or teased felt good. That's why I didn't want to move.

Which meant, of course, that we were standing like that when Bev and Benjamin came back. Bev must have trained at the ninja school for opening doors, because I didn't hear her come in. As soon as I heard their footsteps in the kitchen, I sprang apart from Seth. Not soon enough to keep her from seeing us like that, though.

"Oh, sorry to walk in on you!" Bev said, not sounding sorry at all. She sounded the opposite of sorry, actually.

Delighted. Thrilled. Full of joy that we might have made her a little Jewish grandbaby in her kitchen.

"You didn't walk in on anything," I blurted, which kind of foiled my attempt to be the perfect Fake Girlfriend, but hopefully she'd take it as me being shy. "We're just making French toast. Seth, how's that bread looking?"

"Delicious, Chef," Seth said. "But I think it still needs a few more minutes to finish soaking."

Great. That left me with nothing to do besides stand there and absorb Bev's exultant looks and Benjamin's general affect of "I would rather be anywhere else but here." I dug my pointiest fingernail into the tender skin of my forearm, just to force myself to feel something other than cringe.

It didn't help.

Bev to the rescue. "I've always loved French toast," she said. "I don't let myself eat it often because, you know, all the carbs and sugar, but of course I'll eat yours."

Thank god. I could talk about French toast for hours. "Yeah, it might not be the healthiest breakfast, but it's hard to get more delicious than fried bread with butter and sugar. I was thinking I'd make some syrup out of the berries and some vinegar and citrus zest if you have some, too. It's always a hit when I have it at the café."

"Sounds fantastic," Bev said. "Is that a family recipe?"

It was like the air in the room froze. Except that Bev and Benjamin's expressions didn't change at all, so maybe it was just suddenly freezing for me. I opened my mouth, but ice was lodged in my throat. I couldn't get anything out.

I felt Seth appear beside me before I saw him. "I think the bread is done soaking, Chef. What's next?" His warmth didn't quite thaw me, but it made it possible for me to move. Jerkily, it was true, but I managed to step to the counter and maneuver my fingers into picking up the box of berries.

"Not a family recipe, something I found online and tweaked to my liking," I said, hoping Bev would leave it at that.

But if there's anything you could say about Bev, it wasn't that she was great at taking a hint. She continued, oblivious, "Did you do a lot of cooking with your mom growing up, like Seth did? You said you grew up in the area. Are they still here? Do we get to meet them?"

I closed my eyes, willing the sudden throb behind them away. My first instinct was to hurl the berries at her head as a distraction and then run away, maybe vaulting down the fire escape.

As you may have noticed by now, my first instincts are not always great.

Bugs chewed at my insides. I set the berries down gently on the counter and crossed my arms over my chest. Bared my teeth in what I hoped looked like a smile. "I don't think so. I probably won't see them while I'm here."

Bev looked as if she'd rounded a corner in a haunted house and come upon two zombies chewing each other's faces off. Real zombies, not fake costumed ones. "Oh, my. Why not? I certainly wouldn't begrudge you two taking some time to go see your family."

Seth's hand found my shoulder. "Abby, I just realized I need to charge my phone. Can you show me where you put the charger?"

Huh? I hadn't touched his charger. But it was an excuse

to leave the room and get away from Bev's prying questions, so I let him take my hand and lead me to our shared bedroom. There, without those questioning eyes on me, I was able to take a breath. "I don't know where your charger is."

"I know. It's in the outlet over there. You just looked like a deer in headlights and I thought you might need a break from my parents."

I was able to let out that breath I just took. "It's not that I needed a break. They're really nice people," I said. "And asking about someone's family or where they grew up is a normal question. I'm not saying they were doing anything bad."

"But you don't like talking about your family," Seth said.

I looked away, but I could still feel his eyes on me. "No."

"Don't worry. I'll tell my parents not to bring it up again."

"You don't have to do that," I said. "I'm not some damsel in distress. I really don't mind."

"Are you sure you don't want to talk about it?" he asked. "Sometimes the things you don't want to talk about are the things you need to talk about most." He shrugged. "I won't push. I'll leave it at that."

"Nobody wants to hear about my family drama." Which was convenient, because I didn't want to talk about it.

"I do," Seth said, and he actually sounded like he meant it. I probably should've expected him to say something like that. When I shook my head, it was at both him and myself.

"I didn't have a very happy childhood. What's the point of dredging up all those bad memories?"

"It can help you process it and learn to deal with it in a healthy way," he said earnestly.

Sure. Said someone who had a happy childhood with loving, caring parents. Besides, I had processed it. And I was dealing with it in a perfectly healthy way by not wanting to talk about it or think about it in any form. He'd have room to talk if I'd thrown the berries at Bev, maybe. But I hadn't.

I was fine. Everything was fine. So what if my headache was darkening into a Category 4 and bugs were still chewing at my stomach? That didn't mean anything. I was just hungry from spending all this time thinking about French toast while not eating French toast.

I shrugged. "The bread is soaked enough at this point," I said. "If it soaks too much, it'll fall apart." There was a metaphor somewhere in there if I wanted to think about it a little harder.

"Okay, got it," Seth said. We headed out the door and back out into the hallway, marching past a line of smiling framed Seths growing younger and younger. I was glad he wasn't pushing. Old, even more annoying Seth would probably have pushed or told me something vaguely threatening, like *You can't outrun your past forever.* See? He totally *was* the one who'd changed, not me.

Back in the kitchen, Benjamin had butter sizzling in a pan on the stove while Bev plucked each soaked piece of bread from the dish to lay it out. They looked back at us. "We thought we'd better get started, since if the bread soaks too long, it'll just fall apart."

"Good thinking," I said, stepping up to the counter. I could feel Bev's eyes piercing into the side of my head. "It looks perfect as it is."

To no one's surprise, Bev proved unable to take a really

obvious hint. "So, your family," she said. "If you don't have time to get up there, you're welcome to invite them over here. I'd love to meet them."

"Mom—" Seth said, and as much as I appreciated his willingness to speak up for me—something that I knew was hard for him to do, especially with his mother—I wanted to do it myself. I took a deep breath.

"I grew up in Riverdale. Honestly, it wasn't a very happy time for me. It's part of the reason I moved to Vermont. So I'd rather not talk too much about it, if you don't mind."

"Oh, I'm so sorry, dear," Bev said immediately, and god, I hoped she wasn't going to hug me. Her hands were covered in egg goop, which lowered the probability but didn't entirely eliminate it. "Of course. I won't bring it up again."

The French toast was exceptionally delicious, and, technically, since it was fried in butter, it counted as a Hanukkah food. I chewed slowly, savoring the delicate sugary crust on the outside of the bread and the luscious creamy texture within. It tasted even better knowing that I'd made it over the hump with Bev and Benjamin. They wouldn't ask about my family again; therefore, I didn't have to think about it around them. See? Everything was fine. Everything was *fine*.

15

SINCE WE OBVIOUSLY WOULDN'T BE LIGHTING A menorah with Seth's friends tonight at the Christmas festival, we made sure to light the candles with Seth's parents before leaving. They had their menorah all set up in their window the way you were supposed to, so that it beamed its light to everybody else on the street. A major part of Hanukkah was being loud and proud about your Jewishness, paying tribute to the Maccabees who'd died fighting against assimilation by defiantly sharing your menorah in a world full of Christmas lights.

We were on the seventh floor, so probably nobody could see ours from the street, but it was the thought that counted.

"Bring home one or two of Kylie's ornaments for me," Bev said to us from the couch, where she and Benjamin were sitting on opposite ends, Bev focused intently on some streaming romantic drama while Benjamin was just as intently focused on the thick hardcover in his lap. Bev seemed to be the kind of person who didn't put on pajamas until she was actually in her bed, but she had changed out of her day wear into what had to be expensive fuzzy lounge pants and a sweatshirt. Benjamin seemed to be the kind of person who slept in pressed pants and a button-down, so he wasn't in pajamas, either. "I like to give them as gifts to those who celebrate Christmas."

Seth promised we would, and then we were out into the chill of the night. I'd dressed up a little bit in a burgundy sweater dress, black boots, and a matching scarf, while Seth was in his usual jeans and flannel. But maybe because I was looking fancy, Seth declared we'd be taking a cab instead of the subway.

I wasn't going to lie: I felt a little bit like I was starring in a Christmas rom-com, sitting in the back of a yellow cab as the bright lights of the city whizzed past me, Times Square billboards shouting out holiday specials of TV shows and sidewalk trees strung with twinkling lights, packs of tourists roaming with Santa hats on and glimpses of tall, stately Christmas trees strung with glowing white orbs standing proudly in the lobbies of fancy doorman buildings.

Of course, it ruined the effect a little bit when Seth gallantly opened the cab door for me and I stepped right into an ankle-deep puddle of murky gray slush. RIP, nice leather boots.

I shook it off as Seth helped me up the curb, thanking the cabdriver before he sped away, splashing my boots with more murky gray water. Why did I even bother?

This Christmas market was all the way downtown, smaller than the big, more commercial one in Union Square but just as cheery and festive. A perfectly conical Christmas tree peaked above the booths from the center, garlanded in red ribbons and covered in so many loops of twinkling multicolored lights that I could hardly see the green boughs. The booths themselves weren't much more than tents over rickety wooden tables, but the smells floating out from them were warm and welcoming: spicy gingerbread; oozy melted chocolate; mulled wine warm with cinnamon and cloves. The laughs of children and cheerful calls of vendors echoed from the aisles, too. The whole effect was warm and cozy, exactly what I wanted for my own festival.

I turned to Seth to tell him this, but he was distracted, eyes sweeping the crowd in search of the friend group. His mouth opened in a silent hail as he raised his arm, and just like that, we were getting hugged by a bunch of wool-wrapped arms and squeezed by fleecy fingers. "So glad you could come!" Dan said to Seth, slapping him on the back.

Someone else hugged me lightly from the side. "So glad you could come, too," Freya said to me, her smile a flash of frost pink and blinding white.

I was surprised to feel genuinely happy to see her. It had been so long since I'd had a real friend who was a girl. Not that one night of being nice to each other in a bathroom made us friends. But I'd seen friendships founded on less.

Before I could respond, the Mikes were all on me, and they were introducing their various dates and other friends they'd brought along, who blended into one amorphous mass of sparkling earrings and crisp wool pea coats and boots that were somehow not gritty with dirt and slush. I smiled and said, "Nice to meet you," so many times that the words lost all meaning, making sure to keep by Seth's side so that he couldn't disappear and leave me all alone with these people. Not that he would. And not that it would be so bad if he did.

I just felt more secure having him there by my side.

As if he were reading my mind, he grabbed my hand. I looked over to find him smiling at me, and before I could help it, my lips curved themselves up at him. Of course he hadn't read my mind. He was just remembering that we had to put on a show for his friends.

Christmas music jingled cheerfully over loudspeakers as we made our way into the maze of booths and tents, sleigh bells and bright trumpets. We passed a potpourri seller, the smell of dried flowers and pine making me a little dizzy, then a waffle stand. I didn't know what loaded waffles had to do with Christmas, but, my god, I suddenly realized I'd never wanted anything more than a hot cinnamon waffle filled with cookie butter and drizzled with salted caramel.

"Your eyes are gooey," Seth said. "Like a bride's on her wedding day."

"Only if that bride is walking down the aisle to a hot cinnamon waffle filled with cookie butter and drizzled with salted caramel."

Seth's hand, still in mine, pulled me toward the stand. "Come on."

"Won't we lose your friends?"

"We'll catch up."

The line was long, but it moved quickly. My insides were melting like that warm salted caramel I was dreaming about. Seth glanced down at me, his smile deepening. "You know, you're kind of looking at me like . . ."

"Like what?"

He shook his head. "Never mind." He stepped up to the counter to place our order.

He'd better not have been about to say I was looking at him with those gooey eyes. Because I definitely wasn't. That look was reserved for waffles and waffles only.

And it was fully deserved, by the way: that waffle was delicious. I chewed slowly, hoping I hadn't gotten caramel all over my face. "So good."

"Do I get a bite?" Seth asked, giving me puppy dog eyes.

My initial reaction was to say no, because other people's dirty mouths on my food equaled gross, but I hesitated before the word could come out. He *had* just bought the waffle for me. And somehow I didn't think of Seth's mouth as dirty. Also, more importantly, we had to put on a good show for his friends. His friends who were off somewhere ahead of us.

"Oh my god," Seth said, mouth full. "I, too, would marry this waffle and have little waffle babies."

"You didn't think this through," I told him. "Because the way that ends is with me eating your wife and children."

"A sacrifice I am willing to make. As long as I get a bite."

True to Seth's word, we were able to catch up with his friends. Kylie's face split wide open in a smile as she saw us approach her booth. Like most of the other craft tables, it was a rickety wooden stand cloaked by a red cloth roof, every inch of it displaying her homemade ornaments. "You came!"

As she and the others caught up on what they'd been up to over the last couple of days, I browsed her offerings. I'd never been a crafty person myself, so I appreciated the extra effort that had clearly gone into crocheting and beading and knitting every miniature Santa hat–wearing octopus and red-nosed reindeer and glittery silver dolphin that didn't seem to be celebrating Christmas outwardly at all, which made me feel inclined toward it. I picked it up between my fingertips, rolling it over to examine the tight weave of pearly gray yarn and metallic silver thread. The dolphin's eye gleamed rhinestone, and it was probably just the light, but it seemed to be staring right at me.

"You get a friend discount, if you want it." I jumped when Kylie appeared right in front of me with a toothy grin. "Twenty-five percent off."

I rolled the dolphin around in my hand. I didn't have a Christmas tree. It didn't make sense to buy a Christmas ornament when I didn't have a Christmas tree.

Only just because it had a hook didn't mean it had to go on a tree, right? I couldn't help but picture the bare walls and surfaces of my shitty little apartment. They'd never bothered me before. Honestly, it wasn't like they bothered me so much now. I'd gotten used to them.

But maybe this little dolphin would look nice chilling on my fridge, or hanging out on a windowsill, where the sunlight would make it glitter. Maybe I'd smile when I saw it in a month or a year from now, when this whole adventure was nothing more than a memory, when Kylie had made a whole new stable of ornaments I wouldn't be here to see.

I cleared my throat. What the hell. "I'll take it."

As I tucked the small brown paper bag containing my

new friend into my purse, Seth appeared at my elbow, sipping on what smelled like hot cocoa with a kick of cayenne. "It's not anywhere near as good as yours," he said. "Want some?" I was all sugared out from my waffle and cookie butter, so I shook my head. "Which ones should we get for my mom? She likes to give them to the doormen and cleaning lady along with their holiday tip. Says it adds a personal touch."

By the time we'd selected a cheery turtle with a red-and-green-striped shell and an assortment of safari animals wearing Santa hats, the group was beginning to trickle onward through the festival. I grabbed a mug of mulled wine from a booth on the way, partially because I liked holding the smells of orange peel and cinnamon and nutmeg under my nose—another entry for my spa one day—but mostly because my hands were freezing.

We were standing around, Seth off talking to Dan and a Mike, me content to stand there breathing in the mulled wine steam and occasionally drinking it, when Freya sidled up next to me. Her ears and forehead were covered by her powder blue knit hat, her chin and mouth cloaked by a matching scarf, so that all I could really see were those pale blue eyes and two bright circles of pink on her cheeks. Like Seth, she held a hot chocolate in a paper cup decorated with snowflakes. "The city still treating you well?"

I wondered if "the city" actually meant the city, or if it meant Bev. Either way, the answer was, "Still good. What have you been up to for the holidays?"

Her older brother and his fiancée were in town, she told me, which was nice because they lived in San Francisco and she didn't get to see them much. "They're talking about having a baby soon after the wedding, which is so exciting. I can't wait to be an aunt. I mean, I can't wait to be a mom, but being an aunt will be fun until then."

I stretched my mouth into a smile. I couldn't remember the last time I'd interacted, truly interacted, with a child under ten. Sometimes parents brought them into my coffee shop. They seemed like an alien species, saying things I didn't understand and making expressions that meant the complete opposite from what they actually meant and sometimes letting out sudden, startling shrieks from nowhere that made me jump. It wasn't that I didn't like kids; I just didn't understand them.

But Seth? Seth would be an incredible dad. I could see him patiently teaching a kid how to play T-ball, helping them with math homework, weaving ribbons into braids (after patiently learning how to braid). A contrast to me as a terrible, awkward mom, if I even wanted kids.

"Wow, congratulations to them," I said. A bitter taste rose on the back of my tongue. I took a sip of my mulled wine to chase it away, but it didn't budge. "When's the wedding?"

Freya told me all about how they were planning the wedding for next winter here in Manhattan, and her brother was going to wear a white tux, and they were hoping for real snow but had already reserved some fake snow just in case. "And I'm going to be the best woman, of course," she said. "He's five years older than me, so we weren't all that close as kids, but we became pretty close once he went to college and we were no longer in the same house to fight over everything we could think of. You know, Seth apologized to me."

I blinked. The sudden turn in the conversation had thrown me for a bit of a loop. "What?"

"Seth," Freya said. "He apologized to me for how our breakup worked out. You know, with the ghosting. Just now, when we stepped away for hot chocolate."

While I was looking through the ornaments. It was good of him to keep it between him and Freya, so that she wouldn't feel obligated in front of the group to accept it. "Oh," I said. "That's good, I guess."

"Real relationship or not, you're a good influence on him."

I didn't know why hearing that made me feel so awkward. All I knew was that I didn't want to talk about it anymore. "It's cool your brother made you best woman. Do you wear a suit for that?"

She didn't seem bothered by my own turn in conversation, only chattered excitedly about her lacy blue dress in the same color as the groomsmen's ties. "And what about you, Abby? Do you have any siblings?"

I took a sip of my mulled wine. It was starting to get lukewarm. "No," I said as breezily as possible. "I'm an only child. Do you have any other siblings?"

"No, just me and my brother. Where did you grow up?"

Sweat broke out on my forehead. What was with all these questions? Why did all these people want to know about my past? *It's a normal thing to ask*, the rational part of my brain reminded me, but the rest of me wasn't having it.

Maybe this was why my approach to my past had worked

so well so far: because I wasn't letting anyone get close enough to me to ask these normal, boring questions.

I was getting a tension headache. Category 1.

Part of me wanted to make up an excuse to push Freya away. But I couldn't do that. Not if I wanted to be a Good Fake Girlfriend.

And, honestly? It felt kind of like I was making a girl friend for the first time in a long time. And making a friend felt pretty nice.

"In the area, actually," I said. Having already been through this today, making the words come out was less stressful. "But I wasn't sad to leave it behind. I really like it in Vermont."

She propped her scarf-covered chin on her glove-covered hand. "Ooh, right. I'm kind of jealous of your life. At least the running-a-café part of it. When I was little I used to want to run a bakery, at least until I found out how early you have to wake up every morning and how little you get paid."

I couldn't help but laugh. "Don't those things also apply to being a kindergarten teacher?" I cringed inwardly at myself, hoping I hadn't just insulted her, but she just laughed, too.

"Oh my god, you're telling me. People seem to think I just chill out and play with little kids all day. But do you know how hard I work? I'm teaching them to read and behave in public with other little humans for the first real time in their lives. I bet my job is harder than that of at least half the lawyer and marketer and programmer parents of my kids who think I don't do anything all day."

"Oh my god, same here," I said emphatically. "People think running a café is easy and romantic, that I just chill out whipping up fun drinks and gossiping with the townsfolk. But it's such hard work. I bet I wake up almost as early as a baker, and . . ."

We went on for a while, comparing and complaining about how hard our jobs were. By the time we'd run out of things to say, Freya's hat had slid up and her scarf had slid down, exposing rays of staticky white-blond hair and a chapped lower lip, and I was pretty sure I had a serious case of wild eyes. I took another sip of my mulled wine. To my surprise, I was almost at the bottom of the cup. Also, I had no idea where Seth was. "What are we doing right now, by the way?"

Our group had spread out a bit, and I realized we'd been shuffling along behind them as they slowly moved toward something. Like we were waiting in a line. Freya said, "I have no idea. Hey! Seth!"

There he was. He'd turned his back to talk to one of the Mikes, but he'd been there all along. "You guys seem to be getting along well." The smile he gave us was surprised but pleased, a little guarded. I guess the thought of Connor and Seth interacting gave me similar feelings, even though Seth wasn't even my real boyfriend. Something about the past and present meeting, two people who both knew intimate versions of you from different times.

"We totally are," I said. "Freya is great. She's been telling me all sorts of embarrassing stories about you from when you two were together."

His eyebrows jumped to his hairline. "Please tell me she didn't tell you about the lobsters."

"I was joking," I said. "But now I need to hear about the lobsters."

"Oh my god, okay," Freya said. "So we went away to Maine for a long weekend over July Fourth one year, right? And we decided to host a lobster cookout for all our friends. We went to the store and picked out live lobsters and everything. Only—"

"—only we couldn't bring ourselves to kill them," Seth said, a smile twitching at his lips. The memory might have been embarrassing, but it was also clearly fond. "Freya cried when it came time to put them in the boiling water. So then we looked up other ways to do it, and apparently you can kind of cleave them in half through the brain and that kills them instantly, except—"

"—except Seth got all freaked out by how they moved and couldn't get his knife in place, and he was panicking about cutting into the wrong spot and causing the lobster pain," Freya said.

"So when all our friends got there, expecting some delicious grilled lobster rolls and lobster salad and whatever else, we were just standing there with our live lobsters squirming around the yard," said Seth. "By then we'd named them."

"After various Disney Princesses. We had Belle, Aurora, Jasmine, Cinderella—"

"—Snow White had a big white blotch on her claw—"

"And so obviously, the thought of eating them was a lost cause," Freya said. "We ended up having a ceremonial release and ordering in from the local burger place."

"I know it seems hypocritical, because cows, but at least we didn't know their names," said Seth.

I wondered if they would stop laughing if I told them the one time I'd cooked lobster I'd had no problem tossing that sucker into the water and closing the lid.

I automatically stepped up again when they moved forward. Freya and some of the Mikes struck up a conversation, leaving Seth and me in relative solitude. "Freya told me you apologized to her."

"Yeah. It was long overdue, and I'm glad you pushed me to do it. I'm surprised she told you, though." He raised an eyebrow. "You guys really do seem to be getting along well."

"Is that okay?"

"Of course it's okay," Seth said. "I'm happy about it. You're both people I care about very much."

That awkwardness squirmed in my stomach again. We stepped up once more, following Seth's friends. I asked, "Are we in line for something?"

And didn't need a response, because then I noticed it: the banner proclaiming **MEET SANTA!** in big red letters. Kids dressed like elves in pointed plastic ear bands and forest green outfits flanked a Santa who might have been out of a movie, big and round and red and jolly, with a bulbous nose and full white beard that might actually have been real. "Ho, ho, ho!" Santa called out joyfully into the wind.

I nudged Seth with my elbow. "Why are we waiting to see Santa?"

He shrugged. "Dan thinks it's funny for us all to get pictures with him."

Fine, whatever. The line crawled forward. A Mike and his date went up first, each perching precariously on one of

Santa's knees. It was hard to see who looked most afraid that the old man might collapse. "Have you ever had a picture with Santa before?" I never had. My parents had obviously never taken me, and I'd never gone on my own.

He shrugged again. "Dan used to drag us before I moved."

The Mike and his date finished without crushing any elderly knees and got up, ceding the space to Dan and his friend. Dan leaned in to whisper in Santa's ear. I tried to picture myself doing that, and it felt . . . weird. Not bad weird, necessarily, like I would be doing something wrong. But uncomfortable weird, like trying to put on pants that no longer fit or eating eggplant, which for most people was great but for me made my throat itch.

"I don't know if I want to do this," I said.

"You one hundred percent don't have to do anything you don't want to do," Seth said. Of course not, but opting out when everybody else was doing it would still get me weird looks, make me feel like I alone wasn't part of the group. "Just out of curiosity, what's giving you pause?"

"I don't know, exactly," I said, something in my stomach squirming. And I really didn't. All I knew was that the thought of it gave me that "this isn't quite right" feeling.

I hadn't felt truly Jewish in many years, not until this trip. Maybe it had something to do with that. Not that Jews couldn't go take pictures with Santa Claus if they wanted to—Seth was evidence enough of that. It wasn't like it made them less Jewish. But for me? It just didn't mesh.

I wondered if this was what the Maccabees had felt like

when the king ordered them to start worshipping the Greek gods. Only on, like, a way, way, *way* lesser scale. And with a far smaller chance of ending in blood and fire.

"Yeah, I think I'm going to sit this one out," I said, and saying it felt right: the pants suddenly grew enough to fit, the eggplant morphed into a potato latke. "You should do it if you want, though."

"And leave you sitting out alone? A good boyfriend wouldn't do that."

"Seth!" Dan called out, unfolding himself from Santa's lap, where somehow he'd managed to curl up. "Abby! Your turn!"

Seth stared back at him. Right. Seth's inability to deal with conflict. I braced myself for getting dragged over there no matter how I felt. Which, again, if it took that to be a Good Fake Girlfriend, I could live with it. I grabbed his hand and squeezed through his glove.

Though I'd meant it to communicate how I was feeling, it made him stand up straighter and clear his throat and say, "We're good, man. Freya, Mike, you guys go ahead."

He fell back, shrinking a little bit, as if bracing himself to get yelled at.

But, of course, that wasn't what happened. Dan just shrugged and said, "Okay! Freya, Mike, you're up."

As the rest of the group clustered around Santa and their friends, hollering suggestions on what they should ask for for Christmas, Seth pulled me to the side. Not the side of the crowd but, like, the side of the festival. And not the cool side, the side that guests weren't supposed to be on. The wrong side of the alleyway, the back side of one of the rows, where boxes of extra supplies waited in stacks and electrical cords snaked over the dirt in complex tangles that probably violated several safety standards. The smell of smoke drifted toward us, which panicked me for a second before I noticed the small group of workers taking a cigarette break down the other end of the aisle.

At least this wasn't where they put the trash.

I was a little worried something was wrong with Seth that he needed to talk to me in such privacy, and then I saw his exultant smile. "I did it," he said. "I mean, I know it was such a small thing to basically everybody else with a pulse, but did you see it?"

I cracked a smile back. "Way to deal with conflict in a healthy fashion."

Seth gestured back toward his friends with his chin. "I'm not sure why I didn't want to say anything where they might overhear. It's a little embarrassing, I guess, that it felt like such a big deal to me."

"I get it," I said. "I mean, you shouldn't be embarrassed, but I understand what it feels like when something that feels so big to you feels so small to everyone else." See: being able to answer basic questions about your parents and family.

"Yeah." He smiled down at me again, and I suddenly realized how close we were to each other, so close the edges of our coats were touching, so close I could feel his heat radiating even through all my layers. No, that had to be my imagination. And we were only standing so close because the aisle was so narrow. "And look at you, Ms. Hanukkah Spirit. Refusing to assimilate."

My own smile was tiny, closed-lipped. "Isn't it funny how Christmas and Hanukkah are kind of lumped together because they're both in the winter and became examples of 'the holiday spirit' when they're so different?" I laughed a little, remembering Lorna's vendor friend Fred, dismayed at the actual story of Hanukkah. *Sounds bloody*. Judah Maccabee would hopefully approve of me not wanting to sit on Santa's lap.

He wouldn't approve of you bending to Lorna the way you did on the phone, though, part of me whispered. I did not really want to listen to that part of me, especially not now, with laughter all around us. *You're basically the Jews who said, "Sure, I'll worship Zeus and sacrifice pigs on the sacred altar."*

Okay, I was definitely not as bad as the Jews who worshiped Zeus and sacrificed pigs on the sacred altar. Was it really that big a deal to let Lorna have a few non-Hanukkah things at our Hanukkah festival? It wasn't like Hanukkah was even a major, super important holiday, and my goal with the festival wasn't to present the world with a pure-as-the-sacred-oil vision of the holiday. It was to bring tourists to town and save my café.

My lips parted before I could think too much about it. "Do you think I'm doing the right thing? With the festival?"

I hadn't thought it possible for Seth to move closer, but he did. He leaned in so that his nose practically brushed mine, and yep, now I could definitely feel the heat coming off him, his breath tickling my baby hairs. "What did you say?"

This close, looking him in the eye was almost paralyzing: in the shadows, his were so dark, so deep, that I was afraid I might fall in and never be able to claw my way out. But I couldn't look away, even to use that old middle school trick of talking to the middle of the person's forehead so that it looked as if you were eye to eye but really you weren't.

"The festival. Lorna. You heard our call earlier, where I gave in to her on some of the Christmasy things she wants to make the Hanukkah festival more . . . broadly commercial, I guess," I said. We were only one to two percent of the American population, so basically anything made to cater to us also had to cater to the general Christian population or it couldn't be broadly commercially successful. "Do you think I'm doing the right thing?"

"Do you really have much of a choice when it comes to Lorna?" His lips parted, his tongue dipping out to lick them. Maybe a drop of hot cocoa had gotten caught on his lower lip.

"Did the Maccabees have a choice when Antiochus ordered them to worship Zeus?"

Seth's lips quirked. "I think the stakes are a *little* bit lower in this case."

I didn't laugh. "You didn't answer."

"What do you want me to say?" He shrugged. I could feel the waves of movement in the air. "I think you have to do what's best for you and the festival, and if that means letting Lorna have her way a little bit, then so be it."

"Okay." I still wasn't feeling great about it, but, to be fair, it was hard to feel anything besides how hard my heart was thumping at Seth's proximity. We were so close now I could've stuck my tongue out and swiped that drop of hot cocoa from his lower lip. So close I could touch my forehead to his and breathe in deep that citrusy smell of his. So close I could–

"Abby?" Seth's voice was hoarse. His hand was suddenly on the side of my head, the pressure gentle but firm. My heart skipped a beat. Was he leaning in? Was he going to–

"Seth? Abby?"

I jumped away, my back hitting the canvas wall of a booth. My heart felt like it might leap out of my throat. "Freya?"

Sure enough, Freya was standing there near where we'd come in, poking her head into the aisle, pale eyebrows scrunched in light concern. "What are you guys doing back here? We've been looking for you."

Seth had also moved away into the back side of a tent, his arms now crossed. His body language couldn't possibly have been any more closed off. I almost had to laugh. I couldn't believe I thought he was going to kiss me. Our relationship was fake. We both knew that. Just as we both knew I would be a terrible real girlfriend for him, and he would probably be a terrible real boyfriend for me.

Still. For a second there, it had really seemed . . .

"Kylie's closing up and we're going to head out for a drink," she said. "You guys coming?"

Seth looked at me like he was asking if I wanted to go. I shrugged. "Sure, if you're up for it."

Freya clapped her hands together. Because of her gloves, they didn't make a sound. "Okay, yay! Let's go."

Better not drink anything more tonight, I thought as I trailed after them. Mocktails only. Because clearly my mind couldn't be trusted.

16

SETH'S FRIENDS DIDN'T HAVE JUST ANY REGULAR bar in mind, of course. Like Seth, they had to be a little bit extra.

"I don't even like gingerbread," I groused. It was relevant because I was currently surrounded by it: sheets of it spread on the rickety bar table before me; paper cutouts of gingerbread men hanging on the walls around us; even gingerbread spices flavoring Freya's cocktail, which was sitting right next to me.

Maybe I'd protested too much about my festive gingerbread doodle. Maybe I should've let the gingerbread man drown.

"It doesn't matter if you like it or not," Seth said. "This is a gingerbread house–building event. You don't have to eat it. You probably shouldn't eat it, in fact, since I think it's been sitting out all day."

"Stale gingerbread," I said. "Even better."

Freya nudged me from the side with an elbow. Even though it was warm inside the bar, she'd kept on her ice blue hat, maybe because it looked so good with her eyes. "I agree with your feelings on gingerbread. It's never as good as I want it to be."

The thing was, I didn't even dislike gingerbread that much. Gingerbread was fine. It was just that suddenly, after what had nearly happened between Seth and me in that alley—*had* something nearly happened? Was I imagining it?—the world around me seemed to have dialed the brightness up a few notches. It was like a spotlight was trained on Seth, illuminating every move he made. The way he was aware of his surroundings while walking, shifting from left to right to make sure people had enough room to pass by him. How he looked over his shoulder for me when I lagged behind the group, to make sure I hadn't gotten lost. The way he normally slumped in his seat but, every so often, sat up straight like he'd gotten a jolt from the chair, as if he'd just heard his dad reminding him to maintain good posture or his back would hurt when he got old.

Complaining was my way of trying to revert the world back to its mean. To make me feel more at home in my skin again.

It was not working.

"We can't come to a gingerbread house–building event and not build a gingerbread house," Seth said, and he turned his eyes toward me, and if I met them and committed to sitting right next to him and reaching past him for pieces of decorative candy and feeling the heat of his body every time, I wasn't sure the world would ever go back to its equilibrium.

So, as usual, I fled. Metaphorically, because I think I would've attracted some strange looks if I'd literally fled the bar. My metaphorical fleeing involved clamping onto Freya's fluffy shoulder like she was the hook and I was the fish. "I already said I'd help Freya with hers," I blurted.

Freya glanced at me sidelong. "You did?"

"Yeah, you must not have heard me." It was believable, considering how loud it was in here; "Jingle Bells" was currently blasting from the bar speakers.

She shrugged. "Okay."

As Freya and I gathered materials for our construction, I couldn't stop sneaking glances over at Seth. He had, without much fuss, teamed up with Dan, and the two were currently bending their heads together over what appeared to be an experiment on how high they could build a gingerbread tower without it collapsing into a pile of cinnamon crumbs. He kept throwing his head back with laughter. I wondered what was making him laugh like that.

"Ooh, I didn't even see the snowflake sprinkles," Freya said, peering at the pile of candy I'd assembled. "Those will be so cute."

"And I missed the Nerds," I said, looking at hers. "Those will be . . . so cute, too."

She didn't seem bothered by my stealing her compliment because I hadn't been able to think of anything else. "What do you want to build?"

"Um," I said. "A . . . house?"

"No, I mean, what kind?" she said. "Usually, people decorate theirs in, like, red and green for Christmas, but maybe we could do something for Hanukkah? Since you were saying you guys kind of get the short end of the stick around the holidays."

I was surprised at how much her words touched me. I mean, it was just a stupid gingerbread house that I didn't care about at all, but I felt seen. "Wow. Okay, sure. That sounds cool."

She pushed all the red and green stuff to one side, then reconsidered and picked out some green M&M's and Necco Wafers. "I feel like this will make good grass."

Of course, pushing aside the Christmas stuff raised the question about what decorating for Hanukkah actually meant. "I don't know, I feel like most people I know never really decorated for Hanukkah the way people decorate for Christmas," I said. "I mean, maybe we could do blue and white lights?" We surveyed our collection of candy, most of which was red, green, or white. "Or maybe just put a frosting menorah in the window?"

That semi-decided, we set about constructing our walls, hoping the frosting would hold the confection together. "When you and Seth were dating, did you guys celebrate the holidays a lot together?" I asked.

She squinted at a crack in the sheet of gingerbread she was trying to fit into one of our slots. "Sure, we'd do at least something together. I'd go home for Hanukkah to light the candles with his family, and he'd come celebrate Christmas with mine. I'd go home with him for the Passover seder, and he'd come to mine for Easter. It actually made things easier that we had different religions. Nobody fighting over who gets us for Christmas or Easter dinner."

That was probably true. Though, in my case, we wouldn't be fighting about where to spend the holidays. One, because several Jewish holidays conveniently had multiple nights of celebration; there were two Passover seders and eight nights of Hanukkah. And two, because I wouldn't be celebrating with my family. Seth and I could spend all of the holidays with his family. I could see it now: Bev moaning about being starving on Yom Kippur while Benjamin mused about how maybe he should try intermittent fasting every day; Bev making Seth sing the Four Questions every year at Passover because he was the youngest person at the table and telling him that if he no longer wanted to be the youngest he was welcome to make someone younger.

I glanced back at Seth again. He and Dan had managed to construct a wobbly tower that was at least two feet high; Seth's shoulder flexed as he reached up to stick a gumdrop on the roof.

"How's the fake relationship going?" Freya said in my ear. My eyes instinctually darted around to make sure nobody had overheard, but she'd judged correctly; the music was too loud. "Is it weird that I'm rooting for you guys?"

"Rooting for what?" Somehow the mischief in her voice didn't point toward the answer being *to pull a successful one over on Bev and Benjamin.*

Her eyes twinkled, not unlike Santa Claus in every Christmas movie ever. "No reason."

That was clearly a lie, but I didn't want to push it. Okay, that was also a lie—I *did* want to push it, but something was stopping me. Maybe I was afraid of hearing the answer.

So I changed the subject. "Are you dating anyone right now?"

She glued a gumdrop to the wall of our house with frosting, then grimaced as it fell right off, displacing a Life

Savers candy porthole (we'd decided our house would have portholes rather than windows, because they were a lot easier to make). "Ugh, dating in New York is the worst. I swear they're holding a Worst Guys Ever convention at the Javits every week. That's the only thing to explain the quality of my matches." She shrugged. "But it's okay. I have enough going on where a boyfriend would probably just complicate things anyway." She cocked her head. "Unless you know anyone you want to set me up with?"

I snorted. "Fat chance there." The only guys I knew well enough for that were my fake boyfriend and my ex-boyfriend.

"Have you dated much? Like, for real, I mean?" she asked, and her voice was so nonjudgmental, I found myself spilling the whole story of my relationship with Connor, from those painful stand-up days to our even more painful breakup.

Somehow, among all the word vomit, I found it in myself to marvel at how good she was at listening. She gave sympathetic nods at all the right times, frowned angrily at the moments where Connor was a douche, made *mmm*s of agreement when I told her what I'd done and said in response. It was a skill I'd never had. I was not the sympathetic café worker who listened to all her customers' problems and gave them free coffee when they'd had an especially bad day; I *was* the problem they talked about.

The funny thing about growing up with parents like mine is that I became hyperaware of how the people around me were acting and listening and behaving so that I could be careful not to set them off by doing anything bad, but I never got to figure out the right way to do things instead.

But it didn't seem to bother Freya that I wasn't reacting properly, whatever reacting properly meant, which was another thing that touched me. "What a douchebag," she said. "Good riddance to him."

I had no idea why that made me so defensive. Connor had called me a frigid bitch, for god's sake. "I don't know. It wasn't totally his fault."

"There's no excuse for the things he said to you, whether or not you were a good fit as a couple," she said firmly. Then cracked a smile. "You deserve better. Can you hand me one of those boxes of Nerds? I'm going to make a gravel path to the front door."

I handed over a box of Nerds, thankful that she hadn't lingered on the nice thing she'd said to me. Compliments made me want to puke.

As she laid out a winding rainbow path that looked like something a fairy might walk down, she launched into some stories of recent first dates, one of which was apparently a taxidermy enthusiast who'd worn a stuffed mouse on his shirt like a brooch. "I thought it was real at first. Like, that a real mouse was crawling up his shirt. I screamed and jumped away from the table, and the table next to us saw it, too, and after that, forget it. It was a stampede." She paused and considered. "He was very nice, though. Are my standards too low?"

After what she'd said to me earlier about deserving better, I felt we'd crossed into that level of friendship (?) where I could be honest. "Sorry, but maybe."

I braced myself for her to get insulted, but she only sighed good-naturedly. "And that's not even mentioning the guy who came prepared with a questionnaire aimed at finding out how fertile I am."

Soon enough, our gingerbread house was finished. Freya handed over the tube of frosting with the smallest tip. "You do the honors."

Bending forward and squinting like I was competing at the highest levels of latte art (a real competition I'd once entertained the thought of entering before realizing I couldn't afford the time off and the travel), I frosted a tiny menorah into our house's front porthole. It was so small you could barely see it, but that was okay. Freya and I would both know it was there.

I backed off feeling satisfied, but a crash from behind us told me my fake boyfriend wasn't doing quite as well. Seth and Dan's tower had finally collapsed like a Jenga game, scattering their table with gingery debris and smashed bits of candy. Both Seth and Dan were laughing, showing they weren't too devastated. Seth glanced back at me, mid-laugh, and our eyes met.

Before I could think about it, I leaned in and went to pat him on the back, but somehow that pat on the back turned into a half hug, but he turned just as I was squeezing him to make it into a full hug. My mind blanked for a moment as he held me close, the heat of his body as cozy as a fireplace on a cold day, and then I was right back there at the festival, the smell of hot chocolate on his breath, his lips so close to mine...

I pulled away, cheeks hot. He looked down at me for a second with what might have been concern, but Dan slapped him on the back and pulled him away to demonstrate how they'd reacted to the falling of the tower for Kylie, who must have missed it. That gave me the opportunity to back away and rejoin Freya, who was also looking at me with something like concern. "I just want to make sure you know it's okay," she said.

"What are you talking about?"

"If there's something there," she said, waving her hand vaguely in the air, but I knew exactly what she meant. If there was something there between Seth and me. Something more than a fake relationship.

I opened my mouth, ready to tell her that she had nothing to worry about, but the words stalled in my throat. Because I hadn't totally imagined what had happened between us at the festival, had I? Not that look in his eye, not how close he was leaning toward me, and definitely not how much I wanted him to lean all the way in.

Oh. This was very, very dangerous. I couldn't have feelings for someone like Seth. He'd crack me right open and throw away the key.

Besides, I'd learned that being in a relationship with me was too hard. He'd learn that, too, after a little while, and we'd have a terrible breakup like Connor and me, and I'd lose my friend. My friend who I cared about.

And maybe wanted to kiss.

I took a deep, shaky breath. "I think our Hanukkah house turned out really nice. If I was a gingerbread man, I'd totally live there."

She eyed me for an extra moment before responding. "Sure. I would, too."

And so I busied myself for the rest of the night with creating a tiny gingerbread friend with a kippah and tzitzit, spending all my effort working on something that would go poof when the night was over.

Not that that was a metaphor for anything in my real life.

17

I HAD TO PUT THOSE THOUGHTS ABOUT SETH AND me out of my head. I couldn't be a good friend, or especially not a good fake girlfriend, with them rolling around in there. So I lay in bed that night with my eyes shut tight and took deep breaths, telling myself over and over that this wouldn't be a big deal, that I only had to get through three more nights.

It was very hard to fall asleep.

I woke up after Seth did, meaning I was confronted by his neat pile of blankets and pillow on the floor. Rubbing my eyes, I scrolled through my phone for a bit, answering some emails I'd gotten about the café and the festival, then made a quick stop in the bathroom before padding out to the main space.

Right into the middle of an argument. I was glad I'd taken some time to myself before wading in. Seth was saying, "We really haven't gotten any downtime yet. I was thinking we'd take the day easy, just Abby and me, maybe enter the lotteries for some Broadway shows or head out to Queens for some good Thai—"

"You two get plenty of time just the two of you back home," Bev was saying in response, talking over her son. "You came to New York for family time. Besides, you'll be able to do the event together."

Seth's shoulders were already starting to sag. He might have been able to stand up to his friends, but his mom?

And then he saw me, and something in his eyes flashed, like he was remembering our conversation. He stood up taller. "You should've asked us first," he told Bev.

If I thought Seth's eyes flashed, Bev's eyes burst into flame. Not literally. But I was afraid to get too close to her in case they caught on my hair. "I didn't think I needed to—"

"What's going on?" I asked hastily, hoping to defuse some of this tension. Benjamin, who I realized just now was seated at the kitchen table, looked vaguely disappointed. Maybe that I hadn't brought him any popcorn for the show. Plain, non-buttered popcorn, of course.

Seth and Bev both turned to me, opened their mouths, and unleashed a torrent of words at once. I caught maybe every other one. *Today. Synagogue. Family. Chill. Tired. Cooking.*

I held up a hand. "Sorry, what?"

Seth looked vaguely thrilled, Bev vaguely surprised: maybe that I'd dared interrupt her. Well, it was her own fault. She said, before Seth could speak again, "Every year we take part in a Hanukkah cookie decorating clinic at the synagogue. A bunch of people from around the city from all different synagogues come and participate. There are prizes and things. It's a lot of fun, so I of course signed us up again this year."

"And I said you should have asked us first," Seth said. "Maybe we already have plans." He gave me a questioning look. It was up to me, I guessed.

Honestly, last night had proved there were worse ways to spend a few hours than decorating cookies. And wasn't it my job to make a good impression on Bev? So what if, when she gave me that look of approval, my insides went all warm like my teacher had just given me a gold star?

Still, I didn't want to force Seth into something if he didn't want to do it. A Good Fake Girlfriend wouldn't throw her Fake Boyfriend to the wolves. So I just raised an eyebrow and cocked my head a little bit, doing my best to communicate all of that.

I expected very little. I'd never been called expressive, unless resting bitch face counts as an expression. But somehow Seth seemed to understand it. He gave me a small nod, then turned back to Bev. "Okay, fine. We'll do it."

"Wonderful. It'll be so much fun."

A couple hours later, after eating the leftover French toast (almost as delicious as freshly made), we were setting up in the social hall of their synagogue. Long tables lined the cavernous, high-ceilinged room, with place cards marking each team's designated location. Bev, Benjamin, Seth, and I walked down the aisles of dirty green carpet beneath the huge chandelier, looking for our names.

Bev and Benjamin found theirs first. "Oh, this must be a mistake," she said, looking at the settings on either side of hers. "You two should be next to us."

"Oh, too bad, I wonder what happened," Seth said in such a monotonous rush that I knew immediately he'd called the synagogue ahead of time and requested it. A tiny bit of passive-aggressive revenge.

We found our station at the far end of the room, near the door. Which satisfied me in a sad sort of way. I hated to even think it, but one thing I automatically did when being in a Jewish space was clock the exits. Just in case. We had enough room at the long table where we could stand side by side and only elbow each other if we were both using our elbows at the same time.

The cookies we'd be decorating weren't there yet, but sitting on our station were some basics we'd need for the task ahead: frosting; little tubes of food coloring; a few different kinds of fun sprinkles. It looked as if there were more elaborate decoration options at a table along the side of the room, set up as first come, first serve.

All of my time lounging on the couch watching competition shows on the Food Network after Connor left me was now about to come in handy. "I think our strategy should be to run over and take the most desirable decoration options on that table first," I said in a low voice, leaning into Seth's ear so that he could hear me but the adorable old couple on my left couldn't. "Granny and Gramps over here can't make winning sparkly cookies if there aren't any sparkles for them to use."

Seth looked over at them. Granny and Gramps grinned cheerfully at us and waved enthusiastically in unison over their matching plaid aprons. He looked back to me. "You know, why bother with all the subterfuge? Maybe I should just tackle them if they try to take the sparkles. They can't make winning sparkly cookies if they both have broken hips."

"I didn't realize you were that hard-core."

"To be very clear, I was being sarcastic," Seth said. "You understand that was sarcasm, right?"

I ignored him. "We also want to think originality. Humor is good. Neither of us are super artistic, so we can't rely on making the most beautiful cookies and winning on that. No, we need to make the judges laugh."

"You do realize the prize for this is a gift card to a really mediocre kosher restaurant, right?"

"No, Seth." I tapped the side of his head solemnly. "The prize for this is winning. The knowledge that we are the best."

"Will the knowledge that we are the best cookie decorators among a small subset of Upper West Side Jews help you sleep at night?"

"No," I said. "It will animate the very core of my being."

He shrugged. "Okay, in that case, you run for the sparkles and I'll threaten Granny with our frosting knife."

I held back a smile as a middle-aged woman I assumed was a volunteer approached each table with a box of plain cookies. That smile might have burst fully onto my face if she and I hadn't recognized each other at the same time. My smile evaporated, sinking back into my throat where it formed a lump. Her eyes widened. "Abby Cohen, is that you?"

I couldn't speak. All I could do was nod.

Mrs. Landskroner had clearly aged in the ten years since I'd seen her, but there was no mistaking my old Hebrew school teacher. She had to be in her late sixties or early seventies now, but her hair was still a glossy brown, and either makeup or good plastic surgery had softened the wrinkles around her eyes and mouth. She smiled wide at me. There was a tiny smudge of lipstick on her front teeth. "Well, look at you. You've grown."

Mrs. Landskroner hadn't just been my Hebrew school teacher. She'd been my mom's good friend. As much as my mom had good friends anyway.

I forced a smile. "That's usually what happens after ten years."

She set the white cardboard box of cookies on our station. "And who's this?"

"This is Seth," I said. It probably would have been a Good Fake Girlfriend thing to do to introduce him as my boyfriend, but I couldn't bring myself to do it. Word would get back to my parents, one hundred percent. Mrs. Landskroner would probably text my mom the next second she got to herself. And then what? I'd left here for a reason. I didn't want my parents knowing anything about me.

So I just kept it at that as I grabbed the box of cookies and opened it up, staring down at them as if I'd never seen anything more interesting than plain, slightly burnt sugar cookies in the vague shapes of menorahs and faces and Stars of David.

Mrs. Landskroner touched my shoulder gently. That, plus the scent of her lilac perfume, sent me tumbling fifteen years back into the past.

My skin crawled. I wanted to be anywhere other than here even though I wanted to ask her what my parents had told her about my move to Vermont, how they'd slanted it to make them look good and sad and self-sacrificing and me look bad and selfish and mean.

"Ellen!" someone called from down the line. Mrs. Landskroner's head whipped around. Her hand withdrew from my shoulder, and I had to hold myself back from rubbing the feeling of it away.

"Be right there!" she called back, and then, with a quick smile over her shoulder at me, she was striding to the aid of whatever cookie-based problem the other volunteer was having.

My underarms were suddenly all sticky. How was I supposed to make funny, original cookies when this piece of my past was lurking about?

"Abby," Seth said, his tone that of someone repeating something for the third or fourth time. "Abby, are you okay? You look a little shaken up."

I caught a quick glimpse of myself in the reflective window behind us. To my own eye, I looked the same as always: vaguely annoyed. How could he see anything more than that when I couldn't see it myself? "I'm fine."

But my hands shook as I laid the cookies out on our paper-covered table portion, and I couldn't stop my eyes from darting around me as we planned out our strategy. I volunteered to go grab supplies from the communal table mostly so that I could scope out the room: where the bathrooms were if I needed to flee a sudden approach of Mrs. Landskroner; where all the volunteers were stationed.

Seriously, what were the odds that someone from my past would be here?

Probably not that low, honestly. Even New York City, the biggest Jewish community in the United States, could feel pretty small. Everybody knew everybody. I was probably lucky it wasn't my parents or other relatives popping up here. I might have fainted into my frosting.

Maybe I wasn't as okay as I thought.

I pushed that disconcerting idea away as Seth and I got to work: we had a contest to win, after all, and I'd be damned if I'd tarnish the good name of my café and its baked goods in front of all these people (no matter that I didn't bake most of them myself). I was carefully painting a Star of David into a stained glass beauty when I paused, an idea popping into my head. "What do you think about a cookie-decorating station at the festival?"

Seth didn't pause in his decoration of a menorah cookie. As it turned out, there were only so many humorous things you could do with cookies shaped like that. While I thought turning one into an eight-legged octopus in flagrant defiance of the antisemitic stereotype of the Jew-as-octopus-with-tentacles-all-over-the-world would be both timely and funny, Seth assured me that it would not win the favor of the judges. Which was probably true. "I think it's a great idea."

I knew he wasn't lying because he hadn't hesitated before telling me my octopus cookie idea was terrible. A lightness filled my chest, one that very nearly distracted me from Mrs. Landskroner's poisonous presence. "And it shouldn't be too hard to organize. I can order plain sugar cookies from wherever, and then we just need to make sure we have stuff to decorate them with. Colored frosting, sprinkles, whatever."

"People will love it."

"Hopefully, Lorna will." She'd probably insist on making sure we had candy canes and Santa sprinkles and lots of red and green frosting. "But I'll deal with that when it comes to it."

Fortunately, whatever Mrs. Landskroner's volunteer duties were, they kept her busy for most of the event. I looked up at one point to find an older woman hovering over us, but it was just Bev. "Very nice," she said, eyeballing my stained glass Star of David in particular, which made me proud. "I never thought Seth's children would have any artistic talent, but seems there's hope for them yet."

Another thing we could deal with when it came to it.

An hour later, I was surveying our cookie spread with pride. Our Star of David, menorah, Judah Maccabee, dreidel, and wild card—a face shape that we'd turned into a scarily realistic latke featuring both applesauce and sour cream (didn't want to alienate half the judging pool)—were not just finished, they were gorgeous. "If we don't win this contest, that means it's definitely been rigged. Just like the rainbow cookie one," I said, side-eyeing Granny and Gramps's shakily outlined menorah and splotchy dreidel. I picked up ours to compare, admiring them. "We didn't even need to sabotage any—"

"Abby!" Mrs. Landskroner appeared in front of us again. The lipstick was still on her teeth. "Are you seeing your parents while you're in town? I hope you are. I know your mother misses you."

And that's when it happened. I dropped my cookies. But I didn't just drop them: I lunged fruitlessly to try to catch them before they broke, except I missed. And landed on top of our other cookies, palms first and hard.

Our beautiful winning cookies were nothing more than crumbs now. "Shit!" Absurdly, embarrassingly, tears stung the corners of my eyes.

Seth's shadow fell over me, hovering with concern. "What happened? Are you okay?"

"No, I'm not okay!" I flung my arm out over the table, narrowly missing whapping Mrs. Landskroner on the boob. "Our cookies are ruined!"

"I wasn't talking about the cookies. I was talking about you."

I looked up to find him blurry and indistinct, but you couldn't mistake the emotion in his eyes.

Pity.

Mrs. Landskroner was saying something about how it was such a shame and our cookies had been so beautiful, but I could barely hear her over the sound of my own stomach heaving. Pity. I didn't want his pity. I didn't want anyone's pity. A headache exploded behind my eyes, threatening to make me vomit.

So I finally listened to my first instincts, and fled.

18

IN MY CHILDHOOD SYNAGOGUE I HAD MY DESIGnated fleeing spots for when things got to be too much: the single-stall family restroom; the back corner of the library; the beit midrash. But this was an unfamiliar location. Which was how I wound up in what appeared to be the rabbi's office. You'd think they would've locked it, but no.

I probably should've left, but I didn't want to risk running into Mrs. Landskroner—or anybody else—in the hallway. So I crept past the piles of books on the floor and all the books on the bookshelf—the mark of a good rabbi? Way too many books—and took a seat behind the rabbi's big scrolled wood desk. He or she was clearly much taller than me, since my feet barely touched the floor from the threadbare rolling chair.

Seth would text me eventually when it was time to go, I assumed. I could lie and tell them I'd had a bathroom emergency. Vomiting or something just as gross that nobody wanted to hear details about. Until then I'd just hang out here. If it weren't so dark, and I weren't afraid to turn on a light or use my phone flashlight, I could maybe page through some books. The darkness was good for me right now, though. Better for my eyes than a bright light that would make my headache worse. It had already lessened a little bit just by virtue of getting away here into the dark.

Or away from the cause of the headache. I grimaced. Admitting that to myself was basically admitting that my headaches were caused by . . . stress? Repressed emotions? I didn't know. I didn't want to think about it too hard, because that would mean I really wasn't processing everything in the healthiest way. Not if it was giving me headaches to the point where Seth might start to wonder if I had a lurking brain tumor or something.

There was just barely enough light filtering in through the blinds behind me to survey all the photos on the rabbi's desk. A wedding photo of a bride and groom in puffy ultra-nineties fashion, their smiles tame but their eyes sparkling. Photos of plump babies and children hugging each other. Pictures of the parents and children at a water park, at a high school graduation, all beaming together with the Roman Colosseum in the background. A brightly colored, modern photo of a new baby, showing that the cycle had started all over again.

Something ugly twisted in my stomach. My fists balled in my lap. If I had a little bit less self-control, I'd have picked up one of those photos and hurled it at the wall, felt a mean sort of glee as the glass and the frame shattered all around it.

The door creaked open. I sat up very straight in the chair, rehearsing what I was going to say in my head. *Sorry,*

I know I shouldn't be here. I got turned around. I needed a minute to rest in the dark so that this migraine wouldn't get any worse. I'll go now. Sorry.

"Abby?" But it was Seth. He eased himself inside, something relaxing in his face when he saw me. "Oh, good. I found you."

I tried to take a deep breath, but it hitched in the middle. "I wasn't hiding," I lied. "I just . . . needed a minute to myself, and this was the closest place I found."

He didn't bother asking me why I hadn't tried the bathroom, which had a door that locked. Maybe Bev had been known to bust in on people. It wouldn't surprise me. "Okay." He closed the door behind him. I guessed he wasn't going to judge me, which was a relief. Not that I cared what he thought.

He stepped closer. My chest grew tight, but he didn't come close enough to touch me, which was also a relief, because I was so tight that I might collapse if he did. Instead, he took a seat in one of the cushioned chairs facing the rabbi's desk, which appeared way more comfortable than the bare-bones one I was sitting in. "So," he said. "That woman. She was one of your parents' friends?"

First instinct: I could throw one of the photos at him and make a break for it.

But of course I couldn't do that. That was assault. And if there was anything I wanted less than Mrs. Landskroner bringing news of my fake boyfriend to my parents, it was her bringing them news of my arrest for assault. And also Seth getting hurt. I didn't want that, either. "Yes," I said.

"And my old Hebrew school teacher. But after, like, middle school, she was mostly in my life as my mom's friend."

"So she was part of your bad childhood," Seth said. "Do you want to talk about it?"

My answer was immediate, automatic. "No."

The look Seth gave me in response was hard to read in the shade of the room, but it seemed a little like disappointment. Was he disappointed in *me*? The thought was disconcerting, and I was surprised to realize how much so. When had I started caring what he thought?

My head was throbbing again. It wasn't a Category 3, though, the one his presence had always caused. This was something new and different, something not on the scale. A Category 5.5. Maybe even a Category 6.

I took a deep breath. This one hitched twice. "My parents didn't beat me. It wasn't like that. I didn't go to school with bruises or have CPS called on them or anything. There are people who had it way worse."

I waited for Seth to protest, to tell me that you couldn't compare your life to anyone else's, that my experiences and feelings were all true and valid and *gag*.

But he didn't. He only sat there listening, totally still, as if I were a deer in the woods and one movement might send me running away. And, miracle of miracles, my headache receded a tiny bit, bringing me back to the painful but familiar territory of a Category 5.

The lack of response and the lessening of the pain behind my eyes made it possible for me to go on. "The thing about my parents is that I always had to be on edge around them. You know, that cliché of walking on eggshells, except

I'd describe it more as walking on glass. If you stepped the wrong way it wouldn't just break; it would cut you." I bit my lip. "Again, not literally."

He didn't say anything. Didn't judge. Just listened. My headache receded another half a point. It was kind of spooky. Like speaking these thoughts and feelings out loud was a Tylenol.

"It was like they had all these rules I didn't understand and that didn't make sense and sometimes contradicted one another. Like, sometimes they'd be really happy if I made dinner for them before they got home and would get mad if I didn't do it because they'd come home hungry, and sometimes they'd be furious I did it because I could've lit the house on fire. And they'd punish me for things, but not like the ways my friends were punished. They wouldn't tell me no dessert or ground me or take away my phone or anything; they'd give me the silent treatment. Or suddenly wouldn't drive my friend to activities they'd agreed on and blame me. Or tell people something really embarrassing about me." I cringed again at the memories. "Again, they didn't beat me or anything. There are definitely people out there who have it worse. I'm not trying to say I had it the worst."

Seth finally spoke. "Abuse isn't a competition."

He believed me. He thought it was abuse. My headache receded again, all the way down to a Category 2. The way it was shrinking like this was kind of freaking me out, to be honest. "I talked about it a little bit to my roommate in college, who tried to convince me to go to therapy." I pressed my lips together at the memory. It had felt a little bit like she'd slapped me across the face. Go purposely spill my innermost secrets to someone? Who then might go on to spill them to someone else, who could use them to hurt me? No, thank you. "I didn't, but it was the first time I realized that my childhood wasn't normal. I did a bunch of reading and figured that I didn't need therapy; I just needed to get away from my parents. So I did."

And then I'd made the mistake of coming back. *That* was why I was having all these issues with panicking. Not because there was something wrong with me, or that I'd done something wrong.

Right?

Maybe Seth had a point. Maybe I hadn't processed everything as well as I'd thought. Maybe all I'd done was turn my back and run away and pretend nothing was there. That was the opposite of how I'd dealt with the spiders who seemed to love hanging out in my shitty apartment. Running away from them meant that they were still there to freak me out and make me jump. The way to keep myself from jumping was to force myself to collect them under my designated spider mug with a sheet of paper and dump them outside (because, gross or not, I still appreciated how they ate mosquitoes).

Well. I just had to make it through three more days. Then I could go back to Vermont and never even think about coming here again.

"Therapy doesn't mean you're broken," Seth said. "It's not a bad thing. I've been to therapy, and I've found it really helpful in dealing with hard times and hard things."

I blew a deep breath out through puffed cheeks. "I didn't say that therapy means you're broken or that it's a bad thing. It's just . . . not for me." I didn't understand how Seth could be so unguarded about his vulnerabilities. He was just opening himself up to a world of pain if someone decided to use them to hurt him. Like my parents did. "I'm perfectly happy with my life and how I am."

"Are you?" His voice was mild and not especially judgy, but it *felt* judgy. Maybe because I'd already shared with him more than I'd shared with anyone in a long time. And yes, Seth, I was happy. Really happy. Happier now than I'd been in a long time.

Even if it was only pretend. Only temporary.

I shrugged, ready to instinctively snap back, then stopped myself. He'd listened to me. He'd believed me.

So I took a deep breath. "Thank you. For hearing me," I said. "We should probably go cheer your parents on." I turned, ready to go.

"You don't have to thank me," Seth said to my back. "It's what friends do."

When did that lump swell up in my throat? Hopefully, it wasn't cancer. "Okay."

As we were walking down the hallway toward the social hall, he gently touched the small of my back, as if helping to hold me up. I didn't need the help. I already had my smile fixed on my face like a shield.

But I let it stay there anyway, warm and sure against my spine. Maybe it wasn't the worst thing in the world to be given some help from a friend.

BEV AND BENJAMIN did not win the contest, which she didn't stop muttering about on the way home. "The whole thing was fixed. Of course Eva Hallac got third place. She probably paid off the judges."

"It's the ice caps all over again," I said. Benjamin and Seth both snickered. Warmth swept through me. I'd forgotten how nice it could be to be part of an inside joke. You typically needed to be close to somebody for that. The last time I'd been part of one was . . . when? With Connor?

At home we got to feast on Bev's cookies, which were very pretty but also hard and dry, which prompted more muttering from Bev about what was the point of food looking good if it didn't also taste good. I could agree with that, but what I agreed with more was the large bottle of very fine wine she broke out to soothe her hurt feelings, and the not quite as large but even better bottle of wine Benjamin brought out after from his apparently very secret liquor cabinet. Some fine scotch followed that, and I didn't know the difference between fine and not-fine scotch, but I did appreciate how it made the sharp edges of my day blur even faster than the wine did.

Getting drunk with my fake boyfriend's parents hadn't been on my list of things to do here, but hey, it could've been worse. And wasn't it the Hanukkah spirit and everything?

No. That was Passover, where we were supposed to get drunk to celebrate that we were no longer slaves in the land of Egypt. And also Purim, where we were supposed to get drunk to celebrate that the evil Haman hadn't managed to kill us all.

If getting drunk to celebrate not dying at the hands of an evil tyrant was cool on Purim, why not on Hanukkah? We were pretty much celebrating the same thing. Or so I expounded upon—at great length—to Bev and Benjamin and Seth, who all emphatically agreed and toasted me with another shot.

At some point we lit the candles and sang the blessings loudly and boisterously, Seth's arm wrapped over my shoulder, and screw it: maybe it was the alcohol, but I let myself feel warm and cozy and maybe even snuggled into him a little, had a little spark of joy from the way he looked down at me all pleased and a little surprised. Again: lighting fires while drunk was probably not on the list of Smartest Things to Do in a Small New York City Apartment, but whatever, that was Bev and Benjamin's business. All that was left to me was to watch the candles burning, their flames blurring before me, fuzzy and otherworldly.

Fast-forward another hour or two and both Bev and Benjamin were snoring on the couch, Benjamin's tie askew and Bev's bra strap on full display. Seth and I had abandoned drinking in favor of ransacking the fridge for leftovers, sticking utensils and sometimes fingers into plastic-wrapped remainders of lox, pink and firm; a bag of baby carrots; crusty cardboard containers of lo mein of which I fervently did not want to know the age. I stuffed a mouthful of noodles into my mouth before passing the fork to Seth. Our fingers brushed as he took it from me. I tried to ignore the tingles they left as he said, "It's a scientific fact that nothing soaks up alcohol like leftover carbs."

"Fact." They'd done their job: I could barely feel the buzz of alcohol in my system anymore, and the clarity in Seth's eyes said much the same. I glanced over at his parents. "Should we wake them up and make them eat?"

"Nah, they'll be fine," Seth said. "They never drink this much, though. They're going to be so embarrassed tomorrow morning."

"Assuming they remember anything."

He snorted. "True."

There was nothing else to do at this point besides get ready for bed, so that's what we did. Well, I went and got ready for bed while Seth cleaned up his parents a little—removing shoes, fixing positions so that they wouldn't wake up with pins and needles in their arms. I emerged from the bedroom in the T-shirt and sweats I'd been wearing as pajamas to find him tucking them in with the couch blanket, as tender as a parent toward their child.

That ugly thing in my chest that had made me want to throw the rabbi's picture reared up again. Jealousy. What had I done wrong where I'd never have a relationship like that with my own parents? Why did he get this and I didn't?

It made me think about kids. Not wanting kids for the sake of not wanting kids was totally cool and okay and normal. But sometimes I wondered if I wasn't sure about them because of cool, normal reasons or because I was so afraid of being like my parents.

I shook the feeling away as Seth glanced up at me, a wry

smile on his lips. It wasn't like Seth himself had gone to my parents and made them the way that they were. And I knew that their behavior wasn't my fault. I knew it.

Except maybe if they'd had a different child, a better child, one who knew all the rules and all the right ways to behave, would they still have treated her like that?

Seth was saying something, but I'd totally missed it. He walked off down the hall toward the bedroom and bathroom, leaving me here staring at Bev and Benjamin snoring away. Bev's mouth was wide open, a thin string of drool stretching down her chin. Funnily enough, I would've expected Benjamin to sleep with his mouth closed, but he matched her. Maybe they were more alike than they seemed on the surface.

Whatever. I headed down the hall after Seth, opening the bedroom door to find him in the middle of changing. Again.

I blinked, stunned into stillness for just a moment. He'd frozen, too, boxers on but shirt over his head. Black hair running down his chest, down the stomach, below the belly button . . . "Sorry, sorry," I said hastily, backing up—you'd think I'd have learned after this happened the first time—but he just finished pulling his shirt on and laughed.

"Don't worry. You didn't see much more than you would have in a bathing suit anyway."

I relaxed. He got down on the floor and started punching his makeshift bed into shape. As usual, I grimaced in sympathy at how much his back had to hurt each morning when he woke up.

But that wasn't what I'd blame for what I said next.

Maybe it was the relaxed, friendly way he'd laughed this time when I caught him without his shirt. Like we were friends now, and physical proximity wouldn't be weird, because friends were close to each other all the time.

"You can sleep in the bed tonight if you want," I blurted. Usually, I don't blurt things, and when I do I instantly regret whatever came out, but I didn't this time. It felt right. Fair.

Seth looked up at me from his knees. "Are you sure? I really don't mind being down here."

There are way better things he could be doing from his knees. I flushed warm. "Yeah. Your back must be killing you, and there's plenty of room for the two of us." When he didn't move, I hastily added, "Of course, you don't have to if you're not comfortable with it."

He rose slowly, wincing as his knees cracked. "No, I'm fine with it. We're friends. I've shared beds with my friends before."

And yet, when I'd shared beds with friends in middle school or high school, my stomach hadn't popped and fizzed this way. I scooted over to the left to lie flush against the wall, while he took the outside edge, so far over that half his body seemed to be hanging in the air. "You can come closer, you know." I swallowed, my throat dry. "I don't want you to fall off."

The thing about a full-size bed is that there isn't actually that much room. So when I pushed off the wall so that my side wasn't against the hard, cold surface and Seth wasn't hanging off the edge of the bed, there couldn't have been more than a few inches between us. We were lying on top of the blanket, but even so, I felt his heat push up against me.

I rolled on my side so I could look him in the eye. "Are you comfortable?"

He was on his side, too, his eyes level with mine, which meant his feet must have been hanging off the end of the bed. "I'm comfortable. Are you?"

There was a whole world unspoken in that question mark. So many different things I could say. And I knew that, depending on what I decided, we could go in so many different directions from here. Ones that could lead to that radiating heat coming off him touching my own.

So, naturally, I chickened out. "Not as comfortable as your parents."

Nothing like bringing up someone's parents to kill any heat in the room. Seth chuckled. "That's probably true."

He stared at me. I stared at him. God help me, but that heat sparked all over my skin once more. *Quick, bring up his parents again.*

I didn't listen to that intrusive thought. "You're different than I thought you were," I said.

"You already told me that. I told you I was just as annoying here as I was in Vermont."

"No, it's not that." I paused and held his gaze. His eyes were dark and deep in the shadow of the room; I couldn't even tell where pupil and iris began and ended. I might fall in if I wasn't careful.

When had I stopped being careful? "You're so . . . good,"

I said. "You and your family and your friends. You're so normal and good."

The corners of his lips quirked with amusement. "Thank you?"

He usually picked up on what I was trying to say without actually saying it. Because what I really meant was, *You and your family and your friends, you're so normal and good, unlike me. I'm not normal. There's something wrong with me and I don't think I can ever fix it and be normal like you and I'm sad, so sad.*

"So what you're saying is that I'm not annoying after all," Seth said.

"Ugh." The sadness dissipated. "Don't make me say it."

He scooched closer. One of his hands brushed mine, a gentle touch that sent tingles racing from the tips of my fingers to my shoulder to my heart. "I'm going to make you say it."

"I'm not going to say it." I didn't move my hand, either. Well, I did, but not away—this time I purposefully brushed it against his. His breath went ragged.

"Say it." His lips quirked. Mine did in response, and damn it, what I used to find incredibly annoying now sparked joy. But I couldn't say that. I wouldn't say it. I had to shut him up in another way.

Obviously, I had no choice but to kiss him.

It barely took any movement to close the inches-deep gap between us, but close it I did, pressing up against him like I could melt us together with the heat of our bodies. Our lips were liquid, molten rivers of want and need pulsing against each other, opening and searching and finding. A small groan escaped his throat as I tangled my fingers in his curls to bring his face closer to mine, as if it could get any closer. His stubble scratched my chin, and through the haze of *want want want* the burn heightened the heat inside me.

We were fully pressed up against each other now, one of my legs between his, one of his hands cupping my hip and pulling me in. Against my belly I could feel him stiffening, his hips pushing even harder into me with a pressure that made me gasp. More of that molten heat sparked between my legs, spreading up and down with a hot rush that made me desperate for the bare, slick feel of his skin under these clothes.

And then he pulled back, his other hand stroking my cheek, sending tingles through my chin and down my neck. His eyes were the softest I'd ever seen them: melted chocolate. I'd done that. I'd melted them. "Hey," he said, voice hoarse.

"Hey." Mine was hoarse, too. It was like how bad we wanted each other, how long we'd waited for this, had scoured the both of us from the inside out.

That spark lit again inside me, only this time it wasn't just physical. Maybe this could be real. Maybe it didn't have to end in three days—maybe I really had changed enough where Seth's positive attitude and sunny disposition would forever be no longer annoying but beautiful. Maybe I could really become a part of his family and friend group, and they'd grow to love me and I'd love them back. Maybe I could kiss him every night before I went to bed and he'd decorate my small, shitty apartment and I'd make sure he had coffee and breakfast every morning.

This close, when Seth spoke, I could feel his breath on my face. "I'm going to take that as an admission that you no longer find me annoying."

I sighed. I felt as if I might melt into the bed. Was this what it felt like to relax? If it was, maybe I'd finally take up yoga or something. "Whatever. Fine. I suppose that, at times, I do not find your presence annoying."

"Thank you," he said smugly, but then he ran his fingers through my hair, and it made me want to melt again. My lips found his, and I let myself give in. My body glittered with sparks, some that caught fire where his fingers trailed along my jaw, my collarbone, the curve of my waist.

My own fingers explored his body greedily as we kissed again and again. I wanted to drink it all in: the dip between the muscles of his back; the soft but wiry brush of hair where his shirt rode up on his stomach; the hard cup of his ass. I wanted to feel what they felt like under his clothes, too, and for a moment I went to slip my hand down there, but hesitated. This was his childhood bedroom. Probably not the place for this. So instead I curled up into him, thinking I could stay there forever.

And then, of course, he had to ruin it. Or maybe I ruined it. It was hard to tell. He pulled back to speak. "You're not bad or abnormal, you know. There's nothing wrong with you. I like you how you are."

My stomach clenched, and it was like a door closed inside me. No, it slammed. With part of me caught in it, a sharp, sudden pain.

What had I been thinking? I couldn't do this. I'd already

slipped up and told him too much about me, to the point where he thought he knew what was better for me more than I did myself. This wasn't safe. If this kept going, he'd expect to know more and more, and I'd seen the pain in Freya's eyes when she talked about how he dumped her. I'd felt the pain of being dumped when Connor had left.

And in this case it would be even worse, because I wouldn't just lose Seth. I'd lose the whole community.

I couldn't give him my key. I couldn't let him have access to all the soft, sensitive parts of me that he could hurt.

I wrenched myself away, pulling my hand out of his hair so quickly that a finger caught a curl and he winced. "This was a mistake," I said loudly, as if I could drown out the thumping of my heart.

I looked away so that I wouldn't have to see the hurt flash in his eyes. It didn't help; I could hear it in his voice. "What do you mean?"

Better to hurt now than later. "I mean that this kiss was a mistake," I said harshly, though dialed the volume down so that I wouldn't wake Bev or Benjamin. "We were drunk, and it's late, and—"

"I'm not drunk," Seth said. "And I don't think you are, either."

I pushed away the excuse. "I'm saying that this is a business arrangement and we should keep it that way. There's no point complicating things." My heart squeezed hard in my chest, but I pushed that away, too. It had no idea what it was doing.

He was quiet for a long moment. I took advantage of it to

pull back farther from Seth, pressing my back against the cold safety of the wall. Finally, he said, "If that's how you really feel."

My heart squeezed again. What had it expected? For him to put up a fuss or a grand protest or declare his great love for me? Of course not. This was all for the best. Definitely the best. "It is."

"Okay." He slowly rolled over to his other side, which brought him back to the edge of the bed, facing away from me.

It took me a very long time to fall asleep.

19

I WOKE UP FLUSHED AND SWEATY, ALL TANGLED in the blanket with my forehead cool against the wall, throbbing between my legs from a dream-slash-nightmare that had started with Seth's head between them and ended with him trying to eat me. Literally, with big gnashing teeth and everything. There was probably meaning there, but if I thought too hard about it, I'd never make it out of bed.

Seth already had, I noticed as I rolled over. I wondered when I'd tangled myself in the blanket. Had he let me steal the whole thing and gone cold himself? Or had I wrapped myself in it after he'd gotten up, surrounding myself in his smell?

I didn't know how I'd be able to face him today. I really didn't.

So I stalled while getting ready, brushing my teeth for a full two minutes and then a minute more for good measure, shaving my legs in the shower even though they'd be covered up by my weather-appropriate clothing, making the bed neatly. Which was all for naught when I made it out into the main apartment to find it totally empty. Panic fluttered in my chest for a moment. Maybe they'd all abandoned me. Maybe Seth was out telling them the truth this very second because he couldn't bear the thought of spending one more night with me after The Kiss, and they'd come home stony-faced and annoyed, ready to kick me out. Should I pack my bag? Should I–

A note fluttered on the kitchen table, held down by a granola bar.

Went for a walk. Be back soon. —Seth ♥

He wouldn't put a heart there if he was off telling his parents the truth, right?

I sat down and tried to calm myself. Coffee did not help.

Though it did help me become less jittery to the point where, when they finally did open the door and enter the apartment, I was able to fake what I thought was a pretty decent smile. "Good morning."

"Good morning," Seth said with an easy smile, touching me gently on the shoulder as he walked by. It was enough to almost make me think I'd imagined everything that went down last night. The hurt on his face. The way he curled up on the edge of the bed, trying to get as far from me as possible. "You slept late today."

"Lucky her." Benjamin looked so ravaged that I had to hold back a laugh. It was kind of like he'd spent the night fighting off a swarm of locusts.

Bev looked like she'd been battling beside him, heroically waving her frying pan at the invaders. "Did you already have your coffee, dear?"

I responded by holding up my mug, as if in a toast. "I made some extra for you."

She sighed melodramatically. "Having the Keurig this morning felt like such a step down. I don't know what I'm going to do when you leave. You'll have to come back soon."

That squeeze in my heart again, except this time it felt like she'd physically shoved her arm through my ribs and tried to pulp it herself. My fake smile turned into what I was now positive looked like a grimace. "Or you'll have to come visit us in Vermont."

Only two more nights of lying. I could do this. No matter how shitty it made me feel.

I turned to Seth, ready for a distraction from lying to these lovely people. "What's on the agenda today?"

"My friends are doing this thing if you're feeling up to it," he said. "No worries if you're not. I know last night was kind of a lot, so if you just want to lie in bed all day, no one will fault you."

I cocked my head, trying to read in his face if he wanted to ditch me and hang out with his friends. But for all he'd said about himself being an open book, I couldn't catch anything in his flat mouth and blank eyes.

Well. Guess I had to fall back on what a Good Fake Girlfriend would do. "I think I slept long enough where I outran the hangover," I said brightly. "So let's do this thing with your friends. Whatever it is."

His expression didn't change. Hopefully, that was a good thing. "It's a scavenger hunt around the city. Well, not really a scavenger hunt, because that would involve someone being clever enough to write those kitschy rhymes and dedicated enough to wake up early and go hide clues in places other people won't disturb them. So it's a photo hunt—you're given a list of things to take selfies with. First one to complete the list wins."

"Wins what?"

"Honor. Glory. Pride. A seasonal goodie bag."

Given my loss yesterday with the cookie decorating process, my blood was already beginning to pump hot with the competition. "I'm in."

"Don't worry about us," Benjamin said, collapsing with the groan of a dying car on the couch. "We'll be fine."

We weren't due to leave for a couple hours, so I excused myself to Seth's room to deal with café stuff and festival stuff. As in, literally used it as an excuse. I mean, I did have to do stuff in that regard, but mostly it was an excuse to avoid talking to my fake boyfriend and his real, loving parents.

I sat myself at the desk, facing the window that looked out onto a brick wall. It was because I wanted a view of the outside. Not because I wanted to avoid looking at the bed. The bed where we'd—

Wow. Look at that beautiful brick wall striped with pigeon shit.

My first call was to Maggie at the café. It was late enough in the morning where she should hopefully be between the early pre-work rush and the lunch rush. Sure enough, she picked up on the third ring. I wasn't sure I'd ever picked up on the third ring on the café phone in my life. "Good Coffee, how can I help you?"

"Hi, Maggie, it's Abby," I said. "Is this a good time to chat?"

"Oh, hi, Abby!" Maggie said brightly. "Everything is going well. We're selling a lot of holiday specials. People really seem to love your gingerbread lattes."

Take that, beet-faced flannel man. "That's great," I said, then hesitated. Maggie was really chill about it—no constantly telling me that I should find Jesus so that I wouldn't go to hell, for example—but she went to church every Sunday, not just on Christmas and Easter, and she said things like, *I'll pray for you* when things seemed to be going badly. "Maggie, what do you think about Hanukkah specials at the café in addition to Christmas specials? If you saw a sufganiyot latte—that's doughnut themed—or a gelt mochaccino—that's chocolate—would you try it out?"

"Of course, why not?" was her immediate response. "You might have to explain what it is, since I'm not familiar with those terms, but you did a pretty good job of it just now." She paused, as if reading my thoughts. "It's just coffee, Abby. It's not like drinking one is asking me to convert."

True. Maybe it hadn't been fair to assume that the people who patronized my coffee shop wouldn't be willing to give such things a try. Or to assume that they wouldn't be interested in checking out a Hanukkah festival.

We spent the next ten minutes or so going over business things, what we'd taken in over the course of the week and what unexpected expenses she'd had (somehow she'd run out of whipped cream *again*). It went about as well as could be expected—she hadn't magically turned the place around, but sales also hadn't plummeted in my absence—and I hung up feeling a little more at ease.

It would be so nice if I could afford to hire her again for real, and I could have some occasional time off to go places and do things and let my creativity well refill. Hopefully, the Hanukkah festival would help me do that.

It was with that attitude in mind that I called Lorna next. "Abby, hello," she greeted me. "How is everything going?"

I took a deep breath. "I'm excited about how the festival is turning out," I said. "I've seen a lot of things here that I think we can replicate. For one, I'm thinking about a cookie decorating booth."

That made me think of the lurch of panic in my chest, the flush of shame I'd felt upon seeing Mrs. Landskroner.

But then that was replaced by the vision of Seth finding me, of soothing me, of helping me get through it.

I pushed all those visions away, narrowing my eyes at the brick wall. "I think kids will love it. We can order a big batch of plain sugar cookies in various Hanukkah shapes and stock a bunch of different colored frostings in piping bags with all sorts of sprinkles and edible glitter and other fun things to decorate."

Lorna was silent on the other end for a moment. "I like the idea," she said finally. "But do we need to purchase cookies in specific Hanukkah shapes? What if we got an assortment of generic shapes like squares and circles and then people can draw menorahs or whatever they want on them." It wasn't a question; it was a statement. "I think that would give the booth a wider appeal to the maximum number of visitors."

I wondered if she could hear the grinding of my teeth on the other end of the phone. I'd spent enough of my childhood drawing random things in cutouts of Santa faces or trying to origami a paper Christmas tree into a menorah to know what she really meant. I didn't even have to say it.

But I did anyway. I tried to keep my voice as calm and level as possible. "Lorna, what it seems like to me is that you're trying to make this Hanukkah festival a Christmas festival in all but name."

She was not calm in her response. She squawked, "That's absurd!"

It was unfair that she got to raise her voice, but I didn't. Because if I did, I'd get deemed hysterical or told that I was taking things too personally. So I kept it level as I said, "Every time I've pushed for making things more specific to the holiday the festival is supposed to be celebrating, you've pushed for making them more like Christmas or more 'neutral' so that people can read Christmas into them if they want to."

"That's absurd," she said again. "Name one time I've done that."

I did better: I named all of them. I could practically hear her rolling her eyes through the phone, but, to give her the tiniest amount of credit, she didn't interrupt me until I paused to take a breath. "I'm not trying to make the Hanukkah festival less . . . Hanukkah," she said. *Less Jewish*, is what I heard. "I just want to make sure it's as appealing as possible to the largest number of people."

Less Hanukkah. *Less Jewish.* It always drove me a little crazy that, in media designed to portray Jews—especially

Jewish women—as beautiful or appealing, it always seems like non-Jews are cast to represent us. But when the character is there for comic relief or to embody the more unpleasant Jewish stereotypes? Well. Then we get cast. Because it's all about making sure each piece of media is "as appealing as possible to the largest number of people." Meaning, a real-life Jewish woman wouldn't be appealing enough to be the main character of *The Marvelous Mrs. Maisel* or the movie about Ruth Bader Ginsburg's life, even though she, in real life, was as Jewish as we come.

So my hackles raised as I said, "I don't think that maximizing the Hanukkah means that it won't appeal to people. Maggie, you know Maggie, who took over at my café this week while I'm scouting here in New York, she's not Jewish, but she was excited about the idea of new Hanukkah coffee specials. I think that people are eager to try new things, not just rehash the same old. If they want to go to a Christmas festival, there are plenty of Christmas festivals in the area for them to check out. They're coming to a Hanukkah festival because they want Hanukkah."

Lorna was silent on the other end. My hopes rose a bit, thinking maybe I'd finally gotten through to her, only to hear her bark, "No, the T-shirts go over there!"

Hope faded. She hadn't even been listening. I'd been baring my guts and she hadn't even been *listening*. "Hello?"

"Oh, Abby, are you still there?" She sounded disinterested. "I'm sorry, I'm in the middle of a store redesign. Well, a mini redesign. I'm trying to move all the most in-demand products to the back so that people are forced to go past everything else to find them. You know how it is."

I knew how it was to want to scream. She continued, "Anyway, I have to go. Can we pick this up later? Great. Bye." She hung up before I could say anything back.

I let out a pterodactyl screech and threw my phone at the wall.

No, I didn't. But I wanted to.

Just then, a knock came at the door. Cue a frantic moment where I thought maybe my mind had betrayed me and I had indeed gone nuclear on my phone, only to have Seth poke his head in with a politely quizzical expression. "Hey, we have to leave soon if we're going to make it on time," he said. "My mom made some sandwiches for us to eat quickly before we leave. You ready?"

I could barely bring myself to look at him. I turned, focusing on that trusty brick wall. "Yeah."

After lunch and a largely silent subway ride, we were climbing out at Lincoln Center to meet up with the friend group. The Lincoln Center Christmas tree rose up huge and imposing over the sparkling fountain, glittering white all over. I could only imagine how it would look at night, showcased against the lit-up arches of the massive building, maybe twinkling in tune with the music from inside.

Somehow the friend group had swelled even more since visiting Kylie's booth at the holiday festival, maybe additional people having come home for the holidays. I didn't even bother introducing myself this time. What did it matter, when I'd definitely never be seeing any of them again? But it wasn't like I wanted to stick close to Seth's side right now, either.

I greeted Dan and Kylie, then Freya. She gave me what seemed to be a genuinely happy smile.

As I smiled back at her, Dan trumpeted for everyone to be quiet. "Okay, everybody pair up and we'll hand out the lists!" he shouted. "The first pair to upload all your pics to the shared album wins. I have a great prize for the winners, believe me."

I considered asking Freya or Kylie or literally anyone else to pair up with me, but I knew that would be considered weird—why would I be pairing up with someone other than my boyfriend? Seth appeared just as enthusiastic to be paired with me, or so attested the grim line of his mouth. It seemed I'd finally done it: brought some rain clouds to that sunny attitude.

Somehow it didn't make me feel good.

It took me a second to hear Dan again over the sound of the crowd. "Okay, it looks like we have too many people for it to be pairs, actually," he said. "Let's try groups of three."

Maybe Seth and I would be forced to split up and be thirds for two other pairs. If we could only stall long enough where—

"Hey, you guys need a third?" Kylie asked, appearing between me and Seth. *Damn it.*

Without context or on a dating app, this would be a very different conversation. "Sure," Seth said before I could respond. "Why not?"

With everybody paired—well, tripled—up, Dan began his countdown up front. "Everything on this list can be found within walking distance, between here and Union

Square. That's where we'll meet when we're done," he called. "Okay, three, two, one, here we go!"

I kind of expected everybody to start running for it, but that wouldn't have made any sense, since we didn't know what we were running for. Also, it might have started a mass panic. Kylie and I huddled around Seth's phone, where he'd pulled up the list. It had ten items, all festive. "A skeleton dressed up like Santa, a giant gingerbread man," I read. "Oh, 'something Hanukkah.' Way to be inclusive, Dan."

Seth rolled his eyes. "Any ideas on where we should start?"

"Well, the guy dressed as a nutcracker is definitely going to be in Times Square, right?" Kylie asked. I had no idea. Seth shrugged. "Where else do people dress up in costumes? The Broadway snow globes will be there, too. I've seen them before. And the ice-skating rink is in Bryant Park. The holiday window display is around Saks and Macy's. So we have a general route kind of sketched out. Hopefully, the other stuff will be on the way. Like, I have no idea where we're going to find the holiday train."

I was happy enough to let them take control and navigate, so I just nodded along. And Seth clearly didn't feel like exercising his new conflict muscles without a real reason. So we let Kylie lead us east toward the big department stores, where there would surely be a "window display featuring actual diamond snowflakes."

With Kylie up ahead, Seth drew close to me. "How are you doing?"

"I'm fine," I said automatically, because that's what I

always said when asked the question, fine or not. My mouth opened, ready to ask him the same question, but it closed before I could push the words out. I kind of didn't want to know the answer.

Instead, I said, "Things aren't going to be weird or anything now, right?"

"Weird? Why would they be weird?" He sounded almost offended, which made me tense. "We're friends, Abby. It won't be weird."

The grin rising in his voice offended me more than the offense had. Had our kiss really meant so little to him?

That was a good thing, I reminded myself. It would be nice if we could stay friends after this charade ended. Friends could be casual, someone you met for a drink every so often or chatted with over your morning coffee. It wasn't like you had to share all of your secrets with all of your friends.

He was still staring at me, his grin now beginning to falter at my silence. I'd waited too long to respond. "Good," I said, or squeaked, rather, which was unfortunate. "I'm glad we can still be friends."

"Of course," he said, and then Kylie turned around.

"You guys are so *slow*. Seth, it's like you're not even a New Yorker anymore."

"We walk slowly in Vermont," he said, hustling to catch up to her. "We need to save our energy to run from bears."

As we kept walking, I learned more about Kylie. In addition to her crafty ornament-making side business, her main job was in human resources at a big tech company. "Working there is great," she said. "I barely have to buy food because I just steal everything from the snack fridge. And I exclusively sleep in company gear. The free T-shirts they have lying around for every single event they put on are super-soft."

Plus her health insurance was probably really good. And I bet she had dental insurance. Sometimes I had dreams about being able to go in for a teeth cleaning.

As it turned out, work was how she'd joined the friend group in the first place. She and Seth had been coworkers at a past tech company in Boston, when they were both in-office, and had discovered a mutual love of the local Japanese grocery store before they were both transferred to the New York location. "We'd grab lunch from there every day and made a habit of checking out the fun new snacks," she said. "They had all the stuff my grandparents would bring me from Japan when they visited. Ooh, there's a giant candy cane. Do you guys want to be in the pic?"

"What are the rules again?"

"At least two of us have to be in the picture," Kylie said. "Or it can be a selfie with all three of us, but I think that'll be hard in this case. None of our stubby arms will be able to get in that whole candy cane."

"I'll get the two of you," I said hastily. "I don't love being in pictures. Here, give me your phone."

Kylie handed it over but shook her head. "Don't even try to get out of being in all of them. You have to be in some. We'll have a rotation."

The absolute last thing I wanted to do was stand cheek to cheek with Seth, pretending to smile for the camera, but at least it would be quick. "Okay. But you guys go first."

Seth and Kylie stepped closer to the giant candy cane,

which stood erect and proud before one of the fancy Madison Ave office buildings. They posed before it, hands on hips and huge smiles on their faces. I snapped the pic feeling very, very alone.

As we continued on our way toward the window displays, the frosty air biting our noses and Christmas music jingling out the open doors of designer stores, we grabbed a picture of me and Kylie in front of a train of light-up reindeer decorating the facade of an apartment building. "I have no idea who could live in Midtown like this," I said, shaking my head as Kylie deposited the picture in the shared album. "Surrounded at all times by tourists and a never-ending stream of traffic? My worst nightmare."

"I don't know, if I could afford it, I think the hustle and bustle might be nice," said Kylie. "Just think of the energy."

"Says the woman who lives in the hustle and bustle of Williamsburg," Seth said. "I'm never happier to have moved to Vermont than when I'm back in Midtown. Times Square especially."

"All the people and the lights give me hives," I said. Just a confirmation that I'd also done the right thing in moving to Vermont. You really needed a certain kind of personality to live in the middle of nowhere like we did, a true love of quiet and trees and solitude, a tolerance for nosy neighbors and long drives for essentials and losing your power on days when a bad storm hits.

The streets grew busier as we neared the stores that hosted holiday window displays, slow-walking tourists crowding the sidewalk and gawking at the tall buildings high above them. I sidestepped them, simmering with impatience. One thing that hadn't changed since my move: fast walking.

I did pause and tilt my head back when we neared Saks Fifth Avenue, though. The legendary and legendarily expensive department store was known for its holiday light shows, where its facade was covered in a cascade of multicolored lights that flashed in shapes and patterns along with a Christmasy song like "Carol of the Bells." The actual show wouldn't start up until sunset, but the lights themselves were still beautiful. This year they were shaped like a giant castle.

Seth stepped up next to me. "As much as I like Vermont, I could go for living in a castle like that."

"It looks like Elsa's ice castle from *Frozen*," I said. "You'd probably be very cold."

"Guys, over here!" Kylie called, her fuzzy red glove waving high in the air. "This one's perfect."

It was hard to tell with our untrained eyes and inability to try to smash the diamonds whether they were real, but it was close enough. The skinny female mannequins in their white fur coats and muffs and neon-colored blocky boots were staring up at the ceiling of their window, from which diamond rings and earrings and bracelets glittered on the ends of nearly translucent strings. I said, "Great. How about you two pose?"

"No way," said Kylie. "It's your and Seth's turn. Come on, get in there."

We were friends, I told myself. And we weren't making things weird.

But I still noticed the solid six inches of space left between the two of us as we smiled rictus grins in front of that window.

"Come on, you guys," Kylie said. She bobbed to be seen between the members of a passing cluster of people in matching bright green sweatshirts. "You stand that far apart and you can't even see the diamonds. Act like you like each other." She grinned like she was joking, because she was.

It didn't feel like a joke to me, though. Still, grudgingly, I stepped closer, the arm of my wool coat pressing against Seth's. He took it upon himself to duck his head toward mine, and the end of a curl brushed my cheek. I closed my eyes for a second, taking a deep breath and fighting the urge to tangle my fingers in his hair again.

"Okay, got it," Kylie called. Seth sprang away from me like I'd stung him. I tried not to be offended by that.

As we strolled downtown, we grabbed pictures of me and Kylie with a guy dressed as a nutcracker and Seth and Kylie in front of the Bryant Park skating rink. "That's five," Seth said, scanning through the shared album as he uploaded the last one. "Looks like we're tied for first. Doing great, guys." He raised his eyebrows hopefully. "Maybe great enough for an ice-skating break?"

Wearing uncomfortable knives on my feet while wobbling over an icy surface among people just as clueless about it as I was? No thanks.

Kylie was not as vehemently opposed. "Aw, that would be so cute. You guys hanging on to each other's arms and everything."

I glanced sidelong at Seth. "Actually, the last time we went ice skating together up in Vermont, I nearly decapitated him with my skate."

Kylie's eyebrows jumped to her hairline. "You what?"

"It's not as gory as it sounds," Seth said. "It didn't even sever an artery."

"Imagine how gross that would have been. Blood frozen all over the ice."

"Fortunately, it only nicked me a little when she tripped head over heels and I lunged in to rescue her from breaking her neck," Seth said innocently.

"I don't know," I said. "I feel like my blade wouldn't have even come close to your head if you hadn't also fallen head over heels." We shared a small smile, and for a moment it was like we were back meeting his parents, wildly fabricating stories for the amusement of the crowd.

Except that, since then, we had real stories to tell people about. Real inside jokes we had together. So it was still fun, but . . . I don't know, it felt a little emptier.

"Okay, so what I'm gathering is that we shouldn't go ice-skating or risk losing a limb," Kylie said.

Well, at least I'd won. "Or a head," I told her. "Can't really get a prosthetic head."

The next stop was Times Square for one of the Broadway snow globes. Every year, many of the shows currently playing on Broadway would craft giant snow globes for the public showcasing a key scene; some even had music playing along with them. We passed Elphaba flying up into the snow on her broomstick, Rafiki holding Baby Simba out over a snowy gorge (not super accurate for the Kenyan savanna, I thought), Aladdin and Jasmine flying on their magic carpet.

Kylie stopped short in front of one I wasn't familiar with. "Ooh, since it's your turn and you're a couple, you've got to do this one. It'll be perfect."

The show title in red and black spelled out *Hadestown*, and inside the globe, a young couple clutched at each other with angsty expressions like they were about to be torn apart. Well, I could definitely share the angst. "Whatever," I said, eager to get this over with. Seth stepped up next to me and smiled.

But Kylie didn't hold up her phone. "Aw, come on, you guys. Have a little fun."

"Instructing someone to have fun isn't usually how fun works," I said.

She rolled her eyes. "You know what I mean. Lean into it a little! Come on, pose like them. It'll be so cute. And if we end up tying later on, maybe it'll win us some bonus points."

I took another look at the couple in the snow globe. The girl stood facing me, her face tilting up; the guy—her boyfriend?—stood behind her, clutching her close, his mouth a hair's breadth away from her forehead. Their arms twined together as if they were holding tight against some tremendous force.

If Seth and I were really dating, this wouldn't even be a big deal. So that's how I had to act. I swallowed hard. "Of course. No problem." I tilted my head up at Seth in imitation of the girl in the globe. "Ready?"

His Adam's apple bobbed. "Are you sure?"

"You guys, come on!" Kylie sounded impatient, but I couldn't turn to look at her, because I couldn't tear my eyes from Seth. He opened his mouth, then closed it.

Maybe he wasn't as chill as he was pretending to be.

But he didn't argue. He stepped up behind me, his front against my back. I turned my cheek against the soft wool of his coat, looking up toward his chin, at the scrape of black stubble there, and lifted my arms like I was doing ballet. One tender forearm found its way against his cheek, the other around the back of his head. He wrapped his own arms around them, his fingers tangling with mine.

He looked down at me like if I said the wrong thing, every part of him would unravel. It was lucky we weren't supposed to smile, because I didn't think I could.

"Guys? Guys?" It took me maybe one minute and maybe an hour to realize that Kylie was trying to get our attention. "You did great. We're done."

I cleared my throat. "You can let me go now," I whispered.

He wrinkled his brow at me, looking just as tortured as the guy inside the globe, and I imagined him saying, *I never want to let you go.*

But that was ridiculous. We were just friends, and better for it. His brow cleared and he pulled his arms from mine, letting them fall to his sides. I cleared my throat. "Okay," I said. My voice came out a little rusty. "Where to next?"

20

BY THE TIME WE'D WOUND OUR WAY DOWN TO Union Square and snapped a picture of us with the giant menorah—our "something Hanukkah" that made us feel so included—the sun was beginning to set. We'd stopped briefly for some candied nuts and hot chocolate from a street vendor for a snack, and the sugar was now coursing through my body.

"I can't believe we missed the Santa skeleton," I said, bouncing a little on my toes. We were one of the last groups there, so it wasn't like we'd sped through the city and that was why we hadn't found it. "Maybe we should go back out."

"We are not going back out to search," Seth said, scrolling through his phone. Since Times Square, he'd done an impressive job of not looking me in the eye even once. Even when the two of us had to stand next to each other and fake happiness in front of a gingerbread house display. "Nine out of ten is respectable. Even if we don't win, we—"

"Only one of the other groups found the Santa skeleton

so far, and they didn't get the nutcracker," Kylie reported, also scrolling through her phone. "So we're still in the running."

That was enough to keep my heels on the ground until Dan showed up with his Santa hat on, mug of grog in his hand, the swagger in his step making me confident that mug wasn't his first. "Salutations and congratulations to Mike, Lizzy, and Freya!" he announced. "You've won this Christmas grab bag of fun!"

My shoulders sagged as the winning trio cheered and claimed their grab bag of fun, which seemed to mostly consist of candy. It wasn't even like I had a huge sweet tooth, but I wanted the winning title. "Well. I guess we tried. Even if we lost."

"We did more than try. We did great," Seth said, eyes trained somewhere over my shoulder even as he spoke directly to me. "We got to see so much cool stuff that we wouldn't normally have seen."

True, we probably otherwise wouldn't have checked out the nutcracker display. I'd most likely have nightmares about them tonight, an army of them marching forward on their stiff legs to crack my toes between their creepy wooden jaws.

Besides, how could I not think about this in terms of winning and losing? It was a competition. One team winning meant another team lost. Like in life. People talked a big game about things being fair and a rising tide lifting all boats and whatever, but most things were really just winner-take-all.

"Candy?" Freya popped up with a handful, her rosy cheeks bunched high in a smile.

I really didn't need any more sugar, but this candy probably tasted like winning. "Sure."

I popped the Skittles into my mouth and chewed. Through them, I asked her, "Where did you guys find the Santa skeleton?"

"That was a tough one, wasn't it?" Freya said brightly. She offered some candy to Seth, but he waved it away, eyes trained on his phone. It was buzzing. He stepped away and held it to his ear. "It was kind of hidden down this side street on this goth bar with bats hanging from the . . ."

As she kept telling me about the location, I trained my ears on Seth. "Hi, Mom," he'd answered. "Yeah, we're just finishing up. What . . ." And then he was quiet for long pauses, punctuated occasionally with yeses or nos, I don't knows and I don't think sos. What was Bev telling him?

Maybe she'd found out. About us. I had no idea how she'd done so, but my mind concocted a scenario where she found Seth's diary—because of course someone like Seth would keep a diary, and he probably wouldn't bother locking it—and read with increasing horror about our whole plan. She was telling him now that I was a dirty rotten liar and not to even bother bringing me home because if she saw my face again she was going to smash a freshly baked pie in it and she didn't want to waste a perfectly good pie on me and—

"Abby?" He'd hung up. He was finally looking me in the eye, but from his worried expression, I assumed the worst.

Well, it wasn't like I'd brought that much stuff with me. Surely, he could pack it up himself and bring it down to the—

He was talking. I was missing it. ". . . almost forgot about the Eighth Night Ball," he was saying. I blinked. Right. The big romantic spectacle on the final night of Hanukkah Bev had already bought us tickets to. "She called up her favorite local boutique and got you in just in time for a fitting in an hour, but the hangover hit her hard and she doesn't think she can go with you."

Well. I hadn't expected that. "Okay. I don't mind going by myself."

Or. My eyes settled on Freya. We were friends, right? Or becoming friends? Spending time together one-on-one was how you became better friends. Except maybe she wasn't interested in becoming friends, and she'd make a face and send my heart plummeting.

Seth was saying, "I'll go with you if you want," but he sounded a little like he was volunteering to get his teeth cleaned by a butcher who was considering becoming a dentist.

After tomorrow I'd have no reason to see Freya again, right? So any embarrassment from her saying no only had to last as long as tomorrow. Maybe I could take a tiny leap of faith. Give friendship a shot.

"Hey, Freya," I said. I swallowed my Skittles in a hard, sticky lump. "Any chance you're free after this? And that you like shopping? I'm going to get a gown for the Eighth Night Ball, and I have no idea what I'm doing."

"I *love* shopping." That made one of us. She beamed at me. "Of course. Where are we going?"

Her face lit up even more when I shared the name of the designer, who I didn't recognize. "Ooh, that's some fancy stuff. I have a few things of hers, but they were lucky thrift store finds."

"Oh, wow. I didn't realize." Nervousness fluttered in my stomach. Maybe if I were Seth's real girlfriend I wouldn't mind Bev buying me something fancy and expensive, but being a fake girlfriend? This was basically fraud.

But I couldn't refuse. I already knew Bev well enough to understand that she'd take it as a personal insult. And maybe they'd have a clearance rack I could choose something from. Or I could leave the tags on so Bev could return it once I was gone.

I jumped when Seth touched me gently on the shoulder. "I see you panicking," he murmured. "Don't. My parents can easily afford it, and it makes my mom happy to do things like this for people."

That didn't help. "'Don't panic.' Wow. I didn't think of that," I said. "What great advice. The panic is gone."

If Seth was someone who rolled his eyes, he'd roll his eyes at me. Instead, he just smiled patiently. "She'll cry when she sees you in the dress. Out of happiness. Don't take that away from her."

Whatever. I still felt like I was defrauding an old couple of their money. "What time is the appointment?"

When he told me, my eyes widened. "Dude, that's like now."

"Don't worry," Freya said, linking her arm through mine. "I can get us there on time."

And she did, though it involved throwing ourselves into traffic to beat someone else to a cab, then telling the cab-driver Freya would give him an extra-large tip if he'd stomp on the gas whenever we hit a yellow light. By the time we spilled out of the cab, I was drenched in stress-sweat and my hands were shaking. The perfect combination for trying on fancy dresses.

Freya, on the other hand, continued to look as if she'd never sweated in her life. "Ooh, so exciting," she said, pausing outside the small glass-front boutique to take a picture. Blank-faced mannequins posed in sequins and stoles in the window. "So what's this ball you're going to?"

We entered into a puff of warm air fragrant with the smell of money. When I told the saleswoman who bustled over that I had an appointment in back, she nodded and led me past the clothes on display, which were mostly draped over mannequins like in the window. Did expensive boutiques like this not have racks? Was everything one of a kind?

The thought made me a little queasy, but that was helped by the sparkling water the saleswoman handed us in the back. It reminded me a little bit of the few episodes of *Say Yes to the Dress* I'd seen, only smaller and less white: curtained changing rooms; round poufs for people to sit on; flattering lighting pouring down over multi-angled mirrors. Freya and I shrugged our coats off to set them on a pouf, but before we could, somebody appeared to whisk them away. Hopefully, to hang in a closet and not to steal.

The saleswoman appeared before me again to shake my hand, a wide smile stretching her bright red lips. "I'm Stephanie, and I'll be helping you out today. You must be Abby?"

"I am," I said. Stephanie's handshake threatened to crush my fingers. "And this is Freya. My . . ." I wasn't sure exactly what to call her. She wasn't quite a friend yet, was she? But saying "my fake boyfriend's ex-girlfriend" would probably be weird.

Freya jumped in. "I'm Abby's friend." True or not, the sentence sent a warm glow spreading through me. First Seth, now Freya. Just look at me, making friends everywhere. If only Connor could see this "frigid bitch" now.

"Great," Stephanie said. She turned back to me without shaking Freya's hand. "So you're looking for a dress for a ball tomorrow night, correct? So you won't have time to wait for alterations."

"Correct."

"So if this is a ball, I assume you'll want something formal and elegant. Floor-length?"

"Maybe," I said, having no idea what went into dressing for a ball outside of a Disney movie.

"Any specific design choices or shapes you're looking for? Colors? Special details or materials?" She cast her eyes down my outfit, which consisted of mom jeans and a black sweater. I did not appreciate the judgment curling the edges of those red, red lips. "Sleeves or sleeveless? Neckline?"

I had no idea what to say to any of that. Maybe this was a huge mistake. I needed Bev here to steer me, to tell me what to do. She would love that. "I don't know," I said, taking a step back. "I don't dress up very much."

An awkward silence filled the room. Stephanie surveyed my body again. "Probably an A-line or a ball gown, I'm thinking," she said. "Does that sound okay? Of course, I'll pull a few other options, too."

I didn't even know what those words meant as far as

dresses went. I looked to Freya for help. She gave me a nod, so I gave Stephanie a nod back. Freya said, as if extending a hand in aid, "Abby, I've mostly seen you wear black? Do you want a black dress?"

"Er," I said. "I don't know. Maybe?"

"I'm guessing no pastels and nothing too pale. Anything too pale will wash you out anyway," Stephanie said. "I'll pull blacks and darker, more vibrant colors. What are you planning on doing with makeup?"

"Uh . . ."

"I think that's a good start," Stephanie chirped. "Let me go fetch some options. What size?"

When she went off into the front of the store, I sank onto the pouf with a sigh. The pouf echoed me. "I have no idea what I'm shopping for. I didn't even know this brand," I said. "You should be the one getting a fancy dress for a fancy ball, not me."

Freya let out a dry laugh. "Trust me, if it were me, Bev would not be paying for it." She took a seat beside me, on the very edge of the pouf, her tensed legs holding her up. "I don't know if this ball is new or if I was just not invited when we were dating." She relaxed, giving me a wry smile. "But it's fine. I like the dressing up part, not so much the dancing part. I have two left feet."

"Oh my god, me too," I said. "I think the last time I danced was at my bat mitzvah, and even that was mostly, like, the Electric Slide and the Chicken Dance. I hope I don't waltz into the menorah and light the hotel on fire."

"That would make for a memorable night, at least," Freya said.

I'd already had a memorable night. The kiss.

As if she could read my mind, Freya's eyes widened. "You guys kissed, didn't you?"

I wanted to deny it. But when I tried to shake my head, it wouldn't move. So I gave in. "Maybe. But it didn't mean anything."

"Oh, I doubt that," Freya said. "Seth isn't the kind of person who kisses people casually. If he kissed you, it meant something."

No way. He'd specifically told me it hadn't.

Fortunately, Stephanie showed up towing a silver rack of dresses before we could dissect this any further. "Wow, they all look beautiful," I said without looking at any of them.

Stephanie handed over a slinky red thing that looked like it would come about to my knee. "Why don't we start with this one?" When I went into the dressing room she made to follow me, but Freya stepped in front of her.

"I can do it."

I managed to wiggle into the dress, pull it up inch by inch—Freya assured me it was supposed to fit this way—and then suck in my stomach for her to zip it up.

I knew as soon as we got this dress on that it wouldn't be for me, but after all this effort, I would've felt bad not letting Freya open the curtain and parade me in front of the mirror. Still, Stephanie couldn't miss my wrinkled nose at the sight. "Okay, Abby, you look great, but if you don't *feel* great in it, maybe nothing else this tight," she said. "Let's try an A-line next."

The A-line, a tight gathered black top with a long, chiffony white skirt shaped like an A, definitely felt better in shape even if I didn't love the design. White, for me? No thanks.

Freya went to grab a dress from the middle of the rack. As soon as I saw the material, I shook my head. "I thought we said nothing glittery."

"I just have a feeling about this one," she said, thrusting it at me. Behind her, Stephanie had her lips pursed with disapproval, but she was the one who'd pulled it in the first place. "Let's try it. For me."

Given that she was here taking charge and helping me through this, and without her I'd be stuck with Stephanie and her pursed lips, I couldn't argue with that. So I took the dress into the changing room, shut the curtain, and let her clothe me like a doll.

"I'm just not a glitter person," I was telling her as she led me back out into the main space, but the words stopped short when she shoved me in front of the mirrors and there I was, glittering at angle after angle.

I almost didn't recognize myself. The dress was another simple A-line in shape, gathered at the bust and flowing past my waist to the floor. Its sleeves were loops that circled around my upper arms, baring my shoulders so that my hair could tumble over them or be tied up high to showcase the elegant flow of my throat into my clavicle, which I'd only just now realized was elegant. The dress was black—my favorite color—and covered with tiny chips of what must have been rhinestones, small and subtle and scattered enough where I didn't glow like a disco ball under the lights but instead shimmered whenever I moved.

I looked like a princess of the night sky. I couldn't help but imagine Seth's face when he saw me in it: he'd go slack-jawed, overcome by my magnificence just like a boyfriend in a classic teen movie who barely recognized the nerdy girl after she took off her glasses and straightened her hair.

No, I told myself. Stop it.

"This is the one, I think," Freya was telling Stephanie. I couldn't argue with her, not even when Stephanie told us the price and that Bev had given her her card number to put it on her tab. I'd keep the tags on and return it once the ball was over, I told myself. Bev wouldn't be out anything. What would be the harm?

When I took it off and handed it over to Stephanie to place delicately into a garment bag, it felt a little like I'd lost something. Like I'd seen the ultimate expression of who I could be, and it wasn't me in this sweater and jeans. Like it was a glimpse of who I could have been, for real, if I hadn't grown up the way I did, with the parents I had, if I didn't feel the need to close myself off from everyone and everything.

Would it be weird to walk around in a gown all the time?

"Are you okay?" Freya asked, holding out a tissue to me. I didn't take it; I wasn't crying or anything. Except then I realized that my vision was blurry, so it was either that or a stroke.

I drew in a deep breath. I couldn't take the tissue; that would show weakness.

Except what the hell, Abby? Maybe it was less weak to acknowledge what was happening than to deny it. I took the tissue and swiped at my eyes. The blurry vision cleared up, which was a relief. "Thanks."

"What's on your mind?" Freya asked. It was still just the two of us back here; Stephanie was up front wrapping the dress and processing payment and whatever else.

I hesitated. "Nothing." Then hesitated again. I'd already basically been naked in front of her. She'd called herself a friend. Maybe I could stand to let a little bit of myself out. "I was just thinking about my family."

"Oh, wishing they could be here to see it?" she said sympathetically. "I had a similar thing happen with my prom dress. My mom had to work the night I went shopping, and I was sad she couldn't be there with me."

You know what? It was easier to let her think that than go into the truth. Besides, this night was going so well. I really felt like we were bonding. "Yeah, that's totally it. I haven't seen them in a while."

"But Seth said they lived in the area," Freya said.

"Yeah, it's complicated," I said. I hesitated. Should I go on?

Not with the full truth, definitely. Opening up to Seth had actually made me feel a bit better—or had, at least, made my headache fade—but I trusted him, even though I hadn't known him much longer at this point than I'd known Freya. I thought I might be able to trust Freya someday if this friendship kept developing, but we weren't there yet. "It's been a while since I've seen them," I said again, because that was one hundred percent true. "It's sad. I hadn't thought it bothered me this much, but staying with Seth and his family, it really makes me miss them." That was also one hundred percent true. Even if, when I said I missed them, it was less missing those specific people and who they were than it was missing the idea of the parents I could have had.

Again, the thought struck me: what had I done to deserve the parents I got?

I shook the thought away, imagining Seth's voice in my head. *None of it is your fault.*

"I'm sorry," Freya said. "I don't live in the same place as my parents anymore, but we FaceTime a lot. It's hard to be far away from them. Are you going to see yours while you're here at all?"

Again, I hesitated, that old feeling of irritation bubbling up. How was it any of her business? It was a normal question, though, one I wasn't surprised she'd think given what I'd told her. I went with another half lie. "Probably not. Things have just been so busy, I'm not sure if I'll get the chance. It's too bad."

And it would be too bad, if I had normal parents, a normal relationship with them, a normal family. Like everybody else seemed to.

Freya smiled mysteriously. "Maybe things will work out. Maybe life will surprise you."

Something in my chest twisted hard. Maybe. Maybe one day my parents would turn up at my door and tell me they'd been reflecting on my childhood and that they'd finally realized how wrong they were, and that they wanted to give me their deepest apologies. Maybe life would surprise me and they'd tell me they knew it might take a while for me to trust them, but they wanted to take that time to build a new relationship with me. Maybe I'd finally get to understand what it was like to be part of a real family.

It had been too long since I'd spoken. I cleared my throat. "That would be the most amazing thing."

Ugh. I nearly cringed at myself. When had I turned into someone for whom the maybes were positive? This was all Seth's influence. Normal me would've shut this down right away. I didn't know why I'd already said so much.

Luckily, before Freya could ask any more questions or I could dig myself into an even more ill-advised, deeper hole, Stephanie popped back up. "Thanks so much for shopping with us," she said, handing over the garment bag and a receipt. I carefully did not look at it in fear of having a heart attack that would lead to dropping the dress and getting it dirty. "Hope to see you again!"

She would never see me again. A thought that made me kind of sad, I realized, as Freya and I waved goodbye outside the store and hopped into separate cabs.

Something that also made me sad: even though the sun had already set, Bev, Benjamin, and Seth had waited for me to light the candles. Or maybe sad wasn't the right word. Maybe I was touched, and my body didn't know the difference. All I knew was that my heart squeezed when I entered the apartment and saw them all standing there around the menorah, the candles already inserted and ready to drip wax on the tinfoil beneath.

"Aw, you guys didn't have to wait for me," I said. It was clear who'd selected the candles today by their neat alternating blue and white pattern: Benjamin. Bev's selections were typically more colorful; Seth's a random riot of the oranges and purples that nobody else wanted to include in their setup.

"Of course we waited for you," Bev said, giving me a funny look, as if she hadn't even considered otherwise. "How was dress shopping?"

I held up the garment bag in response. Her face split in a smile. "Oh, I can't wait to see it. I'm sure it's beautiful. I only wish I could've gone, but . . ." She shook her head. "My stomach had other ideas."

"I wish you could've gone, too," I said hastily, before she could fill me in on exactly what other ideas her stomach had. "But I had fun with Freya."

Bev's smile flickered. "You went with Freya? Freya, as in . . ." Her eyes flitted to her son, apparently unable to voice Freya's relationship to him.

"Yup," I said. "Freya and I are friends. I like her a lot."

Seth's eyes were now darting from the menorah to the door, as if judging how long it would take him to make a break for it. I stepped in front of him so that he couldn't go anywhere.

"I see," Bev said. "Well, I'm glad you had a good time. Shall we light the candles?"

Since tomorrow night Seth and I would be at the ball, this was our last night lighting them together. As a family. Well, kind of. Whether we counted as a family or not, I still savored each catch of the flame, each note of our voices raised in song, every flickering reflection of the candles in the glass of the window, the glow of our faces above them.

21

THE MORNING OF THE BALL DAWNED BRIGHT AND clear, which was a relief. No matter what I did with my hair, any rain or snow would've introduced an element of unpredictability. And frizz. Always frizz.

Though it seemed Bev didn't want to leave anything unpredictable. "I made us a hair appointment at my salon for blowouts, if you're up for it. It's at three thirty."

My mouth opened, ready to instinctively agree with her, but what came out was, "I was thinking I might actually wear it curly. Could they help me with that?"

She smiled. "I'm sure they could."

Even though I'd slept in well past Seth, whose floor nest had been cleaned up and folded neatly by the time I cracked my eyes, three thirty was still an interminable number of hours away. Hours I had to fill. Later on, I'd be spending more than enough time in close and awkward proximity to my fake boyfriend who I'd real kissed—time for an excuse. "I think I'm going to go for a run," I said, craning my neck to see past her into the kitchen, where I assumed Seth was.

"That's wonderful, dear. I've never been much of a

runner myself," she said. As if she'd finally caught on to the awkward neck-craning, she added, "Seth and Benjamin went out to play pickleball. They had to go early to snag a court."

My shoulders sagged a little with relief, knowing I wouldn't have to see him first thing, then felt bad for it, because he was my friend. Awkwardness or not, I shouldn't be relieved about not seeing him.

Then it occurred to me that his absence meant I didn't necessarily have to be absent. Though I'd already told Bev I was going running. Going back on that now would probably be weird. "I've never played pickleball."

"Oh, Benjamin loves it," Bev said. "He used to play tennis, but when he realized there was a sport like tennis without all the running he was delighted. He's not much of a runner, either."

To be quite honest, I was also not much of a runner. Other people liked to say that running cleared their mind. Running did indeed clear my mind, but it replaced all those cleared thoughts with a drumbeat of *I hate running I hate running*. But maybe this time, when I really needed a clear head, things would be different.

They were not. Once I'd squeezed myself into the slightly too small exercise clothes I'd packed with me just in case and hauled myself out to Riverside Park, my feet hitting the pavement reminded me exactly how much I hated them hitting the pavement.

At least the scenery was beautiful. Bev had recommended I run on the path beside the river, which was crowded this early on a weekend but not too crowded, probably because it was even colder beside the water than not. I ran north, various sports-like installations and a busy highway on my right and the sparkling slate gray waters of the Hudson on my left. Bikers zoomed past me on the narrow path, many of them delivery guys lugging bags over their handlebars. The air was so cold it hurt my teeth going in and my lungs going out.

I ran—well, jogged—well, jogged slowly—for what felt like an hour or two, then turned that slow jog into a slow walk and checked my phone. It had been eleven minutes. *I hate running.* The thought of continuing filled me with dread, but it wasn't like Bev would check my pedometer, right? I had technically gone for a run, and now I could walk back. Nobody could stop me.

As I'd run north, I'd passed what seemed to be an adult playground with rings, volleyball courts, a soccer field. Now that I'd slowed, I could hear ping-pongy noises from the courts beside me. Pickleball?

I was curious to see Seth and Benjamin play, but I didn't want them to see me and, god forbid, try to make me play with them. I crept up beside the courts, my body hidden by a thick grove of shrubs, and squinted at the players. None were Seth or Benjamin. I stood for a moment, oddly transfixed by the repetitive movement of the ball—was it possible to get hypnotized like this?—and then turned to go.

But not before I heard a familiar voice. "You're better than I remember you being." It was Seth, speaking, presumably, to Benjamin. I turned back toward the courts, realizing now that there were benches set up alongside them for people to sit while, I guessed, they were in between games waiting to rotate back in. "I can't believe we beat that guy with the toupee."

Benjamin snorted. "He talks a big game, but his knees are too old for it. He should take his toupee back to the beginner courts."

"Ouch," Seth said, whistling.

"I say it as I see it," Benjamin said. "So I'll also say, when are you going to ask that girl to marry you? Your mother's already started planning the wedding."

I stopped, rigid, behind the shrubs so that they wouldn't catch a flicker of movement out of the corners of their eyes. I should leave, I told myself. Listening to this conversation would be wrong. I was literally hiding behind shrubs, for heaven's sake.

And yet I didn't move.

Seth snorted identically to his father. "If Mom's already started planning, shouldn't she know when it is?"

"The date's the one missing piece," Benjamin said. "You've been dating for how many months?"

"Is there a standard for when you're supposed to get married?"

"Well, you're getting up there in age," Benjamin said. "It's one thing if you're twenty-one or twenty-two. It's another thing when you're almost thirty. Have the two of you discussed it?"

"So you're saying I need to make an honest woman out of her?" said Seth. "What year is this again?"

"You don't have to get so defensive. You know this is nothing compared to the interrogation your mother will give you the next time you're alone."

"I know." Seth was silent for a minute. I couldn't help but feel a little bad for him right now. It was one thing for me to lie with my presence. It was another thing for a son to straight-up lie to his father about marriage and give him false hope.

Though it was kind of funny that Benjamin thought I needed to be made an honest woman. If only he knew how honest I really was.

Seth finally said, "I'm not sure she feels the same way about me as I feel about her."

Smart. Lay the seeds for our "breakup" now so that it wouldn't come as a shock later. I tried to ignore how those seeds made my stomach kind of lurch.

"I doubt that," said Benjamin. "I see the way the two of you look at each other. It's clear there's love there."

I had to hold back a snort of my own. I certainly didn't look at Seth like I loved him, because I didn't love him. The mere idea of it was absurd.

Right?

I could imagine Seth's mouth twitching in a wry smile, as aware of the irony as I was. The whole thing was hilarious. I wasn't smiling, but that was just due to the ever-present resting bitch face.

But Seth sighed. It didn't sound like he was smiling, either. "There's love on my side," he said. "The other night we kissed and I just . . . I fell so hard, and she pulled away."

My stomach lurched unpleasantly. *This is all part of the fake relationship*, I told myself, but . . . was it? Because we *had* kissed the other night, and I *had* pulled away, and . . .

"She wouldn't be here with you if she wasn't all in,"

Benjamin said. "Eight nights staying in a small apartment with you and your parents? Why would she have come otherwise?"

Seth was silent for what felt like a very long while. He wasn't going to tell Benjamin the truth, was he? My stomach lurched again. I wasn't sure which option I wanted less. Him going back to the lie would show that he had indeed just been fabricating something for his father, which should have made me happy, but instead the thought made me nauseous. And him telling the truth, meaning he'd been telling the truth about his feelings?

Well. That left me feeling shaky. Terrified. Like an earthquake had suddenly struck here in Riverside Park and the world was shuddering around me and pickleball players were screaming and losing their toupees and I no longer knew how to stand up.

If that was the case, though, Seth would catch me. He would help me stand.

He was speaking. "I think she's afraid," he said, and even though I'd just acknowledged the accuracy of that statement, outrage couldn't help but swell in my chest anyway. "I think she's afraid of her feelings and of being really open in a relationship. When I reach out to her, she pulls away. I don't know what to do."

"You can't solve something like that by loving her," Benjamin said gravely. "She has to be the one to take that step. She has to love herself."

This whole conversation was ridiculous. Offensive, actually. I should bound out of my hiding place right now and confront them with the truth. Tell Benjamin all about our scheme so that I could stop this infernal wondering that was making my stomach all soupy and gross.

Because it had to be that this was all fake, just like our dating scheme. Because if it was real, true, then I had to look inward. I had to open up my chest just enough to peer inside and read what exactly my heart was trying to tell me.

I took a deep breath. Before I could make any decisions, a gruff voice by the bench said, "You're up."

Creaking noises as people stood. "Great," Seth said. "Dad, do you think I get bonus points if I knock the toupee off his head?"

Obviously, I couldn't talk to them if they were hitting balls back and forth and at people's heads. That left me to slink away, to ring the bell for Bev to let me in. "You look like you got a great workout," she said brightly as I stepped inside the apartment. It was probably true: my cheeks were red from both the cold and Unwanted Feelings; my hair was all mussed from running my fingers through it over and over during my (long, slow) walk back. "How are you feeling?"

I actually did indeed feel like I'd gotten a workout. My heart was still racing. "I don't know," I said, before I could think about it. "I don't know how I'm feeling."

How did you know if you loved someone? Was it when you felt safe around them? Wanted to share your news and excitement with them before anyone else? Felt comfortable sharing more with them than you'd shared with others maybe ever, even if you weren't ready to crack open your chest and let them dive into the whole bloody mess? Wanted nothing more than to kiss them and touch them and feel the throb of their heart pulsing against yours?

Well, shit. Maybe I didn't need to crack open my chest after all.

I snapped out of it when Bev cupped my forehead with her palm. "You don't feel like you have a fever," she said. "Is it your legs? Did you twist something?"

It occurred to me that she hadn't been asking about my emotional state; she'd been making sure I hadn't hurt myself. Which made me laugh. She looked at me like I was deranged, which maybe I was. "No, I'm great. All of my extremities are doing great."

Seth and Benjamin got back sweaty and red-faced, too, and we had time for a nice lunch—Bev made some excellent spaghetti with a salad—before heading off to our hair appointment. It did not surprise me at all that Bev's usual salon was way swankier than my usual salon, which, to be honest, was less a salon than me trimming my hair in the mirror whenever I got too many split ends. Mirrors covered the walls, multiplying us into infinite versions of ourselves; soothing music that sounded like it should be in a spa played through hidden speakers, and everything smelled like hair cream that cost more than a day of my café's operating expenses.

Bev got her blowout on one side of the salon, and on the other, a hairdresser somehow defrizzed my natural curls and teased them into a half-up, half-down kind of thing with way too many bobby pins sticking into my scalp. Why did people get acupuncture when they could just go to the salon? Head pain or not, what greeted me in the mirror afterward was me, just prettier. The pulled-up part of my hair emphasized my strong jaw and the lines of my cheekbones, and the curly bits that hung free were striking against my pale skin and the elegant slope of my neck. I'd never thought of any part of myself as elegant before this trip, and now here I was doing it two days in a row.

I swallowed a lump in my throat. I'd always rolled my eyes at the makeover scenes in movies, because what really mattered was, of course, on the inside. But maybe it mattered a little bit to have the outside match the inside, at least sometimes.

"You look beautiful," Bev said, making me jump. Somehow she'd snuck up behind me, which was quite a feat, considering I was looking into a mirror. "The two of you will make such a handsome couple. I can't wait for all my friends to see you."

This was our last day together, and after this I'd never see her again. "Bev, can I ask you something? Do you only like me because I'm Jewish?" Something confirming that I was making the right decision, because Seth could've brought home any Jewish girl and Bev would've been just as happy. That I personally didn't matter. "Sorry if that's a rude question, but I heard you didn't like Freya, and Freya is great, so . . ."

Bev stared into my eyes in the mirror. One of her hands found its way to my shoulder and squeezed, fortunately not crushing any delicately hair-sprayed curls. "No, dear, of course that's not the only reason I like you. Is that what Seth said?"

I shrugged. Bev rolled her eyes. "I'm not going to stand here and lie through my teeth; of course I'm happy that he's finally brought home someone Jewish. I know that the world has changed. Just because he doesn't have a Jewish wife or partner doesn't mean he can't be part of the community or that he can't have Jewish children. But I want Jewish grandchildren, I want to light the candles with them and stand up on the bima at their b'nai mitzvot to sing an aliyah for them and teach them all our ways and laws, and I know that's more likely if he's with someone who's also Jewish. I don't want Seth to feel excluded from the community we've spent our entire lives weaving together. But above all else I want him to be happy."

That was not clicking with what Seth had said, but neither had what he told Benjamin at the pickleball court compared to what he'd told me, that our kiss had been just a kiss, and her words rang true. Maybe because she was squeezing my shoulder now like she might crush it if I didn't believe her.

"I didn't dislike Freya as a person," Bev continued. "I didn't think she and Seth were a good fit. She was sweet and polite, but she was too passive. My son needs someone who won't take his crap, who will stand up to him and challenge him. Benjamin and I have worked so well for so many years because our differences complement each other, and we challenge each other to turn us into better people. That didn't happen with Seth and Freya.

"You, on the other hand," Bev went on. "I knew from the moment I met you and you ribbed my son in front of me that you would be good for him. You have the fire he needs, and I can already see that you challenge him. Is he just as good for you? I don't know. I don't know you well enough yet. But I think so, and I hope so. What was your question again? Oh. If I only like you because you're Jewish. No, Abby. I like that you're Jewish, but I like you mostly because I think you're very good for my son."

It was suddenly hard to breathe. The aerosol funk of the salon had crept into my lungs as a fog and was now choking my lungs of all air. Or maybe a lump had risen in my throat and was choking me because I was trying so hard not to cry. Either one.

"Turn around," Bev said briskly. I couldn't not obey her, so I did. And while she probably should have asked me first, she pulled me in for a hug. Her arms closed around my back, pulling me in. Trapping me.

Or that's what hugs usually felt like to me, but somehow this one didn't, even though I was already suffocating. If anything, it eased the pain in my chest. She held me long enough where I could breathe again, even if what I was breathing was her lavender and hair spray scent, and then pulled away. "You look beautiful," she said. "Now let's go home and get you dressed."

I trailed after her into the cab, stomach simmering with unease.

AN UNEASE THAT persisted the rest of the afternoon, as Seth and I hung out and watched the Food Network from opposite ends of the couch, me doing my best not to move so that I didn't ruin my hair. When the time started getting close to the ball, I applied some light makeup—anything else was beyond my capabilities—and, slowly and torturously, managed to shimmy out of my T-shirt without disturbing any bobby pins. I really deserved an award for that. From Seth, whose preparation for the ball consisted of combing his hair and putting on clothes. The differential here did not seem fair.

Still, it was worth it when I regarded myself in the mirror. I was no longer the princess of the night sky.

I was the *queen*.

"Oh, you're just stunning," Bev said, clasping her hands together. "Isn't she, Seth?"

Seth, garbed in a black tuxedo that was somehow both slightly too long in the arms and the most dashing thing he could be wearing, had no words for me. He just nodded, an odd look I couldn't quite read shimmering in those hazel eyes. I wanted to gaze into them. I wanted to drown in them.

I couldn't handle the intensity. I looked away.

"Very pretty," Benjamin said gruffly. From the way Bev sighed dreamily, I gathered that was the equivalent of a regular person throwing confetti and gushing out a thesaurus's worth of synonyms for beautiful.

I wondered how they'd balanced each other out over the years. If before they'd met, Bev had been overly volatile and anxious; if Benjamin had been totally closed off and taciturn. If over the years they'd challenged each other, brought out the best in each other and smoothed out some of the rough edges, balanced each other in a way that made them both better, happier people.

Before my brain could push it away, I let myself wonder if that was true. If Bev had been right back in the salon when she'd told me she could see how Seth and I brought out the best in each other. Because hadn't I been feeling happier, more comfortable, here with him than I had maybe ever before? I felt prouder in my Jewishness, too, and more open—okay, so I didn't feel more open exactly, but I had opened up at least a little bit, and it hadn't killed me. Yet. And Seth. Seth had been able to deal with conflict in a small, manageable way, true, but he'd still dealt with it in a way he hadn't before. Was that us bringing out the best in each other?

Stop thinking about it, I tried to order myself, but I couldn't help picturing me and Seth in ten years, twenty years, thirty years. Maybe Seth would never be entirely comfortable starting conflict or striding right into it. Maybe I'd never be an open book—which was fine, because who wanted everybody reading my insides anyway? But maybe we'd be able to bring out those parts of each other the same way Benjamin and Bev had. Maybe . . .

"The Uber's here," Seth said, snapping me back to reality. "You ready, Abby?"

I waited a second before turning to him just to make sure my eyes weren't glittering with tears, then let him take my arm. I just had to get through tonight. Then I could figure out what all these confusing feelings meant. Or, better yet, I could not. I could just shove them away and pretend they didn't exist.

Except that somehow the thought didn't feel as appealing as it usually did.

22

THE EIGHTH NIGHT BALL TOOK PLACE IN THE ballroom of a hotel Seth had been shocked I'd never heard of. "It gets name-dropped on, like, *Gossip Girl*," he said. "It's where all the fancy people stay. Seriously, do you live under a rock?"

"Seriously, how have we never discussed that you've watched *Gossip Girl*?" I retorted. "Seriously, how have we waited this long to discuss Derena and Chair and how Jenny Humphrey deserved better?"

"Okay, but Dan Humphrey was a psychopath, right?" Seth said. I nodded with so much force I was afraid my curls might come out. "And everybody just treated him like he wasn't? And then he got a happy ending? I'm worried about Serena's future, honestly."

We debated the whole Uber ride to the hotel, but all conversation ceased as Seth opened the door for me and motioned me out with a grand gesture.

And just like that, we were in a fairyland. White marble steps climbed above the sidewalk into columns that made me think of the Met. Twinkling lights were strung everywhere, glowing against the dark, and warm, inviting light beamed out of the hotel's large arched windows. Chatter escaped the open doors, and so did notes from what sounded like a string quartet. I held up one side of my skirt so that I could walk up without tripping, because I could just imagine what Bev's friends would have to say about me doing a full face-plant down the steps of the fancy hotel.

We showed our tickets at the door and then we were inside, which took my breath away. The ceiling of the hotel ballroom stretched unfathomably high overhead, hung with glittering crystal chandeliers and painted with the blazing glory of a sunset. Arched mirrors decorated the gilded walls, reflecting all the people in gowns and tuxes sipping bubbly flutes of champagne and snacking on mini latkes topped with crème fraîche and caviar. A string quartet was indeed playing away, right now to a jazzy version of "Ma'oz Tzur." In the center of the room, set up high on a platform, shone a golden menorah the size of a very large dog.

Before I could grab a champagne flute or a latke, Seth snagged one of the waitstaff to take some pictures of us in front of the giant menorah. "My mom will pitch a fit if we don't take enough pictures," he said. "I've learned it's easiest just to get them out of the way early."

It was hard to blame her. I wanted pictures of Seth looking like this, too. Something about the tux in its stark black and white made my stomach go all warm. We posed in front of the menorah, smiling as the waiter turned Seth's phone this way and that as we tried not to touch each other. Or at least, that was me.

Seth retrieved his phone and swiped through the

pictures to make sure we weren't blinking in all of them. "Perfect," he said, then waved at someone behind me. "Hey!"

I turned around only to be enveloped by a cloud of flowery perfume and damp skin. When the cloud dissipated, I realized I'd been hugged by a woman maybe a few years older than us, accompanied by a man around the same age. Both had sleek dark hair and sharp, narrow features. They could've been siblings, but the way he was rubbing her back said they definitely were not.

"If it isn't Seth Abrams, showing his face in New York City again," the woman said affectionately. Her dress was long, tight, and pink, with rosettes bursting around the shoulders. "How's Vermont? You moving back yet?"

"Definitely not," Seth said, just as affectionately. He gave her a loose side-hug. "Abby, this is Emily and her boyfriend, Hugo. I've known Emily basically since I was born; we went to Hebrew school together. Emily, this is my girlfriend, Abby."

"I was hoping I'd get to meet you!" Emily cried. I hoped she wasn't going to hug me again. "I've heard so much about you through the temple grapevine. I assume it's not true that you're already pregnant and are planning on naming the baby after Bev's parents?"

"Definitely not." I echoed Seth. "It's nice to meet you."

Seth and Emily spent a few minutes catching up on their lives—Emily was a doctor in obstetrics and gynecology up at Columbia, her sister had just gotten married, she'd gotten a great deal on an apartment in Morningside Heights with a slight mouse problem but that could be dealt with—and then Emily turned to me. "I heard you run a café," she said.

"That's so cool. I always wanted to have a bakery when I was younger."

I'd definitely had people say that to me in a condescending way, but she sounded genuinely enthusiastic. I smiled at her, trying to counter my resting bitch face. "I do. Thanks."

She squinted sidelong at Seth and leaned in like she was going to whisper, though she spoke at full volume. "I'm more amazed at how you got him here, though. Especially in a tux! The kid wore jeans to his own bar mitzvah."

I raised my eyebrow. "Bev let that happen?"

"She didn't have a choice after I threw my suit pants down the garbage chute the morning of," Seth mumbled.

Okay, that was a story I was dying to hear more about. But Emily was talking again. "He didn't go to prom both because of the suit and because he didn't dance. I wasn't surprised at all when he moved to Vermont. He belongs in jeans and flannel all year."

I raised my other eyebrow. "He didn't protest about coming tonight." I thought for a moment. "Okay, he didn't protest *much*."

Emily elbowed him gently. "Oh, really? What's so different about this night?"

"Compared to all other nights?" Seth asked. "Well, we eat matzah instead of bread, we—"

"It's not Passover," she interrupted, rolling her eyes. "Fortunately, since I've had about ten of those mini waffles so far. You should definitely grab one of them before they stop circulating."

"We're definitely going to eat about a pound of those each," Seth said.

Emily's eyes widened. "Speaking of circulating snacks, I'm seeing the latkes with salmon roe on the other side of the room and I'm not letting them get away again. Catch up with you later? Oh, before I forget." She pulled out her phone and extended her arm, crowding her face between Seth's and mine. I barely had time to smile before she snapped the selfie. "Okay, see you!" Another cloud of perfume and damp skin and she was off, moving faster than I could've ever moved in heels like that.

"My mom's probably already seen that selfie," Seth said, turning back to me. "She'll be delighted."

Probably way more delighted than when Seth threw his bar mitzvah suit down a trash chute. "Really, though, I'm curious," I said, and I wasn't entirely sure why I was chasing the subject, just that I wanted to know. "If you really hate dressing up and dancing so much, why come tonight? We could've skipped it."

The corner of his mouth twitched. "Dressing up and dancing isn't so bad." A beat of silence where I just stared at him. "Okay, it was the expression on your face after my mom told us about it. You lit up like you were Cinderella finally getting an invitation to the ball, without even having to wear glass slippers that could easily break and end in a gory mess-slash-amputated foot. Seriously, didn't the fairy godmother know those were health hazards?"

"I always assumed they were magical unbreakable glass," I said, mostly because I couldn't say anything else without a lump rising in my throat. Actually, I didn't need to say anything—there it was. I coughed, trying to clear it out.

"Seriously, you didn't have to do this for me. I would've been totally fine not going."

"I know I didn't have to," Seth said. "I wanted to."

Is this love? The thought wormed its way into the back of my brain. *Doing something you really don't want to do for the sake of someone else?* Just to see them happy?

The string quartet launched into another interpretation of "Rock of Ages," this one a little slower and more serious, as Seth smiled at me, then held out his hand. "Dance with me?"

I blinked. The dazzle of the room left golden impressions on the backs of my eyelids. "I thought you didn't dance."

The corner of his lip quirked in a smile. "I'll dance with you."

"You don't have to."

"I want to." His hand didn't waver. "I want to dance with you, Abby."

I couldn't do anything but nod.

Seth swept me up in his arms, moving us back into the dancing crowd. He didn't seem to be doing any particular step, no waltz or tango or polka (not that I'd want him to be doing the polka; it was just one of the only dances I could think of), but his movements were fluid and elegant, his hands sure against my shoulder and my hip. Surprising for someone who claimed he didn't dance. I wrapped my own arms around his shoulders, linking them loosely at the back of his neck, where his curls tickled them.

In this moment, focusing on the motions of my feet and my body, trying not to bump into any other couples or trip over Seth's feet or the hem of my dress, my brain couldn't dwell on anything else. Couldn't make me deny anything else. I was forced to realize one single truth without trying to push it away.

I was happy. For the first time in a long time. Really, truly happy. Really, truly content. Really, truly comfortable.

And I didn't want it to end.

That was enough of a thought to distract my brain. Sure enough, without constant minding, my feet got tangled between Seth's ankles. My hands came loose as I toppled, ready to catch myself.

But I didn't have to catch myself. Seth caught me. Pulled me back up. Murmured in my ear, "You okay?"

I opened my mouth to respond. Couldn't think of what to say. No, I wasn't okay; my entire life strategy was crumbling before my eyes and I was in the midst of an existential crisis while dressed as the night sky queen. Yes, I was okay, more than okay; I was happy, comfortable, safe, open.

In love.

The thought sent terrified shivers through me. I had to squeeze the words out through a throat that suddenly felt more like a drinking straw. "I need some air," I choked. Air, sure. Any air where I couldn't smell him, feel him.

It took some wrenching to pry Seth's hands off my hip and my shoulder—he was holding on extra tight, maybe afraid I'd fall again—and then turn around in what I hoped looked like a controlled fashion and not utter panic like I was feeling inside. Picking up my skirts so that I wouldn't fall again, I strode through a blur of lights and wavery violin notes toward an opening on the far side of the room.

"Abby! Wait!" Seth called behind me. I didn't stop, though my feet did stutter for a moment, as if they'd rather listen to him than my brain. It was hard to blame them. Sometimes I didn't like my brain, either.

The opening led to a corridor lined with conference rooms and business suites. The doors were all locked with a code, and the straight lines left nowhere to hide, so I kept moving. The end of the corridor led into a lobby, which was empty aside from a bored front desk attendant who barely even spared me a glance. Among the frilly potted trees and trickling fountains, I sank into one of the couches. My bare shoulders immediately stuck to the leather.

Deep breath in. Deep breath out. I tried to focus on the magazines splayed out before me on the table. *Golf Fancy. Architectural Digest. Bon Appétit.* They looked like all the magazines Bev and Benjamin had on their table, which sent me spiraling again, struggling to pull enough air into my lungs.

"Abby?" Seth said from behind me. I turned to find him panting in his tux, which meant he'd probably gotten his fancy shirt all sweaty. He'd have to pay for dry-cleaning, and it would be all my fault. See? He'd be better off without me.

That voice wasn't as convincing as it had been before.

"Hi, Seth." My words sounded tinny. "I just . . . needed some air."

He laughed, but it was an uncomfortable laugh, like he wasn't sure how much he should pretend to believe me. "You looked like Cinderella running away at midnight. Are you going to turn into a pumpkin?"

"Cinderella didn't turn into a pumpkin, that was her carriage," I said in the automatic way of someone who'd watched every single Disney Princess movie multiple times as a child. Maybe this was it, how I could spin it. Princesses ran away.

But queens? Queens stayed to face the facts. And I wasn't a princess. I was a queen.

"I hope Cinderella will accept my deepest, most sincere apologies," Seth said. "How about you? I hope I didn't do something to make you run away. If it was the dancing, we don't have to—"

"Seth." I stood up and turned to face him, balling my fists at my sides for strength. "I ran away because . . . because . . ." I couldn't seem to get the words out.

But, looking at his soft eyes, his patient expression, I knew I had the time to. I pulled in a breath so deep I was worried it might snap my bra. "Because I have real feelings for you and I don't know how to deal with them." I let all the words out in a torrent. Hopefully, they wouldn't drown him. Or me. "I'm not used to this. I don't know how to open myself up to someone else, but I want to, because I'm in love with you."

The shock of that last phrase was enough to snap my mouth shut. My heart pounded in my chest so hard I thought I might vomit it up. What had I been *thinking*? In *love*? My face heated, little prickles spreading over my forehead. Great, I was sweating all over. Now I was going to have to pay for dry-cleaning, too, before Bev could return my gown.

My mouth opened again and the words started coming

out, whether I wanted them to or not. "I know I'm probably not what you pictured. I'm not open and nurturing and emotional like you, and I probably never will be, and I'm prickly, and I'm grumpy in the mornings, and I always see the glass as half-empty, and I don't like talking about my feelings, and . . ." I trailed off.

Seth raised an eyebrow. "Are you done?"

I nodded.

"Good," he said, taking a step closer to me. This close I could smell that lovely, irritating, delicious scent of oranges and campfire, which clung to him even through the dusty tux his father had dug out of his closet. "Because there's a lot you forgot. You're brilliant, and funny, and driven, and ambitious. I know you like to think you're cold and calculating, but you're really not; you're caring and you like to help people, no matter how much you try to hide it. Being around you makes my heart race and my brain work hard, because you make me want to be a better person. To be someone who's worthy of you." He paused. "Oh, and you're beautiful, too. Can't forget that."

All those things he was saying were spiking my blood pressure, that side of my brain telling me, *He's wrong, he's lying, you're not worth it.*

I ignored it. I took a step closer. Now I couldn't just smell him; I could feel the heat of him, warming my front like an actual campfire. "I still find the positive attitude a little annoying sometimes," I said. "But I want it to keep annoying me."

He stepped even closer, placing our faces inches apart. I could see his spiky eyelashes, the tiny beauty mark near his right eye, the little patch of hair he'd missed shaving on the line of his jaw. "Oh, by the way. Almost forgot," he said. "I'm in love with you, too."

I don't even know who kissed who, but it didn't matter. Our lips were moving against each other's, our bodies pressed together. I didn't care who saw us. All I wanted was to be here, with him, our limbs entwined and our fingers tangled in each other's hair and the wet heat of his mouth on my own.

I felt that mouth smile beneath mine. "It's hard to kiss you when you're smiling," I whispered.

"You're smiling back," he whispered. It was true.

Did we have to go back to the ball? I kind of wanted to stay here forever, but I would settle for the rest of the night. Why go back to Seth's childhood room when we had an entire hotel above our heads, one with comfy king-size beds and no parents within earshot? One whose rooms probably cost more than my rent up in Vermont?

Stop thinking about logistics. For once, I listened to myself, and lost myself in how it felt when his beard rubbed my chin, the tender way he cupped my cheek, the—

"Abigail? Is that you?"

That familiar voice might as well have been a bucket of cold water thrown over my head. I wrenched away from Seth, my stomach lurching into my chest.

No. It couldn't be.

"Abigail, it *is* you."

I turned slowly, trying to keep from screaming, and yes. There they were.

My parents.

I'm not going to lie: I had occasionally googled them over the years to see if they were dead. I'd come back with photos of them on social media with friends, so I knew vaguely how they'd aged, but it was still jarring seeing them here in person with those extra years painted on their faces. My mom's dark pixie cut was going silver above her ears, and her cheeks were thinner. My dad had packed on a belly, and the bags under his eyes had gotten pouchy.

My mom stepped forward. Her lips stretched into a smile. "What a surprise. Or is it? Did you remember that we liked to stay here whenever we went out for a night in the city? Some part of you must have."

I could barely hear her over the sound of my heart thudding inside my skull. Since when had they ever come here? I knew it had been a lot of years, but I couldn't imagine that, unless they'd won the lottery or something, their financial situation had changed all that much. I'd never heard of this hotel before, that much I knew.

Or had I? Somehow speaking with my parents always made me unsure what I knew and what I didn't know.

Mrs. Landskroner popped into my head. Maybe after seeing that Seth and I had been at the cookie decorating event, she'd struck up a conversation with Bev and Benjamin. Learned that Seth and I would be here at the Eighth Night Ball. Leaked the information to my mom.

I cleared my throat, which was suddenly very dry. "You never came here," I whispered. I *did* know that. I *wasn't* crazy.

The smile my mom gave me was an apologetic one. "Of course we've come here, Abigail. You must remember." She turned to Seth. "Our Abigail is a lovely girl, but you may have noticed that she sometimes has trouble with the truth."

Oh, god. They hadn't changed a bit. This was like I'd stepped into a nightmare.

Seth's hand found my back, reinforcing it, giving me strength.

But not enough. I ran. Again.

23

I DIDN'T THINK ABOUT WHERE I WAS GOING, I JUST raced blindly from the room. Fortunately, not in the direction I'd come from, because I think the sensory overload of that ballroom might have made me full-on collapse. Honestly, I didn't even remember the journey or how I got there; I just found myself in the hotel gym, the lights flickering on above me as I burst inside. It was empty, but it still smelled like sweaty socks and rubber. Trying to slow my heart rate so that it wouldn't explode, I set myself down on one of the weight benches.

My phone buzzed in my clutch. I didn't want to look at it, but I did. It was Seth. **Abby, where are you?**

Just as I let out a deep, shaky breath and started preparing myself to respond, the gym door creaked open. I jumped to my feet and braced myself for whoever was going to come in, so tense the weights on this machine could have fallen on me and probably just bounced off, but it was only Seth. "There you are," he said. "What was that? Those were your parents?"

I nodded, unable to speak. And then, because it seemed

very important to ask, "Did you believe them? When they said I had trouble with the truth?"

Seth's face pinched with concern. "Of course not. After what you told me, I'd never believe a word they said." He was quiet for a moment. "Did you think I might?"

"No. Yes. I don't know." I shook my head. "My parents spent years warping everything around me. Playing games with my head, making me think I was crazy, punishing me for breaking rules I didn't know existed. I didn't know what was normal, and what wasn't. All I knew was that it was safest—not safe, nothing was ever safe—if I didn't share anything with them, because anything extra they knew they could use against me." I wasn't talking about this specific meeting anymore. I wondered if Seth knew that. I wanted him to know that. "So I was always afraid to share things with people. With friends. With you."

Something glittered in Seth's eyes. It took me a second to realize it was fury. It took me another second, one where I almost shrank away, to realize it wasn't aimed at me.

That gave me the courage to go on. "And I think it became a habit I couldn't break. One I didn't want to break. Because what was the point? I never thought it was worth it to let people in. Or maybe it's that I never found anyone worth it."

"You've opened up to me," Seth said softly.

I had. Maybe not as much as he would have, or a "normal" person would have, but I'd opened up and let him in. "And I think that's why I freaked out so much when we kissed," I told him. "The first time. Because I knew I was letting myself open up, and I panicked that I'd get hurt. But

I . . ." I took a deep breath. "I'm starting to think it might be worth it. At least a little bit. With you. And I don't want to close myself off again."

"Oh, Abby."

But I wasn't done. "Losing my parents and closing myself off from the world didn't only mean losing my family," I said. "It meant losing the community I'd grown up in. It meant not feeling Jewish anymore. And it felt like a part of me was missing, like I'd lost a leg without noticing and just accustomed myself to hobbling around without it. But coming back to the community through you didn't just make me want to be with you; it made my leg grow back. Or maybe gave me a really good prosthetic. This Hanukkah made me remember everything I was missing. And I don't want to lose it again."

Seth cupped my chin between his hands. "Abby," he said tenderly. "Whether or not you choose to be part of your family, or whether you're part of my family, you're always part of *this* family. The Jewish family. You can never lose your place here. You can't get rid of us. You're *home*."

It had been years since I'd cried for real, anything beyond a few tears while slicing an onion or getting teary when I was panicking really hard. But now the tears welled up and overflowed, spilling down my cheeks and splashing onto the rubber mats of the floor. My instinct was to duck my head and turn away, like somehow I could make it so that Seth hadn't seen, but I forced myself to stay upright. Stay strong. Let him see. I knew he wouldn't think I was weak for it. Hell, he'd probably say something inspirational about how strong I was being.

"Crying is a sign of strength, you know," he said earnestly, and the tears melted into laughter. I nestled my cheek against his chest. He'd already have to get the tux dry-cleaned; a few tears—okay, a lot of tears—wouldn't permanently stain. "It's a scientific thing. The tears move stress hormones out of your body or something. It makes you feel better."

These tears must have been transporting years' worth of built-up stress hormones, then, because I could feel the tension in my body melting away. Not all of it, obviously—crying wasn't some kind of black magic. But enough of it where I felt like I could be a little vulnerable again. "I don't know if I want kids." I took a deep breath. "I've never felt a superstrong urge to have them, but I don't know if that's because the only way I know of raising kids is how I was raised, and I could never do that to a kid."

"I don't know if I want kids, either," Seth said. "If I do, it won't be for years, at least. So we can figure that out later."

I backed away a step so that I could look him in the eye. His hands fell from my cheeks to his sides. I missed their warmth. "Does Bev know that?"

Seth huffed a laugh. "You'd know if my mom knew. You'd have been able to hear her head exploding all the way from Vermont."

I couldn't handle not touching him for one more moment, so I took his hands in mine. "Then, you and me . . ."

"You and me," he said, a smile spreading across his face. I matched it with one of my own.

Which faltered after I remembered what was waiting for us out there. "My parents are still here. I can't . . ." I'd cracked myself open. I was vulnerable. Who knew what they might be able to dig out of me? It would probably be bloody. I imagined them cracking open my rib cage, inspecting my heart and lungs and viscera. As much as I wanted to go before them and show them how well I was doing without them, there was a significant chance I'd just crumble and revert back to my old self. I'd already panicked when I heard my mom's voice.

Seth squared his shoulders. "I got this. Thanks to you." He squeezed my hand. "Wait here. I'll tell them you want nothing to do with them."

He wouldn't have been able to do that before. Maybe he hadn't been kidding when he said I'd influenced him for the better. I nodded, not trusting myself to speak.

He gave me one last hug, and then he was gone. I sat back down on the weight bench, then gave in to the exhaustion tugging at my limbs and laid down all the way, staring up at the weights hanging above my head. This was probably dangerous. I didn't care.

From my supine position, I heard the door creak open again. That was fast. I turned my head, expecting Seth, finding instead an elderly man wearing a sweatband and shorts so short I was treated to a full outline of his package. He raised an eyebrow when he saw me on the weight bench, my sparkly dress brushing the floor. "Wow. That's dedication."

Dedication. I snorted a laugh and swung around so that I was sitting back up. "I'm just taking a break from out there."

"I get it," the old man said, stepping up on the treadmill

and turning it up higher than I could've gone on a good day. "It seems like a lot."

But it was only a lot because of my parents. I hadn't felt that overwhelmed by the rest of it, I realized. On the contrary, it was really nice to be surrounded by my culture and people, to not have the menorah and Hanukkah music be a small side plot to the usual giant Christmas trees and endless permutations of "Jingle Bells" or "Silent Night." If anything, that was dedication, getting an event like this off the ground.

An event like my Hanukkah festival. I knew suddenly what I had to do.

I didn't expect Lorna to pick up this late, but she did on the second ring. "Hello?"

"Hi, Lorna," I said, tone brisk and professional. "I have to talk to you about the Hanukkah festival."

"Oh, that," she said. "I've actually had some more ideas I wanted to talk to you about. There's this guy who does ornament decorating, and I know that Hanukkah trees aren't a thing, but I do know a lot of people have Hanukkah bushes, so I think—"

"Lorna," I interrupted. "When I said I have to talk to you, that's what I meant. Not that you have to talk to me." I stopped, both a little shocked and thrilled I'd dared to say that to her face. Well, to her ear.

She must have been shocked, too, because she didn't say anything in response. So I forged on. "Listen. This is what we're going to do."

When I hung up the phone, the old man on the treadmill, legs still pumping faster than they had any right to, looked over his shoulder and gave me a slow clap. "That's right. You tell her."

He had no idea what was going on, but it felt good anyway.

Seth chose that moment to return. His square jaw was even squarer with determination than it usually was. "All right. It's done." He held out his hand.

I took it. "Conflict looks sexy on you."

He twirled me. My skirt fanned out in a circle, catching the gym lights and twinkling like the stars. It would've been magical if I hadn't almost tripped over a stray barbell. "Come on. Let's get back to the ball."

And, as the bright lights of the gym transformed into the twinkling golden lights of the ballroom, as the sound of the old man puffing on the treadmill turned into the most beautiful violin moaning "Light One Candle" that I'd ever heard, as the entire ballroom's voices rose up in song to fill each arm of the golden menorah with even more golden light, I didn't think I'd ever been so happy.

Epilogue

The End of December

CORRECTION: THE PINNACLE OF HAPPINESS WAS not the night of the ball. It was now. To be fair, every day since the ball had been a new, shining high of happiness.

Gag me.

Still, if there was any night to be super ultra grandpa corny, it was tonight: the opening of the Hanukkah festival I'd spent the past few weeks frantically cobbling together. I took a deep breath as I scurried around my apartment with my tote bag, gathering everything I'd need tonight. Hand sanitizer? Sure. Another thing of hand sanitizer in case the first one ran out? Why not. Pepper spray? Who knew what might go on at the area's first Hanukkah festival—couldn't be too careful. Gum? Didn't want to walk around with oniony latke breath all night.

"Maybe you want to throw some sunglasses in there, too," Seth said from behind me. "You never know if for the first time ever the sun will decide to come out at night."

I knew perfectly well that he was making fun of me, but now I thought that maybe I *did* need sunglasses. What if the spotlights were so bright that they made me squint and I missed something?

His hand found my upper back and rubbed in soothing circles. "Relax. It's going to be amazing."

"Or it's going to be a disaster." My heart flipped at the thought. There were so many things that could go wrong. One of the vendors driving up from the city could have blown a tire en route and not had the signal to call me and let me know, or we hadn't gotten the word out to the right communities and nobody would show—

"It's not going to be a disaster," Seth said firmly. "It's going to be amazing."

He couldn't know that, but I'd learned by now that there was no use in arguing with him about whether the glass was half-full or half-empty. I drew in a deep breath, setting my very heavy tote bag down with a thump. A tube of ChapStick rolled out and disappeared with a plink under the couch, but that was okay. I had two others in there just in case.

Trying to distract myself from the feeling of impending doom, I took a few deep breaths and tried to remind my brain that the odds of everything going wrong like that were actually very low, something my new therapist had recommended. I'd only started talking to her virtually a week ago, but I'd promised Seth that I'd give therapy a real go before declaring it useless. More importantly, I'd promised that to myself. So be it.

Wind howled outside. I braced myself for the chilly gust sure to come through my terrible cheap windows, but I remained warm. I blinked. That was distracting enough that all thoughts of how much of a disaster tonight might be fled. "Are my windows less drafty or is it just me?"

"Oh yeah, forgot to tell you," Seth said. "I was so cold the other night that I resolved to fix them. It actually wasn't that hard."

"Who knew you were so handy?" I certainly hadn't.

He shrugged modestly. "YouTube helped. It's amazing how many things you can do when you just watch a video on how to do them. You're welcome."

"Thanks."

"I already said you're welcome. You ready?"

I took one last glance around the apartment, then down at myself. I'd selected jeans, one of Seth's ugly Hanukkah sweaters we'd brought back with us just for this occasion—the one with the light-up menorah—and my warm puffy jacket to go over the ugly Hanukkah sweater so that nobody would actually have to see me wearing it. It was the spirit that counted. "I guess."

"It's going to be amazing," Seth said for the third time, opening my front door before I could protest that I needed just one more—

Wait. I actually did need just one more thing. Before putting on my muddy boots, I darted over to the kitchen counter and palmed the knitted dolphin Kylie had made, tucking it away in my pocket. It wasn't like I believed in good luck charms or anything, or like I found its presence on me comforting, or thought of it fondly. It was just a fun thing to have around.

(I'd named him Judah Maccasea.)

It was a quick drive to the site of the festival. I spent it looking out the window and taking deep breaths. Snow-topped trees flew by, perfuming the air with pine even through the closed windows of Seth's car. He said, "Perfect weather. Enough snow on the ground to be appropriately festive, but not enough to impede travel."

"It's cold, though," I said. "People might not want to come out in the cold."

"It's winter in Vermont. People know it's going to be cold."

I opened my mouth to argue, then closed it. Why bother? Maybe he was even right. I mean, nobody came to Vermont in the winter expecting a tropical vacation.

My heart lifted as we drove over the bumpy gravel of the parking lot, because the field was glowing with light. I could see the giant blow-up menorah, the fake flames high and proud, even from here. Since it wasn't actually Hanukkah, we wouldn't need to light anything, so I'd gone with the money-saving option.

Though I wouldn't should we do this next year, because, if the event was a success and we did it again, it was going to be held on the actual holiday. That was one thing I'd insisted upon to Lorna during our phone call. We could extend it through winter break if we chose to, but I wanted to be able to light the menorah every night with the crowd. Everybody singing the blessings together like that was important to me and, I imagined, to them.

As we got out of the car, the speakers were already playing the selection of Hanukkah music Seth and I had painstakingly gathered from all around the Internet. Live music—a band headed by the bass player from the Eighth Night Ball, who told me he and his singer and guitar- and keyboard-playing friends knew all the same songs—would begin in a bit, when hopefully the attendance would be at its peak.

"Everything looks good," Seth said. He wrapped his arms around me, pulling me in for a quick hug before the madness set in. "How are you feeling?"

My immediate reaction was to say panicked, or nervous, but honestly? Everything did look good. I'd done all I could. Now I just had to hope the people would come.

Over the next hour, they did. The vendors started setting up. I greeted the cookie-decorating people, Benjamin's friend from Boston with his homemade menorahs (I had my eye on one sculpted out of wire flowers if it didn't go quickly), the performers who'd be telling the Hanukkah story every half hour on the hour. The smells of frying dough and potatoes perfumed the air. There were a few minor hiccups—a missing electrical cord; some spilled applesauce—but nothing that couldn't be remedied by Seth making a quick run to the local hardware store and supermarket.

Obviously, I had to stop by my own booth first. Maggie had been delighted to help out for the festival, and had dived into the job of making the Hanukkah specials I'd dreamed up absolutely perfectly every time. Since the festival was at night, I'd made sure to have plenty of decaf options on hand, as well as some spiced-up options for anyone who wanted to slip a little rum or vodka in their chocolate gelt latte or latke-ccino (one of the perks of living in a small town is being on a first-name basis with the guy who does liquor licenses).

I spent the rest of the time running around, getting forms signed and checking on all the details, but during a rare quiet moment I found myself standing at the edge of things, my hand in the pocket of my coat, stroking the small, fuzzy head of Judah Maccasea the dolphin (not for comfort or anything; just because it was fuzzy and fun and, *fine*, he was my good luck charm). I didn't want to get my hopes up too high, but traffic at my café had been up by a fair amount this morning, mostly unfamiliar faces.

Unfamiliar faces that I started to see trickling in as the gates officially opened. Locals were scattered among them, curious at the new event in town or here to help work the booths, but mostly they seemed to be real tourists? Which was great? Exactly what I'd wanted?

I wasn't sure how to deal with getting exactly what I wanted. My first instinct was to run away, or to tell myself that I hadn't wanted it that bad anyway.

Mark that down on a note for my next therapy session. For now, I just rubbed Judah Maccasea's head and smiled.

"Ticket numbers for the first half hour are looking good." Seth magically popped up beside me as I was succumbing to the delicious smells wafting over from the drinks booth and taking my first sip of a mulled apple cider. "I just checked in at the gate and they're already above what we were hoping. It should only get better from here."

"Don't say that," I said. "You never know."

But he was right, something that I was always still grudging to admit even when it was true. Numbers grew steadily, and soon the festival was bustling: families walking around crunching on latkes and arguing over the best toppings;

people waiting in a long line at the decorate-your-own-Hanukkah-cookie booth; guests applauding the guys telling the story of Hanukkah (and applauding even more when one of their fake beards fell off). A punk rock rendition of "Sivivon, Sov Sov Sov" filled the air, kids singing along as they skipped down the aisles, begging their parents for menorahs made out of porcelain dinosaurs or bags of specialized gelt showcasing world currencies.

I'd done a really, really good job. I hoped Lorna would agree. I headed toward her booth, which, I saw as I got closer, was one of the few without a line.

She looked up hopefully as I approached her stand, which was full of the same generic Vermont-themed T-shirts and candles and soaps that stocked her store. "Oh, hey, Abby," she said, pasting on a smile. "Seems like everything is going well."

She was being nice. I tried to hold the smugness back when I replied, "It is. Numbers are even higher so far than we'd hoped."

Our call—which I'd nicknamed the come-to-Jesus call, despite the context (there was only so much societal Christianity I could overcome)—from the Eighth Night Ball had gone about as well as could be expected. I'd told her firmly and clearly, drawing on the spirit of the Maccabees and how they refused to submit to assimilation, that I'd ensure the standards of vendors and make sure that we didn't run over budget, but that I was going to make this a real Hanukkah festival or we wouldn't be doing it at all. No Christmas trees. No ornament decorations. No Santa. I was going to make this festival loudly, proudly Jewish.

She'd tried to protest, of course, but I'd shut her down each time. "If you want to run a Christmas festival, then run a Christmas festival," I'd said, and the old man on the treadmill had punched his fist in the air as if for emphasis. "If you want me to run you a Hanukkah festival, then this is how we're going to do it."

And she'd listened. Had she been entirely happy about it? No. But I'd been firm enough that she didn't bother arguing. Well, she did, but I'd shut her down and gone about running this festival my way.

To her credit, she hadn't protested further. I made a quick scan of her goods on display and picked up a maple leaf–shaped soap to buy. I could give it as a gift to someone next time Seth and I went down to the city. Her smile was tentative, but it lit up her face. "Thanks, Abby." New beginnings and all that. I smiled at her in return, backing away and into somebody.

"Oops, sorry," I said, turning, only to see that it was Connor.

He gave me a lopsided smile that creased his freckled cheeks. "Hey, Abby. Congratulations. The festival is great."

For once, I didn't want to run away from my ex. "Thanks, Connor," I said. "That means a lot."

"I didn't realize how much fun Hanukkah was," he said. "You never celebrated it when we were together. Now I kind of wish we had. How have I gotten to be almost thirty years old without tasting a latke?"

I had to laugh. "They are pretty great, aren't they?"

"Hell yes." He nodded at me. "Congrats again. I'm really happy for you."

"Thanks," I said. I was really happy for me, too.

Back to my rounds, where I put out a fire between two fighting families at the funnel cake booth (not a literal one) and put out a fire at the latke stand (this one literal). So I was sweaty and a little smoky when I was enveloped in hugs by Seth's entire family and friend group.

"Surprise!" Bev said, pulling back. She was only wrinkling her nose at my stench a little. Benjamin stood behind her, tall and stiff in his wool pea coat. He smiled at me and gave me a nod when I smiled back.

"You came!" I said, genuinely surprised as Dan and some Mikes and Kylie started slapping me on the back and hugging me and, yes, wrinkling their noses at my stench.

"Wouldn't miss it for the world!" gushed Kylie. She grinned wide as I showed her Judah Maccasea in my pocket. "I'm glad he's helping. Don't forget to feed him latkes. He prefers sour cream."

I gasped. "Blasphemy! We're an applesauce family!"

Dan and the Mikes stepped aside to check out the doughnut booth (well, one of the three doughnut booths). Kylie followed, yelling something about making sure to get her a Boston cream.

Behind them, a beam of light shone down from the moon, illuminating Freya in its frosted glow. I didn't even resent it; I was so happy to see her. "You came!" I gushed, and she was such a good friend by this point that she didn't even try to hug me. I loved her for it.

"Of course I came!" she said brightly. "I wouldn't miss it for the world."

"You know something else you shouldn't miss?" I said.

"A sufganiyot latte. Tell Maggie I sent you and she'll give you extra jelly."

"I'm not sure how appetizing that sounds in the context of a coffee, but I'll trust you on that." She wandered off, hands tucked into her white fake fur muff.

Bev stepped up beside me, her round face as luminous as the moon. "Seth told me about your plans for the community center up here."

I nodded, mood brightening even further. "Yes!" It was still in the early stages, as in more thought than plan, but the goal was to get started for real once the festival was over. Our Southern Vermont Jewish Community Center, that was. I had no idea how many of us there were up here, but there had to be at least a minyan scattered around. I'd find them, assuming they wanted to be found—but probably not through an online dating app. And we'd form a community. I didn't know what it would look like. I certainly wasn't qualified to start a synagogue, and I wasn't sure I wanted to belong to one right now anyway.

But I did want my community back. My family back.

Bev squeezed my shoulder. "I'm happy to refer you to any of my friends in the city for advice if you have questions. They'd be thrilled to help out."

"Thank you so much," I said. "I'd love that."

The night went on, and the festival grounds continued to bustle. The tourism board members found me, one by one, to enthuse about how much business they were getting, both from tourists stopping by the stores in town and through the booths many had set up here, which I'd encouraged. I loved that the bookstore owner had special-ordered copies of *The Matzah Ball* and *Eight Nights of Flirting* and *Larry's Latkes*, and that the antique store owner had brought all his candlesticks and even a few menorahs he'd dug up. They were part of my community, too, and it meant a lot to have them come out for me.

The rest of the night whirled by in klezmer music and sparkling lights and the smell of oil. Around closing time, I found myself at Seth's side, watching the final performance of the Hanukkah story. The fake-bearded guys were feigning mostly convincing shock at the fact that the oil had lasted for eight days. "It's a miracle!" one cried. "A miracle of the oil!"

Seth pulled me tightly to him, his lips pressing against my forehead. Tingles ran through my hair. "This is amazing," he said, then moved in for a real kiss on the lips. "*You're* amazing."

The miracle of the oil was great and everything, sure. But me falling in love? With Seth? That was a miracle, too. And, if you asked me, it was even better than doughnuts.

Acknowledgments

The winter holidays are my favorite time in New York City. The twinkling lights everywhere you look! The Christmas tree salespeople who make the sidewalks smell like freshly cut pine! The general air of joy and festivity! Thank you so much to my publishing team for helping me share my love of the season in book form: Kristine Swartz, Mary Baker, Tara O'Connor, Dache' Rogers, Elisha Katz, Christine Legon, Liz Gluck, and Colleen Reinhardt at Berkley; Merrilee Heifetz, Rebecca Eskildsen, and the rest of the team at Writers House; and Petra Braun for the absolutely dreamy cover.

Thanks a latke to all the friends and family who helped keep me sane through the publishing process, with a special shoutout to the Berkletes (especially Jo Segura for her feedback on the synopsis) and the NYC Writer Commiseration Station. Jean Meltzer, thank you a plateful of latkes for your blurb, your support, and for being such an encouraging light when I was figuring out whether I could write this book. Many latkes with applesauce, sour cream, and smoked salmon to Katie Shepard for not just helping me with the synopsis but also coming up with the perfect title of this book. Apologies to my (very good) parents for (once again) writing a book about terrible parents. I promise they are not based on you.

Jeremy, thank you forever for being my love story. And Miriam—having a baby in the middle of writing this book might have made it harder to finish it, but I wouldn't have had it any other way.

LOVE YOU A LATKE

AMANDA ELLIOT

READERS GUIDE

Discussion Questions

1. Significant themes in both the story of Hanukkah and the story of this book are assimilation and fighting against a greater power or society that wants you to change important parts of yourself in order to fit in. The stakes might be drastically different in each story, but they both end with an anti-assimilation message. Do you agree with this message and how Abby handled her disputes with Lorna?

2. While the bulk of the book's action takes place in New York City, both main characters prefer their home in small-town Vermont. What are some of the positives and negatives of living in the city, and same for a small town? Which do you prefer?

3. When Abby first hears about Freya, Seth's ex, she's wary and thinks their relationship will be a cold and perhaps antagonistic one. By the end, they're quite close friends, meaning Abby's first impression is proven wrong. When was a time you've changed your mind after a first impression, whether it was about a book or something that happened in real life?

4. As the book discusses, food plays a large role in many Jewish holidays. Aside from Hanukkah and its (delicious) fried menu, what are some other real-world examples of when specific foods play important roles, whether it's for a holiday, an event, or an occasion? What do you think makes these particular foods such vital markers or participants in the examples you've named?

5. Bev says that one of the reasons she and her husband have had such a long successful marriage is that their differences complement each other and help challenge them to become better people. She thinks the same is true of Abby and Seth. What do you think? When you look at your relationships with romantic partners, close friends, or family members, do you think that's true of your life?

6. Abby is adamant for most of the book that her relationship with Seth and his family has not changed her, but she admits by the end that she's wrong. How did you see her change over the course of the book, and do you think her changes were for the better? How about Seth's evolution over the course of the book?

7. The thread of Abby's relationship with her parents is not neatly resolved by the end of the book—she does not tell them off in a cathartic way, and they do not come around to understand all the pain they've caused her. How do you feel about this part of the ending? Do you think she handled it the right way? Do you think they will ever meet again?

8. Imagine an epilogue that takes place during Hanukkah five years after the close of the book. Where do you think all of the characters are now, and why?

KEEP READING FOR A PREVIEW OF

Sadie on a Plate

BY AMANDA ELLIOT, AVAILABLE NOW!

MY LIFE HAS THIS IRRITATING HABIT OF THROWING its biggest changes at me while I'm completely in the nude.

Exhibit one, ten years ago: I was seventeen and enamored with a boy my parents hated, all for the completely unfair reason that he skipped school most days to smoke pot behind the local 7-Eleven. I'd snuck him up to my room, deciding against the back door in favor of the tree outside my window because it seemed so much more romantic. We were in the throes of quiet passion when my door flew open.

"Sadie?" my sister said, and her mouth dropped open. She was four years younger than me, so I would've felt bad for traumatizing her if I wasn't so busy screeching and scrambling for my clothes or a sheet or anything to cover up our naughty bits.

"Get out of here!" I grabbed the closest thing within reach—an old soccer trophy—and hurled it in her general direction for emphasis. It landed with a thunk on the rug, which made her jump and blink her eyes. "Get ouuuuuuuut!"

"Okay. Fine." She blinked again and adjusted her glasses. As she turned to go, she said over her shoulder, "By the way, Grandma died."

Exhibit two, six weeks ago: I was getting out of the shower when I heard my phone ding with a text. It was charging on the nightstand, so I picked it up on my way to the dresser. All I saw on the lock screen was that it was from Chef Derek Anders, my boss, and it started with, **Hey Sadie** . . . I sighed, figuring he was probably asking me to come in for a last-minute shift on the line. I entered my PIN and read the whole text.

Hey Sadie, I'm sorry but we're going to have to let you go.

Exhibit three, five weeks ago: I was walking around my apartment eating Nutella out of the jar with my fingers for breakfast, psyching myself up to put on fancy professional clothes and head out for my nine a.m. interview at the temp agency. My phone rang with a 212 number, which I knew was New York City, and the only reason I picked up was because I thought that the temp agency had its headquarters in New York and maybe they were calling to cancel the interview because *what are you thinking, Sadie, all you've ever done is work in restaurants and all you've ever wanted to do is have your own, why are you trying to get an admin job at some obnoxiously hipstery tech company?*

It's not like I want *to work at a tech company,* I argued silently with the temp agency. *It's that I've been blacklisted for the near future from the entire Seattle restaurant scene and need some way to earn money until all this fuss dies down.*

The temp agency scoffed in my head. *Yeah, okay. Like you could do a fancy office job. All you can do is work the line, and now you can't even do that anymore. You're worthless.*

I picked up the phone, my shoulders already drooping. "Hello, this is Sadie Rosen."

"Hi, Sadie!" It was a woman on the other end, her tone far too chipper for this hour of the morning. "My name is Adrianna Rogalsky, and I'm calling from *Chef Supreme.* Is this a good time?"

I almost dropped my phone. "Yes!" I cleared my throat, trying to keep from squeaking the way I did when I got too excited. "I mean yes, this is a good time."

"Great!" Adrianna chirped. "I'm calling to tell you that the committee really liked your application and your cooking video. Would you mind answering a few more questions for me?"

My eyes involuntarily darted to my bookshelf, which consisted mainly of cookbooks. I spent too much time in restaurant kitchens to cook much from them—or at least, up until a week ago I had—but I liked flipping through them to gather ideas and marvel at the food photography. Five were written by winners of *Chef Supreme,* and four by runners-up and semifinalists. I'd watched every episode of all six seasons, seated on the edge of my couch to goggle at every cooking challenge and winning dish and contestant who cried when eliminated.

Season three's winner, Seattle's Julie Chee, was my culinary idol. Derek, my boss, had taken me by her restaurant after-hours one day. She'd laughed when I told her how I'd been rooting for her all season, patted my head like I was a little kid, and then cooked me a grilled cheese with bacon and kimchi. It was the best night of my life. Right after that, I'd started dreaming about competing on the show myself.

"Hello? Sadie?"

And if I didn't get on my game, that dream was going to evaporate like a pot of boiling water forgotten on the stove. I mean, I didn't really think I was actually going to make it on the show, but it wasn't like I was going to hang up on someone from *Chef Supreme*. "Sorry!" I said. "Bad connection for a minute there. Yes, I'd love to answer some questions." I shook my head and grimaced. Love? *Love* was a strong word. I should've said I'd *be happy* to answer some questions. Now Adrianna was probably—

Talking! Already! "Your application from six months ago says that you're a sous-chef at the Green Onion in Seattle?"

I cleared my throat. "Well, um." This was not off to a great start. "I was a sous-chef there until last week. I decided to leave to . . . um, pursue personal business opportunities." Another grimace. Personal business opportunities? What did that even mean?

I really wished I wasn't naked right now. I knew Adrianna from *Chef Supreme* couldn't see me through the phone, but I still felt way too exposed.

Fortunately, job-hopping is fairly common in the food

world. So Adrianna just said, "Great. And how would you describe your personal style?"

I hoped she meant food-wise and not looks-wise, because my personal fashion style consisted mainly of beat-up Converses, thrift store T-shirts, and constant calculations on how far I could go between haircuts before crossing the line from fashionably mussed to overgrown sheepdog. "At the Green Onion, I was cooking mostly New American food with some French influences and a bit of molecular gastronomy," I told her. "But my own style, I'd say, is more homestyle, with Jewish influences? Not kosher cooking; that's a different thing. I'm inspired by traditional Jewish cuisine."

Paper rustled on the other end. "Right, the matzah ball ramen you cooked in your video looked fantastic. We were all drooling in the room!"

I perked up. Forgot that I was naked. Forgot that lately I was a walking disaster. "That's one of my go-tos and will definitely be on my future menu. I've been experimenting lately with putting a spin on kugels . . ."

As I chattered on, I could practically see my grandma shaking her head at me. Grandma Ruth had cooked up a storm for every Passover, Yom Kippur, and Chanukah, piling her table till it groaned with challah rolls, beef brisket in a ketchup-based sauce, and tomato and cucumber salad so fresh and herby and acidic it could make you feel like summer in the middle of winter. *Pastrami-spiced* pork *shoulder? Really, dear?*

I shook my own head back at her, making her poof away

in a cloud of metaphorical smoke. I had that power now that she was dead and buried and existing primarily as a manifestation of my own anxiety.

". . . so in that way it's really more of a cheesecake with noodles in it," I finished up. My blood was sparking just talking about my food; I had to do a few quick hops just to burn off some of that excess energy.

"I love your passion," Adrianna said on the other end of the phone. "So, I take it that opening your own restaurant is hashtag goals for you?"

"Hashtag goals," I agreed. And my shoulders drooped again, because that was a dream that was never going to happen now. After I got fired by the Green Onion and the chefs at all the other restaurants worth working at learned why, I became the joke of Seattle's restaurant industry. Who wanted to invest in the local joke?

She asked me a few other questions, pertaining mostly to my schedule and availability (there were only so many ways to say, "I'm free whenever you want me, considering I no longer have a job"). I continued to pace around my apartment, circling the coffee table, bare feet padding over the rug. And then, "It's been lovely to speak with you, Sadie."

I stopped short, my shin slamming into the table leg. I swallowed back a curse. "It's been lovely to speak with you . . . too?" I finished with a question, because I couldn't ask what I really wanted to ask. *Is this it? Did I not meet whatever criteria you have? What's wrong with me?*

"We'll be in touch soon," Adrianna said. "Have a great day!"

I did not have a great day. Because of Adrianna's call, I

was fifteen minutes late to my interview at the temp agency and arrived all sweaty and panting from the rush to get there on time. The interviewer's lip had actually curled in distaste as she touched my damp, clammy hand. The sugar rush from the Nutella had worn off by the time I hurried back out onto the street, and I was starting to feel a little shaky, but the only place to buy food in the vicinity was a coffee shop where I was forced to choose between a stale bagel and some slimy fruit salad.

And that wasn't all. As I chewed (and chewed, and chewed, and chewed) on my stale bagel with too much cream cheese caked on, I ran into an old friend. Like, literally ran into an old friend, as in our bodies collided as I was trying to catch the bus.

"Oh!" I knew it was her as soon as I heard that raspy voice, earned from years of smoking in alleyways behind restaurants. Her eyes widened as she took me in: the sweaty strands of hair sticking to the sides of my face, the thrift store blazer that still smelled like the eighties, even though I'd washed it twice and taken the shoulder pads out. "Sadie! How are you . . . doing?"

I gritted my teeth at the false sympathy in those big blue eyes. "Hi, Kaitlyn. So you heard?"

Kaitlyn leaned in, bringing the smell of smoke with her. I fought the urge to step back. Even after years working in restaurant kitchens, where most everybody was a smoker at least when drunk, I hated the smell. "Of *course* I heard. I'm surprised you're still here. Not here in SoDo, like, in Seattle."

"I'm still here," I said through a clenched jaw. Kaitlyn Avilleira and I had quasi-bonded in our early twenties, a little over five years ago. We were the only two women on the line at Atelier Laurent, and we had to have each other's backs if we didn't want to get banished to the pastry kitchen.

Having her back didn't mean I liked her.

"That's really strong of you." Kaitlyn pulled me in for a one-armed hug that might actually have been an attempt to strangle me. "I'm rooting for you, girl!"

I gritted my teeth in a smile. This was the song and dance of our relationship: seeing who could pretend harder that we *did* like each other, because we were busy fighting so many stereotypes about women on the line that there was no way we could fulfill the one where the only two women were enemies. "Thanks, Kait!"

An uncomfortable silence settled over us. I looked in the direction of the bus. No, I *stared* in the direction of the bus, willing it with my eyes to appear.

Alas, I had not developed any magical powers in the past few minutes.

"We have to get drinks sometime," I said. "And catch up. It's been way too long."

"*Way* too long," Kaitlyn said. She tossed her long, shiny brown hair. Her eyes sparkled, and her cheeks were naturally rosy. *She* never had to wear blush or undereye concealer to keep coworkers from asking her if she was sick. "Wait till I tell you about working for Chef Marcus. He works me like a dog." She trilled a laugh. "I almost wish I could take a break like you."

I clenched my jaw and told myself that I couldn't hit her or I'd get arrested, and going to jail was really the only way I could make my situation worse. Well, that, or moving back in with my parents in the suburbs, into my childhood bedroom with the shag carpet and no lock on the door.

"Well, I'd better be going," Kaitlyn said, just as I was saying, "Well, I'll let you go." Our words clashed, and we both laughed nervously before hugging yet again. "You should finally open that restaurant now that you're free and have all this time," Kaitlyn said as she backed away. "I'll be there opening night!"

Thankfully, she was off before I had to respond. I made a face at her back. Of course I wanted to open my restaurant now that I was *free* and had *all* this *time.* But opening a restaurant either took lots of money, which I didn't have even before the whole unemployment situation, or a bunch of rich investors willing to throw their money away on my behalf, which, again, I *wished.*

The bus was delayed, obviously, and it took me twice as long as it should have to get home, the whole time crammed in next to a manspreader who kept giving me dirty looks for trying to sit in three-quarters of my own seat. I stared hard out the window, watching the warehouses and industrial lofts turn into the residential buildings and parks of Crown Hill. By the time I stumbled through the door of my apartment, I was done with today. I pulled off my clothes, dropping them in puddles on the floor, so that I could shower the stink of failure away and then eat something for my soul. Like more Nutella out of the jar.

My phone chimed. *It's probably the temp agency already rejecting me,* I thought glumly, digging it out of my bag. Sure enough, it was an email.

But it was from Adrianna Rogalsky of *Chef Supreme.* And

it started with, Hey Sadie, just like my firing-by-text. *Fantastic.* I took a deep breath as I clicked it open, readying myself for yet another important food world person to tell me how inadequate I was.

> Hey Sadie, I enjoyed our conversation earlier. Upon further discussion with the *Chef Supreme* team, we'd like to fly you out to New York for some more interviews and cooking tests to determine whether you'd be a good fit to compete on *Chef Supreme* season 7. Would next Wednesday work for you?

I dropped my phone. *OhmyGodohmyGodohmyGod.* What if I'd just shattered my phone and I couldn't afford a new one and I couldn't get back to Adrianna and . . . and . . .

I picked it up. It wasn't even cracked. I opened an email and wrote Adrianna back about how yes, I'd love to come in whenever they needed me because it was my dream to be on *Chef Supreme* and I couldn't wait to meet—

Backspace. I cleared my throat. Okay, take two, and be more professional this time. Hi Adrianna, thanks for reaching out! Yes, next Wednesday still works for me. I look forward to receiving the flight information.

I sent it off, chewing nervously on my lip even as I tried to talk myself down. *They probably have a hundred people come in to audition further for each season's twelve slots. And seriously, if they have a hundred people to choose from, why the hell would they choose* you*? Maybe you shouldn't even waste your time. Is it too late to email Adrianna back and cancel?*

I spilled this all on my parents the next night at dinner. I kept my eyes on my plate of eggplant Parm, and not just because my sister, Rachel, who sat across from me at our kitchen table, tended to chew with her mouth open. "So it probably won't actually turn into anything if I decide to go," I said. "But on the off chance it does, it could mean a new start for me. The goal is really not even to win, but to get noticed."

"Get noticed by who?" asked my mom. She set her utensils onto her plate with a clink. My dad followed suit. Only Rachel was left chewing. Loudly.

I let myself look up and look left, at my mom, then right, at my dad. I was an uncanny mix of the two of them: deep-set dark eyes and big boobs like my mom; a round face and thick, wiry brown hair like my dad. Unlike Rachel, who was a blond, blue-eyed giraffe. Even sitting, the top of her head nearly brushed the brass light fixture hanging over the table.

I cleared my throat. "Get noticed by anyone, really. The top four is the sweet spot. They get noticed by the public and by investors. Are offered their own restaurants and fancy executive chef gigs."

My dad shook his head. "Do you really think you're ready for that?" His eyebrows were furrowed with both love and concern, but his words hit me like a kick to the stomach. I pursed my lips and stared over his head, at the row of porcelain chickens in a perpetual march across the counter. "You've been through a lot lately. And you're still so young. I'm just worried about you, honey. Maybe going on TV in front of the whole country isn't the best idea right now."

"I'm not that young. I'm twenty-seven." I blinked hard, trying not to cry. "You don't believe in me?"

"Of course I believe in you," my dad said. He sounded wounded by my very suggestion. "I think you could win. I *know* you could win. But you've spent the past few weeks huddled up crying. Maybe next—"

"I think that's exactly why you *should* do it, Sadie." My mom's eyes were fiery as she reached out to grab my hand. Her squeeze made me sit up straight. "Follow your dreams. Why the hell not, right? Make it to the top four. Get noticed. Never work for a shithead man again."

Relief swept through me, lightening the weight on my shoulders, and that was just about enough to convince me that she was right. That I *should* do this. "I haven't even made it on the show yet," I cautioned.

"But if you do . . . This is what you've always wanted. Don't let it go."

I was pretty sure what I wanted to do, but I looked at Rachel anyway. Grimaced at the chewed-up mass of eggplant Parm that greeted me from her tongue, then the raised eyebrows of a question. She grinned without swallowing. "Do it."

So I got on that plane Wednesday with my heart hammering and my head held high. Jet-lagged and sleepless, I talked to producer after producer, random person after random person. I cooked more of my food for other random people, and sometimes they liked it and sometimes they chewed slowly and expressionlessly and nearly made me scream with anxiety. I sat down with a psychologist or a psychiatrist, I wasn't sure exactly, and he introduced himself too quickly and I thought that maybe asking him to repeat himself would get me a black mark, and I tried to seem a lot less crazy than I actually was, which in turn made me paranoid that he'd see right through me, so I tried to seem a little crazy but not *too* crazy, and—

Well, anyway, they flew me back to Seattle and didn't even make me wait impatiently for weeks and weeks before they told me I got in. While I was changing into my running clothes, naturally.

Was it that I spent far more time naked than the average person? Either way, nudity never failed.

Author photo by Cassie Gonzales

Amanda Elliot lives with her husband and daughter in New York City, where she collects way too many cookbooks for her tiny kitchen, runs in Central Park, and writes mysteries under the name Bellamy Rose.

VISIT AMANDA ELLIOT ONLINE

AmandaPanitch.com

AmandaPanitch